I0689536

DRAGON DREAMS

DRAGON DREAMS

DRAGONS OF BOSTON BOOK I

CHRIS A. JACKSON

Copyright © 2019 by Chris A. Jackson

Cover Design by Melissa McArthur

All rights reserved.

No part of this book may be reproduced in any form or by any electronic or mechanical means, including information storage and retrieval systems, without written permission from the author, except for the use of brief quotations in a book review.

This book is a work of fiction. Any resemblance to any real person, living or dead, is purely coincidental.

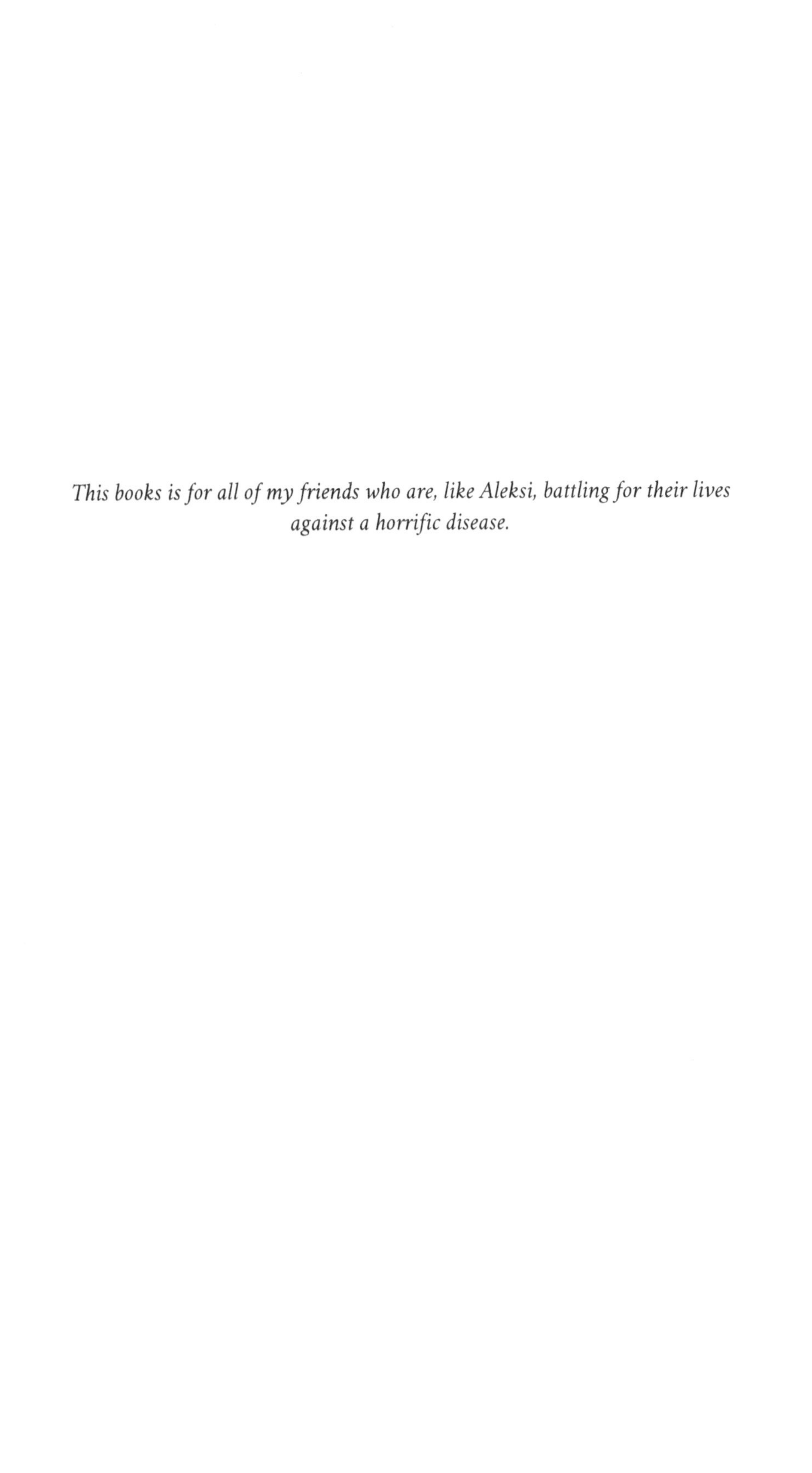

This books is for all of my friends who are, like Aleksi, battling for their lives against a horrific disease.

She huddled in a warm nook of rock, sheltering her new daughter under her wings. Wind howled overhead, icy and harsh, but heat radiated up from the ground and from her body to keep her daughter warm while the changes molded her fragile flesh and bone into her new shape.

Calm. Warm. Sleep, she thought, remembering her own birth, the confusion, painful changes, hunger. Soon, she would hunt again and bring back more meat. Soon, when her daughter's changes were near complete, they would part, never to see one another again. They would each seek out more humans to protect from the predators of the world, from other humans, and make more daughters. Such was their way.

The ground rumbled, which was why this nook was warm, a haven in this bitter frozen landscape. It was not the ideal place to make a daughter, but it was either that or kill the poor thing. The girl's human family had perished, and only chance had brought her salvation...of a sort. When the pack of carnivores that had killed the other humans were scattered and slain, she had been alone. She would not have survived long. This was the kinder fate, by far, but she remembered the horror in the poor girl's eyes as the leathery wings enfolded her.

Calm...warm...sleep...

The earth shook, harder this time and longer, and she lifted her head to peer out. The sky was grey, but it was not cloud that blotted out the sun. Worried, she examined her daughter; the changes were nearly complete. *Soon...soon you will fly.*

Not soon enough.

The earth heaved up beneath her, and her worry flashed into panic. She looked up the slope and saw a sheet of grey death falling down upon them. With a shriek, she flung herself up, her wings clawing the air to escape the deadly cloud. As she streaked away, she glanced back, lamenting her poor doomed daughter huddled there in the rock. The poor thing would never know the joy of her new life. She would never fly, never hunt, and never make a daughter of her own.

She would never know what it was to be a dragon.

1

Death was her milieu.

Aleksi breathed in the faint scent of formalin and plaster of Paris, a contented smile tugging at her mouth. The musty scents of quiet repose, the chill echoes of remembered life; these were the things she lived for. The catacombs of museums' deep basements and repositories, more than any other place in the world, were her home. Here she could think. She could look thorough the old disused or forgotten samples, caress the ancient fossilized memories of organisms that had passed from this Earth. Here she could dream without interruption. Only here did she feel truly safe.

Here, no one would ask her why she never went out, why she didn't have a boyfriend, or think her strange for preferring science to social interaction. From her earliest disconsolate excursions into the museums of Manhattan in an effort to escape the yelling, the smell of alcohol, the ridicule, this had been her refuge. Museums were cleaner, quieter, and friendlier, with their long-desiccated denizens, than the bustling, noisy, onerous world of the living. There was death in paleontology, but there was also peace.

Her latex-covered fingertips brushed the faces of the closed drawers, her eyes scanning the numbers on their cards, the paper yellowed with age. She found the number she was looking for and smiled. The wide, thin drawer' slid open, and the protective plastic shield folded back to reveal rows and rows of fossilized therapsid bones. Cynognathus' link to Megazostrodon, the evolution of mammal-like reptiles to true mammals, could easily lie in this drawer, tucked away and forgotten, unrecognized and undiscovered for a hundred years.

Aleksi removed a jeweler's loupe from her pocket—a present from her father upon her graduation from NYU, and the only thing he ever gave her that she actually used—flipped on the tiny LED light, and leaned over the samples. This was where the real finds were in paleontology today, not digging through strata or imaging with sonar. Thousands upon thousands of poorly categorized samples waited to be discovered in the repositories of the great museums, miss-labeled and long forgotten. Modern paleontologists tended to believe what they read, and the label on the drawer cover clearly stated, "Various Therapsids," but what if they were wrong?

Finding a doctoral dissertation in a drawer was also much easier, cheaper, and cleaner than applying for a grant to visit some distant site in Nebraska or China. Too much traveling, too many airports, and *way* too many people. No, Aleksi was not a digger, she was a discoverer, and she preferred to do it alone, in the peace and quiet of these cool, dim places, away from people and interruptions.

As if to remind her of her fallacious notion, her phone twittered in her back pocket. The list of people who had her number was short, and there was no way her parents would be calling her in the middle of the morning. That left her roommate, her landlord, the graduate coordinator, and her advisor as the only likely potentials. She retrieved the interruptive implement and saw that it was only a text. She stripped off one latex glove and swept the screen. The message was from her advisor, Dr. Oliver.

"Oh, please not now…" Aleksi tapped the screen to retrieve the message with a cringe. Whenever Dr. Oliver called, it meant more work.

The message simply read: "My office pre 10AM today, pls."

The time display on her phone read 0945.

Aleksi swore under her breath, tapped in "BRT" and hit send. Luckily she was in the archives and not working at home, which was a ten-minute bike ride in good weather. The recent snow had her walking, which meant closer to twenty.

Aleksi stuffed the phone back in her pocket, closed the drawer, and hurried out of the repository, a hundred possible nightmares trundling through her head. She was scheduled to take her qualifying exams this semester, and had to teach a lab, as well as finish up her own compulsory course schedule. If Oliver piled any more work on her, she wouldn't get her dissertation proposal in on time. As she pushed the heavy door open, a voice surprised her.

"Did you find what you were looking for?"

Aleksi started before she recognized the young man as one of the curator's assistants. He was smiling like they were old friends or something, but she barely knew him, didn't even remember his name. She only met his eyes for an instant before she looked down. "Oh, um, no. I got called away. Sorry." She grabbed her heavy coat and brushed past him up the stairs.

"See you later then," he called after her.

"Um, maybe. Sure." Aleksi hurried up and burst through the double doors of the Museum of Comparative Zoology into the blustery Cambridge winter.

Skeletal trees and a few snow-shrouded evergreens dotted the deserted quad along Oxford Street. Winter break had sent most of the undergraduate population home for the holidays. Only faculty, maintenance staff, and a few die-hard graduate students remained on campus, which made the place almost as peaceful as the repository.

Aleksi shivered as the biting wind tried to invade her layers of clothing, but cold and wind were nothing new for her. She stuffed her hands in her coat pockets and strode around the corner of the museum toward the glass and steel megalith of the Northwest Science Building. The sciences departments had outgrown the more traditional red brick buildings, and many of the faculty offices had moved to this larger and more modern facility. The Organismal and Evolutionary Biology Department, of which Aleksi was a part, made up only a fraction of the School of Arts and Sciences, and there was little real organization to the offices of the faculty. One might have thought that proximity to primary buildings of their field of study would dictate location, but politics, grant funding, and prestige played greater roles. The NWS building was newer, plush, flashy, and very "front page"; consequently, the higher profile faculty resided here, Dr. Oliver among them.

The wind intensified as she approached the gap between Conant Hall and the NWS building, her long coat flapping in the frigid air. Aleksi ducked against the onslaught and yanked open the huge glass door without taking her hand from her pocket. The metal handle would be cold enough to stick to her hand, and she hadn't donned her gloves. She dashed up the stairwell on her left to the third floor—she detested elevators; too close, and people always wanted to talk—and entered the long, polished hallway dotted with lecture halls, labs and offices. Dr. Oliver's office, one in a suite of four, stood open. Aleksi heard her advisor talking in that voice that said she was on the phone, so she peeked cautiously into the room.

Oliver sat at her desk, phone wedged between her shoulder and ear, tapping on her computer and talking at the same time. She was the queen of multi-tasking. Oliver saw her, and waved her in, pointing at the phone and mouthing the word, "Lawson", the graduate director. Aleksi entered, her nerves jangling. If Oliver was talking to Dr. Lawson about *her*…

"Okay, fine." Dr. Oliver waved at a chair. "Yes, she just walked in, and I know she'll pick up the ball on this. Right. Thanks, Daniel. Later, then." She ended the call and smiled; a bad sign.

"Thanks for coming in, Alexi," she said, mispronouncing her name, as usual. "Lawson called with a minor issue, and I thought you might be able to solve it for me. Have a seat."

"An issue?" Aleksi shuffled in and sank into the indicated chair, clenching her hands in her pockets. "I was just working on my project, and I—"

"I thought you might be, and that's why I texted." Oliver made a dismissive gesture with one hand, as she always did when she thought whatever had just come out of someone's mouth was irrelevant. "The January at GSAS schedule is all set, but we've had a fall-out. Jim Felton was going to give a series on the new paleosciences virtual library system, but he had to cancel. Family emergency. Out for the semester. I know you're familiar with the system."

"But we agreed that I'd use winter recess to—"

"Oh, I know, Lexi," Oliver interrupted, mangling her name even worse, making the contraction rhyme with 'sexy', a taunt throughout her mortifying high-school years. "But that was before this emergency. It's only a two-week series, and you don't have any classes to teach during the recess, so you'll have time." She glanced at her watch and began shutting down her computer.

"But I was hoping to do some imaging during the recess. I've just found some Therapsid samples that might be—"

"Oh, don't *worry*, Lexi; you'll have *plenty* of time for that. The series doesn't start until the eighth, and you said you weren't going to be away long for the holidays, right?" She stuffed a folder and some other items into her bag, obviously having decided that the issue was settled. She stood and rounded the desk. "I appreciate you picking up the ball on this, Lexi. There's plenty of time for your imaging analysis. I've got to go, so we can talk about this later."

Aleksi stood, opening her mouth to object, but Oliver was already past her and standing at the door. She knew there would be no other discussion; it was set. There went her winter recess.

"I've emailed you Jim's outline, though you know the system well enough that you'll probably be able to wing it." Oliver ushered her out and locked her office door. "Oh, and because Jim's out for the semester, Lawson needed someone to pick up his general bio lab, too. I knew you could teach it in your sleep, so I put you in for it. You can use the extra money, I'm sure."

Aleksi gaped at her in shock. "But I'm *already* teaching the Comp Zoology lab, and I'm taking my *qualifying* exams this semester."

"Oh, you'll do *fine*, Lexi. You won't have any problem with your quals, and they're both just labs." She dropped her keys into her bag and fixed Aleksi with a stare. "I've *already* bent the rules allowing you to fulfill your teaching requirements with lab courses. You *should* have to teach a lecture, you know."

Aleksi clenched her anger between her teeth. Heat rushed to her face at that same old threat; Oliver knew Aleksi didn't like teaching lectures and used that as a bludgeon every time she piled on more work. Oliver also knew she would fold under the pressure of a confrontation, which only made Aleksi angrier.

"I know that." Aleksi hated the crack in her voice, the weakness. She clenched her hands until her nails bit into her palms.

"Then we don't have a problem, do we?" Oliver gave her a tight smile and turned to go. "Lawson will email you the course outline, and you should get in touch with the course coordinator before he leaves for the holidays." Oliver walked away without another word.

Aleksi stood there shaking. Oliver had just increased her workload by half and obliterated her winter recess, but Aleksi was angrier with herself than her advisor. She had never been able to deal with situations like this, and Oliver knew it. She caved every time, and it only got worse the longer she let it continue. A thousand similar discussions with her mother screamed through her mind, the results always the same: submission, capitulation, surrender. She trembled, her vision blurring with unshed tears.

"Aleksandrovna Rychenkna?"

She started at the perfect pronunciation of her name and whirled, sniffing and blinking, mortified that someone had been watching her in mid-breakdown. A man stood in another open office door, and she recognized him immediately.

"Dr. Hutchinson!" She wondered if he'd heard the entire discussion, and her embarrassment doubled. "I'm sorry, I..." She bit her lip; why was she apologizing, and for what?

"I didn't mean to startle you, but I couldn't help overhearing." He nodded down the hall where Dr. Oliver had gone and cocked an eyebrow. "You shouldn't feel bad about that; she runs roughshod over all her students. That's why most of them abandon ship by their second year. You've lasted longer than most."

"She does? I mean, I didn't mean to..." She faltered again, fixing her eyes on his feet.

"Don't worry about it. I won't tell her she's a bitch if you don't."

She gaped at that, opened her mouth to say something, but couldn't imagine defending Dr. Oliver. Dr. Hutchinson saved her from more embarrassment by changing the subject.

"You took my class on Cryptozoology last spring, right?" At her nod, he asked, "That was the first time the course was offered, and I didn't get much feedback. What did you think?"

"I, uh..." Her mind stumbled at the question; he wanted *her* opinion on *his* class? "I enjoyed it. It wasn't what I expected going in, and you made it fun."

"Good. Most scientists think it's a bunch of bunk. You know, Bigfoot and the Loch Ness Monster, but I wanted to introduce the discipline in a new light." He leaned against the door jam and crossed his arms. "Look, Aleksi, I'll be frank with you; I think it's crappy how Oliver's treating you, and I want to make you an offer. Actually, I was going to email you yesterday and got sidetracked. I'm about as organized as the average train wreck. Then you showed up here, so I thought I'd just ask."

"Ask?" She wondered what kind of offer he was talking about. Probably more work, and she was already swamped. "I don't think I can take any more projects on right now, Dr. Hutchinson."

"I'm not trying to pile more work on you, Aleksi," he said, once again pronouncing her name perfectly. "This wouldn't be on *top* of what you're doing with Dr. Oliver, but *instead* of."

"Instead?" Realization struck through her unease. He wanted to take her on as a student, to be her advisor. He wanted to steal her away from Oliver. "But I've already got a project, and I'm right in the middle of—"

"I know, imaging Therapsids." He pursed his lips and stared at her for a heartbeat. She fixed her eyes on his shoes again. "Tell you what; let me buy you a coffee and give me thirty minutes to explain what I'm offering. If you want to stay with Oliver when I'm through, I won't tell a soul. But I *guarantee* I can get you out of January at GSAS, and probably find someone to take the freshman bio lab. I can *also* promise you a finished dissertation proposal by mid semester."

"I…uh…" She looked up at him, trying to figure out if he was serious or just trying to manipulate her like Dr. Oliver, promising to help only to get work out of her. It certainly wouldn't hurt to hear him out. She bit her lip, promising herself that she wouldn't get seduced into another project with no light at the end of the tunnel. "Okay. I'll listen."

"Great. Let me grab my coat and we'll hit Buckminster's." As he retrieved a long black coat from a rack behind the door, she peeked into his office. He wasn't lying about one thing, anyway; the place was a train wreck. He shrugged into his coat and locked the door. "Besides, I'm a sucker for their apple Danish, and it's way past time for second breakfast!"

"*Second* breakfast?" She followed him down the hall toward the stairs.

"Sure! One of the seven meals: breakfast, second breakfast, elevenses, lunch, tea, supper and dinner." He looked at her for a response, but she just shook her head. "Don't tell me you never read *The Lord of the Rings*."

"Oh. No. Sorry, I've never been much for make-believe."

"That's okay." He rounded the first landing and smiled back at her. "I've never been much for reality, so we should balance each other out nicely."

She didn't know what to make of that but forced a weak smile. He was so different than Dr. Oliver, so casual and friendly. A niggling suspicion twisted her insides as she followed him down the steps and out into the bitter cold Cambridge winter. Why was he being so nice to her? He must want something.

<hr>

Thirty minutes later, her head buzzing with her second Cuban Blend coffee, Aleksi knew exactly what Dr. Hutchinson wanted. He needed someone who could read and transcribe Russian fluently, had expertise in paleontology, and specifically archival research of previously mislabeled or poorly categorized samples. Her parents were immigrants, and she spoke Russian as well as English, and she'd spent a third of her life in the archives of museums.

Dr. Hutchinson intended to examine and re-categorize of a number of Ursus species samples taken from a bone bed in northeast of Siberia in the early 1900's. Due to the state of unrest in Russia at the time, the samples were sent to the US in a freighter and found a home at the Harvard MCZ. Some were cleaned and displayed, but of the four original samples, two were stored. The bone bed included a number of species, and many supposed Ursus samples. He wanted to do morphological and, if possible, DNA analysis of the samples and compare the results with those the Knapp group had published years ago in Molecular Ecology. There were four possible projects involved in the bone bed samples, and she could choose which she wanted.

And he was taking possession of the samples in less than a week.

"The transfer's already lined up." He downed the last of his coffee with a shrug. "I'm working with Quinton Neilson. He said he knew you."

"I didn't know he…um. Yeah. We've met." Aleksi had met the curator of the MCZ during a trip to Cambridge when she was in college. She'd been doing work study with the American Museum of Natural History, in Manhattan, and helped with a transfer of some samples. In fact, Quinton had suggested she apply to Harvard for graduate studies.

"He said I should look you up. Problem is, the holidays. If you were planning to go home to Brooklyn for Christmas, you probably won't be here for the transfer."

This was all moving so fast, her head was spinning. She hadn't even agreed to take on the project, and he was asking about her holiday schedule. "I *was* planning to go home for the holidays, but…" She dreaded going home, not because her parents wouldn't be delighted to see her, but she knew how the visit would end up. Yelling, accusations, ridicule, and tears. Then she realized what Dr. Hutchinson had just said. "You know I'm from Brooklyn?"

"I told you I was planning to contact you about this anyway. I did my homework on you; Suma Cum Laude at NYU, senior project in vertebrate paleontology archival and repository systems, published in the Journal of Paleontology. You finished your undergrad in three years, cleping out of most of your freshman requirements, and got college credit in high school for work study at the AMNH. You *also* carried a twenty plus credit hour load every semester. You're fluent in Russian; your parents are immigrants who came over right after the wall came down.

You were born in the states, in Brooklyn, where your parents live and have a jewelry shop. Oh, and you've managed to escape New York without a discernible accent, which is commendable." His tone made the last bit a joke, but she was already blushing and examining her coffee cup, uncomfortable with the list of her dubious accomplishments.

"Don't take this offer lightly, Aleksi," he said, suddenly serious. "I need someone with me on this, and I searched the entire graduate program for the right skill set. You're so far ahead of anyone else that there was no *choice* involved. It's either you, or I have to hire a translator and probably two technicians, and stand over their shoulders throughout the process. But I need an answer."

She looked up at him, but then shied away from the intensity of his stare. She let her eyes roam over the virtually empty café, the sterile white décor, all angles and recessed lighting. It felt stark, hard and unfriendly, and she found herself thinking of Dr. Oliver. If she changed advisors, what would the repercussions be? Would Oliver insist to the graduate coordinator that she teach lectures to fulfill her requirement? The teaching requirement had to be fulfilled by the end of second year, and she was already slated to teach a lab, two now, this spring.

"Can I..." She looked back at him and faltered again, looking down at her empty cup. Clenching her hands under the table she forced herself to speak. "I need to think about this. There could be...problems."

"If you're worried about Oliver..."

"I am, but it's not just that. I just need a little time." She lifted her eyes furtively. "Would...could I give my answer tomorrow morning? It's just such a big decision, and so sudden, I need to think."

"Tomorrow's fine, Aleksi. I work out at Malkin from six to seven, then hit Peet's Coffee for breakfast. We can meet there, or you can just email if you prefer."

"I'll...um...email you in the morning. With the weather, I'm on foot, and Peet's is on the other side of the square from my apartment." She cringed; she didn't want to appear lazy, unwilling to walk an extra five blocks.

"That's fine, Aleksi. Good." He downed the rest of his coffee and stood. She lunged to her feet, her chair making a horrible screech on the floor. She flinched but he seemed not to notice. "I'll look forward to your answer. Thanks for listening."

He held out his hand.

"Oh! Sure," she stammered, hesitating only a heartbeat before shaking his hand. His grasp was firm and steady, whereas hers was probably trembling and sweaty. "No problem. I'll email you first thing."

"Great." He released her hand and grinned. "Well, I better get back to the grindstone. Still going over final exams."

"Okay. And thanks, Dr. Hutchinson, for the offer, I mean." She stuffed her hands in her pockets and clenched them.

"I hope we can work together, Aleksi. I think it'd be good for both of us." He smiled again as he donned his coat and then turned to the door.

She followed him out, fingers fumbling to button her coat against the blast of arctic air that greeted them. Outside, he said goodbye and started off toward the NWS building. She stood there for a moment, her head still buzzing from caffeine and the surprising offer. She shivered and looked around the stark, white and gray landscape, the ruddy brick buildings of the MCZ, the Hoffman Lab, and the pillared edifice of the Mallinckrodt building. She remembered her first day here, how daunting it had all seemed, how fearful she'd been, so out of her element. Now it was familiar.

Things change with time, she thought. *Perceptions, architecture, even species evolve; but people pretty much stay the same.* She had no doubt that if she stayed with Oliver, she would continue to pile on extra work and ignore Aleksi's research, stringing her along as someone she could manipulate. But would working with Dr. Hutchinson be any different? He seemed nice, honest, and he certainly needed her help, but she could have said the same about Dr. Oliver when they first met.

She needed to think.

Aleksi started back toward the MCZ, thinking to go back to the repository and her drawer of Therapsid specimens, but stopped. If she did change advisors, the project she'd planned would go by the wayside. That was almost a semester of tedious research that would be useless. She cringed again and decided to walk home. If she went back to the MCZ, she'd get caught up and not think about Dr. Hutchinson's offer. She fished her hat and gloves out of her coat pockets and pulled them on, heading north on Oxford, easing into her accustomed long-legged pace that would take her home in twenty minutes.

2

J ulie?" Aleksi nudged open the door, already ajar, and peered into the apartment. "Julie, you here?"

"Oh, shit! Lex?" Julie's tousled blond mop of hair poked out from her bedroom door, and she grinned. "Sorry! Thought you were working on campus all day!"

"I was, but I—" She froze as Julie ducked back into her room and slammed the door. She heard some scuffling and a male voice. Heat flushed to her face and she turned away. "Sorry!" She closed the door and hurried into their little kitchen.

This wasn't the first time she'd interrupted Julie with a man; at least this time they were in her bedroom, not on the sofa. She fiddled in the kitchen, starting to make coffee out of reflex then realizing that more caffeine was the last thing she needed. She poured a glass of orange juice and almost dropped the glass as Julie popped around the corner.

"Didn't mean to leave my door open, Lex. Sorry about that." She finger-combed her hair and straightened her sweater; red cashmere that hugged her like a glove.

"I thought you were leaving for the holidays this morning." Aleksi tried to ignore her vivacious roommate. She liked Julie, but they were complete opposites.

"I was, but then Vic came over to say goodbye, and we um…well, one thing led to another."

"What dear Julie is trying so eloquently to say," Vic appeared behind Julie and wrapping his arms around her waist, "is that she lured me into her boudoir and proceeded to honor me with a little farewell fuck."

"Vic!" Julie slapped at his hands as they quested under her sweater. "Stop it!"

Aleksi turned away and busied herself exploring the cupboard, hating her shaking hands and the blush that warmed her cheeks.

"Why?" Vic laughed, clearly enjoying Aleksi's discomfort as much as Julie's protests.

"Because I *said* so!" Julie turned and gave him a shove, apparently honestly irritated with his juvenile behavior. "I'm sorry, Lex."

"Don't worry about it." Aleksi shrugged and continued rummaging through the cabinet, deciding on an early lunch more out of the necessity to occupy herself than any real hunger. "Just close the front door next time, please."

"Oh, did it not latch?" Julie cringed and glared at Vic, who just shrugged. "Sorry about that."

Aleksi settled on peanut butter and jelly and began slathering bread with both. Julie took the hint, long used to her unease with such situations and usually considerate. She urged Vic back, and Aleksi heard the bedroom door close. She finished making her sandwich, grabbed her glass of orange juice, and retreated to the farthest corner of the apartment so she wouldn't have to listen to the two having sex.

She plopped down on the couch near the bay window, took off her boots, and stared out at the wintery landscape. She took a bite of her thoroughly unappetizing sandwich and tried to focus on Hutchinson's offer. Was it genuine, or did he just need a workhorse to whip?

Iggy rattled his cage, having smelled the food, and she reached down to unlatch the door. She kept the iguana's cage near the radiator because he liked the heat and got some sun through the window. The two-foot-long green lizard hopped up to the cage door and climbed up her arm, his long, curved claws finding easy purchase on her sweater. He hopped off her shoulder to the armrest of the couch and started for her sandwich where it sat on a folded paper towel.

"Iggy, be good!" She snatched the sandwich out of the iguana's reach. "You'll get some, but only if you're a good lizard, understand?" She dabbed a little jelly on a finger and let him lick it off. He settled down on the armrest and waited for his next treat, content to be spoiled rotten. They shared the sandwich, Aleksi eating the bread and peanut butter, Iggy concentrating on the jam. This was grape, his favorite.

While they ate, Aleksi watched the winter winds knock snow and ice from the trees and thought about her morning. If she changed advisors, how would that look on her record? Would Oliver make her life a living hell? Would it delay her progress toward her PhD, or actually hasten it in the long run? She was already halfway through her second year and still without a firm dissertation project, mostly due to Oliver's continued rejection of one proposal after another. That, too, might be one of Oliver's tactics, and one of the reasons she had a poor record of retaining graduate students.

When the sandwich was gone, she lifted Iggy and took the empty glass and soiled paper towel back to the kitchen. Iggy squirmed, knowing all too well that this was the room where food came from, but she kept a firm hold on him and risked a tiptoe dash past Julie's door to her own room. She retrieved her laptop and hurried back to the front room, trying to ignore the noises coming from behind Julie's door. Evidently, Vic was receiving quite a farewell, but knowing they were doing it in there only made Aleksi uncomfortable and acutely aware of her own nonexistent social life.

She took her lizard and her computer, both of which she related to better than most people, back to the couch and reclined. Placing Iggy on her chest and the laptop on her legs, she patted the iguana while the computer booted up. In no time Iggy was warm and happily torpid, and she was busy researching her prospective new advisor.

Initially, she didn't learn anything new; his curriculum vitae was impressive enough. Dwayne Hutchinson, Associate Professor of Paleontology, PhD in Evolutionary Biology from Princeton in 1998, and an M.Phil in Molecular Biology from SUNY Stonybrook. He was from Seattle originally, and got his bachelor from Washington State. Some students thought he was some kind of tree-hugging activist, but his reputation was solid. He had an impressive publication record, six papers in just the last two years —three of those published with his own graduate students as first authors —and worked with other university departments all over the world. He was currently involved in the litigation over a pipeline project as an expert witness and had defended half a dozen previous cases that tended toward environmental protection. Dr. Hutchinson was the epitome of a Harvard professor: brilliant, multi-disciplinary, prolific, active, and professional.

But Dr. Oliver would have fit those categories as well.

For the rest, Google provided a huge number of hits when she tagged his degree onto his name. There was plenty of negative press associated with his environmental protection standpoint. He was being sued by one of the contractors associated with the pipeline project, though it looked like a pressure tactic. He'd pissed off a few corporate big-wigs in the past few years. Deeper, about five pages deeper, she found that he'd divorced a couple of years ago. Not that it interested her, but she found herself wondering why. Things like this sent red flags up in her mind, though she knew plenty of "happily married" couples who were a mess. Case in point: her parents.

She glanced up from the screen when the front door closed.

Julie came into the front room looking a little sheepish.

"Hey, Lex. Sorry about before." She sat on the other end of the couch and smiled.

"Don't worry about it." Aleksi smiled back; she couldn't be mad at Julie for having a little fun, and Vic was her latest fun thing. She checked the time on her computer. "You going home today, then?"

"Yeah, I was gonna take off in a bit, but I just wanted to apologize first. Vic can be a real dick sometimes. I just wanted to make sure we're okay before I take off."

"We're okay."

"So why are you back from campus so early?" Julie asked in one of her usual spur of the moment changes of subject. "I thought you were gonna to be gone all day. You're lucky we weren't doing it in the kitchen or something."

"*Please* don't do it in the kitchen, Julie! I have to eat in there."

"Oh, I'm *kidding*. So, what's up? You look a little 'deer in the headlights'."

"Do I?" After rooming together a year and a half, Julie noticed these things more than most people, but it still bothered Aleksi that she somehow looked upset. "Well, something happened this morning that could be good, but I have to figure it out."

"Find something good in the repository?" Julie's honest interest in the details of Aleksi's life was one thing that made her over-the-top perkiness tolerable. At least she'd stopped trying to set her up with men, and when that failed, women.

"No. Oliver called me in and dumped a January at GSAS session on me, then told me she's giving me a freshman Bio lab, too."

"You are fucking *kidding* me! Lexi, you *can't* teach two labs, GSAS, finish your proposal, *and* take your quals all in one semester!"

"Well, I might not have to." She turned her computer so Julie could see. "After Oliver took off, Dr. Hutchinson asked me if I'd like to change advisors. His office is right across the hall, and he heard the whole thing. He's got a project that's got my name written all over it, and he promised me a finished proposal by mid semester if I do it."

"No *way!*" Julie peered at the screen and her manicured eyebrows arched. "Oooo, yummy! Maybe *I'll* change advisors!"

"Julie!" Julie just laughed, so Aleksi let the comment slide. "Anyway, he's got some samples from Siberia that he's transferring from the MCZ, and he needs someone to transcribe the notes and work up the find. He said he'd get me out of the January seminar and maybe even the freshman bio lab."

"That's awesome!" Julie sat back and knitted her eyebrows. "So, what's the problem?"

"I just don't know if I should do it." She bit her lip and patted Iggy on the head. "I mean, I'm a year and a half in with Oliver, and jumping ship now might look bad."

"Aleksi Rychenkna, if you don't do this, I will slap you silly!" Julie glared at her. "Oliver's been riding you like a rented mule for a year, and all you ever do is take it. This is *perfect* for you!"

"It *seems* perfect, but it could be more of the same." Aleksi shifted, and Iggy lashed his tail in discontent at the disturbance. "What if Hutchinson only wants a translator he doesn't have to pay for?"

"Why don't you ask one of his students what he's like?"

"That's…" Aleksi stopped and blinked at Julie. "That's brilliant! He has four students now, and if I email them all, I might get an answer before tomorrow morning." She switched screens and did a search of the graduate student body.

"Why the rush? What's tomorrow morning?"

"Tomorrow I have to give him my answer." Aleksi had the four students' names, and was surprised that she had met two of them. She started composing individual emails to each.

"Again, why the rush?"

"Because he's transferring the samples on the twenty-sixth."

"And *you* get out of going home for Christmas! *Bo-nus!*" Julie knew what Aleksi's home life was like, but saying it like that just made Aleksi feel guilty.

A few hours later Alexi had two replies from Hutchinson's students. Both glowed with praise, urging her to take the offer, which she found surprising. Grad students tended to be jealous of their advisor's time, and sharing with an additional student cut that time by a significant percentage. She wondered at first if Dr. Hutchinson might have contacted them and coached them on how to respond to her inquiries, but then realized that she was being paranoid.

In the interim, she researched the project that Hutchinson had outlined, but there wasn't much. The digger, a Russian paleontologist named Sagadeyev, had not made the trip to the United States with his specimens. The subsequent years of unrest had left him destitute and working in a factory. He had died during the October revolution. Then Aleksi looked into each of Hutchinson's four students and discovered that one of them, Lonnie Westinghouse, was due to graduate at the end of the year. This explained part of the others' willingness to encourage a new addition; Lonnie was leaving, so a new student wouldn't change Hutchinson's workload.

She had just about made her decision when she received a third email, this one from Lonnie. It was short, but direct. She read, "Aleksi: Take it! He's been worrying about this project for a month! He needs help! You're perfect for it. L."

"Well, I guess that about does it." She fired off a thank you and sat up.

Iggy was back in his cage, and Julie was off to her parents' house in Connecticut for the holidays, so the apartment was hers. A glance out the window confirmed that it was already dark, so she closed the blinds and went to the kitchen to brew coffee and think about dinner.

Two heaping scoops of espresso in the filter, water, and push the button, then she opened the fridge and grimaced. Neither she nor Julie enjoyed cooking, so there wasn't much. She peeked under a foil wrapped dish and winced at the congealed mass of three-day-old tuna-noodle bake. She closed the fridge and went for the freezer. A box of frozen pizza hit the counter like a brick. She retrieved the Frisbee-like object from the container and cut it in quarters. Three went back in the freezer, and one went into the microwave. She paced the three short steps back and forth across kitchen, trying to compose her emails to Dr. Hutchinson and Dr. Oliver in her head.

"You're putting it off, Aleksi." But she wasn't stalling about the emails as much as the phone call to her parents.

She went to the bathroom while her dinner spun circles in the microwave, feeling an empathy with the whirling slice of pizza. Washing her hands, she glimpsed herself in the mirror and cringed. She scrubbed her face, hoping to add some color to her pallid features. She rinsed with hot water and rubbed vigorously with a towel, but other than adding a flush to her skin, the face staring back at her remained unchanged.

"A wonder Hutchinson didn't take one look and change his mind."

She often wished she could change her appearance, not to look more attractive, but just more professional. Unfortunately, she didn't know how or what to change. Makeup had never been her style. Her hair, a dirty blond that she hated, she generally tied back and forgot about. Her ears were pierced at her mother's insistence, and her father had made a number of very pretty earrings for her, but she rarely wore jewelry. Another sore point with her parents, who thought she should be married with kids by now.

The microwave dinged and she retreated from her damning reflection to the solace of strong coffee and hot pizza. Dinner for one.

She sat on the couch to eat, drafting her email to Dr. Hutchinson. Finally satisfied, she double checked it, added his address, and sent it off. The pizza was gone and her cup was empty, so she got up for a refill. Back on the couch less than a minute later, she stared in surprise at a reply from Dr. Hutchinson. She opened it and read.

Great, Aleksi! Welcome aboard. Would you like me to tell Oliver the news, or do you want to do it?

I'll round up the troops and we'll have an orientation meeting at Grendel's tomorrow evening. Say, 5PM for happy hour? First round's on me. We can all talk about the project, and maybe split up the work. I'll see what I can do about the January at GSAS series and the freshman Bio lab.

Thanks for the quick reply. I'll start the ball rolling...
Hutch

She stared at it, astonished that he'd offered to inform Dr. Oliver of the change. Was this for real, or some kind of test? If she took him up on the offer, would he think her weak or lazy? Was he manipulating her already?

"Shit." She had to answer him soon; he knew she was at her computer and would expect a prompt reply.

She made a decision and typed, "Thanks for the welcome, and the offer, but I'll notify Dr. Oliver of my decision. Tomorrow at 5pm is fine. Looking forward to meeting 'the troops'. Aleksi."

She double checked it and hit send. The last bit was a lie, of course, but she had to say it. She would rather a trip to the dentist than sit in a bar during happy hour. She tapped her foot and clenched her hands, staring at the screen. The reply popped up and she opened it with shaking fingers.

It read, "Cool. Offer's open if you change your mind. See you tomorrow. Hutch."

That was too easy. Then she realized that she had to write Oliver tonight and tell her she was leaving. Fortunately, she was much better at email than talking to people in person or on the phone. Of course, that reminded her that she still had to call her parents.

3

No, Mama, I *can't* come home. This is just too important, and Dr. Hutchinson can't change his plans." She listened to her mother go on as she poured coffee and pushed the toast down, then went to the fridge to find something for Iggy. She took out some romaine, celery, a squishy tomato, and a few grapes. By the time she had the knife in her hand and his bowl ready, the gushing concern that she was working too hard had devolved into questions, then blame.

"I wish I knew where I failed you. We'll have to change all our plans, and Christmas is only in three days! How could you *do* this to us, Aleksen'ka?"

"I didn't know until last night, Mama. I'm sorry." She diced a piece of lettuce, and a half stalk of celery one-handed, then held the phone with her shoulder to dice the tomato. "Dr. Hutchinson only asked me yesterday morning and I had to think about it."

"Think? What's to think about? High time you left that *cyka*, Oliver."

Aleksi nearly cut her finger; that was twice in twenty-four hours that someone called Oliver a bitch.

"So, this Dr. Hutchinson, is he single?"

"I don't know, Mama, and it's not like that." She cringed at the lie and started cutting the grapes in half. The toast popped up.

"Not like what? Is it wrong to ask?"

"Yes, it is, Mama. This is a *professional* relationship and that's all it's ever going to be." Throwing all of Iggy's food into a bowl, she retrieved the toast, slathered peanut butter on, balanced the plate, Iggy's bowl, and her coffee, and headed for the front room.

"I wish you could come home, Aleksen'ka. Is your work so much more important than your father and me that you can't even see us for Christmas?"

"I'd have to come back the day after, and the trains are packed." That at least wasn't a lie; travelling to New York for the holidays was always a mess, and she dreaded hours on a crowded train.

"Papa could drive you."

Aleksi heard her father swear fluently in Russian in the background. "No, Mama." Aleksi put her coffee and her plate on the table and Iggy's bowl in his cage. He pounced on the food like a starved crocodile. *At least I made someone happy this morning.* "Papa's busy with the shop, especially this time of year. Maybe after the holidays I can come for a visit."

"And when will that be? When you have *time* from your busy schedule?"

"Mama, please don't start." Aleksi collapsed on the couch and stared at her breakfast while her stomach did flip-flops.

"Don't start? She cares more about old bones and her precious *Harvard* degree than her own mother, and she says don't start!"

Her father yelled at her loud enough for Aleksi to hear clearly, and her mother yelled back that he was too lazy even to drive a few hours to bring his own daughter home for Christmas. Aleksi held the phone away from her ear until the yelling subsided. She knew better than to hang up on her mother, but by the time she could speak and be heard, her breakfast was cold.

"Mama," she tried when the yelling had diminished. When she received no answer, she stood and took her coffee and toast to the kitchen. The bread hit the garbage, and her coffee went into a thermal travel cup. She headed for her room and grabbed her coat and boots. "Mama, I can't talk any longer. I have to go." That, finally, got a response.

"Go? Go where? You have no classes, and no research to do!"

"I have to study Dr. Hutchinson's project. We're meeting this afternoon with his other students to discuss it." That was partly true, at least. She could do the research here, but it was a good excuse to end the call. She would go to the library.

"Well, if you have to go..." Silence hung like a burial shroud on the line. "Call us when you know when you can come to visit, Aleksen'ka. It would be nice to see you."

No, it wouldn't, she thought, guilt twisting her gut. "I will, Mama. I'll call you in a few days."

"We love you, Aleksen'ka," her mother said, driving another nail through Aleksi's heart. "And we miss you."

"I'll look for something after the holidays. Hug Papa for me. I love you, Mama. Bye."

Aleksi hit 'end' and stuffed her phone in her coat pocket, then sat on her bed and jammed her feet into her boots. Sniffing back tears, she cinched the bows into knots. She went back to the kitchen, grabbed her computer bag, pocketbook, gloves, hat, keys and her travel cup, and left the apartment. It would be a cold walk to campus, but she needed the time to think, and maybe the frigid air would freeze her tears.

Y ou sonofabitch!" Oliver burst into Hutch's office without so much as a knock, red faced and fuming. "You *stole* my student! What makes you think you have the right to take Alexi away from me? I ought to file a formal grievance with the graduate coordinator!"

"Feel free, Marilyn, but I didn't *steal* anything from you." He had been expecting her to be upset, maybe even angry, but she was positively livid. "I have a project that I thought she would be interested in, and she accepted."

"And you don't think that's stealing? Where do you get off thinking you can take whatever you want around here?"

"It's not stealing, because Aleksi is not a *thing*. She's a *person*, and is capable of making her *own* decision whether or not to stay with her current advisor or seek a new one." He placed his hands flat on his desk and reminded himself to keep his voice calm. Experience had taught him that raising his voice during a discussion, even when you were being yelled at, only made things worse. "If you started treating your students more like people and less like draft animals, they'd probably stick around."

"I do *NOT* treat my students like draft animals!"

"No? You loaded an extra lab *and* a January at GSAS seminar on a second year PhD student who doesn't have an accepted dissertation proposal yet, and has to take her comps this semester." He cocked his head and smiled at her. "*That's* overloading. File a grievance with the graduate coordinator, Marilyn. Please."

"Was that a *threat*?"

"No. That was a promise. Aleksi's a brilliant student and you were treating her like cheap labor. If you file a grievance against me, I'll file one right back against you. I think our records with our students speak for themselves."

"This isn't some backwater state college, Hutch; this is *Harvard*! Students are expected to *work* to earn their degrees here!"

"And how exactly would you know that, Marilyn? You've never attended a backwater state college." She glared at him, but he just smiled back. Oliver was Ivy League, through and through, and had never attended a public school in her life. She thought that made her better than everyone else, which only made her worse. Then he remembered that had Aleksi graduated from NYU, and the pieces fit together. "Is *that* why you were driving Aleksi into the ground, Marilyn, because she went to a state college?"

Oliver's face flushed red, and he knew he'd scored.

"I was *NOT* running her into the ground! She's capable of more than she thinks she is, and I was *challenging* her. That's how you make a student better. You're not doing yours any favors by coddling them, you know!"

"Ah, thanks for that. I'll just make myself a note." He grabbed a Post-it and actually wrote as he said, "Do not coddle students. Got it! Was there something else, because I've got a lot of work to do. This *is* Harvard, after all."

"Fine. Play your little games, Hutch, but if I find out you took her just to have someone to warm your bed, I'll have your ass kicked out of this university before you can say coitus interruptus."

He pushed down on the top of his desk and stood, truly angry now, but refusing to show it. "This discussion is over, Marilyn. Please leave. Now."

She sneered, looked him up and down as if he was a stain on her shoe, then whirled and stalked out. Her office door slammed hard enough to rattle the pictures hanging on his wall. Hutch sat down slowly and took a deep breath. He closed his eyes and took another, calming his mind and letting the stress and anger flow away with each exhalation. It was a simple yoga maneuver, but it worked. Three more breaths and he was centered, calm, and serene.

The truth was, in the two years since his divorce, he had had one very brief relationship with a student, but not one of his own, and not even in the College of Arts and Sciences. She had been a law student and it had lasted all of two weeks. The brief relationship had raised a few eyebrows, even though he'd broken no rules. Regardless, he'd broken it off—the attraction for both of them had only been physical anyway—and vowed to himself to keep his relationships extracurricular. *No sense in giving people like Dr. Oliver ammunition.*

He settled into work and put the issue out of his mind. He had more important things to do.

Aleksi gripped the steel handrail and eased down the icy steps into Grendel's Den. With a deep breath to steady her nerves, she nudged aside the heavy door. Dozens of conversations washed over her like a breaking wave. She fought down the urge to flee, jammed her hands in her pockets and scanned the confusion of light wood, tile table tops, and way too many people. She checked her phone for the time; just after five PM. Maybe she'd misunderstood.

The basement restaurant had been a Harvard square institution for forty years, but wasn't much to look at. In the summer they put tables outside, but in winter the bar was small and crowded. Aleksi had been here a few times, usually to grab a sandwich at lunch and sit alone at one of the tiny tables, ignoring the crowd and being ignored. It was crowded now because of happy hour, but Grendel's happy hour was half price food, not drinks. It was feeding time in the jungle of higher education, and the animals were hungry.

An arm waved from a corner table and she spotted Dr. Hutchinson. She worked her way through the crowd and stepped up onto the raised back section of the restaurant. The table was already festooned with drinks, but no food. How long had they been here? Had they been talking about her?

Dr. Hutchinson waved at the single empty chair and grinned. "Glad you could make it, Aleksi," he said as she struggled out of her heavy coat and sat down. "One of the team couldn't make it, but three out of four isn't bad for winter recess. This is Lonnie Westinghouse, my senior student."

"Hi!" Lonnie grinned and stuck out a hand, her teeth looking too white against her dark skin. She wore her hair in tight plaits with beads that clattered as she moved. Aleksi shook the hand, surprised at the woman's strength.

Dr. Hutchinson waved to the two men. "John Alvarez, who's in his third year, and my youngster, Bob Tomlin, who's still got that confused look every first-year shares."

"Hey! I do *not* look confused!" Bob, young with short dark hair and a pleasant round face, scowled at his grinning supervisor. "I'm just...pensive."

"Terrified is more like it." John nudged the other with a smile that looked sinister with his short cropped black goatee and mustache.

"Terry Price, another third year of mine, couldn't make it. He flew out yesterday for California, but you'll meet him in January."

"Nice to meet you all." Aleksi forced a smile and tried to relax. She knew their faces from the web, and even knew where they'd done their undergraduate work, their majors, their areas of study, and their GPAs. She felt a little guilty about spying on them, then wondered if they had done the same to her.

"Welcome aboard!" Lonnie lifted her beer in toast.

"Thanks."

"I took the liberty of ordering nachos and quesadillas, but if you want anything more, feel free." As if on cue, a waitress arrived with two huge platters and everyone moved their glasses to make space. "The quesadillas are vegi. Hope you don't mind. What are you drinking, Aleksi?"

"Um, I don't usually..." The others were all drinking beer of various shades, but Aleksi had never liked beer. She thought about ordering a soda, but didn't want to seem like she wasn't one of the team, and ordering wine might seem aloof when the others were drinking beer. The waitress made a face and rolled her eyes, clearly impatient. "Irish coffee with no mint, please."

"Damn! Why didn't *I* think of that?" Bob made a face as the waitress scratched a note and whirled away. "On a day like this, that would be perfect."

"Because you're a herd animal, like the rest of us," John replied. "Hutch orders beer, so we all follow suit. Obviously, Alexi is the only one here with any originality at all."

"Or she doesn't like beer." Lonnie flashed him a look that Aleksi couldn't interpret. "And it's *Alek*si, not *Alex*i, right?"

"Oh, it doesn't really matter." She unwrapped her napkin from her silverware and clenched it in her lap.

"Sure, it matters," Lonnie said with another smile. "I wouldn't want people to call me Loony, though a few have on occasion."

"And they're still alive?" John asked, sipping his beer.

"I didn't say *that*, and yes, it was a *bitch* hiding the bodies!" The others laughed, and Aleksi found herself liking Lonnie's sense of humor.

"I can't tell the difference." Bob knitted his eyebrows. "The two sound the same to me."

"The difference is subtle," Dr. Hutchinson said, suddenly serious. "'A-lek-si' breaks the last syllable before the s sound, and is correct. 'A-lex-i' breaks it after, and isn't. Is that right, Aleksi?"

"Um…yeah, that's right," she stammered, uncomfortable with the scrutiny of her name. "Thanks, Dr. Hutchinson."

"Ooo, she broke rule number one!" Bob grinned and lifted his glass. "Shame, shame! Two demerits!"

"I'm sorry, I—" The others were laughing, and Aleksi felt heat flush to her face.

"Doesn't count." Dr. Hutchinson took a portion of the nachos and a quesadilla, motioning the others to dig in. "She doesn't know the rules."

"Rules?" The waitress arrived with her coffee, and Aleksi took a sip. It was hot, strong, and sweet, the Irish whiskey biting her tongue. She vowed to only have one.

"Rule number one," Lonnie held up a finger, "states that, outside of formal academic situations where potentially anal-retentive faculty members are present, Dr. Hutchinson will only be addressed by his official nick name, Hutch. Any violation of this edict will earn two demerits and invoke rule number two." She raised a second finger.

"And what's rule number two?"

"Violators of rule number one will buy the next round!" they all chimed in unison, loud enough to earn some glances from the surrounding tables.

"But you didn't know the rules, so you get a freebie," John raised his glass with another devilish grin. "*This* time."

"So, now that we're introduced and have everyone's name straight, let's go over this new project and see if we can get some work done."

Dr. Hutchinson, *Hutch*, she reminded herself, outlined the Siberian bone bed project and what he hoped to accomplish. Aleksi listened, gauging everyone's moods. At the mention of work, they all shifted to more somber faces, though Lonnie seemed less attentive than the others. She finished her beer and flagged down the waitress for another. Aleksi sipped her coffee carefully and nibbled one of the quesadillas.

"So, Lonnie's off the hook because she's defending her dissertation in March, and will be *utterly* insufferable after that," Hutch said when the summary was complete.

"*Damn* right!" Lonnie grinned, accepted her beer from the waitress, and lifted it in toast.

"But the rest of you are decidedly *on* the hook." Hutch looked at Bob who cringed like he knew what was coming. "Bob is our molecular guru, and will be isolating, PCRing, and sequencing DNA from the samples."

"Which means piecing together about a *million* fragments." Bob made a face.

"True. As well as full isolation precautions with the samples to avoid contamination. This project, he hopes, will provide enough secondary data for a dissertation proposal, but the primary Ursus analysis will be Aleksi's. We've got to get her proposal in before the end of the semester. John will handle some of the more esoteric statistical analyses, but that won't kick in for months. Aleksi will be handling the lion's share of the initial workload. That means working up the samples, imaging, categorizing everything by morphology, transcribing all the notes and, hopefully, finding enough tissue for the DNA isolation."

"Better you than me," John said.

"I'd rather scrape bone than do stats." Lonnie gave Aleksi a nudge.

"Me, too," Aleksi agreed.

As Hutch continued with the plan, she found herself smiling. She liked them, all of them; they were friendly and seemed competent. A team, working together instead of competing, and she was a part of it. She had to admit, it felt good.

                                    4

____

leksi grasped the handle of the door to the Northwest Science
building and pulled, but it was locked. *Of course it's locked, idiot.
It's the day after Christmas. The whole university's closed.*

Christmas… She'd spent the day alone in her apartment, reading and
playing with Iggy. She'd given him some hot-house grown hibiscus for his
present, and he had gorged until he could barely move. Her own
Christmas dinner had been grilled ham and cheese and pretzels. She
drank Irish coffee, read every word of Dr. Hutchinson's proposal until she
knew it backward and forward, and fell asleep on the couch. It was the
best Christmas she could remember, simply because she had spent it
alone. Except for one phone call to her parents, a half an hour of guilt and
ridicule, it had been perfect.

She pulled one glove off with her teeth and fumbled her ring of keys
from her coat pocket. They were so cold they stuck to her fingers. She
found the right one and opened the door, careful to pull the metal handle
with her gloved hand. They'd had another Arctic blast, and Cambridge
was a solid block of ice.

She pulled off her other glove and unbuttoned her coat as she climbed
the stairs. The heat inside the buildings had been turned down, but it felt
positively torrid compared to outside. She turned down the short hall to
Hutch's office, and found his door closed. Immediately, she wondered if

she'd made a mistake with the time. Was she late? Early? Was this the wrong day?

Aleksi reached for her phone to check her schedule, but stopped when she heard laughter from behind the door. They were inside.

Anxiety gripped her stomach. Were they talking about her? Should she listen through the door? What if they were and she overheard something bad? What if they opened the door and she was caught?

Stop it! Near panic attacks like this were nothing new, but why now? She knew everyone in that room. They were working together, professionals, scientists; she was being an idiot again.

Aleksi clenched her hands into fists and forced herself to knock. The door opened before her knuckles rapped a third time, and she found herself staring into the wizened features of the MCZ curator, Dr. Quinton Neilson.

"Aleksi!" Quinton stepped back and waved her into the office.

Inside, Bob Tomlin and Hutch stood from their chairs, both of them smiling. *Had* they been talking about her? A wall of heat and the scent of coffee buffeted her as she stepped inside, and she realized why the door had been closed. Hutch had a space heater running.

"It's good to see you again." Quinton stepped aside and closed the door behind her.

"And you, Dr. Neilson," she said, forcing a smile.

"Now, stop that." He grinned to Hutch. "I told her the first time we met to call me Quinton, but it didn't take. Aleksi was doing undergraduate work study with the American Museum of Natural History in Manhattan, and came up to tell us how to reorganize our archives." He laughed and Aleksi blushed, opening her mouth to protest. "Oh, don't. I'm just kidding. Well, it won't be long before I can call *you* Dr. Rychenkna, from what I hear."

"It'll be a few years yet." She lowered her gaze and clenched her hands in her pockets. They *had* been talking about her.

"Don't worry, Aleksi. We didn't talk about you much, and it was all good."

She gaped at Hutch for a moment, then stammered, "I didn't...I mean I wasn't..."

"It's true." Bob grinned and looked sheepish. "It *was* all good. You're like a Stepford student. Makes a poor lab geek like me feel inadequate."

"I..." She stared at Bob. He was joking. He had to be.

"Well, we're not here to chat, but to get you your samples." Quinton gave her arm a squeeze and nodded to the door. "Let's get over to the MCZ and see what we can find, shall we?"

Hutch finished his coffee and they all grabbed their coats. He unplugged the heater before they left and followed the curator down the stairs and out into the bitter cold.

"I requisitioned us some muscle." Quinton keyed them into the museum and ushered them inside. "One of the assistants who wanted to earn some overtime."

"Good." Hutch grinned at his two students. "I did tell you the samples were big, didn't I?"

"Cave bear bones usually are, aren't they?" Bob chuckled.

"It's not just the bone that's heavy. It's the rock bed." Aleksi had worked on some bone bed finds that weighed tons.

"She's right." Quinton led the way down to the archives in the basement, the primary storage facility for the museum, four floors of nothing but storage. "These are merely huge, not truly gargantuan, so we should be able to manage."

They kept descending until they were on the bottom level. Out of the stairwell, they stopped to divest their coats, gloves, scarves and hats. That musty, dusty, repository scent caressed Aleksi's senses, and she felt better.

After her first high school field trip to the American Museum of Natural History, Aleksi had taken every chance to hop the train and spend her meager allowance on the entry fee. After the fifth time the night guards had to force her to leave at closing time, one of the curators had suggested that she should arrange a work study project with her school.

The experience had changed her life.

"I don't get down here often enough." Quinton said as they passed through a pair of double doors into the meticulously climate-controlled archives, row upon row of shelves, racks of drawers, a library of once living creatures waiting to be discovered. "You won't find *this* on the Internet, ay, Aleksi."

"Exactly," was all she could say.

"Impressive." Hutch squinted down the rows of cabinets and open racks that held larger specimens. "How many samples in the whole facility?"

"Including those on display, about a quarter million." Quinton motioned them down the rows of racks toward the back. "Most are entomological and small vertebrates, of course. Space is a problem. There's some pressure to consolidate some of the larger samples, put them in long term, off-site, storage, but we're fighting it."

"I wondered why my request for the bone bed samples was approved so quickly. You need the space." Aleksi thought Hutch might be trying for sardonic, but she knew he was right.

"That's part of the reason," Quinton admitted. "The other is that the samples haven't been worked up properly." He smiled at Aleksi. "And now that I know Aleksi's going to do the work-up, I'm even more satisfied with the arrangement."

Aleksi studied her boots as they walked.

"Stepford student. What did I tell you?" Bob nudged her elbow, and gave her a wink, his whisper jovial and his smile genuine.

"You may not think so, Aleksi, but you already have a good reputation with the work you've done at AMNH, so don't be modest." Quinton checked a sheet of paper and the numbers on the racks. "Ah, here we are. Right down here." He turned between two columns of steel shelving.

A man stood half way down the row, his back to them, one hand resting on the shelf. A yellow trolley stood beside him, the kind Aleksi recognized for moving heavy samples through tight spaces. The man wore a lab coat and had meticulously trimmed short brown hair.

"Ah. Derrick. Good of you to come." The man turned, and Aleksi recognized him. The same museum assistant she'd seen the other day when she left the archives, the one who seemed too friendly.

"My pleasure, Dr. Neilson." His eyes flicked over them and he smiled, teeth perfectly white and straight. "I hadn't intended to go home for the holidays, and I'm happy to help."

"You found the specimens, I see." Quinton peered at the labels on the rack.

"Yes. This, these two, and the bottom one there." Derrick touched four wrapped crates. The last box he tapped was about six feet long, three wide, and occupied an entire section of shelving.

"Those *are* big." Aleksi thought they would need a forklift just to get it down.

"Holy crap." Bob sounded a little stunned. "I mean… that's a lot of stuff. Don't we need a forklift or something?"

"Oh, don't worry about loading them," Quinton said, pulling a pair of latex gloves from a nearby dispenser. "We've got Derrick to do that. He'll get a lift later, but we can have a look at one of the smaller ones. Give me a hand, Derrick. We can lift this smaller one down."

"Sure."

Quinton and Derrick donned latex gloves, and Aleksi backed away. The crate they picked was only about three feet long, two deep and a foot high. It was on a waist high shelf, so the two men had no trouble lifting it down, though she noticed the strain in Quinton's face as they did so.

"Well, that was heavier than I thought it would be," the older man said, straightening with a grin. "Nice to know that I can do a little of the heavy work. Now, let's see."

He worked the crate's simple latch and opened it to reveal a fitted Ethafoam insert. He lifted the top layer with care. Inside, instead of the dark preserved bone that Aleksi expected, they found only a thick casing of plaster of Paris.

"Not much to see, I'm afraid. Like I said, most of this wasn't worked up." Quinton grinned at Aleksi. "I'm afraid you've got your work cut out for you, dear."

"Are they all like this?" She was surprised that they'd allowed this to sit so long without even removing the shipping matrix.

"Oh, no. I think half of the entire shipment was at least cleaned up. I'll have to look at the records again. But these four are yours."

There was also a large tag, yellowed with age, inside an acid-free plastic bag, and Aleksi recognized the Cyrillic letters. He lifted it out and showed her. "This one's for you, I think."

She put on gloves and took the document. There were actually several pages in the bag, but she wasn't about to open it here. "Collection notes. Date, location, conditions, personnel…"

"They should each have such a sheet, I think." Quinton peered at the page inquisitively. "We'll just put it all back and let you transcribe it under more controlled conditions. The pertinent information is in the database."

"Of course." She put it back in the case.

"Well, if even half of the samples are like this, you really *do* have some work ahead of you." Hutch cringed and shrugged. "Sorry, Aleksi. I didn't think they'd be this bad."

"Don't be." She ran a gloved hand over the thick mass of plaster of Paris. It was almost as if she could feel the bone within asking her to free it from its long sleep. She stood and stepped back, and realized she was smiling. "It'll be fun."

"Fun? Chipping through a foot-thick block of plaster?" Bob looked at her like she was insane. "Are you kidding me?"

"I see that you really don't know Aleksi quite yet." Quinton patted her on the shoulder. "She isn't a digger, she's a finder. If there's something to be found in these old samples, she's the one who can."

Aleksi blushed under his praise and studied her shoes, but she couldn't keep the smile from her face. "What can I say? It's what I like to do."

"And it's exactly what I need, Aleksi." Hutch took a deep breath and let it out slowly. "Well, we better get to it."

"We'll load this first one onto the trolley, and Derrick will load the rest with a lift." Quinton started to move to help Derrick lift, but Hutch put a hand on his shoulder.

"Let me help Derrick with that, Quinton."

"Well, all right." The curator backed away with a chuckle. "The last thing I need is a herniated disc." Quinton patted Bob on the shoulder. "Don't ever get old, my boy."

"I don't think age has as much to do with it as muscle." Bob grinned. "I'm a lab geek. I don't lift anything heavier than a pipettor most days."

As the two men lifted the sample onto the cart, Derrick caught Alexi's eye and smiled again with those white-perfect teeth. She looked away, pretending to show interest in the paperwork Quinton was examining. Something about Derrick unnerved her even more than most men. Maybe it was his smile, those perfect teeth, or his perfect hair and smooth, chiseled features. He was too perfect. Way too perfect to be paying attention to her.

"If you all can manage this one to your lab, I'll have the next one loaded by the time you get back, and I can follow you with the lift." Derrick cinched the straps around the case, unlocked the trolley's wheels, and pulled a handle that inclined the bed to near vertical. "That should make it easier to get around the corners."

"Thank you, Derrick. We should be back shortly."

While they left the archives, Aleksi glanced back to find Derrick smiling at her again, as if the expression was pasted on his face. She looked away, swallowing her unease. She had work to do.

L ast one, I promise." Quinton flipped a page on the form and pointed to the yellow sticky labeled, 'Sign Here.'

Hutch scrawled his signature and clicked the pen closed. "What's this section about first-born male child? You sure this is legit?"

"Don't suggest that. The powers that be might just put in a contingency clause." Quinton stuffed the sheaf of forms into a folder and stood from behind his desk. "So much paper in this digital age, but everyone needs their original. Take care of those specimens, Hutch, and don't let Aleksi get over her head. From what I understand, she's good at that."

"No worries, Quinton. If anything, taking this project on has *cut* her workload. Oliver was overloading her."

"That's what I heard, too." Quinton held out a hand, and Hutch shook it. "Take care, Hutch. I better get home before my wife divorces me for working on a university holiday."

"Right." Quinton's comment reminded him of something he'd been putting off. "Will I see you at the faculty New Year party?"

"Probably, but it depends on the weather." Quinton reached for his coat. "Why couldn't I curate a museum in Florida?"

"I hear there's a position opening at Gatorland." Hutch grinned.

"Sounds perfect."

They left Quinton's office and went their separate ways, the curator home to his wife and Hutch down to the basement lab of the MCZ annex. Aleksi and Bob should have all the samples squared away by now with Derrick's help. First, however, he had to take care of one unpleasant task. He pulled his phone from his pocket, brought up the directory, and punched a number he hadn't called in almost a year. As it rang, he secretly wished it would go to voicemail, but today wasn't his lucky day.

"Hutch? What's wrong?"

God, he hated caller ID. "Hello, Persephone. Nothing's wrong. Why would something be wrong?"

"You only ever call when something's wrong." She sounded busy, which was pretty much her status every waking hour. "Sorry. What's up?"

"I was thinking about the faculty New Year party and wondered if you had plans." *Please, please be busy.*

"I'll have to check my schedule." There was a long pause, which he refused to break. "I always *did* enjoy those parties, and you look so dashing in a tux. So, how are things in Cambridge?"

"Quiet. Winter recess, you know. I'm at the MCZ right now."

"You're *working*? They don't give you a recess just so you can dig up more bones, you know." She'd always given him grief for working too hard, though he had taken every holiday and vacation day he'd earned while they were married. Persephone had not held a job a day in her life and didn't understand people who did.

He often wondered what they'd seen in each other to begin with. She was from old money, and he was middle class. He worked hard to make a name for himself and build a career, and she had been born with a name and only worked hard to maintain her reputation as a socialite. They'd met at a fundraiser for the school where he learned she had a love of cryptozoology. Unfortunately, she found academics boring, except for the parties.

"Well, these bones were in the archives of the museum, so I didn't even need to get my knees dirty."

"I remember you used to *like* dirty knees, at least when they were mine."

"Ha! Well, I see your sense of humor hasn't changed." There were a few things he remembered about Persephone with fondness, but there were far too many unfond ones to counterbalance those. She'd gotten bored with him, and when Persephone got bored, she became petulant and dangerous. "Call me when you figure out your schedule."

"Will do," she chimed, then added, "and thanks for calling, Hutch. It *would* be good to see you again, and I'm not joking."

"You, too, Persephone. Bye."

"Bye, Hutch."

He pressed End and took a deep, calming breath. Honestly, he didn't know why he'd invited her. Their divorce had been amicable. She had more money than many small countries, so there was no alimony, and there were no children to fight over. More than anything, he thought it would have been rude *not* to invite her, and he shouldn't go alone. The one thing Persephone loved above all others was a formal party where she could be the center of attention. He wasn't really looking forward to the faculty function, but had to attend for political reasons. He could do a lot worse than to walk in with Persephone on his arm. If he was lucky, she'd be surrounded by physicians and lawyers, and he could ditch her. He dropped his phone in his pocket and headed down to Aleksi's lab.

Aleksi brushed her fingers against the door of room B-5 in the MCZ basement and turned the key in the lock. *My lab*. The thought brought a thrill of excitement. Her first impression of the place had been less than thrilling, but at least it was hers. Hers and two other technicians' who worked for the museum. Shared space was the only space they could get, and she felt sorry for the other technicians. She was going to make a hell of a mess in here.

She held the door open while Derrick and Bob maneuvered the last and largest of the four samples through. It barely fit. They wheeled the huge slab between lab benches and other projects underway. There were two fume hoods set into one wall, and open air-handling conduits hanging from the ceiling. Her portion of the space, about a quarter of the entire room, was walled off by plastic sheeting to keep the dust she would generate contained.

"Here. Let me get that." She held the sheeting aside for the trolley, and the two men wheeled the heavy crate through.

"I can't believe you're going to do all this yourself." Bob stood aside while Derrick locked the wheels and brought the crate back to horizontal, then wheeled the portable electric lift into position.

"It'll go faster than you think. Plaster is easy. Once we get down to rock, things will slow down." She and Bob watched nervously as the technician lifted the lid off the crate and pried up the foam. She cringed at his brisk movements. "Need any help?"

"No." Derrick glanced at her and she saw a flash of something in his eyes that might have been annoyance before he flashed that smile again. "I'm being careful. Trust me."

"Sure." She bit her lip as he attached the straps to the lift's hook and pushed the button that engaged the electric motor. Its whine deepened as the sample came free of the crate.

"Jesus H. Christ that's huge." Bob chuckled nervously as Derrick pulled the trolley and the empty crate away, then maneuvered the lift until the sample hung over the table. "I hope the table will take it."

"Sorry about the cramped quarters, but it was all we could get." They all turned at Hutch's voice. He pulled the plastic sheeting aside and stopped dead. "Don't let me interrupt."

"No problem, professor." Derrick smiled that patent smile again and lowered the specimen down onto the table. Unhooking the straps, he turned that smile on Aleksi. "See? I told you to trust me."

"Thank you." Aleksi breathed a sigh of relief and helped maneuver the lift and the trolley out of the curtained space.

"I'll help Derrick take these back." Bob smiled and waved. "Call me if you need anything Aleksi. I'm setting up the genetics lab for the next week, so I'm not far away."

"Um…sure."

"Thanks, Bob." Hutch gestured Aleksi back to the personal protection equipment station set up outside the plastic barrier. "So, first things first. You know the procedures, but I've got to cover them."

"Sure." She followed him to the cart laden with paper and latex.

"Nobody goes in without gloves and particle mask." This, she knew, was more for the protection of the specimens than her; any contact with the fossils could contaminate them with human DNA. "A gown isn't mandatory, but unless you want plaster and rock dust in your clothes, I'd recommend one. Any time anyone's working, eye shields *are* mandatory and ear protection if you're using power tools." He put on gloves and a particle mask, and she followed suit.

Hutch pushed open the overlapping plastic sheeting and stepped inside the enclosure. The four samples dominated the space. One was in a partial state of exposure, and one was completely free of any restraining shipping matrix, though there was still quite a bit of rock to be removed. The last two were just huge blocks of plaster with their documents lying beside them in flat plastic pouches. All the tools and equipment she would need were set up along the bench that ran around the periphery of the lab.

"I know I don't need to tell you to document everything. There's a digital camera set up for you there." He gestured to an imaging setup, a simple digital camera on a frame with a gridded base for reference. "Photograph all the field notes first, that way you can transfer the files and work on transcribing them at home. There's plastic for your laptop if you want to work here, too. *Nothing* leaves the lab without approval."

"Of course." She glanced at him. "Don't worry, Hutch. I know the rules." She'd spent thousands of hours in labs like this, probably more than he had.

"Sorry. I know you do." He took a deep breath. "I'm just stressing a little. Big project, big grant, big responsibility." He smiled behind his mask, his eyes crinkling. "You sure you want a PhD? The first thing they do is stick you in an office and tell you to start delegating all the fun stuff."

"I'm sure." Something was bothering him, without a doubt. Did he doubt her abilities? She didn't dare ask. "I better get to work. I've only got a few weeks before classes start."

"Oh, that reminds me." He grimaced. "I got you out of January GSAS, but the freshman bio lab is a bigger problem. Lawson's being a pain about it, and if I take it off your shoulders, I'll have to double load someone else. I thought of Lonnie, but she's defending her dissertation this semester, and it wouldn't be fair. I'll try to find someone to take it, but it might not happen until a few weeks into the semester."

"Okay." Freshman biology lab really wasn't much work, but it meant at least ten hours a week in set up, take down, and paperwork. That time had to come from somewhere. "It might slow things down here some."

"Understood." He looked around at the samples and shrugged. "Maybe I can free myself up a few hours a week to help you here. Been a while since I got my hands dirty."

"Sure." She wasn't sure she liked the idea of working side-by-side with her advisor. Too many cooks could ruin a project. There was only one thing that she felt obligated to say. "As long as I get my proposal in on time and can prepare for my quals."

"That I can promise you, Aleksi." He looked her in the eye, serious as stone. "You have my word on it."

"Thanks." She looked away, uncomfortable with his eyes on hers. "Well, I better start taking pictures."

"Right." He turned away and pushed open the barrier, then turned back. "Oh, and when we need to take anything for CT or X-ray there's a ton of paperwork involved, so let me know as soon as you can and I'll start the ball rolling.

"No problem."

"Okay, then. Don't work too late. Let me know if you need anything."

"I will." Aleksi watched him leave, his shape murky though the translucent plastic barrier. Alone and safe, she got to work.

5

———————

Hutch burst into his office and threw his coat in the general direction of the rack. He barely had time to do his email before he had to meet with the graduate coordinator about Aleksi's schedule. The thought of her in her oral qualifying exams worried him. She seemed too introverted to handle it. With any luck, the meeting wouldn't last long. He had to get home, get cleaned up, and put on a tux. The faculty party started at seven.

"Five hours of standing around dealing with stuffed shirts…"

He booted up his computer and reviewed his snail mail while his email downloaded. *Nothing that can't wait,* he decided, filing the stack in his "to do" pile. Not many emails, either. Maybe there was hope for a cup of coffee before his meeting. He scanned them and cringed. One was from a Persephone, and the subject was 'Party Time!'

"Shit." He hadn't heard a word from her since he'd invited her to the party and thought she had gotten a better offer. Now this. He read it quickly. She would meet him at his place at six thirty, ready to go. "Fucking perfect!"

"That doesn't sound good."

He glanced up to see Lonnie Westinghouse leaning against his door. "Jeez, Lonnie! You scared the shit out of me! What's up?"

"Just dropped by to talk about my dissertation defense, but if you've already got too much on your plate…"

"This? Don't worry; nothing serious. My ex is coming to the faculty party tonight."

"I thought she was long gone."

"Yeah, well, I'm an idiot. I invited her just to be nice, and she just accepted." He sighed. "Nothing like the last minute. Not your problem. What's up with your dissertation?"

"I was thinking that I'm pretty much ready to roll except for a few details. If we can manage to move the date up a few weeks, I can take that bio lab for Aleksi, and maybe help her with the samples a little. I'll just be writing otherwise."

"That would be awesome, Lonnie. See what you can do about scheduling."

"Herding cats, you mean?" She rolled her eyes. "I'll see what I can do."

"Great, but don't tell Aleksi until it's settled. Don't want to set her up for a fall."

"Sure, Hutch. Bummer about the party. Some of the grad students are getting together at Dudley for drinks, junk food, and watching the ball fall." She grinned at him. "Come by if you get bored."

"I might. Thanks." It sounded like a hell of a lot more fun than a night with Persephone and a room full of stodgy professors.

"Great. See you there, maybe." She waved. "Good luck with Persephone."

"Thanks." He grimaced at the thought of an evening with his ex-wife.

Beautiful…" Aleksi's latex-covered fingers brushed the dark rock and fossilized bone.

She'd translated the field notes, stored all the old documents, and removed the shipping matrix from three of the four samples. They were still embedded in rock, but the plaster casting had been removed. She could see her treasures now.

Not a bad start for less than a week. It was late, and Aleksi was getting tired, but one sample remained untouched; the largest one. Before she could begin the more delicate task of chipping and grinding away the concealing rock, she had to remove the plaster from the last sample. If she didn't, she'd just have to clean up the plaster dust twice.

She stretched her aching back and neck and glanced at the clock. The sunlight through the basement windows had faded hours ago. It was just past eight. *I'll just get a good start on the last one and call it a day.*

She moved her tools to the last bench and looked over the largest of the four samples. Big enough to fill a coffin, it weighed several hundred pounds. She was glad she wouldn't have to move it. She lifted the bone saw, a device designed to cut bone or plaster casts with a blunt-toothed vibrating blade, and flipped it on. The trick with this step was to go slowly. She knew from the cover sheet the approximate dimensions of the sample within, but she'd read erroneous cover sheets before, and had seen samples damaged by overzealous technicians. She estimated that she had at least three inches of plaster to cut through, but her first cut would only be a half-inch deep.

She sliced down the middle of the block, blinking through the plaster dust. After pausing to wipe her safety glasses, she made another pass parallel to the first, same depth, six inches to the left, and connected the two cuts top and bottom. She then inserted a broad bladed chisel and tapped it with a hammer. The plaster was layered with canvas, like most samples preserved in the early twentieth century, and if she gauged her cuts right it would come off in sheets. The six-inch swath came out in pieces. She'd been right; there was a layer of heavy canvas beneath. She vacuumed the area clean and retrieved a pair of sheers. The canvas was heavily waxed, a primitive moisture barrier before the advent of plastics, but even so, one side was moldy. As she cut along the periphery and lifted the material free, however, she stared in surprise at what lay beneath.

Directly in the middle of the block, still partially covered by the outer layer of plaster, a canvas-wrapped bundle lay in a square recess.

"What the hell?" She peered at the package.

It had been completely encased in waxed canvas, then plastered over. But what was it? She reached for the bone saw, intending to cut it free, but then realized what she was doing and cursed under her breath.

"Pictures first, idiot!"

She removed the plastic hood that protected the photographic equipment from dust and lifted the digital camera from its mount. After placing a ruler next to the package for scale, she climbed onto a stepstool and took several photos. Evidently, this sample hadn't been X-rayed, or they'd have found this earlier. She snapped more pictures, her mind filled with visions of Faberge eggs and other national treasures secreted out of the country to save them from the chaos of Russian revolution.

Returning the camera to its hood, she retrieved the bone saw and cut around the assumed outline of the package and lifted the plaster free. After more pictures, sheers parted the waxed canvas and she folded it back. The entire package measured only about eight by six inches. She vacuumed the dust away and took more pictures, then gingerly lifted the bundle free. It was only an inch thick, and even before she put it down under the camera, she knew it was a book.

"Curiouser and curiouser," she muttered as she changed to clean gloves.

Snapping photos at every step, Aleksi unwrapped the package. As she removed the last layer of fine cotton cloth, her face split into a grin beneath her dust mask. It *was* a book, with a plain brown leather cover and high-quality stitched binding, but without a single marking on the cover. She lay the cloth aside and took more photos, front back and spine. It was in excellent condition for a hundred-year-old book. Then, holding her breath, she gingerly turned the cover over. The inside page was blank.

"Huh?" She stared at it for a moment, as if willing some hidden message to appear, then snapped a photo and reached for the page. The fine parchment was yellowed at the edges but turned without cracking. The next page was blank, too, and her mistake dawned in her mind.

"Idiot." She closed the book and turned it over. With no markings on the cover, she'd flipped the back open first. With the same care, she turned over the front cover, and caught her breath. Elegant Cyrillic writing greeted her eyes.

"Императорская Санкт-Петербургская Академия Наук," she read, "*The Imperial Saint Petersburg Academy of Sciences*. Personal Journal of Dr. Andriy Loktev. Entries – January 1912 -" There was no completion date. Even more curious, this was not the journal of Dr. Sagadeyev, who had collected the bone bed samples.

She snapped a photo and turned the page. She was tempted to begin reading the dated entries, but knew it would be easier and better for everyone if she simply photographed the pages and transcribed them to English later. That way, the data was safe, even if the book was somehow lost or destroyed. As she flipped the pages and snapped photos, however, she noted the dates and locations. This sample wasn't from Sagadeyev's Bratskoe Vdkhr site at all, but from a site on the Kamchatka Peninsula, hundreds of miles away. She paused to read snippets here and there; the excitement of the narrative infectious. Loktev described the site in detail, down to celestial fixes of his location and topographic sketches, an ash deposit exposed at the edge of an ice field, a strange place to dig for fossils. She snapped photos and turned pages, then gasped at the sketches of the excavated sample. It was encased in pyroclastic ash, like something from the Pompeii exhibit. Only one bit of bone, a tooth exposed by recent erosion, hinted at what lay beneath. They had not removed the ash, but had encased the sample where it lay, rushed by the oncoming winter.

She snapped photos and turned pages.

September 24th, his team boarded a ship at Palana, and sailed to Vladivostok, where they met Dr. Sagadeyev. The last entry read like the confession of a mother giving her child up for adoption. Learning the climate of the political landscape and the storm that was coming, Loktev had encased his journal in with the sample and sent them off to America with Sagadeyev's specimens. His hopes were to join them there one day, to discover the hidden treasure he had pulled from the earth.

The last third of the book was blank.

"Well, if this isn't a holy crap moment..." She closed the book with reverent care and placed it in a special acid-free plastic bag for storage. Simple exposure to air, dust and moisture would destroy it in time, though it was currently in excellent condition. The data was safe in the camera. She stretched again and looked at the clock. Ten thirty. Too late to call Hutch about this and her stomach was growling like a hungry wolf.

She copied the photos from the camera to a flash drive, then backed them up on the photo setup's external hard drive as well. The files were too big to easily email, so she would just email him what she'd found and show him tomorrow. For now, she needed to eat.

Aleksi removed her gown and stuffed the flash drive in her pocket, then vacuumed the dust from her hair, knowing she must look like a pastry chef after a food fight. Outside the dust barrier, she doffed her gloves, mask and safety glasses, washed her hands and face in the lab sink, grabbed her coat and bag, and headed for the door, dreaming of reheated pizza, Irish coffee, and the pages of the newly discovered treasure in her pocket.

6

The bracing cold air hit Aleksi like a five AM wakeup call. It had been a long day, but the excitement of the discovery and the blast of chill air shattered her fatigue.

That and the noise.

"New Year's Eve," she muttered with a shake of the head.

Aleksi had few good memories of the holiday. People tended to drink too much, get way too friendly, and wake up in the morning regretting both. Consequently, she tried to avoid invitations, or claim that she had already been invited to other celebrations, then sit home and ignore the blaring music and loud voices cheering in the New Year.

Tonight, however, with excitement still pounding in her head, the music blaring from the Law School residence halls seemed like a crowd of cheering spectators celebrating her find. She laughed at the notion, and stuck her hands in her pockets, lengthening her strides for home.

Then her phone vibrated.

"Damn." She'd turned it to vibrate and left in in her coat pocket that morning. She pulled off a glove and swiped the screen: two calls from her mother and, a text from a local number she didn't recognize. "Double damn!" She hadn't called home since Christmas day. Well, that could wait until tomorrow; her parents were in bed by nine thirty. She pulled up the text and saw that it was from Lonnie Westinghouse.

It said, "Where R U?" and was two hours old.

She tapped in, "Sorry. Work. Sup?" and sent it. She stuffed the phone in her pocket, but only took a dozen steps before it vibrated again. She pulled it out without breaking stride; she had a date with an Irish coffee.

"Party @ Dudley. Hutch is here."

"Not much for NYE parties." She sent it, but then stopped. If Hutch was there, she could tell him about the journal she'd found. *But drunk people, music, crowds...* Before she could make a decision, her phone vibrated again.

"He's in black tie! Can U say incriminating photos?" Lonnie had attached a picture of Hutch, drink in hand, tie hanging around his open collar. His mouth was open and he was gesticulating. A dark-haired young woman stood at his elbow, gazing at him as if he had just agreed to father her child.

Aleksi smiled; she was starting to like Lonnie's sense of humor. She sent, "BRT! 10 min."

She did an about face and stuffed the phone in her pocket. Harvard Yard was noisy. Students who had not gone home for the holidays were having a stereo contest. There were a few shouts and one obscene invitation, but she ignored them and just kept walking. Lehman hall, which held Dudley House Graduate Center and the Dudley Café, occupied the corner of the yard. She heard the music before she even cracked the door.

It wasn't as loud as the battle of the stereos, but it was loud enough to make conversation a shouting contest. A big screen TV displayed Times Square in all its gritty splendor, but there were fewer people here than she would have expected. Long tables laden with junk food and alcohol lined one wall. Lonnie approached with a pitcher of sangria in one hand and two cups in the other.

"Aleksi! You made it!" She wrapped her long arms around Aleksi without spilling a drop of the liquid. "Stash your coat and have some of the worst sangria in the free world!"

Aleksi tried not to shy from the wobbly embrace. She liked Lonnie, but wasn't a hugger. After removing her coat, she reluctantly accepting one of the cups.

"You going prematurely gray, or working with a plaster saw?" Lonnie lifted her glass in toast. Aleksi could tell this wasn't her first drink of the evening.

"The latter." She sampled the sangria and stifled a cough. "Holy—"

"The chem geeks made it. I think they used anhydrous ethanol and grape soda." She took a sip and grimaced. "Revolting, isn't it?"

Aleksi took another careful sip and had to check her gag reflex before swallowing. "God, it's disgusting! I can't drink this."

"I thought Russian's drank straight vodka."

"We do, and it's *way* better than this."

"That's okay. Just pour it back in and get whatever you like from the bar." She gestured toward the bottle-laden table. "Oh, and there's food, sort of. Come on."

She followed Lonnie to the table and cringed again. There was a huge cooler of various beers, bottles of cheap wine, and a plethora of hard liquor and mixers. *No Irish coffee tonight,* she thought, looking at the decimated food table. There were half a dozen empty platters, several bowls of chips and dip, a vegie plate, and some chicken wings that looked radioactive. *And so much for dinner.* She filled a paper plate with tortilla chips, ladled on some kind of cream-cheese based dip, and took some wings, carrots, and celery.

"No drink?" Lonnie looked at her like she was damaging the party. "Come *on*, Aleksi, let me pour you *something*."

"Um, okay." She scanned the table and espied a familiar red and white label. After emptying her cup back into Lonnie's pitcher, she filled it with ice, then poured in a measure of Stolychnia and topped it with tonic. "Better?"

"Much better." Lonnie wrapped an arm around her shoulders and, much to Aleksi's horror, steered her toward the crowd.

"You, um, said Hutch was here?" Aleksi scanned the group but couldn't see anyone in a tux. She balanced her plate on her cup and tried a chip. The dip was loaded with herbs. She hoped they were the legal kind.

"Yeah, somewhere. He's got law students swarming all over him." Lonnie leaned in close. "He dated a grad student over there a while ago, and she evidently talked to her friends about him. The women are circling like sharks."

"Oh?" The thought of a bevy of female lawyers stalking Hutch struck her as amusing.

She spotted him in the middle of a group of students, not *all* of them women, but most. Lonnie elbowed her way right in, something Aleksi could never have done, and touched Hutch's arm.

"Look who I dragged in out of the cold!" Lonnie waved a hand at Aleksi and in an instant every eye in the group was on her. She stood there with a plate of chips in one hand and her plastic cup in the other, a deer in the headlights.

"Aleksi! Wow!" He grinned and waved her into the group. "Everyone this is Aleksi Rychenkna, my newest grad student. Aleksi, this is...well... just about the whole law review. We've been talking about the lawsuits over the pipeline project. It's a legal nightmare."

"Oh, sure. Hi." She took a sip of her drink to mask her discomfort at being the center of attention, however brief.

"Is that *plaster* dust?" Hutch stepped over and reached up to touch her hair. "Tell me you didn't just get out of the lab."

"I...Oh! You won't *believe* what I found." Aleksi suddenly remembered the journal and her reticence vanished. "One of the samples isn't from Bratskoe Vdkhr. It's from Kamchatka! Some digger named Andriy Loktev found it at the base of the Nalychevo volcano."

"*What?*" Hutch nearly dropped his plastic cup. "After all that paperwork, we took the wrong sample? That's impossible!"

"I thought so, too. All the cover documents said it was one of Sagadeyev's four samples, but I found a journal under the first layer of plaster on the biggest one. I photographed the whole thing and read a little. He put his specimen on the ship with Sagadeyev's at Vladivostok when he found out what was happening back in Moscow. He worked for The Imperial Saint Petersburg Academy of Sciences, and was afraid the revolution would destroy his work. They changed the cover documents instead of adding a whole new shipment manifest."

"Quinton is going to have a coronary." Hutch shook his head and took a healthy swig of his drink. "I want to see these pictures, Aleksi. What is the sample, anyway?"

"I've got them on a stick." She balanced her plate on her cup and pulled the jump drive out of her pocket. "And they're not fossilized. Or, at least, I don't think so. The sample was buried in a pyroclastic ash deposit. He only found it because a tooth was exposed by erosion."

"A tooth? What kind of tooth?" Hutch turned to the rest of the group, whose attention in their conversation had waned. "Anyone have a computer?"

"Uh, sure." One of the law students dug in his bag and pulled out a tablet. "Whadaya need?"

"Mind if we look at some pictures with it?" At the raised eyebrows around the group, he rolled his eyes. "*Work* pictures."

"Oh, sure. Just don't delete anything, okay?" The student booted up the tablet, logged in, and handed it over.

"No problem. Thanks!" Hutch steered them toward two lounge chairs away from the crowd and they sat. While he inserted the stick and pulled up the files, he asked again, "So, what was this tooth?"

"There's a sketch in the journal, about two thirds back. Loktev thought it was a carnivore, but he didn't have much more information. He didn't want to excavate through the ash cast in the field, so he encased the whole thing in plaster. He was going to take it all to St. Petersburg and work on it there, but that never happened." She balanced her plate on the arm of her chair and munched a chip. Her empty stomach grumbled at the mixture of junk food and alcohol as she watched him flip through the photos. "There!"

"A canine! Holy crap, look at that! Is this to scale?"

"I don't know. The journal is about six by eight, but I didn't cut down to the sample itself. I knew you'd want to see this before we did any more." She watched Hutch resize the photo to match the dimensions of the journal. The sketch of the curved canine was about an inch long, but only showed the portion that was exposed from the ash. The detail of the sketch was excellent, and there were two different views. "Carnivore?"

"Looks more like a primate tooth. I've seen macaque canines like this, and baboon even bigger." He squinted at the Cyrillic notes. "What does this say?"

"He describes the recurve edge of the tooth. He says it's sharp, like a razor."

"That *does* sound more like a male macaque. Big cats and bears have peg teeth." He chuckled. "Sorry, I know you teach comparative zoology; I'm just being a prof."

"No problem." She wasn't about to tell him that she didn't need a lecture on vertebrate morphology. "But there's no way it's a macaque. Flip forward a few pages. There. He's got sketches of the cranial section with all the alluvial deposit removed. The ash formed a cast like the ones at Pompeii. It's probably less than an inch thick. The shape is all wrong and it's too big."

"Hmmm." He sipped his drink and frowned. "You're right. We should image the whole thing and get a full body picture, but..." He leaned back and looked at her. "I'd love to study this, Aleksi, but we have to tell Quinton what we've found before we do anything else."

"Oh." Aleksi realized that he was right. They weren't even supposed to have this sample. "You think he'll want it back?"

"Probably. This isn't what we were looking for. And even if the museum *did* let us keep it, we've got no funding, and you've got a dissertation to work on."

Aleksi could see it in his face; there was interest, but reluctance, too. She bit her lip; she was more interested in this sample than all of the Ursus data. It was an unknown. It might be a dead end, but they would never know if Quinton took the sample back. Then a thought occurred to her, and she heard herself speaking before she could stop.

"What if we could get funding from the MCZ to work this up?"

"It would still take time, Aleksi, and your dissertation proposal is due, not to mention your comp exams. You can't do it all."

Her mind raced. "How about this: we ask Quinton for permission and money to do a basic workup on the sample, just imaging and clean up, maybe some DNA work if we can get it, just to identify what we've got. I'll continue on the workup of the Ursus samples until we know what this one is. If it's something I can use for my dissertation, I'll apply for a grant, and you bring Bob into the Ursus project for his dissertation. It's mostly genetics, anyway; he'll love you for it. I'll help him with the grunt work, and he can do the DNA isolation and PCR on this sample when we have something ready for my proposal."

"And if this turns out to be a dead end?"

"Then we send it back to MCZ basement, and I've only lost a couple of weeks."

"You're sure you want to do this, Aleksi? I mean the workload..."

She flipped the tablet to the page that displayed Loktev's sketch of the entire sample prior to encasing it in plaster and showed it to him. "I'm sure."

"Holy..." his eyes widened at the sketch. The outline was vague, but its sinuous shape and long forelimbs were clear. "What the hell have you dug up, Aleksi?"

"I don't know." The warm glow of discovery filled her like a drug. "But I want to find out."

"*There* you are!"

Both of their heads came up at the accusative cry. A dark-haired woman strode toward them, flipping open the buttons of her voluminous fur coat. Beneath, she wore a deep blue evening gown that plunged at the neck, and a glittering necklace of blue and white stones. Her hair was coifed into an intricate pile of curls, and gems to match her necklace dangled at her ears. Her eyes flashed at Hutch with more fire than her jewelry.

"Dwayne Hutchinson, you *ditched* me!" She shrugged out of her coat and flung it at a chair.

"Persephone!" Hutch stood, looking apologetic. "Sorry. You seemed to be having a good time, and something came up."

Aleksi stood and started to back away, but the woman's eyes pinned her like an insect in a collection before they snapped back to Hutch. *This* was Hutch's ex-wife? She'd seen her picture on the Internet while researching Hutch, but never dressed up for a formal party. If the jewelry was real, it could have financed Aleksi's college education. What was she doing here?

"Something came up? What could come up on New Year's Eve, Hutch, but another party?" She flung a hand at the room full of graduate students. "You got a better offer and left me hanging with a bunch of stuffy academics."

"Actually, Aleksi here was working this evening, and found something interesting." He reached for the tablet as Aleksi stood there stunned. He was using her as an excuse. The computer slipped from her numb fingers, and he flipped to the page with the drawings. "See?" He held it for her to see.

"Working?" Persephone looked first at Aleksi, then down at the screen. "*Nobody* works on New Year's Eve. What are you trying to…"

As she peered down at the screen, Hutch caught Aleksi's eye and mouthed, "Sorry," with a cringe and a shrug. Aleksi looked away. She didn't like being used as an excuse. Then Persephone's eyes widened, and her voice changed.

"Oh *my*! That's…" She bit her lip and cocked her head, peering at the illustration. "That's *something*. It's all in Russian, too. What is it?"

"We don't know yet." Hutch took the tablet back, though Persephone seemed reluctant to let it go. "The journal was hidden in a specimen unearthed about a hundred years ago. It was buried in an ash deposit in Kamchatka. Aleksi wants to find out what it is."

"Aleksi…" Persephone pinned her again with those intense eyes and smiled with perfect teeth. "Well, since Hutch is too big a boor to even introduce us, I'll do so myself." She held out a hand. "I'm Persephone Terris. I assume you're one of my ex-husband's students."

"Yes." Aleksi shook her hand, one of those finger-only greetings that always seemed fake to her. "I am."

"And from the look of the dust in your hair, he wasn't lying about you working." Persephone brushed her hand on her dress as if she's been contaminated. "You poor dear. Hutch, how *could* you make her work on New Year's Eve?"

"Oh, he didn't. I just…like to work." Aleksi bit her lip, wondering why she was defending Hutch after he used her as his excuse.

"You *like* to *work*?" Persephone looked at her as if she'd grown horns and a tail.

"Some people *enjoy* working, Persephone." Hutch's tone stated clearly that this was an old argument. "She's got a dissertation project and her comps to do this semester."

"Oh, all right. I'm sorry." Persephone waved a hand in a dismissive gesture. "Well, you came here to work, and *I* came here to party, so have fun. I'm sure *someone* in Cambridge isn't working!" She snatched up her coat and flung it on. "But next time you invite me to a party, I expect you to stay there with me."

"I'm sorry, Persephone. I should have told you when I left."

"Yes, you *should* have." She glanced at Aleksi, then back to Hutch. "Goodnight."

"Goodnight." Hutch watched her go, then turned to Aleksi. "I'm sorry I did that. I needed an excuse and I panicked."

"That's all right." It wasn't, but Aleksi couldn't call him out on it.

"No, it's really *not*." Hutch shut down the tablet and handed her the flash drive. "You've really dug up something interesting, Aleksi. If you want to pursue this, we will, but if it gets to be too much for you, you have to promise me to let me know."

"I will," she said, having no intention of doing so. "I promise."

Persephone stared out the window as the streetlights flashed past in flurries of snow. New Year's Eve had not ended as she'd hoped; she hadn't seen Hutch in almost a year, and she'd hoped to lure him to bed for old times' sake. There had been a lot of good times between them, and even better times with him between the sheets. Now he was hanging out with young nerdy graduate students, probably seducing a new one every week.

Let it go, Persephone… She closed her eyes and sighed. She'd agreed to the divorce, though it had been more of an effort to keep him isolated from her other life than any lack of interest in him.

My other life… The images she'd glimpsed on the computer swam behind her eyes. *Life from another age. Watch for anything unusual, anything unexplained. Not all of mythology is myth…*

She'd been eighteen, but her great-grandmother's words came to her like she'd heard them yesterday. And she'd spent her life devoted to the family calling, watching for unexplained mysteries. What better way to look into mysteries of ancient life than by marrying a paleontologist? It had seemed simple, elegant even, but had become too complicated. Hutch found her curiosity of cryptozoology strange and asked too many questions. But this. This could be something important.

The rented limo pulled up to the gate and the privacy window lowered. She handed the driver her key card, and he swiped it and handed it back. The wrought iron barrier rolled open and he drove through, closed circuit cameras following their progress. He parked near the foyer and hurried around to hold the door and an umbrella for her, though it really wasn't snowing that hard.

She thanked him for the escort, pressed the intercom and said, "I'm home." The door clicked open, and she stepped inside. The hall light came on and the door closed and locked behind her. The house staff were either in bed or out ringing in the New Year, but that was fine with Persephone. She didn't need a butler tonight.

She took off her coat and checked the monitor beside the front door just to make sure the limo left through the gate. It did. She flipped through the screens from one camera to another but didn't see a soul. The security system was completely automated, of course. The fewer people who knew her family's secrets, the better.

Persephone flung the ermine coat in the general direction of the closet and hurried to the stairs down to the cellar. Motion sensor lights flicked on as she descended, teetering a bit on the steps. Champagne and high heels didn't mix. She click-clacked through the maze of draped shapes—decorations, furnishings, and shelves of knickknacks out of season—to the wine cellar door. Another card swipe and a key code popped the lock, and she stepped inside the cool room, closing the door behind her. Past the spotless racks of bottles, she finally reached her goal, a nondescript door with another keypad and a print scanner. She punched in the code and pressed her thumb to the pad. The light flashed green, and the door lock clicked.

She turned the handle and stepped into the Sanctum.

Down a sterile hall, she thumbed open another door. Dark paneling, subdued lighting, soft carpets of fine Oriental silk, and books defined the room's décor. A modern adjustable bed and a lift system were the only overt hints that this was more than just a secret library or den. Several large flat screens dominated the wall opposite the bed, now displaying a mosaic of silent star scape. Persephone stepped softly to the side of the bed.

The occupant looked barely human.

Skeletally thin and wizened beyond imagining, her great-grandmother's lips were as thin as a razor, her skin the texture of parchment, creased with lines so deep that they had to be meticulously cleaned to stave off infections. Her eyes, sunken in their sockets, were closed in sleep, breathing barely perceptible. An oxygen cannula lay under nostrils that flared with every shallow intake of precious air. Her hands lay folded over a blanket, knuckles like walnuts, nails yellowed with untold years.

Persephone leaned down to whisper, "Gi-gi."

Her eyes opened, and the face became even less human, irises of bright lavender, almost luminous in the dim light. Those eyes swiveled to look at her, constricting to focus, and she blinked once. The coloration wasn't normal, of course; a byproduct of one of the family's earliest discoveries, the one that had earned them the millions that had blossomed into an international multi-billion-dollar empire. *All thanks to some long-dead African witchdoctor...* One day, Persephone would be faced with the choice of becoming something not quite human in exchange for the staggering intelligence her great-grandmother possessed. She hadn't yet decided whether to take it or die human.

The razor-slit mouth twitched open to whisper, barely audible over the quiet whir of the oxygen generator. "Persephone." The voice reminded her of the rustle of dried corn husks in autumn.

"Yes, Gi-gi." She reached out to lay a hand on her ancestor's. The wizened skin felt like the touch of the sun, warm, dry, alive. "I may have found something important."

She blinked again, her hand twitching under Persephone's. "Tell me."

"My...former husband has found the remains of a strange creature in the repository at the Museum of Comparative Zoology. It was encased in plaster, mislabeled, and undiscovered until recently. A book was found from a Russian paleontologist describing the find. The illustrations were nothing I've ever seen before."

The wizened hand moved under hers, the knobby fingers unlacing. "Show me."

Persephone tensed, then nodded. "Yes, ma'am." She lifted the hand, warm and soft, yet as fragile as the shell of an egg, and bent down to press the palm to the side of her head.

Her great-grandmother drew a breath, lips parted, and those luminous eyes closed. A sharp headache blossomed between Persephone's eyes as she recalled the images she'd seen on the computer, the artful drawings and Cyrillic writing. Her memories became both of theirs.

"Yes..." Those eyes opened again, and Persephone lowered the hand back. "Interesting. You must pursue this. Bring me the book."

Persephone massaged her temples to score away the pain. "I can't, but I may be able to bring you a copy."

One razor lip curled from yellowed teeth. "Digital?"

"Yes." She knew her great grandmother didn't care for digital copies, but even getting that would be difficult. She might have to sleep with Hutch to get it. *A dirty job, but someone has to do it.* Memories tingled through her, and her lips curved into a smile. "To get it, I will need to be *persuasive.*"

"Then be persuasive." The hand lifted again and the fingers touched a control pad in the side of the bed. She tapped out a code, and a drawer opened in a bookshelf. Inside, a velvet-lined case with three tiny vials of clear liquid. "Use it sparingly, and only at need."

"Thank you, Gi-gi." Persephone lowered her hand and patted it there, bending to kiss his wizened brow. "Rest now. I'll take care of everything." She took one of the vials from the drawer and left the Sanctum.

7

Derrick was starting to grow impatient, and he knew from experience that impatience led to recklessness, and often dire mistakes. *Control...* He girded his impulsiveness and climbed the stairs to Neilson's office. *Patience...* He'd been hasty before, and it had cost him. *One simple mistake...* He rapped on the door and opened it.

"Yes?" The old man looked up from his computer screen. "Oh, Derrick. Yes. Welcome back. Did you have a good holiday?"

"Yes, I did." Not a lie, exactly. It had been fun slumming through Boston's clubs on New Year's Eve, and the two drunk sluts he'd brought home had been entertaining. Now it was back to work, buttering up this old fuck to get into the graduate program. "I brought those files you asked for. The new acquisitions from Mexico." He held up a jump drive. "With the room we've got in the repository—"

"Oh, yes, about that." Dr. Neilson tapped his computer screen. "You'll never believe this, but one of those samples we gave to Dr. Hutchinson wasn't even the right one."

"Not the right one?" He'd loaded those samples himself and checked the papers. "What do you mean?"

Neilson glanced up at his tone then made a face. "Oh, don't worry, Derrick. Not your fault. It was miss-labeled from the start. Some Russian digger forged the documentation, and it was never even X-rayed. We had no way to know. Ha! Aleksi must be dancing a jig or a...oh whatever those Russian dancers dance. She found a journal encased in the largest of the four samples, and the illustrations are remarkable." He turned his monitor for Derrick to see, flipping through the pages of pencil sketches and Cyrillic writing.

"That's..." He caught a glimpse of one illustration, a recurved tooth. "What *is* that?"

"That's just it. We don't know." Neilson took the drive from Derrick and transferred the files to his computer. "Aleksi's translating the journal, but it'll take some time. They want money to work it up, but I can't see any way to give it to them. It's a shame, really. If we had the money, her dissertation project would be in the bag. We'll probably have to take the sample back and wait for funding."

"That *is* a shame." *Money...* That, at least, he had. *Time to pony up again, daddy...* This might be exactly what he'd been looking for. If it was returned to the repository, he could pimp his father for a grant to work up the sample, and he'd have an instant dissertation project.

Derrick accepted the drive from his boss and turned to leave, resolving to return to the curator's office later. He'd watched Neilson log on enough times to crack his password. Once he had the file, even if the sample didn't come back to the repository, he'd find out a way to make it his baby. Maybe he could seduce that nerdy chick into doing all the work for him. He might have to fuck her to get there, but he'd make the sacrifice. *PhD, here I come...*

W*aiting...*
Aleksi worked on the Ursus samples by day and translated the journal in the evenings, while the newly discovered mystery sat on the lab bench untouched. She and Hutch had spent New Year's Day crafting the plea to Quinton. The curator had responded with shock that such a blunder had taken place on his watch and promised to pitch their plea for funding to the MCZ board of directors, but that was all he could do.

The ensuing silence was deafening.

Every morning she came into the lab and glared at the block of plaster, yearning to delve its secrets. Then she would spend the day working on the bone bed samples, her mind dancing with images of the sketches in the journal. Bob Tomlin came by several times to take samples, and was busy with the laborious process of decontamination, extraction, cloning, and amplification of the fragmented DNA. It would be weeks before they had any meaningful data.

"Aleksi!"

She nearly dropped the high-speed rotary tool she was using, and turned to find Hutch and Bob standing at the opening to the dust barrier.

"Got a minute?" Hutch waved a single sheet of paper.

Her stomach did a flip. By their strained smiles, it wasn't good news. "Sure." She removed her dust mask, ear protection, and goggles. "What's that?"

"Permission." Hutch handed over the sheet of paper, a printout of the email from Quinton outlining the board's decision. "But they won't pay for it."

"Damn!" She scanned the document. "But we only need twelve thousand dollars! They spend more on paper *towels* in a year!"

"Come on, Aleksi. It could be worse. They could have insisted we send it back." Bob tried to smile but failed.

"They might as well have said no." Aleksi handed back the paper, her frustration burning through her usual reticence. "Where are we going to get twelve thousand dollars? It'll take *months* to get a grant, and we don't have the time!"

"About that." Hutch crumpled the paper and flung it at the nearest recycling bin. "I may have an idea, but it's...not somewhere I really wanted to go."

Aleksi and Bob traded a glance and a shrug.

"Don't keep us in suspense, Hutch. You know someone with that kind of money?" Bob grinned hopefully.

"Yeah. I used to be married to her." He fished his phone from his pocket.

"Persephone?" Aleksi bit her lip at her outburst, remembering the woman at the New Year's Eve party.

"Yep." Hutch tapped his phone and brought it to his ear.

Aleksi traded another questioning look with Bob, but he had never met Hutch's ex-wife.

"Persephone! Hi!" Hutch turned away and started to pace the lab floor. "Well, I thought I'd make a peace offering to make up for my bad behavior. How about lunch?"

Pause.

"No, not McDonalds. Someplace nice. You pick." He looked at them and raised his eyebrows. "Dinner? I don't know, Persephone. I know your taste, and the school doesn't pay me *that* much."

Another pause, and a look of surprise widened his eyes.

"All right then, if you insist. You wouldn't mind if I brought two of my students along, would you?"

Aleksi opened her mouth to protest, but Bob touched her arm and put a finger to his lips. She bit her lip and jammed her hands into her pockets to clench her fists. *Dinner with Persephone? Is he joking?*

"I've got a little proposal that I think you might be interested in. Right up your alley. Cryptozoology and a mystery novel all wrapped into a tale of the Russian Revolution." Hutch stopped to listen then nodded. "I promise, not too much shop talk."

More listening and Aleksi gritted her teeth.

"All right, then. Seven sounds perfect. We'll be there." He ended the call and grinned. "We're having dinner at the Chart House tonight."

"Hutch, I—"

Bob touched her arm again. "You *really* think she'll hand you twelve grand?"

"Persephone spends more than that on a weekend trip to New York." He slipped the phone into his pocket, his grin unbridled. "She's a cryptozoology nut behind the glitz and glamour, and I think we can pitch it to her the right way. I'll tell her she can name it if it's a new species."

Bob made a face. "Hutch, the chances of it being a new species are about one percent of *zero*."

"I know that, but she doesn't."

Aleksi just stared at him. Hutch was turning out to be secretly manipulative, a quality she knew all too well from her previous advisor. "Hutch, I really don't want to go to dinner. I'd only embarrass you."

"No, you won't, and this is *your* dissertation, Aleksi." He shrugged. "Think of this as a preparation for your oral exams. If you can't face down Persephone Terris, you'll never be able to confront your dissertation committee."

"But..."

"It's just dinner, Aleksi, not the *Inquisition*." Bob gave her a nudge. "It's not like the woman's a demon from hell or anything!"

"Well, she *can* resemble a succubus on certain occasions, but she's not that bad." Hutch grinned. "Wear something nice, both of you. I'll pick you up about six thirty."

"Right." Bob nudged Aleksi again. "A night on the town! What a deal!"

"Right." Aleksi bit her lip as they left and turned back to her work. She put her goggles, earmuffs, and mask back on and picked up the rotary tool, but her hands were shaking too badly to work. The prospect of dinner with Hutch and his succubus ex-wife had her stomach in knots.

8

———————————

Persephone Terris turned toward them as Aleksi and Bob followed Hutch into Chart House bar. A martini glistened in her manicured fingers, her dress of deep red complimenting her figure and a necklace of pearls and garnets perfectly. Her lips matched the hue of her dress to a tee, and her hair looked right out of a beauty salon. Aleksi tugged her simple blazer straight and tried not to put her hands in her pockets.

"Hutch!" Persephone spread her arms as if to embrace him, then just touched his shoulder with her free hand and kissed his cheek, though her lips never actually touched. "You look *wonderful*! Oh, and you've brought your little friends!"

"Hello, Persephone." Hutch stepped aside and gestured to Aleksi and Bob. "You met Aleksi Rychenkna on New Year's Eve, and this is Bob Tomlin, my first-year student."

"De*light*ful to meet you both." Persephone extended a hand and gave them each a stiff-armed, fingertip greeting. She looked Bob up and down as if she might take a bite. "You're both so *young*! Right from college to graduate school?" She inspected Aleksi, too, her gaze lingering on the cashmere sweater she'd borrowed from Julie.

"Yes." Aleksi recovered her hand and clenching it tight. "I went to NYU."

"Aleksi's a New Yorker," Hutch offered.

She wasn't about to correct him by saying she was actually from Brooklyn.

"*Really?*" Persephone beamed a ten-thousand-dollar smile and touched her arm. "Dear, we simply *must* talk!" She breezed past them to the maître d's desk, martini still in hand. "And you, Robert?"

"Yes. Straight from University of Houston to Harvard."

"A Texan and a New Yorker?" She laughed musically. "We may start another civil *war.*"

"They're on the same side this time." Hutch followed the hostess to their table overlooking the white sheen of the frozen Boston Harbor.

They sat with the two men facing each other with Hutch beside his ex, which meant Aleksi was staring right across at Persephone. She swallowed and clenched her hands under the table.

"And I'm not *from* Texas, I just went to school there." Bob took his seat, looking mildly terrified. "I'm from Utah."

"Well, I hope you took away the best from both states." Persephone raised a hand, and a waiter materialized as if by magic. She finished her martini and handed him the glass.

"The best from both?" Bob asked.

"Why yes. Men from Utah have the reputation of satisfying multiple wives, and *everything* is supposedly bigger in Texas, right?" Her teeth gleamed.

Bob just stared at her with an open mouth.

"Persephone, be good." Hutch's tone was only half jovial.

"I'm *always* good, Dr. Hutchinson." She nudged him and laughed. "Oh, come *on.* A harmless bit of fun. Have some wine and loosen up a little." She accepted the wine list from the waiter and ran a crimson nail down it.

Aleksi traded glances with both men; Bob managed a terrified smile, but Hutch's jaw was clenched. He looked angry. Aleksi took her napkin from her plate and clenched it in her lap.

"Let's see, Hutch is a vegetarian, so he'll probably order fish. Robert, you look like a red meat kind of man, am I right?"

"Yes."

"Oh, good. They do a prime rib here that's lovely. And Aleksi? Red or white?"

"Red, please." She kept her eyes fixed on her plate.

"And I'm feeling like lobster, so… Well, I suppose we better have one of each." She rattled off two wines that Aleksi had never heard of and handed the list back.

Dinner was only mildly hellish. Aleksi concentrated on her food, which was admittedly delicious, sipped her single glass of wine, and tried to listen without opening her mouth. Fortunately, with Persephone at the table, nobody else had to worry about carrying on a conversation. The woman chatted on subjects ranging from fashion, "That sweater is *lovely*, dear, but that blazer hides your figure," to cosmetics, "Your hair's so simply done. I know *just* the man to give you a proper do," to politics, "I had such high hopes for our new governor. Good breeding and all, but he's such an *idiot* when it comes to money!"

An occasional nod and smile kept Aleksi safely out of the conversation.

Then Hutch and Bob both left the table.

"So!" Persephone sipped her wine as Aleksi stared in horror at Hutch's retreating back. "Are you two fucking, or is this just a student-pupil relationship?"

"I...*What?* No!" Aleksi swallowed, her stomach clenching on her meal. She'd asked so casually, like 'pass the salt', it had caught her off guard. "We're *not*. He's my advisor."

"Well, *that's* a shame. You really should, you know." She finished her wine and put the glass aside. A waiter materialized to refill it. "He's *very* good in that department. There's always young Robert. He looks positively delicious, and you, my dear, are *desperately* in need of a good fuck."

Aleksi gaped again at the casual obscenity, then looked down at her plate. "I'm...not..."

"No? Well, *that's* a shame, too." She called for a desert menu. "You don't mind if I take Hutch home for a little fun, do you?" She bit her lip and cocked her head with the question.

"Um...no. I don't care." The woman's audacity astonished her, but Aleksi was recovering. Obviously, Persephone was trying to shock her, but why? Probably for the entertainment value. "I didn't know you two were still, um, involved."

"Oh, we're not." She made a gesture. "The *last* thing I need is another *relationship*, but I'm not the type to pass up an opportunity, and New Year's Eve was rather disappointing."

"Of course." She wondered if this was some kind of revenge for Hutch ditching her. There was no way she could tell Persephone that he actually hadn't left to meet her for work. Not if there was any hope of getting her to donate so much money for their cause. She wondered how far Hutch would go to secure that money.

"Well, that's settled then." Persephone sipped her wine and smiled at Aleksi as the men returned from the bathroom.

Aleksi passed on desert, unsure if her roiling stomach could handle anything sweet.

"So, I asked you out to bring up Aleksi's discovery." Hutch fixed Persephone with a businesslike stare. "You remember those pictures you saw at the New Year's party. The Russian journal?"

"Vaguely." Persephone flipped a hand. "Some kind of unknown sample hidden in the repository, wasn't it?"

"Yes. We'd like to work it up. You know, imaging and DNA analysis, to apply for a grant, but the museum has no money to spare."

"So *that's* what this is about." Persephone beamed. "You need *money!*"

"Not a lot. I wouldn't ask if time wasn't so important. Aleksi wants to use the find for her dissertation proposal, and that has to happen before the end of the semester."

"I tell you what." She sipped her wine and smiled. "You can pitch me the project during the ride home." She lifted her glass. "I've had too much to drive. You can drive my car, and the kids can take yours. That way, we won't ruin this lovely meal with shop talk. You brought a computer with the pictures, didn't you?"

"Um, yes." Hutch sounded uncomfortable.

"Perfect!" She swirled her wine and sipped as the waiter returned with three deserts and a coffee for Aleksi. "Ooo, chocolate and red wine. The two together are positively *sinful,* don't you think?" She speared the corner of a dark chocolate torte with her fork and took the bite into her mouth.

Aleksi sipped her coffee and tried to ignore the woman. *Succubus indeed.*

I'll call you later." Hutch lifted the laptop bag out of the back of his car and lowered his voice. "I may need you to rescue me."

"Should I bring torches and pitchforks?" Bob grinned and accepted the keys.

"Funny." Hutch tried to relax as he put his computer into the back seat of Persephone's Jaguar and got behind the wheel. The car smelled funny, some kind of air freshener or leather treatment that made him want to sneeze.

"Alone at last." Persephone rested a hand on his arm as Hutch shifted the car into gear. "Where *shall* we go?"

"I thought I was driving you home." He pulled out of the drive and merged with the slow winter traffic.

"If you want to. We could look over your proposal there, or find some nice little place to have drinks."

"Persephone, I don't think—"

"I don't want you to *think*, Hutch. That's what the drinks are for." She turned the heat up and unbuttoned her coat.

"I shouldn't have any more. Two glasses of wine is enough."

"Enough for what?" She reached out to run her nails down the back of his neck.

Hutch suppressed the tingle that ran down his spine. *Enough to tolerate your company*. He shrugged her hand off and craned his neck to change lanes. "Persephone, please. I'm driving."

"Oh, all right." She sighed and reached back between the seats. He couldn't help but glance down at her gaping dress. He knew she was doing it on purpose. "I'll check out your pictures while you drive." She sat back up with his computer in hand and a sultry look in her eye. He hoped she hadn't caught him looking. "Or, I could check something else out." Her nails brushed his thigh.

"Persephone!" He brushed her hand away, cursing the uncontrollable physical response to her touch.

"Oh, *fine*." She flipped open the tablet and stabbed the power button. "The man who sold me this car said driving it was better than sex, but I never thought he was *serious*." The screen came to life, lighting her in the passenger seat. "You sure you wouldn't like to try both at the same time?"

"I'm sure."

"Have it your way." She sighed and tapped keys. "You really should change your password occasionally."

"I will now. Thanks. The file's on the desktop. It's labeled 'Locktev Journal'."

"Got it."

He navigated through the maze of downtown, turned onto Tremont, passed Boston Common, and continued into Back Bay as she flipped through the pages. Persephone came from old money, and was never likely to sell the family home. He had loathed the place during their marriage, and she'd agreed to buy the condo in Cambridge. He'd gotten it outright in the divorce without a fight.

"These illustrations really are beautiful. This guy was an artist as well as a digger."

At least she was off the subject of sex. "Most naturalists were in those days. Cameras were few and far between, and barely portable."

"Where did you say this was from? My Russian is a little rusty."

"Kamchatka."

"And you really think it's something unusual?"

"It sure looks strange from the sketch on page seventy-three, but we don't know. DNA analysis should narrow it down. If it didn't get cooked from the ash fall, that is." He fell silent, and she didn't fill that void. He glanced down occasionally, but she seemed engrossed in the journal. He turned onto her street.

"And how much do you need from me?"

"We asked the MCZ for twelve thousand to get things started. That includes CT scans and DNA analysis. The preliminary data, if it's promising, should get us a grant. I'll apply for enough to pay you back, so this would be a loan." He glanced again, and noticed she was looking at the illustration of the entire specimen. "Something, isn't it?"

"It *is*."

He pulled into her drive and held out a hand for her key card. She closed his computer and retrieved the card from her pocketbook, but instead of handing it over, she reached back between the seats again to put the tablet back in its case. He refused to look at her this time. She looked up at him as she moved back into her seat, looking disappointed. She held the card between two fingers.

"You're not driving anymore." She reached for his lap.

"No, Persephone." He caught her wrist and pushed her hand away.

"Then come in and have a drink with me while we…negotiate my donation to your worthy cause."

"I don't think so." He put her hand back in her own lap. "Not a good idea."

"Why not?" She reached back to run her fingers along the back of his neck. They were very warm, and he felt another tingle down his spine that sent blood rushing from his brain to all the wrong places. "I won't tell, and it'll do you good. I can feel all that suppressed energy built up in you. I'm just offering you a little release; no strings attached."

Hutch suppressed the surge of desire that burned through him, the urge to accept her offer, to take her right here in the car, then again inside. *No!* He gritted his teeth. *Not gonna happen.* "There are always strings attached, Persephone." He shrugged her hand away, and shifted in his seat, suddenly uncomfortable. "You're an *expert* at strings."

"Strings, ropes, handcuffs, whatever." She gave him a sultry laugh. When he didn't respond, she went into pout mode. "Oh, come *on*, Hutch. It's not like you'd be plowing virgin soil, you know. When did you turn into such a prude?"

"I'm not a prude, Persephone. I just don't think it's a good idea."

"Because you're asking me for money, and having sex with me would make you feel like a whore?"

"Something like that."

"Then let's make it a formal agreement." She leaned in, her lips an inch from his, her chocolate-wine scented breath warm in his face. "Come inside and fuck me, and I'll write you a check for twenty thousand dollars. That'll make you the highest-paid whore in the city."

"And if I don't?" He glared at her, tempted to get out of the car and walk away.

"Maybe you can send over your little friend, Aleksi. *She* might put out for her dissertation if you won't."

"Persephone! That's…" He had no words to describe it, but she did.

"Blackmail? Dishonest? Immoral?" She flicked the key card under his nose and ran her hand over his crotch. "*Incredibly* tempting?"

He pushed her away and glared. "I'm sorry, Persephone, but no." He opened the door and got out of the car.

"You're *kidding* me!" Persephone stared in wide-eyed shock as he opened the back door and retrieved his computer. "Dwayne Hutchinson, get your ass back in this car!"

"No. I don't perform sex for money, Persephone." He slammed the door.

"Wait!" She was out of the car in a flash, her coat flapping in the icy wind. "Hutch, *wait*, God damn it! Forget it! Here!"

He turned back as she slammed her bag onto the top of the car and pulled out a tiny folded book of checks. A gold pen flickered in the security light as she scrawled something and ripped one free.

"Here! Take it." The check fluttered in the wind, Aleksi's dissertation ready to fly away if Persephone let go.

"This is a *loan*. I'll pay it back once we get a grant."

"I don't *care*, Hutch. Spend it on whatever you like." Persephone stepped forward and stuffed the check into his coat pocket. "No strings." She rounded the car and swiped her key card. The gate rolled open.

"Drive the Jag home. I'll have someone come get it in the morning." She walked up the drive without looking back.

Hutch pulled the check from his pocket. It was made out to him for the sum of twenty thousand dollars.

"Persephone!"

She stopped and turned, clutching her coat closed. "What *now*, for Christ sake?"

"Thank you." He held up the check then put it in his pocket.

She shook her head and laughed. "Take me to *lunch* sometime!" She walked up the drive, and the gate closed behind her.

Hutch got back in the car, backed out of the drive, and drove half a block before he parked beside a snow bank and fished his phone from his pocket. He punched Bob's number.

"Hutch?"

"Yeah. We got it. Twenty thousand."

"Twenty thousand!" He heard Bob and Aleksi cheering over the phone. "Thanks Hutch!"

"No problem. Tell Aleksi I've scheduled imaging for Tuesday. We've got to arrange the movement of the sample. Tell her to get with Quinton. I'm taking Monday off."

"Great! No problem! G'nite Hutch."

"Good night." He ended the call, pocketed the phone, and pulled the Jaguar out into traffic.

Persephone punched up the slide show and slipped the remote control into her great grandmother's withered hand. "It's all there for you, Gi-gi."

"Yes." Her ancient fingers flexed, and the screens began to flick past. "You were very persuasive, my child. Thank you."

"I did my best." *And still failed...* She'd transferred the file to a stick while she perused the images in the passenger seat. Persuasion had nothing to do with it. In fact, the pheromone had failed her utterly. How Hutch had refused her, she had no idea. She'd used it before, and had men groveling at her feet.

Why did you do it, Persephone? Why try to seduce him? You had the damned files, just write him a check and stay friendly. But no, you had to call him a whore. Now he hates you.

She'd been asking herself that since walking up the driveway in the cold. She knew the answer; she was lonely, and when she didn't get what she wanted, she became petulant. The knowledge didn't make it any easier, and certainly didn't solve her loneliness.

She left the Sanctum and climbed the stairs to her own solitary abode. She found her nightgown laid out on her bed with elegant precision, a glass of seltzer water and two pills on her nightstand. In the morning she would be herself again, the powerful socialite ready to take Boston by the balls and get her way.

Right now, she felt like shit.

9

The word "disappointment" didn't quite cover it.

"Empty? What do you mean, empty?" Aleksi looked at Hutch and Bob, then at the imaging technician. "It *can't* be empty!"

"Look for yourself." The woman gestured to the screen where two images were displayed. "We got good penetration, but there's nothing inside. No bones, anyway. You can see the outline of the ash cast, but inside…nothing."

"Not quite nothing." Hutch instructed the technician to zoom in on one area of the image. "Look here; there are teeth, though they're faint, and you can see shadows here and that might be some jaw structure. It's not intact, but it's something. Fragments, maybe."

"But how could the bones just disintegrate like that?" Bob asked.

"Temperature," Hutch said with a grimace. "Some pyroclastic casts found in Herculaneum had nothing inside but splintered bone. The ash was so hot that the body fluids boiled and the bones fractured. If that's the case here, we're not going to get any DNA." Hutch squinted at the display again as Aleksi's heart sank; no bones and no DNA meant no project. "But I can't really see any detail here."

"Well, at this exposure…" They looked at the technician. "Sorry, but I had to punch through all that plaster and ash if you want to see anything at all."

"What about a CT?" Bob asked. "Even if we can't get a picture of the skeletal structure, we should be able to get a three-dee image of the ash cast outline."

"Good thinking."

Three frustrating hours later they had a picture of what lay inside the block of plaster, or, more precisely, what didn't lie within.

"How can this have happened?" Aleksi peered at the confusing image. "It's like it completely crumbled to dust.

"I don't know," Hutch admitted. "The cast of ash formed and solidified before the tissues collapsed completely, so we have an outline. There should be bones, at least fragments, but it's like the entire skeletal structure just crumbled. Some reaction to heat and cold cycling, maybe. Not much left."

"We have the location of the dig from the journal. We could look at data from glacial cores as close as we can get to the site and correlate weather cycling data."

"Very good idea, Bob, but we need to date the sample to do that." Hutch squinted at the image and shook his head. "And there's not much left to do that with."

"Except for the teeth." Aleksi pointed to the points of white in the black field where the specimen's head had been. The shadows that Hutch had thought were the remnants of bone on X-ray, were now revealed to be nothing but crumbled layers of dust. But along the edges, imbedded in the ash, a few points of interest remained. "If we get anything at all, it'll be there."

"Not much to work with, I'm afraid." Hutch straightened his back with an audible pop and turned to the technician. "Can you compile a three-dee composite from these? We need a big picture to send back to the curator."

"Sure."

"You going to ask for suggestions?" Aleksi's hopes felt like they were crumbling to dust, just like the specimen had. "We can at least remove the plaster and get some samples for aging, can't we?"

"We can, but should we? If we remove the plaster, the entire thing could crumble."

"But if we don't, we've got nothing." There was a quaver of desperation in her voice that she hated. "I could expose the teeth and we might get some radiocarbon data. Morphology might give us a species, and *maybe* some DNA." Tooth roots and even plaque were treasure troves of genetic information.

"Let's bounce that off of Quinton first, Aleksi." He rested a hand on her shoulder for a moment, smiling in sympathy. "Their sample, their rules."

"All right" *Which means another week waiting for the damned directors to make a damned decision.*

"Here's your big picture." The technician waved a hand at the wide flat-screen. "Pretty weird stuff."

"What the *hell*?" Hutch's voice held a note of wonder that Aleksi had not heard before.

She peered at the screen, and a chill climbed her spine. The rotating three-dimensional image resembled nothing she'd ever seen before. The shape was slim, but curled up into a ball, twisted into a contortionist's nightmare, the sinuous neck canted back, long forelegs flung up at odd angles. What looked like shreds of tissue trailed from the elongated third and fourth digits of the forefeet. The hind legs were drawn up in a fetal posture, and hard to discern, the feet long-toed with what might have been claws.

"What *is* that?" Aleksi traced a finger along the outline of the elongated digits of the forelimbs.

"Don't touch the screen, please." The tech scowled at her.

"Sorry." Aleksi stepped back, her arms folded as she stared at the image on the screen.

"I'll just put this on a stick for you, and you can look at it all you want. I've got another scan to do today." The tech put a stick in a USB and started the process, but the image continued to rotate on the screen.

"Have you ever *seen* anything like that before?" Aleksi looked at Hutch, but he hadn't heard her. He stood transfixed, as if staring into a hypnotist's crystal ball.

"Hutch?" Bob said, touching his arm.

"Huh? Oh, sorry." He looked at them both then back to the screen. "No. I've never seen anything like this in my life."

<hr>

By the time the specimen was back in Aleksi's lab, the winter sun had set. Hutch ushered Bob and Aleksi to his office to call Quinton. Bob sat in the upholstered chair in the corner and Aleksi paced, biting her nails. She was a wreck, but Hutch didn't know how to calm her down. He tapped in Quinton's number and put the call on speaker.

"Hutch? What's up?" Quinton sounded like he was in the middle of something.

Hutch checked the time and cringed. "Sorry to call after hours, Quinton, but we've had quite a day and I'm sending you some files." Hutch was already uploading the huge CT image files onto a shared university mailbox. "You'll never guess in a million years what we found."

"No, I probably won't, and I quit playing guessing games twenty years ago."

"Okay, then, I'll just tell you; there was nothing inside but dust and a few teeth."

"Not funny, Hutch." They heard the sound of cutlery clattering on a plate. "You wouldn't be calling me in the middle of dinner if you hadn't found anything."

"Not trying to be funny. The space inside the plaster was completely degraded. No bones, no fossilized remnants, but the CT gave us a *very* interesting three-dee image of the thing's outline. I'm uploading that into the shared mailbox now. Give it a look and call me in the morning."

There was a long silence. "That good, huh?"

Hutch looked up at Alexi and winked. "That good, Quinton. Nothing I've ever seen before. Aleksi's itching to cut the thing open for dating, morphology, and genetic material from the tooth remnants."

"And the journal?" Quinton asked. "How's that going?"

"I'm still working on it," Aleksi put in, pausing in her pacing for a moment. "I can send you what I've got so far, but there's probably another week of work, and classes start Monday. I won't have as much time to work on it once semester begins…"

"All right, all right. I get it. I'll have a look at these pictures and get back to you in the morning, Hutch. Don't send any of the journal until you've got the whole thing translated, Aleksi. *We're* not in a hurry."

They said their goodbyes and Hutch hung up.

"He sounded mad." Aleksi bit her nails and resumed pacing, still obviously wound up tight. "Maybe we should have waited to call him at the office."

"*Relax*, Aleksi." Hutch shut down his computer. "I'll bet you both lunch at Grendel's that he takes one look at that image and gives us the go ahead."

"I'll take that bet!" Bob's eyes flashed at the mention of food and lurched to his feet. "Come on, Aleksi, I'll buy you a slice of pizza."

"I don't know, Hutch." Aleksi bit her nails some more. "You think so?"

"I know Quinton, Aleksi. He's a *scientist*. When *he* sees what *we* saw on that CT, he's going to be as curious as we are." He pulled his laptop out of the docking station and stuffed it into a carry bag. "Wanna bet?"

She shook her head. "No, and I'm starving."

"Excellent!" Bob grinned and grabbed her arm, steering her out of the office. "Let's go!"

"See you for lunch." Hutch watched them go with a little flicker of warmth. Bob seemed able to break through Aleksi's shyness. He hefted his computer bag and headed for home.

An hour later, in his kitchen, Hutch had just started making dinner when his cell phone chirped. He answered with a grin. "Couldn't wait until morning, Quinton?"

"You've got the go ahead, but be damned careful, Hutch." Quinton sounded both elated and worried. "I've never seen anything like this in my life. Don't screw this up."

"We'll be careful."

"Just the teeth for now, right?"

"Yes, just the teeth, and just enough to get the samples we need."

"All right. Goodnight then."

"Goodnight, Quinton." He tapped end and punched up Aleksi's number.

"Is he going to let us do it?" Aleksi sounded positively frantic.

"Yep. Is Bob with you?"

"Right here. Let me put you on speaker."

The sounds of a busy restaurant came through the phone.

"Okay, we meet at Grendel's for planning at eleven. We don't have much to work with here, and this could be something that's never been described before. That means precise measurements and photographic documentation the whole way."

"We can get measurements from the CT images, and outline a plan for exposing the teeth and taking samples." Hutch could tell by her tone that Aleksi and Bob had already been discussing the task. "The exposed tooth from the journal is probably already contaminated with human DNA from the original excavation. We can take that one for morphology, and the others for genetic data."

"We'll discuss it at lunch. You two *relax* tonight. We've earned a night off."

"Um…yeah. Okay. G'nite Hutch."

"Goodnight." He ended the call and flipped his Portobello in the pan, feeling a little strange. *Bob and Aleksi?* It could happen, and they would be good for each other.

L*ocks, keys, security cameras, passwords… It's like nobody* trusts *anyone around here.* A key slipped into the lock of Quinton Neilson's office door and turned. Click.

"Paranoia…" Derrick Penningly slipped through the door and locked it behind him for the next pass of the security guard.

He had little more than contempt for campus security. It had been no better at Princeton, and he'd hacked their system in his junior year. He had spent two years delving the files of half the faculty; tests, research, even email—which turned into blackmail when he found an assistant professor with an inbox full of explicit bondage pictures of him with another man.

At the curator's desk, his rubber-gloved fingertips tapped in Neilson's password. *Patience…careful…* He'd overheard Neilson talking to one of his cronies about what the Hutchinson team had found. "Like nothing I've ever seen before." It sounded like a perfect doctoral project for a brilliant young scientist from Princeton.

He found the file he was looking for and pulled it up. The image loaded slowly then came to life in a 3-D rotating display.

"What the *fuck?*" Was this some kind of a hoax? It looked like something out of some geek fantasy game, half bat, half human. He checked the other imaging files, but none were as good as this one. X-rays didn't show any skeletal structure at all, but he could see the outline of the plaster cast. The images were genuine.

"I gotta get a look at this thing. There's got to be more data." And Derrick knew only one place he could find it: Hutchinson's laboratory. But he didn't have keys. He might sneak in somehow for a peek, but what he really needed was free access, time to copy their research files, figure out how to horn in.

But he had to be careful.

Patience… The sample wasn't going anywhere. *Got to figure out how to*

*make a play for this. Maybe get in with one of Hutchinson's students. Let them
do the grunt work, then scoop it up.*

Then he remembered the mousey woman, Aleksi, so afraid, so vulnerable, so fucking needy. A smile spread across his lips like blood flowing
from an open wound. "Yeah. She's my key." He didn't know how, exactly,
yet. Get close, sidle up, be friends, then get her in the sack at his place
where he could get some pictures, maybe even video. Then he could ride
that bitch all the way to his degree.

10

With a rising whine of the bone saw, Aleksi made her first cut into the plaster cast of the mystery specimen. Sleep had come hard, and she'd finally rolled out of bed at five in the morning. A quick shower, toast, and coffee put her in the lab at six. Three hours of measurements, markings, photographs, and calculations using the grid overlay with the CT and X-ray images from her laptop, and she was ready.

"Measure twice, cut once." The old carpenter's adage served her well. As she cut into the slab, she knew the exact position of the blade with respect to her goal. Hutch and Bob had volunteered to help, but she had declined. Bumping elbows with a couple of men while wielding a power tool wasn't a good idea.

The scream of the saw died, and the first layer lifted out. She cut the waxed canvas away with a pair of sheers. Beneath lay more plaster, five centimeters of it. Although tempted to make another cut with the bone saw, she put the heavy tool away, took pictures, and picked up the Dremel. The hand-sized tool was fitted with a router bit that would only cut half a centimeter deep. The tool spun at up to thirty-five thousand RPM and gouged through the soft plaster like a knife through cheese, lessening vibrations that might damage the fragile ash cast within. She made several passes, removed the dust with a vacuum, and took more pictures and measurements.

So the morning went.

The head-end of the specimen looked like the terraces of a miniature strip mine when a call of, "How goes it?" startled her out of her work. She looked up to see Bob Tomlin standing in the gap of the dust barrier, a brown paper sack in one hand and a tray with two tall cardboard cups in the other.

"Beware nerds bearing greasy burritos and caffeine."

"Second breakfast?" She stretched and put the Dremel down.

"More like lunch." He gestured to the clock; it showed twelve thirty. "You missed second breakfast *and* elevenses. Not good for a busy hobbit."

"Right." Aleksi stripped off her protective gear and did a quick pass with the shop vac.

"Inside or outside. It's cold, but the snow's stopped."

"Outside. I could use the fresh air." A quick rinse at the sink, and she grabbed her coat and followed him up the stairs.

They settled on the back steps of the MCZ. He handed her a coffee and pulled out the burritos. She took a sip and sighed with the rush of double strength caffeine.

"So, how goes it?" His breath came out in clouds as he handed over one of the paper-wrapped monstrosities. The burritos were a full two inches thick and the paper was soaked through with greasy goodness.

"Slow." She unwrapped the thing and took a bite. Her mouth exploded with spicy shredded pork, refried beans, and tangy cheese. She closed her eyes in bliss and chewed. "These are glorious. Thanks."

"No problem. Hutch offered, but I figured he'd bring you a tofu burger, so I took the duty. He said you'd work right through lunch if someone didn't remind you to eat." Bob sampled his own and smiled. "Besides, he paid."

"I wish he wouldn't do that." She sipped her coffee and took another bite. The excitement of last night, sitting with Bob and planning, eating pizza and talking about the project, had made her comfortable around him, but this morning the old anxiety had returned.

"Don't worry about it, Aleksi. He's not hurting for cash. Not with an ex like Persephone."

"She was...different." A niggling anxiety clenched her stomach. *Are you two fucking...* If Persephone thought that, had it happened before? Was that why they got divorced? Had Hutch cheated on her with a student? It didn't seem possible, but Lonnie had said he'd dated a law student. Should she be more careful around him? Avoid being alone with him?

"You're too nice. She's a spoiled rich bitch." Bob took another bite. "So, do I have to threaten to take away your coffee, or are you going to tell me how the work's going."

She gave him an update of her progress, more comfortable discussing work. Unfortunately, there wasn't much to tell yet. "The closer I get, the slower it's going to go."

"I know, but it's hard waiting when we know what's in there waiting for us."

"You mean when we *don't* know. The more I look at that CT, the more I wonder if this might be more than one specimen. Like the bone bed. The shape's just too crazy, like some kind of pterosaur, or..."

"I don't think it's that old." Bob munched as he spoke. "I did some searching through geological data from that area. Nalychevo's last eruption was only twenty thousand years ago, give or take."

"Ice-age." The CT image had plagued her restless sleep, but she couldn't think of anything that resembled the twisted form. "Gigantism? Some mutation? Chiroptera maybe..."

"Maybe it's Batman." He grinned and nudged her knee. "I'm more curious why there are no bone remnants. Even if the ash was superheated, we should have skull sections and metacarpals. I'm dying to get my hands on something I can extract DNA from. Bone marrow or teeth are just about our only hope."

"We'll get some." Sudden confidence swelled up inside her. Or maybe it was just the caffeine. She finished the monster burrito and wiped her hands on a paper napkin.

"You better wash before you touch anything in the lab, or all I'm going to get is pig DNA." He nudged her knee again with his own, a simple gesture, friendly, nice.

Nice... Her confidence melted like snowflakes on a hotplate. "Right." She dropped the napkin in the bag and sipped her coffee, staring at her hands wrapped around the paper cup.

"Aleksi, it was a joke."

"Oh, sorry. Yeah, I just can't stop thinking, you know." She liked Bob, felt comfortable talking to him, but... *But he's nice and I'm Aleksi.* She stood. "I need to get back to work. Thanks for the lunch. It was delicious."

"No problem." He stood and wadded up the trash, cradling his coffee in his other hand. "You going to eat dinner or should I come back with pizza?"

"I'll go home for dinner." She raised her coffee in toast. "Can't get exhausted. Tired means mistakes, and we can't afford any."

"Good." He toasted her with his coffee. "Give a call if you need any help."

"I will." She knew she wouldn't. Aleksi waved as he left and turned back to the safety of her lab and her solitary work.

<hr>

Power tools gave way to tiny picks and scrapers when she got close to the ash cast. This was the painstaking part, where she could really screw up if she wasn't careful. She worked steadily, and finally removed a piece of plaster to reveal a layer of gray ash.

"Score!" She paused to stretch and look at the clock. It was five thirty. "Damn." She took a series of photos, some careful measurements, and went back to her computer. The screen came up with the measurement grid overlay superimposed over the merged images of the CT and the X-ray. She'd broken through about a centimeter from the exposed tooth, just as she'd planned.

"Three hours," she estimated with a glance at the clock. She had put in almost twelve hours, which had been her self-imposed limit for one day's work. She didn't feel particularly exhausted, and after the huge lunch, she wasn't hungry either. "Just a bit more." She set a timer for nine PM, knowing she would lose track of time, and got back to work.

The plaster yielded easily to her picks, and though bits of the ash cast came off as she progressed, she knew from the journal that it was fairly thick. A fleck of translucent golden material appeared in one of the chips of plaster and ash, maybe pyrite or gypsum. She placed the chip aside and continued to dig.

A wedge of pearly white appeared with the next chip she removed.

"About damn time!" She grinned under her dust mask, retrieved the camera, and took a quick picture, then examined the tooth with her jeweler's loupe. It was smooth and hard, not fossilized, but resistant to her pick. "So, if *this* survived, where did your bones go?"

From the drawings and the CT, she knew that the exposed portion was about three centimeters long. With any luck, she could expose the rest and slip the tooth free with little difficulty. She took pictures as she progressed, careful to avoid pressing or prying right on the crescent of white. So far, it hadn't even wiggled. As it emerged, she noted that the tip was still needle sharp, the back edge like a razor, just as Loktev described, like a male baboon or macaque's canines.

"So, maybe you're a boy." She took a series of close-up photos before attempting the last bit of plaster. Minutes later the tooth hung suspended only by the ash cast. She retrieved a pair of hemostats, padded their textured jaws with gauze, and took a firm grip on the tooth. "Now come to mama." She applied gentle pressure.

It didn't budge.

"Well, that doesn't make sense." If the supporting bone had degraded to dust, the tooth should only be held in place by the ash cast. She put down the hemostats, retrieved her pick and started to chip carefully at the cast around the tooth. Tiny pieces crumbled away from the surface, but a millimeter or so in the stuff became hard, like fired clay. She frowned.

"All I need is a couple of teeth to figure out who you are." She worked on the gray deposit surrounding the tooth. A piece came free, and more of the glittering mineral came with it in a fine dust. Another piece yielded, and she thought the tooth wiggled ever so slightly. "Yes! Now I'll get you."

She applied the hemostats again and pulled. Nothing.

"Why you dirty rotten piece of..." She stopped pulling and glared, but the tooth just sat there, taunting her. "Fine. We'll do this the hard way." She retrieved her pick and inserted it the crack between the tooth and the ash cast.

The lab timer went off.

Aleksi started, and her pick moved against the tooth like a tiny lever. Something cracked and the crescent of white fell free of the ash cast, glittering golden dust drifting down from the hollow it had occupied.

"Shit!" She reached to catch the falling tooth without thinking.

As her hand closed, the needle tip pierced her latex glove and her palm. A gasp of surprise escaped her lips, and she stared for a moment at the bloody white tooth protruding from her hand.

"Well, *fuck*." The world turned gray at the edges and closed in around her. As she fell into darkness, all she could think was that she had contaminated the sample.

Y ou look like crap."

Aleksi blinked at Julie as she doffed her coat and put her bag down. "Thanks." She thought about returning the complement, but it would have been a lie. Julie was dressed in a short black skirt with leggings, and a green sweater that hugged her like a coat of paint, her hair an intricate chaos of curls. "You going out?"

"Hel-lo. Just got in. It's past midnight, Lex." Julie looked at her like she was stupid. "You okay?"

"Midnight? Yeah, I just..." She looked at her hand, trying to remember something. Her palm itched. "Just tired."

"No kidding." Julie turned to her room, unbuckling her belt and unzipping her skirt on the way. "Did you at least eat dinner this time?"

"Dinner? Um, no. I had a big lunch." Aleksi headed for the kitchen, thinking only of coffee, though her stomach rumbled at the mention of food. She had work to do on the journal. She started fumbling with the coffee maker but couldn't seem to remember how to work it.

"You are *not* making coffee!" Julie stalked into the kitchen wearing a pink terry robe and fuzzy slippers, with striped socks.

"I've got work to do." Aleksi fumbled with the coffee filters, trying to separate just one from the pile. Her hands were shaking, and she couldn't manage it.

"You're working too hard, Lex. You're dead on your feet." Julie took the coffee filters from her and put them away. "You need food and sleep, or you're not going to be worth a damn tomorrow. Come on, let me make you something. What would you like?"

"I'll...uh. I'll make a grilled cheese." Aleksi opened the fridge. "I've got to work on the journal and get some sleep. Tomorrow's a big day." She couldn't remember why tomorrow was important, but she knew it would be. Cheese, bread, butter, pastrami and a jar of green olives landed on the counter. She reached for a knife.

"Oh no, not the way you're shaking. You'd cut your hand off. Here!"

Aleksi sighed and backed away from the counter as Julie took the knife from her hand. She scratched her itchy palm and shivered. "No male company tonight? Where'd you go?"

"Movie and dinner at Brad's apartment."

"Who's Brad? I thought you were dating Vic."

"I am, but he's out of town until Sunday. Brad's just a friend." Julie gave a little shrug that said that Brad was the kind of friend she shared a bed with occasionally, and started preparing the sandwich, piling on meat, thick slices of cheese, and sliced olives. "You can't expect me to spend the last few days before the semester cooped up in my apartment."

"Why not?" Aleksi poured herself a glass of water and drained it, surprised that she was so thirsty. She rubbed her palm on her jeans. "That's what I'm doing."

"Because unlike you, all work no play makes Julie a cranky bitch." She buttered the bread and dropped the sandwich in the hot skillet. "You should take some downtime, Lex. You've been busting ass non-stop. You're gonna crash if you don't."

"I'm fine, Julie." She poured herself another glass of water and drank half. "I'm pacing myself."

"Pacing yourself into a coma." Julie flipped the sandwich as the cheese started to melt. "You're going straight to bed after you eat this…thing, young lady. Roommate's orders."

"Yes, *Mom*." Aleksi put everything back in the fridge in exchange for a jar of dill pickles and filled her glass with milk. She didn't remember drinking the rest of her water, but the cold glass felt good in her hand. She heard a hiss from the pan; the cheese had melted just enough to run. The smell was heavenly, and Julie slipped it onto a plate. A pickle and a tall glass of milk and she had dinner for one.

"That's disgusting." Julie wrinkled her nose at the plate. "That's basically a fat sandwich. I don't know how you stay so thin."

"Twelve-hour days digging for fossils." She took her dinner to the front room. "Thanks, Julie."

"Just get some sleep, okay?" Julie folded her arms and looked worried. "No more work tonight."

"No work, I promise." Iggy rattled his cage, and she leaned over to open the door and haul him out. "I'll just have dinner with my boyfriend here and hit the sack." She rubbed his chin and fed him a tiny bit of melted cheese. He gobbled it down and bobbed his head.

"A lizard is *not* a boyfriend." Julie made a face. "I'm not even sure it's a pet. Can't you get a cat or something cuddly?"

"Iggy's cuddly." Aleksi took a bite of her sandwich and fed him another bit of cheese.

"In a scaly, slimy, cold-blooded kind of way."

"He is *not* slimy." Aleksi folded her legs and let Iggy find a comfortable spot while she ate.

"Just don't let him loose again." Julie turned and retreated to her room, closing the door behind her.

Aleksi finished the sandwich, feeding Iggy bits of cheese until the plate was clean. She leaned back, letting Iggy lay on top of her, warm and contented. She didn't intend to fall asleep there, but the next thing she knew, she was dreaming...

She's walking through the apartment, the air cool on naked skin. Iggy sits on the back of the couch, and she wonders how he got out. She picks him up. He's warm. She kisses him and puts him down in his favorite spot on the window sill, but the light is moonlight, and he glows. She walks to Julie's door and reaches for the handle, but stops as she sees the blood on her hand. Oh yes...she was bitten by...something. She touches the handle of Julie's door and it turns easily. The moonlight streams in, illuminating Julie's form on the bed, her hair a tousled mess, the curve of her body clear beneath the blanket, like a fossil wrapped in plaster. She draws the blanket back, curious why Julie doesn't wake. She leans down, inhaling the scent, listening to the beating heart, the rush of blood, and knows what she has to do. Daughter... She spreads her jaws and sinks her long, recurved teeth into Julie's flesh.

11

A leksi!"

"Wha—!" She bolted upright, the taste of blood still in her mouth, eyes wide with panic. Light streamed in the window and Iggy lashed his tail with displeasure at her sudden movement; he'd been asleep on her chest.

"Aleksi, it's morning. You fell asleep on the couch."

"Damn!" She grabbed Iggy before he could bolt and blinked at the sunlight streaming in. "What time is it?"

"A little after eight." Julie looked worried. "You look worse than you did last night."

"I feel worse," she admitted, her voice hoarse and her head aching. She sat up and put Iggy in his cage for the day, a process that he did *not* appreciate. "Tell me there's coffee."

"I'll make you some if you tell me you'll take the morning off and get some more sleep." Julie folded her arms.

"No can do. I've got work to do, and I'm behind." She struggled to her feet and wobbled a little. The floor didn't want to stay level. "I'm going to jump in the shower. Could you *please* put some coffee on?"

"Fine, but don't slip and break your neck!" Julie turned to the kitchen, her fuzzy pink slippers swishing along the rug. "If I have to call the paramedics to come haul your naked ass out of the bathtub, I'll take pictures and post them on Facebook!"

Aleksi muttered something caustic and wobbled her way to the bathroom. One glance in the mirror and she knew Julie wasn't joking; she looked even worse than she felt, which was saying something. Her face was pale, her eyes red rimmed and dark circled. She stripped and stepped into the shower, scrubbing the lingering plaster dust out of her hair and trying to wake up.

For some reason she couldn't seem to get the water hot enough, and by the time she felt clean, it was running out. She stepped out of the tub shivering and toweled dry. The floor seemed slightly more stable as she padded to her room in the towel and donned clean clothes. The glorious aroma of fresh coffee pervaded the apartment when she emerged, dressed and feeling almost human.

"You are my savior, Julie." She entered the kitchen and took the huge cup of steaming brew from her roommate's hands. The scalding cup felt good against her palms. She inhaled the aroma and took a cautious sip.

"You still look like death warmed over." Julie poured her own cup. "You want some toast or something?"

"Mmmm, I don't know. I'm hungry, but..." she opened the fridge and frowned. She really didn't have time to cook anything, and toast sounded terrible. She peeled a couple of slices of pastrami out of the package and wolfed them down. *Wonderful...* She grabbed two more slices. "I'll pick up a bagel or something on the way in."

"Promise me you'll eat something. You look like you're coming down with the flu, and I *so* don't need a sick roommate, three days before the semester begins." Julie sipped her own coffee and glared.

"Your concern is touching." Aleksi finished the meat and rushed through her coffee, enduring more glares from Julie. "You're just worried that you'll catch it."

"Damn right I am." Julie retreated to her room.

Aleksi finished her coffee and went to the bathroom to brush her teeth and blow-dry her wet hair. Blinking at her reflection, she remembered the dream. She looked down at her hand. There wasn't a mark on it. In her dream, it had been bleeding, but that was ridiculous. She still had no recollection of leaving the lab or her walk home. Working late to expose the tooth and setting a timer for nine PM were clear, but nothing after that.

So where did three hours vanish to?

"Maybe I *am* working too hard." She bundled up in coat, scarf, gloves, and hat, grabbed her bag, filled her travel cup, and headed out into the blustery Cambridge winter.

Looking around the lab felt like looking into a mirror and not seeing a reflection. Everything was perfectly orderly, all her tools put away, the sample with its exposed section right there. The tooth that she remembered working so hard to expose the previous evening lay on the table in a small Ziplock bag. It even looked like the floor had been cleaned of plaster dust.

And Aleksi had no memory of any of it.

She donned her gear and went to the table. The tooth was bigger than she'd thought it would be, as long as her finger from needle tip to the fractured root. There was even a little tag in the bag labeled with a designation number in her hand writing, but she had no memory of writing it.

"I am definitely losing it." She lifted the bag to examine the piece of her vanished memory.

The entire base of the tooth was splintered. If heat did that, there would be little chance of finding DNA. *Bob's going to be disappointed.* The tip looked like a dagger, the back edge sharp like a male macaque's canine. Her palm itched, and she put the bag down to rub her gloved hands together.

"Well, it's not like there's not more work to do." She booted up her computer and put it in its protective plastic bag.

She checked the digital camera, viewed the last few pictures, and remembered taking them. She took more photos, of both the tooth and the recess where it had resided, holding up a small plastic ruler for scale. She then explored the recess with a blunt probe, holding a small plastic weighing boat beneath it. A few fragments of the shattered tooth clattered into it, accompanied by a good bit of strange, almost iridescent residue. She took it over to the dissecting scope for a look.

The tooth fragments, if that was what they were, showed no signs of any residual tissue, and the dusty residue looked more like flakes of some mineral than any kind of bone or soft tissue. She put the boat's contents into a small baggie with a label, sealed it, took more pictures, and got back to work. There were four more tooth remnants of reasonable size according to the CT scan, and with any luck she could have them exposed by lunch.

A ny luck?" Hutch peered through the gap in the plastic barrier, trying to keep the plaster dust from the rest of the lab. He lifted the brown paper bag. "I brought lunch."

Aleksi looked up from her work and blinked at him, chalky dust caked around her goggles. Her hair looked wet and matted with dust. "Some, but not promising." She put down the Dremel, and he saw that her hands were shaking. "I extracted the tooth that was already exposed last night, and the entire base is splintered. I've exposed two more, but I didn't want to extract them until you had a look."

More nervousness, or fatigue? he wondered. "You okay, Aleksi?" He put the bag down and donned a mask and gloves. "You look pale."

"Oh, I'm fine." She clenched her hands, a nervous gesture he'd noticed before. "I think I might be fighting a bug. Nothing serious."

"Well, you've been working awfully hard." He came in and picked up the baggie with the tooth. "Don't forget that you've got classes next week. You should probably knock off and get some rest." He peered at the tooth and took it over to the dissecting scope. "This does look like a big primate. I'd say macaque."

She wiped her brow and blinked. "Yeah, that's what I thought, but Kamchatka's way out of their home range. What do you think about the broken end?"

"Probably heat fracturing. The tooth root and the surrounding bone marrow may have vaporized with the heat of the pyroclastic ash. If that's the case, all the soft tissues would have vaporized. It's a wonder there's anything left at all." He turned the scope's light off and put the bagged tooth back on the table. "Bob's not going to get any DNA."

"I know." Aleksi pulled the paper gown off and pitched it in the trash, then vacuumed the dust from her jeans and boots. When she stood up after, she wobbled and steadied herself on the edge of the table.

"Aleksi? You *sure* you're okay?" He stepped closer. The plaster dust around her goggles and in her hair was caked because she was sweating.

"Yeah" She took a step back. "Just a little dizzy. Stood up too quick."

"You look pale and you're sweating." He reached up to put a gloved hand on her brow, but she pulled away. "Aleksi, hold still. I just want to see if you're running a fever."

"I…um…okay."

He pressed his palm to her forehead. "You're burning up. Come on."

She followed him out and they doffed their masks and gloves. He peered at her face and shook his head. "I can't tell if that's plaster dust or if you're really that pale. Come over here and wash up."

"I'm *fine*, really." She went to the lab sink to washing her hands and face, and she didn't wobble, so maybe she was telling him the truth. His hands might have been cold from outside. She dried with paper towels and turned back to him.

"You're still pale." He looked at her closely and frowned. Her eyes were bloodshot. "You look fevered."

"I'm just a little tired. Need a break."

"Well, I brought you something to eat, but I don't think you should go outside. You'll get chilled. How about the steps?"

"Sounds good. Did you bring coffee?"

"Of course!"

They left the lab and sat on the steps to the first floor. He handed her a paper cup and watched her gulp the steaming coffee. Two wraps came out of the bag, his vegie, hers chicken with lettuce, beans, sprouts and avocado. She looked at it dubiously and tried a bite, then chased it with more coffee. Hutch ate his own, trying not to stare at her as she ate. She got about halfway through the wrap and put it aside.

"Thought you were hungry."

She looked at him, then stared at her hands clutching her coffee. "I was…I just…maybe I'm getting a cold or something. It just doesn't taste good." She drank more coffee.

"Tell you what." He finished the last of his own wrap and crumpled the paper. "I'll help you extract the teeth you've got exposed, and we'll let Bob see what he can get out of them. We should give him some of the ash as well, and some of that debris from inside, for analysis. Then you go home and get some sleep. The morphology can wait."

"But I've got so much—"

"No buts, Aleksi. If you get home and can't sleep, you can work on the journal, but I'm not about to have you work yourself into the hospital just to finish this project."

"All right." She looked down, obviously upset but unable or unwilling to argue with him.

I almost wish she would.

"Come on. Finish your coffee, and we'll get to work. You'll have to watch me, though. Been a while since I used a Dremel."

"Okay." She gulped coffee but wouldn't look at him.

Working together, they had the other two teeth removed in less than an hour. The second canine was more intact than the previous, and a bicuspid was fractured down the middle. The canine might yield some genetic data, so Hutch took it with him, promising to deliver it to the molecular biology lab.

"Let me drive you home, Aleksi. I'd rather you didn't walk in this cold, not if you're fighting the flu."

"Oh, I can..." She looked at him and froze, then looked away. She looked scared. "Okay."

"I'm parked in the Oxford garage." He reached for his coat, wondering why she would be scared. "We don't even need to go outside. Come on."

A leksi followed him upstairs, wondering if she was making a mistake. She felt terrible, knew that walking home would be stupid, but dreaded getting into a car with him. Persephone's blunt question came back to her. Would he come on to her? Was this a trap? She clenched her hands in her pockets.

Her knees trembled from the climb. Thankfully, his car was on the same level as the walkover. She got in the passenger side and let the soft leather seat envelop her. Her eyes closed just as second, and a tiny snippet dream of eating a thick, rare steak flashed through her mind. She jerked awake with her mouth watering.

"You okay?" he asked as they pulled out onto the snowy street.

"Yeah, just a little drowsy. You didn't buy me decaf, did you?"

"I wouldn't dare."

He drove to her apartment in silence, which was fine with her. The heated seat radiated soothing warmth into her. She closed her eyes again and breathed in the scent of the car, leather, his aftershave, and a little hint of something else. *Flying low over trees, the scent of danger...*

"Here we are."

She jerked awake and rubbed her nose, banishing the strange dream. "Thanks, Hutch. I'll email you tomorrow."

"If you're not feeling any better, stay home. Really! I mean it. You can postpone your first freshman bio lab if you need to. Just get the students' emails from Lawson and set up a make-up lab."

"It's not until Monday. I should be fine by then."

He waved and she closed the door. She watched his shiny green Prius pull away, and noticed that his plate read, "TREHUGR." She shook her head. *Perfect.* She felt stupid for worrying about Hutch coming onto her. He wasn't likely to risk his career for someone like her.

She made it to the third floor after two stops, her knees shaking. Fumbling the key in the lock, she lurched into the apartment and called out, "Julie?", but got no answer. She stashed her bag and took the rest of the disgusting wrap that she'd saved to the front room. She picked off the bits of chicken and dumped the rest of the vegies into Iggy's bowl. He sniffed it, but evidently had the same opinion as she, then tried to escape his cage.

"Sorry buddy, not right now." She stood up too quickly and stumbled before the dizziness passed. "Mom needs to eat something or she's going to pass out."

Aleksi went to the kitchen and looked in the fridge, but it hadn't spontaneously generated the steak she had fantasized about in the car. She took out the rest of the pastrami, some cheese and some spicy mustard. She intended to make a sandwich, but started munching, cutting thick slices of cheese, wrapping them in pastrami and dipping them in mustard. Before she knew it, both cheese and meat were gone, and her stomach had stopped growling. Sated, she went to the couch, kicked off her boots and lay down, pulling a thick afghan down from the back.

"Just a nap," she mumbled, resolving to make some progress on the journal when she woke.

Flying again. Tall pines sweep beneath her in vistas of green. Taiga, the Aleksi in her thinks. Figures move among the trees, crashing through the subtropical undergrowth in panic, bushes and small trees crashing aside at their wake. Prey...meat... She stoops. The trees slip past her, brushing her sides, her wings, her long lithe body. She nears one of the creatures—titanothere—smelling its panic, tasting its fear. The beast breaks left in a wild evasive maneuver, but she twists after it, making the turn with much less trouble. Her teeth flash and salty warmth floods her mouth. Bones crunch in her jaws and she feels the death shudder through her entire length as her teeth pierce its spine.

She checks the surrounding wood then bends her sinuous neck to feed. But the flesh has changed, and she finds herself staring into the startled face of Dr. Hutchinson. He blinks at her, his flesh whole, warm against her skin. She feels him stir between her legs, and desire rises like a warm flood.

"Aleksandrovna, I don't think—" He's speaking Russian. Then he cannot speak at all, as she blocks his words with her mouth.

12

———————

Beware of advisors bearing gifts." Hutch dangled the specimen bag as he turned into the corner of the molecular biology lab that Bob had been assigned.

Bob looked up from his computer and grinned. "Got something?"

"Maybe, but it doesn't look promising." Hutch put his shoulder bag down and retrieved the other two samples he'd taken from Aleksi. "This tooth might have something. I also brought some of the ash cast for analysis and a bit of the residue from inside, though I have no idea if it's anything that you can analyze."

Bob peered at the samples. "Wow. Not much left, huh?"

"Not a lot." Hutch nudged the tooth with the remaining root. "I'd try that first, but since the debris is already broken up, you might try just a simple DNA extraction. If we don't get anything, we'll have to rely on morphology to figure out what this thing is."

"No such thing as negative data." Bob squinted at the tooth skeptically. "Man, that's quite a chopper! Never seen anything like that, before."

"It looks like a big macaque canine." He pointed out the features as he spoke. "Carnivores generally have peg canines for grasping. They're never this sharp, and they don't have this honed trailing edge. Male macaques use them for display and fighting. They're used more as weapons than for eating."

"That CT didn't look like a monkey." Bob cocked an eyebrow at him. "Unless you mean one of the ones from Wizard of Oz."

"Oh, and this is probably all you're going to get for a few days. Aleksi's fighting off some kind of bug. She looked terrible."

"Really? She looked fine yesterday."

"Looks like the flu." Hutch shrugged. "Pale, feverish, shaky. I took her home and told her to get some rest."

"Wow. Right before the first week of the semester. That *sucks*!"

"Yeah, well, she's been pushing too hard and hit the wall. If she actually gets some rest, she should be able to kick it soon."

"Maybe I'll bring her a care package," Bob said with a grin. "Chicken soup or something."

"That'd be nice, but don't guilt her for staying home." Then he realized that Bob probably had no idea where Aleksi lived. "Her apartment is up off of—"

"I've got it, Hutch." At his questioning look, Bob explained. "I checked her out before our first meeting at Grendel's. And don't worry; I'm not going to guilt her for getting sick."

"All right. Just don't catch it." He waved and left the lab, wondering if all of Bob's interest in Aleksi was all professional.

———

Aleksi woke in a cocoon of sweat-drenched clothes and blankets, wondering where the hell the dream had come from. She blinked at the dark room, the drawn curtains and the dim light from the kitchen. She smelled something cooking. Her mouth was dry, and she still felt like something that had been run over by a truck and left beside the road to die. She rolled over and made an involuntary grunt at the weight of blankets and comforters covering her. Finally, she managed to heave up to a sitting position, her head spinning.

"You alive?"

She looked up to see Julie standing with her arms folded. "No." Her voice came out hoarse. "I'm dead. Did you bury me in all these blankets?"

"Well, when I came home you were shivering, so I figured you were chilled. You look like a train wreck."

"Thanks." She tried to stand up and failed, her legs still tangled in blankets. She gave up. "What smells good?"

"Chicken soup. Some guy, uh, Bob Tom-something, came by with a care package."

"Bob Tomlin? He came *here*?" Aleksi rubbed her eyes. She didn't feel like she had the flu. Her breathing was normal and there was no cough, but every joint ached and her head was pounding.

"Yeah, but don't worry, he didn't get close enough to see the wreckage. He is kind of cute, though." Julie's smile told Aleksi that she was thinking below the waist.

"Great." She tried again and managed to make it to her feet. Her shirt was soaked through with sweat and her hair was a mess. "I need a shower. Thanks for the blankets. I didn't mean to crash on the couch."

"Don't worry about it. Just don't cough on me."

"Not coughing, am I?" Aleksi managed a weak glare. "I don't think it's the flu. I just feel achy and dizzy."

"Well, you've got chills and sweats. You're running a temp, for sure."

"I'll check it."

"You want your soup in the front room? You've already infected the couch, so you might as well sleep there."

"Okay. Thanks, Julie."

"Just don't expect this level of care once the semester begins. And if you get me sick…"

"Yeah, I know, you'll take pictures and post them on Facebook."

"You got it!"

Julie retreated to the kitchen and Aleksi went to her room. She peeled out of her sweaty clothes and threw them all in the hamper, donning a thick terry robe and picking out her most comfortable flannel pajamas. If she was going to sleep on the couch, she needed something softer than jeans. In the bathroom, she risked a look in the mirror and cringed. Her eyes were bloodshot, and her face was puffy, her hair a sodden rat's nest streaked with plaster dust. If Bob did see her like this, at least she wouldn't have to worry about him ever finding her attractive.

She dropped her robe and stepped into the scalding shower, letting the hot spray soak away her headache and ease her inflamed muscles and joints. It seemed like only minutes before the hot water started to fail, so she turned it off and stepped out before she could get a chill. She felt better, and toweled off briskly, though straightening up quickly still made her dizzy. The fogged mirror exempted her from her reflection. She brushed her hair out and used the blow-drier, knowing that wet hair would give her a chill. Warm and reasonably comfortable in layers of flannel, she ventured into the kitchen.

"Oh, no you don't." Julie pointed at the front room. "Kitchen's off limits until you're not running a temp. What was it, by the way?"

"I forgot to take it." She went back to the bathroom and recovered the digital thermometer from the cabinet. It only took a moment, but the read out displayed 104.5, which was ridiculous.

"Must still be hot from the shower," she said, as she went back out to the front room. "I'll take it later." A huge bowl of soup sat on the coffee table in front of the couch. Beside it sat a big cup of a lemony smelling concoction. "What's this?"

"Thera-flu, also from your care-package provider. He said it's guaranteed to knock you out for eight hours."

"Great," she muttered, sniffing the liquid skeptically.

The medication tasted worse than it smelled. The soup, however, was delicious, with huge pieces of roast chicken and lots of noodles. She was surprised when the bowl was empty. She drank the cup of lukewarm medication down with a grimace. Her stomach was full, but she still felt hungry, as if she had a craving that could not be sated by the soup. She took the dishes to the kitchen, and Julie just pointed at the sink. She put them in and went back to the bathroom to brush her teeth. The taste of toothpaste almost made her ill, so she did a quick job, retrieved her bag and her pillow from her bedroom and went back to her sickbed. Julie came in with a scowl as she booted up her laptop.

"You are *not* working tonight."

"I need to notify the course coordinator that I might have to reschedule my first lab. I'll be off in ten minutes."

"Ten minutes." Julie looked at her watch. "Starting now."

"Yes, *Mom*." She sent a quick email to the course coordinator for freshman biology, requesting the email list for her students so she could schedule a make-up lab, checked her email, which only yielded half a dozen unimportant messages, and logged off. She closed the computer and put it on the coffee table. "Ten minutes?"

"Eight minutes thirty-two seconds. Now get some sleep."

"Yes, Mom." She lay back and tried to get comfortable. Unfortunately, with all her aches and pains, it was impossible. After a half an hour of tossing and turning the medication took hold, and she finally eased off into a fitful sleep.

She's on the green line, and it is rush hour, standing room only.

Of course, she's naked. Why wouldn't she be?

She remembers this as if it has happened before and wonders why she isn't embarrassed. A man with a briefcase and a Wall Street suit is looking at her. She avoids his eyes, because that is what New Yorkers do.

The train comes into a station, but it is not her stop. The doors open; people get out and others get in. Wall Street suit is now right next to her, his briefcase held like a shield, but not between them. It is held to hide what his other hand is doing. He slides his palm up her abdomen and cups her breast. She feels it, can detect the tiny ridge of callus on his thumb. She wants to knock his hand away, but can't.

Another hand, another man in a Wall Street suit, grabs her ass. She glares, but it's the same man. There are two of him...no, there are four...eight...she is surrounded by him, all of them reaching for her with their calloused hands, and she is defenseless to fend them off.

Then, she isn't.

Her claws rake through them like scythes, ripping grey flannel, skin, flesh and bone. Warm blood spatters her, a coppery taste on her lips. The rest of the passengers all look at her, but there is no panic, no shouts or screams.

They watch her as she bends down to feed.

Aleksi woke shaking, sweat pouring down her face and the coppery taste of blood still on her tongue. She fought her sodden bedclothes, the damp blankets, and lurched to sit up. The dream was still fresh in her mind, the taste like raw meat, an open wound that hurt when she touched it but itched when she didn't.

"God damn fever dreams."

She flung the blankets off and wobbled her way to the kitchen. Three glasses of water and her parched mouth finally tasted only of sleep and stale toothpaste. The clock on the microwave displayed 1:28. Her stomach rumbled, but she was still nauseous from the dream. She hoped that the memory would fade soon. She opened the refrigerator, but there was nothing to eat; a Tupperware container of left-over soup, some potato salad in a supermarket plastic cup, a few vegetables for Iggy. The cabinet yielded more promising results. She pulled down a can of tuna, opened it, and ate it with her fingers. She drank another glass of water to wash it down and dropped the can in the garbage.

She felt like she was still in the same dream, as if the man in the flannel suit would walk into her kitchen at any moment and she would have to kill him. She blinked, realizing she was leaning on the kitchen counter half asleep.

"Gotta get some sleep," she muttered.

The box of Thera-Flu sat on the counter. She put water on and made a cup, then opened the freezer and pulled out the bottle of Stoly. *Fuck my liver, I need sleep.* She topped off the steaming brew with vodka and drank it down.

She put everything away and stumbled back to her nest. Her bedclothes were still damp but she felt better. She lay down and sleep took her mind down a long dark spiral.

At the bottom, her dreams waited patiently.

13

T his is *so* not going to work." Bob removed the vials from the centrifuge and took them to his lab bench.

He'd gone through the extraction process for two samples, one from the tooth root, and the other from the seemingly cremated soft tissues from within the ash cast. Now, for all of his effort, he had two miniscule pellets of something that was *supposed* to be DNA. If there was any at all, as with all ancient DNA, it would be fragmented. On top of that, they had no idea what this organism was. Consequently, Bob planned to use what he called the shotgun technique, treating the samples with a number of primers, short DNA sequences that matched known sequences in the genomes common to millions of species, and would begin the replication process that would amplify the unknown DNA. The segments would then be sequenced and matched against the vast database of known sequences in Genbank.

If there's any DNA at all. Bob suspected that the temperatures of the pyroclastic ash had denatured anything organic, but science didn't work on supposition. If they found nothing, they would know for sure, and would resort to the scanty morphological data to identify the sample.

Bob split each sample into six separate tubes, then treated each with a different set of primers. Twelve tubes went into the PCR block where any DNA would be amplified into a large enough sample to be sequenced. The process would only take a couple hours, but the block would automatically chill when finished, so Bob could come back in the morning to run the sequences. He turned it on and checked his watch.

"Crap! Two thirty?" He blinked and rubbed his eyes. "Time flies when you're having fun."

He stripped off all of his protective gear and left the lab.

Inside the tubes, two disparate types of DNA began reacting with the primers. One strand was human, and the other was not. What no scientist would ever believe was that both segments of DNA belonged to the same organism.

***

Hutch lurched out of bed, wrenched from a deep sleep and completely disoriented. Only after a few ragged breaths did he realize that his phone was ringing. He glanced at the clock.

"Shit." He snatched it off the night table. Calls at three in the morning were never good news. "Hello!"

"Hey Hutch." Persephone's voice cut through the haze of panic like a knife.

What the hell was she doing calling at three in the morning? She wasn't the type to do a post-party drunk call.

"Persephone? What's wrong?"

"I wanted to apologize to you for the other night."

"At three in the morning?" Maybe she was drunk.

"Is it? Oh damn. I'm sorry, Hutch. I just got in, and I've been obsessing about what I said the other night. Look, I had too much to drink, and my mouth was running the show without my brain. I just wanted to say I'm sorry."

"Okay. Apology accepted." He couldn't very well stay angry at her after she'd given him twenty thousand dollars. He sat on the side of his bed and rubbed his face. "Don't worry about it, Persephone."

"So, we're good?"

"Sure. We're fine."

"You don't know how good it makes me feel to hear you say that. I thought I'd really fucked things up. Let me make it up to you. I'll buy you lunch at that little place you like in Cambridge. The one with the rooftop garden."

His brain stumbled. Now *she* wanted to buy *him* lunch? Suspicion chewed through the fog of sleep. "Um, look, Persephone. I don't want to send you mixed signals here. I'm still not interested in getting back together, okay?"

"Don't worry, Hutch. I'm not after a relationship here. I just thought we could stay friendly. I'd like to know how that project I'm funding is going, too. Did you find anything in that mystery sample?"

"Um, yeah." His mind did another flip flop. Now she wanted to talk about the project? "Look, Persephone, can I call you when I'm awake. We can have lunch if you want, but I can't even think straight right now."

"Oh, okay. Sorry. I always forget that you're a morning person. Give me a call around ten and we'll set up lunch. You can bring your computer and show me what you've found. Sound good?"

"Sure. That's fine."

"Okay then! Goodnight, Hutch. I'm glad we're okay."

"We're fine, Persephone. Goodnight." He punched end and silenced his phone, thinking that was perhaps the strangest phone call he'd ever gotten. His head hit the pillow, and he was asleep in seconds.

Sunday morning brought big surprises. Bob's first came when a simple test with a spectrophotometer told him that the PCR had worked; there was DNA in all of his samples. His second surprise came when he called Hutch to announce the good news, but got no answer. Hutch was always up early. Bob left a brief message and hung up. He thought about calling Aleksi, but realized he shouldn't disturb her rest.

He prepared the samples for sequencing, which meant a second PCR run with specialized nucleotide bases. When they were done, he picked one of the tooth samples and started it running. It wouldn't be finished for a few hours, so he put the other samples in storage, cleaned up the lab, and caught up on his logbook. He was only halfway through, however, when the sequencing computer chimed a warning.

"Here we go." He wheeled his chair over to the screen.

The sequencer was still running, but the result was muddled. There were two segments of amplified DNA in the sample instead of one. Both started with the same primer sequence, but a few bases after that the sequences diverged, and he had a double result for every base thereafter. He'd seen this before when there was DNA from more than one critter in a sample. It generally manifested as a few bases difference in the code, but these two were vastly different. He cross checked the primer sequence with the one on the kit documentation, and it was right. The primer was for a highly conserved bit of "nonsense" DNA common to most eukaryotic organisms.

"No such thing as negative data," he reminded himself, and let the sequencer run. He could separate the two sequences later by cloning them into bacteria and then excising and resequencing the cloned segments, but that would be time consuming. He would see what he could salvage from the other samples first.

He tried Hutch again, but still got no answer. He checked his watch, decided it was time for lunch and left the lab. Maybe he'd bring Aleksi another care package.

14

Aleksi woke to a wonderful smell and whispered voices from the kitchen. She tried to sit up but a startling weakness pervaded her aching limbs. But that smell had her mouth watering. She swallowed, cleared her throat and said, "You can stop whispering. I'm awake."

"Hey! It's alive!" Bob Tomlin poked his head around the corner and grinned at her. "I was just about ready to have you stuffed and put on display in the MCZ."

"If that glorious smell is what I think it is, I'll forgive that comment." She scrunched up against her pillow until she was almost sitting up.

"Burritos as big as your head!" He retrieved a bulging paper sack from the kitchen. "I would have brought coffee, too, but I didn't figure you needed caffeine."

"You're forgiven." She tried to smile but was afraid all she managed was a grimace. "I'm starving."

"See what I mean?" Julie followed Bob out of the kitchen with a plate and a big glass of water. "Weirdest flu I've ever seen. No cough and she's hungry, but she's *got* to have a fever."

"Add in aches, weakness, and some *wicked* fever dreams, and you've got it." Aleksi rubbed her eyes and accepted the brimming glass of water. Her hand trembled so badly that she spilled a bit before it reached her lips. She downed half without pausing for breath. "Thanks, Julie."

"Sounds more like an infection than the flu." Bob unwrapped one of the huge burritos, put it on the plate and handed it over. "Need a knife and fork?"

"No way." She lifted the huge thing, took a bite, and rolled her eyes. It was wonderful.

"I thought the flu *was* and infection." Julie looked at Bob and crossed her arms.

Aleksi knew Julie wasn't actively flirting, but she was one of those women who didn't have to. She was wearing an old Harvard Tee shirt and jeans, and was sexier than Aleksi ever could dream of being. She almost laughed at Bob's sudden blush.

"Uh, yeah, you're right. It's a viral infection, but this sounds more like Mono. No nausea, so it's not food poisoning." He looked back at Aleksi. "If we were in South America or even Florida, I'd say Dengue Fever, but the only living mosquito within a hundred miles is probably in the entomology lab. Think we should take you to the med center?"

"Not on your life. They'd stick me with needles, charge me a thousand dollars, and tell me to get rest and drink fluids." She took another bite and chewed. "This is the best medicine I've had all day."

"So, you're some kind of *medical* paleontology student?" Julie gave him a wry look.

"No." Bob blushed a little less this time. "Dad's a doctor, mom's a doctor, and you couldn't pay me enough. Working with sick people all day? Yuck!"

"Thanks." Aleksi took another bite and chewed.

"Sorry." Bob blushed again. "I didn't mean you."

"Never mind. You brought me food. You can say whatever you like." She drained her glass and sighed. "So, how goes the lab work?"

"Oh, cripes! I almost forgot!" He grinned. "We scored DNA, and not just a little."

"No way!" Aleksi nearly dropped her burrito.

"Yep. I ran six primers on one tooth and the stuff from inside the cast and they all came up positive. I've only sequenced one, but there are two strands, and they're way different."

"What was the primer?"

"A highly conserved junk region. I'll have to clone it to get both strands, then we can run a blast on Genbank and see what we've got."

"That's weird. Contamination, maybe?" Aleksi's mind was spinning. "Which piece of the specimen was it from?"

"The tooth that wasn't exposed. Hutch figured that if it was still intact, there might be something in it, and that it had the least chance of contamination. But PCR worked on the inside stuff, too."

"So it must not have been a very hot ash fall." She ate more Burrito, trying to think, but her mind was muddled with fever. "Did you look at the ash cast material?"

"Not yet. I'll have to use the mass spec for that, and scheduling's tight." He shrugged. "If the ash wasn't that hot, the thing might have suffocated, but…"

"But if it died of asphyxiation, why no bones?" she finished for him.

"Exactly. If I have to clone this to get a clean sequence, we won't have an answer for a week or so." He furrowed his brow. "You *are* taking a couple more days off, aren't you?"

"Well, I—"

"She's not leaving this apartment until her fever's gone." Julie glared at her. "Even if I have to take pictures and—"

"Post them on Facebook. That threat would have bigger teeth if I actually *had* any friends, you know." Aleksi took another bite of her dwindling burrito.

"Oh, but I've got thousands!" Julie flashed a predatory grin. "And they'd *love* to see pics of my sick roommate. I could even take a video of you snoring and drooling and put it on YouTube!"

"Fine." Aleksi ate and glared, then asked Bob, "What does Hutch think about the sample?"

"He doesn't know yet. I tried to call him but his phone's off."

"That's odd." Aleksi finished the last of her burrito.

"Well, it's Sunday. Maybe he's just taking a day off." Bob took the plate and glass, since Julie was showing no sign of wanting to touch anything that might be infected with whatever had laid Aleksi low. "I'll put the other burrito in the fridge for later. You want more water?"

"Please." She watched Julie follow him into the kitchen and had an unaccustomed pang of jealousy. She shook it off and suppressed a shiver.

"You canceled your labs for the week, right?" Bob returned with the full glass.

"Just Monday's Freshman Bio." She accepted the water and drank some without spilling this time. "I should be back on my feet by Wednesday for Comparative Zoology."

"Don't push yourself. If it is Mono, you could be down for more than a week."

"I'll be fine in a couple of days, I'm sure. Thanks for the food."

"No problem. Let me know if you need anything else. I mean it."

"Thanks."

"No thanks necessary. Just get well. The teamwork thing doesn't work if half the team is flat on her back with a fever." He smiled and retreated to the kitchen.

She listened to Bob and Julie whispering for a bit, but she couldn't concentrate enough to follow everything. She heard water running and imagined him doing the dishes for her. She snuggled down in her nest of blankets and felt another pang of jealousy. She knew Bob was just being nice. He was always nice. She closed her eyes and let her mind drift. Her last cognizant thoughts before sleep were how strange it was to have people who actually cared for her. She wondered why it should make her feel jealous.

Flying again, but this time the canyons and forest are the rooms and furniture of her apartment. She soars around the living room, perching high on this or that, scanning the vista for danger or prey. Iggy looks at her from his cage, and she smiles at him, her dear friend. She soars through the kitchen, down the hall and around her room, but there is no one else here.

Julie's door is closed, but sounds come from within. Aleksi knows those sounds, has heard them before from Julie's room, and she frowns. The doorknob turns in her hand.

She soars into the room and takes a high perch, peering down at them on the bed. Skin against skin, Julie and Bob moving in carnal synchrony, beautiful and fragile. She watches, confused at the feelings this evokes in her. She feels warm and tingly inside, but also angry.

Why angry?

A thrill of danger chases up her spine as they climax together and collapse in a tangle of sweaty arms and legs.

Hutch stomped the snow from his boots and stepped into the Daedalus Bar and Grille's sweltering, noisy, fragrant, and wonderful interior. Great food and a really fine selection of craft beers had made this place a local favorite for years. In summer, the roof would be as crowded as the downstairs, with brimming window boxes full of flowers and friendly wait staff. In winter, the theme shifted to one of warmth, noise, flavors, and shoulder to shoulder seating.

Not Persephone's kind of place.

That elicited suspicion. If she wanted to buy him lunch, why not one of her usual haunts with white linen and crystal? The answer was simple: she wanted something. He hoped it wasn't him.

"Hutch!"

The call over the murmur of conversation snapped his eye to the bar. Persephone waved him over with a beaming smile.

Once more into the breech… He loosened his coat and strode forth to do battle, his defenses up.

For the first time in recent memory, Persephone wasn't dressed to show off her money; a simple sweater, tights with boots, and sedate rings and earrings. She greeted him with a real hug and a kiss on the cheek.

"Great to see you, Hutch." She waved him to a vacant barstool. "The place is jammed, so I thought we'd just hang at the bar if that's okay."

"Sure." That was another surprise. Persephone didn't 'hang' anywhere, and he'd never known her to eat a meal from a barstool. "You trying to turn over a middle-class leaf or something?"

"No. Just blending in." She waved the bartender over. "What's your poison?"

He glanced at the taps. "Harpoon IPA and a couple of menus."

The bartender handed over the menus and went to draw his draft.

Persephone raised her wine glass as his beer arrived. "So, formal apology time: I'm sorry about the other night, Hutch. I'm over the top sometimes, I know. I hope you can forgive me."

"I'm not mad about it, Persephone." She touched his glass to hers and sipped his beer.

"Yes, you are, and you have every right to be. I've got a big mouth."

He waited for the punchline, one of her lewd innuendos that he knew so well, but she didn't go there. He glanced up from his menu and found her looking at him with a strange expression he couldn't read. He knew her moods, and this was a new one.

"I *was* mad, but I'm not anymore, okay?"

"Okay." She looked at her menu, then back. "I've been…having some problems lately, and…well, it was just me being stupid."

That was new, too. Persephone never admitted to having problems. Problems were things that poor people had. "We're all stupid every once in a while."

The waiter returned and he ordered a Portobello burger. She ordered a chicken Caesar, and an uncomfortable silence descended. They both sipped their drinks, and he remembered why they'd gotten divorced. Initially it had been fun, *she* had been fun. Rich, generous, gregarious, and witty, it had been hard to say no to her, but he didn't like parties, and she accused him of being a workaholic. They had nothing in common but sex, and she got bored easily. He'd started coming home to an empty condo and messages on the phone that she was busy and would sleep at the house. When it boiled down to seeing each other only two or three nights a week, he'd finally asked for a divorce. She'd thrown a tantrum at first, of course, but then agreed and gave him more than he asked for in the split.

And now she's having problems...

"So, this project I'm funding is going well, you said?"

"Oh, well we just got started, but yes." He realized that there was one more thing they had in common; their mutual love of cryptozoology. "In fact, you'll get a kick out of this." He pulled his computer from his pack and fired it up.

"Tell me you found the Loch Ness Monster on a mountain in Kamchatka and I'll write you a blank check if I get to name it." She scooched her stool over so they could both look at the screen.

"Not quite, but we're not sure yet." He pulled up the CT image and waited for it to load. "The weirdest thing was the CT results. The sample is an ash cast like the ones in Pompeii. You know the ones I mean?"

"I've seen pictures." She cringed. "That one of the woman sheltering the child always makes me want to cry."

He glanced at her. Was *that* her problem? Was Persephone having biological clock issues? She'd never struck him as maternal, but people changed with age. "So, like those, the hot ash basically created a cocoon around our specimen, but the shocker came when we did a CT and found nothing inside."

"Nothing? What, like it vaporized?"

"Yes, but even the bones were nothing but dust. Only a few teeth and fragments were left, so our hopes of getting any DNA are pretty dismal. But look at the three-dee rendering of the scan." He tilted the screen to give her a better view.

"Oh, *my*!" Her eyes widened and she put down her wine glass too hard. "That's...Hutch, what *is* that?"

"No idea." He grinned at her fascination, admitting to himself that he'd missed her enthusiasm for these things.

"Are those *wings*?"

"They do look like some kind of elongated digits, maybe with a membranous webbing, like a bat, but the body shape's all wrong. The hind limbs are too long and the teeth really look like a big male primate's. Here." He pulled up the photos of the large canines under magnification.

"Wow!" Her eyes gleamed and she leaned in, one hand on his leg, but not a hint of a come-on. "You don't suppose I could have a copy of those, do you?"

"I can't, Persephone. I'm sorry, but if this ends up on some fringe crypto website next to pictures of Nessie and Sasquatch, I'd be in trouble."

"Come *on*, Hutch." She leaned back and cocked one plucked eyebrow. "I *paid* for this, you know."

There it was again, the spoiled child coming out. "I can't let the cat out of the bag before I know if it's a cat or a canary." He closed his computer as the bartender arrived with their meals.

"What if I offer to fund the entire project, soup to nuts?" She grinned and grabbed his wrist before he could put the computer back in his bag.

"You don't give up, do you?"

"No, but I'm offering to fund your project." She let go and turned to her meal. "You could name your own price, Hutch."

"We don't even know what this thing is yet."

"Well, when you find out, let me know and we'll work up a figure." She ate a bite of salad and chased it with a sip of wine.

"You're serious."

"Of *course*, I'm serious." She ate another bite. "Get your DNA analysis done and call me with a plan. We'll negotiate. I get to unveil your Kamchatka mountain monster, and you get funding."

He laughed at her, surprised by her generosity. "Tell you what. I'll think about it, but it's Aleksi's project, not mine."

"Oh, I'd rather do business with you, Hutch." She cringed. "I don't think she likes me much."

"Why?" That was a warning bell; Persephone didn't think *anyone* didn't like her.

"I kind of embarrassed her the other night by accident, I think." She gave him a chagrined face.

"Persephone, what did you say to her?"

"Well, she's young and attractive, even if she doesn't *know* it, and I thought you two might be..." She waved a hand. "...you know. So I asked her."

"You *didn't*!"

"Well, she said you weren't, so no real harm done."

Hutch just stared at her.

"Oh, come on, Hutch. She's a big girl." She sipped wine and gave him a look. "What?"

"You astound me, that's all." He leaned in and lowered his voice. "You really think I'd sleep with one of my grad students?"

"Oh, come on, Hutch. You know me. I think everyone's sleeping with everyone." She laughed musically. "And more than half the time, I'm right!"

"Well I'm not."

"I know. That's what she said." She grinned at him. "Don't worry, Hutch. Even if you were, I wouldn't hold it against you. Hell, I wouldn't hold it against *me*!" She did a little shimmy on her barstool and sat up straight. "That girl can wear a sweater, let me tell you."

"Don't you *dare* seduce my student, Persephone." He knew she might do it just for fun or spite.

"Oh, I *won't*." She made a face. "She's *so* not my type."

"You have a type?" He couldn't resist.

"Now who's being petulant?" She laughed and returned to her meal. "So, when do you get DNA from this thing?"

"*If* we get DNA, we should…" That reminded him that he hadn't heard from Bob yet, and really should have. "In fact, we should know by now if we have any. Hang on." He fished his phone out of his pocket and saw that he had two missed calls. "Damn!"

"What?"

He punched up the voicemail and glared at her. "*Someone* called me at three AM and I turned my ringer off."

"Oh?" She gave him her best look of innocence.

He ignored her and listened to the message.

"Hey, Hutch. Sorry to bug you on Sunday, but we scored some DNA on the samples. I'll be in the lab if you want to come down and have a look."

"Well, I'll be damned." He pulled up the second message.

"Weird results here, Hutch. Swing by when you can."

Hutch put his phone away and took a big bite of his burger.

"Well, tell me."

"We got DNA." He chased the bite with beer and took another. He wanted to rush to the lab, but wouldn't waste a perfectly good lunch.

"That's good. So what is it?"

"No idea yet, but Bob said it's weird."

"Well, weird is good, too, right?" She bit her lip and cocked her head. "Right?"

"Yes, Persephone, weird is good."

W hat did you get?"
Bob turned as Hutch entered the lab and started putting on isolation gear. Before the mask hid is features, he saw the excitement there. He wished he had better news.

"More than we bargained for, I think." Bob finished what he was doing, put his pipettor aside, and picked up his logbook. "You want the long version or the Cliff notes?"

"Short version first."

Bob described his results so far; the spectrophotometer readings indicating the presence of DNA in the samples, and the muddled results of the first sequence. As it turned out, very little of the two strands of DNA were similar, but there was a lot of crossing over, short shared segments, then longer ones that were different.

"I think we have contamination, but I can't figure out from where."

"Was this a tooth or the debris from inside?"

"A tooth, why?"

"Plaque, maybe." Hutch looked at the sequencer. "What are you running now?"

"I just started one of the debris samples." Bob went to the sequencer and looked at the results. "This one's better, but there's still a lot of doubling. Not as bad as the first, but..."

"It's still too much to get a decent sequence. If you're going to run a search in Genbank, you need a clean run of three or four hundred bases."

"Well, we're not getting that." Bob pointed to the screen, which showed a significant percentage of doubling in the signal. "Not even close."

"We've got to figure out what's going on here." Hutch leaned back and Bob knew what he was going to say. "Clone these two into E-Coli and get solid runs of both strands. Then do a search on Genbank."

Bob cringed. "It'll take a week or so."

"Well, you can sequence the rest of what you've got in the meantime. If you get a solid segment from that, you can run a search on it. Otherwise, we're cloning."

"Roger will-co, boss." Bob stood and stretched, then realized that there was a little more information that Hutch might be interested in. "Oh, and I went by Aleksi's place. I brought her some food. She's really looking rough. Fever, chills, aches, the whole bit."

"Did she cancel her labs?"

"Monday's, but not the comp zoo one yet. She thinks she'll kick it by Wednesday."

"Not likely." Hutch's brow furrowed. "I could probably take her Wednesday lab, but I've got a big meeting on Thursday."

"Don't look at me! I don't know crap about comparative zoology. I barely passed it as an undergrad!" That wasn't exactly true; he'd gotten a B. He just hated dissections.

"Really? Well, you know what they say: you never really learn something until you teach it." Bob could see Hutch's evil grin right through his mask. "Maybe fall semester."

"I *knew* I shouldn't have opened my mouth!"

"I'll make sure Aleksi's lab is covered, don't worry. I just hope she kicks this quick, otherwise we're going to get behind."

"Well, don't tell *her* that. I think she's feeling guilty enough already."

"I thought she would be." Hutch headed for the door. "No worries, Bob. We'll sort it all out and get things back on track soon enough." He peeled out of his gear and looked back. "And don't push yourself too hard. The last think I need is *two* sick students."

"No worries there, doc. I'm the lazy one, remember?"

Hutch just laughed as the door closed behind him.

⁂

Gi-gi's warm palm against Persephone's head brought her memories to the fore. The rotating image of the CT scan, the photographs of the curved canine teeth, Hutch's scent as he leaned close, the warm tingle in her stomach with his thigh under her hand.

Her eyes snapped open with the piercing headache and she jerked away. She'd given too much. "I'm sorry. I was only…"

"Be at ease, child." Those thin lips drew up in the corners. "Enjoy your youth. Your pleasure pleases me."

Persephone hid her embarrassment behind a mask of submission.

"This thing they've found…I've never *seen* anything like it before." That, coming from Gi-gi, meant that it was unknown to the world of science. "There are…*myths*, however, that speak of such creatures."

"Myths?" Persephone knew from experience that there were often cores of truth in myths.

"Yes...Kur, in Sumer, for one." The ancient woman's eyes fluttered, a sign of fatigue. "The specimen...acquire it for me."

"That will be difficult." Stealing a six-hundred-pound specimen from a lab in the MCZ would be more than difficult. More like impossible. And it would put Hutch's career on the line. "Would a...*piece* of the specimen suffice?"

"No. All of it. We must *not* let this be found by the government...*any* government. They can't be trusted with such treasures."

Persephone swallowed hard. *The things I do for this family...* "I'll do my best."

15

Aleksi woke to full daylight streaming in the windows and a blur of memories. She blinked the sleep from her eyes and sat up. She had slept, *really* slept, for the first time in days. Her bedclothes were dry and warm; no fever, no sweats, and no memories of recent fever dreams. She still ached, but that was probably due to so long in bed.

"Thank God." She checked the time; just past nine in the morning, but she honestly didn't know what day it was. She did know two things, however: she was ravenous, and she *really* had to pee.

"Julie?" No answer.

Her laptop lay on the coffee table, so she opened it and turned it on. While it booted, she took all the rumpled blankets and her pillow to her bedroom and dumped them in a pile. Laundry would wait. She stripped off her pajamas, grabbed a clean robe and hurried to the bathroom. When she was done with nature's call, she washed her face and hands, and caught her reflection in the mirror.

"Not quite so deathly." She had some color at least, even though her hair resembled a rat's nest. She stopped by the kitchen to start coffee and went to her computer. The date in the corner said the twenty-second, Wednesday.

"Shit!"

She'd lost a whole day somehow. Her Comparative Zoology lab was scheduled for ten AM *today*. She pulled up her email and scanned the messages. All but two of her freshman biology lab students agreed on the time she set for a make-up lab, and those two had already made up the lab in another section. Good. Then she saw the message from Hutch titled Comp Zoo Lab.

"Double shit!" She pulled it up.

Aleksi,

Looks like you're not going to make Wednesday's lab. There is no one to cover, so I'll take it for you. Hope you feel better soon.

Hutch.

She checked the clock again; it was quarter after nine. She could just make it. She grabbed her cell phone, punched Hutch's number and dashed for the shower. He picked up on the third ring.

"Aleksi! How are you?"

"Hi Hutch. I'm good. I just woke up." She turned the water on and dropped her robe. "Fever's gone and I just read your email. I can make the lab, so you don't have to cover."

"You sure? I talked to Bob yesterday, and he said you were out cold."

"I was. I finally got some sleep, and the fever broke. I'm fine. I can make the lab, but I've got to hurry, so..." She felt the water, but it took forever to get hot.

"But you've been out, Aleksi. You haven't had time to review the material."

"I've got last semester's notes on my computer and the lab's already set up. I can do this, Hutch. It's the worm lab, right?"

"Yeah, it is. Well, okay. If you're sure..."

"I'm sure, Hutch. Thanks." Another thought struck her as she stepped into the finally hot spray. She turned, trying to keep her phone dry. "I'll call you after the lab. I'd like to get caught up."

"To tell you the truth, Aleksi, I'm swamped. I've got a huge meeting tomorrow on the pipeline project. Catch up with Bob, and I'll meet with you both on Friday."

"All right. Oh, and thanks for offering to cover, Hutch. Oliver would *never* have done something like that."

"Not a problem, Aleksi. I'm just glad you're feeling better."

She signed off and took the fastest shower in human history. Clean, she dashed to the kitchen in a towel, threw some bread in the toaster and cracked two eggs into a skillet. Four thick slices of bacon joined the eggs. She put a cover on the skillet, grabbed a few vegies for Iggy and took them to his cage. He ignored her, obviously despondent for being ignored for three days.

"Sorry, buddy. Mom will be back in a few hours, and we'll play, okay." He blinked, ignored the food and lashed his tail. "Fine. Be that way."

Back in the kitchen, she poured coffee and willed her breakfast to cook faster. Impatient, she got dressed while it cooked. When her toast popped up, she tilted the contents of the skillet onto the two crisped slices and dug in. The bread tasted a little funny, but the loaf hadn't looked moldy. She shrugged and wolfed it down between sips of coffee. Reasonably sated, she filled a travel cup, put the plate and skillet in the sink, grabbed her coat and bag, and left the apartment.

In the sink, raw egg dripped from the cold skillet. In her rush, Aleksi had not turned on the stove.

———

The Comparative Zoology lab started off like clockwork, but it seemed to Aleksi that the clock was running at half speed. She flashed through the introduction, the syllabus, the quiz schedule, grading, and make-up options in barely ten minutes.

"Any questions?" She scanned the twenty faces. They looked a little stunned. One of the faces in the back looked vaguely familiar, then another student raised her hand. "Yes?"

"Um, I didn't get the syllabus email."

"Your email address?" As the girl gave it, Aleksi typed it in, attached the syllabus and sent it. "You've got it now. You might want to check to make sure the lab coordinator has your correct email. Anything else?"

There were no other questions.

"All right, then. Platyhelminthes, Nematoda, and Annelida. Pair up and boot up your workstation computers and the dissecting scopes. Gloves are on that bench, and our wormy subjects are in the buckets over there. Please take one of each and follow the dissection guide on your workstations. If you have any questions, problems, or anything at all, speak up."

She guided them through the dissections using diagrams and illustrations projected from her computer onto a screen at the head of the classroom, using a laser pointer as she walked around the class, offering help, advice, and generally keeping everyone on track. She found herself listening to several low-voiced conversations as she talked, and picked out the students who seemed genuinely interested versus those who were just going through the motions.

The fellow she thought she'd recognized surprised her as she passed his table.

"Hello, Aleksi."

"You're..." His face registered, and she gaped in surprise. "Derrick? You're in Comparative Zoology?"

"Surprised to see me?" He smiled, his teeth perfectly white, perfectly straight. The girl he had paired with looked from him to Aleksi with wide eyes.

"Yes." She shrugged off her surprise. "I thought you worked for Dr. Neilson."

"Oh, that's just until my grad school application goes through. I'll be in the paleosciences program next year." That smile again.

"Really! Why are you taking Comparative Zoology then?"

"Oh, I finished up at Princeton and took a year off. I'm taking Comp Zoo as a non-degree course. It gives me a chance to check out the programs and pick an advisor, and I can maintain my student status. You know."

"Sure." She certainly understood why he wanted to maintain his student status. Deferring loans and the student healthcare perks were reasons enough. "You didn't take Comp Zoo as an undergrad?"

"No, but I didn't have to." He shrugged. "I was going to do med school but changed my mind."

"Oh." She knew what that meant, too. He'd bombed his MCATs. "Well, good to see you."

"Hey, I'd like to talk to you after class about advisors, if you don't mind. It's tough to know the sharks from the tuna, if you know what I mean."

"I'm really kind of swamped today." That wasn't a lie. She had five days to catch up on.

"Let me just buy you a coffee. It won't take long, I promise." That smile again...

Aleksi suppressed a shiver and hoped she wasn't having a relapse. "Sure. Okay." She said it more to end the conversation during class than any real desire to help him out. Something about Derrick gave her the creeps.

She kept up her instructions as she circulated the room. Whenever he caught her eye, he smiled with those perfect teeth and sat up in his chair a little. In fact, every time she looked his way, he was looking at her.

I so don't need this. She smiled briefly back, thinking that she better nip his interest in the bud. She was too busy to deal with a creepy stalker. The notion that she would never have thought about blowing off a stalker a week ago didn't enter her mind.

---

*S**omething's different…*** Derrick considered Aleksi critically, analyzing, composing his plan. The mousy woman he remembered seemed to have lost her fear. When she looked at him he could see discomfort, but the fear, that anxiety, was missing. *Doesn't matter. She's my way in, that's all. A year from now she'll be a strung-out addict selling herself on the street, and I'll be working her project. All I have to do is play her right.*

He worked through the ridiculous class, cutting open the worms and dazzling the young woman he'd paired with. One never knew when one might need a pawn. The class ended and he accepted the girl's phone number, promising to call her to study. Then he waited outside for Aleksi.

"Still up for coffee?"

She jerked at his question, her eyes snapping to his in surprise, pupils dilated. "Oh, Derrick. Right. I'd forgotten. You know, I'm just slammed in the lab. I've been out a few days, and I've got a *ton* of catching up to do."

"I'll throw in a bagel. Come on, I found a great little place. I just want to pick your brain about advisors." He gave her his best smile again and watched her eyes. Her pupils constricted, and she looked away, then back. *Unease, apprehension, yes, but no fear or anxiety.*

"All right." She shouldered her bag. "But I might opt for a piece of pizza instead of a bagel."

"Great!"

As they walked to Dudley Café, he regaled her with his life story. Magna cum laude from Princeton, Ivy League family back four genera-tions. "Old money, you know." He made a face like being rich was a curse.

She just nodded and seemed disinterested. He didn't understand. Money and prestige generally lit women up like a white phosphorous grenade. Maybe she was a dyke. That would make this more difficult.

"So, you're working with Dr. Hutchinson." They sat down at a free table, he with coffee, and she with two slices of meat-lover's pizza. "How's that going?"

"Good." She picked meat and cheese off the crust with her fingertips.

"He's the environmentalist guy, isn't he? Working to block that trans-Canada pipeline?"

"Um, I don't really know much about his work outside the university, but he's already got five students, so I don't know if he'll be taking anyone new."

"Oh? That sucks. He's popular."

"Is he?" She shrugged.

"I thought I might get my pick, but it looks like all the good advisors are overloaded." He looked at her and cocked an eyebrow, smiling again. "Got any recommendations?"

"That depends on what you're interested in?"

He launched into a detailed dissertation of his entire research plan, utterly fabricated, of course. She nodded and kept stuffing meat and cheese into her mouth, sipping coffee. He worked his way around to working at the MCZ, and how that had opened his eyes to the wonders of paleontology. Then he popped the question.

"I heard that you found something that was mislabeled in the repository? Some long-lost specimen from Kamchatka?" Her eyes darted up from her plate. "What was *that* all about?"

"It was mislabeled in Russia and ended up here." She shrugged again as if she didn't care. "We got an outside donation to look into it, but we don't know much yet."

"Wow, what a blunder. I almost took the heat for that mislabeling until Neilson told everyone about that diary you found."

Her eyes flashed up again. "How did you find out about the diary?"

He didn't like that tone but covered easily. "Oh, Neilson showed me the pictures you sent him. Pretty freaky stuff."

She looked down and shrugged. "Just a case of mistaken identity, I think. Happens all the time." She ate some more then paused and looked up as if she'd just had an epiphany. "You know, I think you might have something in common with Dr. Oliver. You should look at her research and see if it fits your interest."

"Really?" He smiled, wondering if she'd shifted subjects to throw him off, but he'd asked her about advisors, so he couldn't easily defer. "You think so?"

I*'m so going to hell for this*, Aleksi thought. "Oh, absolutely! She's really brilliant, and I happen to know she's got an opening for a graduate student."

"Wow. Thanks!" He gave her that smile again, and she swallowed hard.

"Hey, I'm sorry, but I really do have to run. I'm swamped." Aleksi stood up. "Thanks for the Pizza."

"Oh, okay. Sure. No problem." He stood. "See you around."

"See you next Wednesday then." She took her coffee with her but left the two denuded pizza crusts on the table.

Two texts later, Aleksi knew just how much she'd missed. She hurried to Bob's lab to get caught up to speed.

"Hey Bob!" She left her bag and coat at the door, and reached for a surgical mask and gloves.

"Aleksi!" He got up from his bench and looked her up and down. "Wow! You're alive!

"Told you I'd kick it! No small thanks to you and your care packages." She snapped her gloves and ran her fingers together in a long-practiced motion to work the air out. Her knuckles ached. "Ready for a little catch up."

"I can't believe you made your lab today. Yesterday I was about ready to take you to the hospital."

"I can't believe I lost a whole day." She joined him at the bench. "What'd I miss?"

"So, we've got significant coding differences in all of the samples. Definitely two species' DNA here, but every shared base pair means a potential cross-over of the sequence, right?" Bob waved a hand at the sequencing data and sighed. "That means cloning to split them up before we can get anything big enough to match to Genbank. The *good* news is that nothing is as fragmented as I thought it would be. I used short, conserved primers and all got hits. I'm beginning to think the reason the CT looked so weird was that there are two organisms in that cast. I've got all the bugs cooking right now, and I'm waiting on mass spec time for the ash cast sample. I've got a friend in Geology who's willing to have a look at the results and give an informal opinion…for a favor."

"What *kind* of favor?" Aleksi could tell from his reticence that the favor wasn't something simple. She hoped he wasn't making promises. That was how research papers accumulated authors who hadn't really contributed.

"Um...well...I kind of promised I'd introduce him to Lonnie." Bob blushed, and she could see his grin despite his mask. "He met her at the New Year party, but he's kind of shy."

"Great!" She laughed, wondering how Lonnie would react. "Just don't tell her she's the payoff for a mass spec analysis."

"Do I *look* like I want a splenectomy?"

"Probably a *vasectomy*, if I know Lonnie."

They both snickered, and she noticed that Bob was looking at her strangely. "What?"

"Nothing. Just surprised to see you so perky all of the sudden. You seem...I don't know, happier or something."

"Well, not feeling like crap probably has something to do with that." She didn't really feel any different, but she knew what he meant. She felt at ease, as if recovering from the illness had left her without any worries. She knew she had plenty to worry about, but it all seemed to make sense, as if she could easily prioritize things now. "So, we're looking at what, a week before we get anything?"

"Maybe Monday, if I work over the weekend."

"Well, I'll be working, too, so don't feel bad. I'm behind on the translation, and I should probably get back to work on the bear samples until we get some data on these."

"Okay. Maybe we can commiserate over burritos or something."

"I'll buy this time," she said, moving toward the door. "I owe you big for the care packages. They saved my life."

"Sounds good!" He grinned. "See you later, then. We're meeting with Hutch Friday morning. He said he'd emailed you."

"Right. Later." She stuffed all her protective gear in the trash and left the lab with one last wave. Her only worry was the strange mixture of warmth and foreboding that was churning in her stomach talking to Bob.

A remembered dream, bodies moving together, sweat and flesh, passion so thick she could taste it.

The door clicked closed behind her and she leaned back against it, dizzy with the vision. *What the Hell?* Her heart was pounding in her chest. *Julie and Bob?* She looked back over her shoulder through the glass panel in the door, unsure if the vision was a dream or a memory.

***

Hey, Julie!" Aleksi called as she burst into the apartment, one arm cradling a bag of groceries. She heard music from the front room, which meant her roommate was exercising. She poked her head around the corner and grinned. "You must have gotten my text. You working up an appetite?"

"Damn right." Julie was doing some kind of complicated stretch that looked more like a form of midlevel torture than exercise. "You owe me big, and I'm going to *collect*."

Aleksi showed her the bag. "New York strips and all the fixin's."

"You should get sick more often! I've got like twenty minutes of this, then I've got to shower."

"Perfect." Aleksi went to the kitchen and began unloading supplies. "I'll nuke the potatoes and catch a quick shower, then do the rest while you're in there."

"Don't you *dare* use all the hot water this time!"

"I won't, I promise."

Aleksi prepped the potatoes and put them in the microwave, then pulled the two huge steaks from the white paper wrapping. Her mouth watered as she trimmed the fat to a quarter inch, stabbed them with a fork and put them in a Tupperware with a little white wine, Italian dressing, and garlic salt. She flipped them a couple times, then snapped on the lid and put them in the fridge. Wadding up the butcher paper, she couldn't find the fat she'd cut away.

Must have pitched it already. She licked her lips without thinking about the flavor of meat still in her mouth.

Aleksi hit the shower—after five hours in the lab she needed it to get the rock dust out of her hair—and was drying off just as Julie finished her torture session.

She poked her head in the bathroom as Aleksi was drying her hair. "Any hot water left?"

"Plenty!"

"There better be." Julie ducked out.

Aleksi finished drying and looked in the steamed mirror. A swipe with her hand cleared the image, and she paused. *Is that really me?* She turned sideways. *I must have lost some weight while I was sick.* She grabbed her clothes and her towel and went to her room. In fresh clothes, she felt like a new woman. Tucking in her fleece top she found her jeans a little loose around the waist. *Huh, definitely lost weight.*

She finished in the kitchen, making a salad and broiling the steaks just enough to sear the outside and leave the inside red. She poured two glasses of red wine as she heard the shower turn off.

"Payback!" Aleksi met Julie at the bathroom door with one glass held out.

"Ah! Sweet!" They clinked glasses and sipped. "Mmm, not bad!"

"I splurged and went over the ten-dollar mark." Aleksi turned back to the kitchen to check on things. "You like rare, don't you?"

"Medium rare, not bloody." Julie followed her, finger combing her wet curls. She took a deep breath of the seared meat smell. "Oh, my *God*, that smells good."

"Just what the doctor ordered." Aleksi took one of the steaks out and slid the other back under the broiler. "About a minute if you want to get dressed."

"I'm good." Julie leaned against the wall and sipped her wine, flapping the lapel of her fuzzy pink robe. "Still overheated from the torture session. I can't believe you're feeling so good so quick! This time yesterday, I was measuring you for a casket."

"You know, I have *no* memory of yesterday." Aleksi doled out salad and prepped the potatoes. "Everything on your potato?"

"Just a little sour cream, if it's low fat."

"Buzzkill." Aleksi shoveled sour cream, bacon bits, chives, salt and pepper on hers. She loaded the other steak and lifted both plates. "Bring the wine, oh tender of the ill and incapacitated."

"Ha! You *are* feeling better!"

"Positively giddy with it." She put the plates on the coffee table and went back to get forks and knives while Julie took a seat on a throw pillow and topped off their glasses. Aleksi sat on the couch and lifted her glass. "Here's to not feeling like crap!"

"I'll drink to that."

They did, and then dug into their steaks. Aleksi sliced off a piece of the barely seared meat and popped it into her mouth, chewing with bliss. A visceral memory flooded her mind—*warm flesh between her teeth, the coppery taste of blood on her tongue*—She blinked and swallowed forcefully. *What the hell?* She looked at the steak as if it were a freshly killed ungulate waiting to be devoured.

"You okay?" Julie sipped her wine and wrinkled her brow.

"Yeah. Yeah, fine. Why?" Aleksi tried some of her baked potato, but it didn't taste right, as if the sour cream had turned or something. Julie was eating hers with no complaint, so she sipped some wine to clear her palate.

"You just turned kind of white all of the sudden."

"Oh?" Aleksi tried another bite of steak and had no strange visions. The meat was delicious. "Maybe I forgot what real food tasted like."

"Beats Ramen noodles." Julie took a bite of the salad, which reminded Aleksi that it was on her plate. She ate some, but it was kind of like eating air compared to the steak. "So, if this is my payback, how are you going to compensate your friend Bob? Something similar, or did you have something more intimate in mind?" Julie grinned and sipped her wine.

"Burritos." Aleksi cut another bite of steak and popped it into her mouth. "And get your mind out of the gutter. We're friends, that's all. We're going to be working too close for anything else." She chewed and thought for a moment.

Bodies moving together, sweat and flesh, passion so thick she could taste it.

She looked at Julie and felt that tug in her stomach again. *Dream or memory?* "Seems to me that you had your eye on him, though."

"Well, like I said, he's cute in a kind of nerdy fashion." Julie shrugged. "Not my type, really."

"You've got a type?" Aleksi grinned. *It must have been a fever dream. Still…* "You mean other than having a Y chromosome?"

"Oh, *nice!*" Julie put her wineglass down and tried to look hurt. "I rescue you from a lingering death, risking my *own* health in the process, and you accuse me of being a wanton woman!"

"Would that be wanton or wonton? I really don't think Bob's into Chinese food, but if you dipped yourself in soy sauce, I'm sure he'd try a nibble."

Julie burst out in laughter, staring wide-eyed at her. "Oh my *God*, where did Aleksi Rychenkna get a sense of humor?"

"Told you I was giddy." She took another bite of steak and closed her eyes in bliss. "Seriously, though, if you're interested in Bob, I'll let him know. He'd be better for you than *Vic*." She made a face.

"I'll think about it. Don't tell him anything."

"My lips are sealed." Aleksi closed her eyes, recalling the dream again. Maybe she could make that happen. She thought of Bob and Julie together and couldn't suppress a smile. *Yeah, they'd be good for each other.*

When they were finished with their impromptu feast, Aleksi cleared up the dishes—she'd only eaten a couple of bites of her potato and half her salad—and they both got back to work; Julie reading some ancient script on Mesopotamian opera, and Aleksi checking her own class schedule and pulling up the journal for more translation. She confirmed the makeup lab for her freshman biology students, and started in on the journal. Iggy rattled his cage, and she brought him out to play, as promised, feeding him bits of her leftover salad and scratching his chin. He settled down in her lap, his favorite spot, while she painstakingly translated Dr. Andriy Loktev's journal.

Friday morning, Bob and Aleksi met with Hutch in his office. Bob looked tired and frustrated, and Hutch's hair was wet. The weather had changed, a warm front turning snow to cold rain and slush. They were due for more cold tonight. She could smell the hint of soap and aftershave on Hutch and realized that he must have come straight from the gym. Both of them held huge brown paper cups, the aroma of coffee almost aphrodisiac.

"Good morning." Hutch smiled, but she could see that he'd been working late, too. There were dark circles under his eyes.

They both said good morning, and Bob raised an eyebrow at Aleksi. "What, no coffee? I thought you were a confirmed caffeine addict."

"Way ahead of you; I was up early and finished the journal. Any more coffee and my head will explode." She passed a flash drive to Hutch. "You already have the original scans, so I just put the translation on there. I put all the illustrations and footnotes in the document."

"Good reading?" Hutch asked, sipping his coffee and booting up his computer.

"Actually, yes. More like a memoir than a log-book." She smiled at the memories of the flowery language, conjecture, and supposition in the journal; nothing like a modern lab journal.

"So, where do we stand with the samples, Bob?"

"I'm trying to figure out why we've got anything at all, Hutch." He rubbed his eyes and pulled a sheaf of papers from his bag. "I got some feedback from my friend in Geology on the ash cast results. The ash is pyroclastic, but not all the minerals show pyrogenous origins."

"So it might not have been as hot as we thought."

"It *can't* have been," Bob said shaking his head. "There's not nearly as much DNA fragmenting as we expected. I might not be getting clean sequences, but I'm getting long ones. I don't know why I'm getting two different copies from every primer, but I was thinking that we might have two organisms, which might explain that weird CT image. But whatever it is, it wasn't cooked."

"I was thinking that could be due to the climate of the find." Hutch turned to Aleksi. "Did we get an exact position from the log book?"

"If you believe it, sure. Within a few miles or so, on the slopes of Mount Nalychevo, at about forty-five hundred feet."

"Permafrost?" Bob asked, his eyebrows arching again. Tissue could be amazingly well preserved if it never thawed.

"It's the only explanation I can think of. Does the journal mention anything about the temperature?"

"Sure. It was cold, and they were in a hurry to avoid the onset of winter, but they didn't mention permafrost."

"Well, we can match with climatological data from the dates in the journal, then look backward with our isotope dating. Unless all of our data is due to contamination by the original diggers, we've got DNA, and we'll be able to sequence it eventually, which is more than we thought we'd have." Hutch finished transferring the journal and handed her back the memory stick. "What about the bone bed samples? How's that progressing?"

Aleksi launched into her work on the bear samples. She'd isolated five individuals already and was working on a sixth. All solidly fossilized. She could give samples to Bob whenever he wanted them, but this DNA, if they got any, would be fragmented, which meant a lot of work on Bob's part for any meaningful data. After another ten minutes of discussion of how best to proceed, Hutch started looking at his watch.

"Okay, so at least we've got a direction." He shut down his computer and pulled the laptop out of its docking station. "I'll send the translation to Quinton and catch him up on our progress this afternoon. Sorry to dash off, but I'm meeting with a legal team this morning, have a lecture at eleven, and wining and dining a congressman who's trying to help us drum up support for the pipeline intervention."

They took the hint and packed up to go. "Oh, right! How goes the battle?"

"It's complicated." Aleksi could see the worry in Hutch's eyes. "I get frustrated when money trumps the environment. Don't get me started."

"More raping and pillaging in the name of the economy?" Bob asked.

"That and more."

"Well, I don't think you should—"

"Oh! Hi!"

Aleksi turned at the voice and found herself staring at Derrick Penningly.

Oh crap! She forced a smile. "Oh. Hello, Derrick." She realized that Dr. Oliver's office was across from Hutch's and cursed herself for mentioning her old advisor to him. Thankfully, Oliver's door was closed. "You looking for Dr. Oliver?"

"Yeah." He smiled with those perfect pearly whites and shrugged. "I emailed her and she said to come by during her office hours, so here I am during office hours, and no Dr. Oliver. Hi, Dr. Hutchinson"

"You work for Quinton Neilson." Hutch shook his hand. "You helped us move the specimens, right?"

"Yep. I'm in the graduate program next year."

"Derrick's in my Comp Zoo lab class. He's looking for an advisor, and I told him that Dr. Oliver might have an opening." She gave Hutch a conspiratorial look and he nodded sagely. "And you remember Bob Tomlin."

Everyone said cordial hellos, though she noticed a decidedly cool stare from Bob.

"Well, I might as well just come back later." Derrick shrugged and flashed that salesman smile again, and Aleksi fought the urge to step back. While there was no doubt he was good looking, his manner set her teeth on edge. He *reeked* of privilege. "She probably got hung up somewhere."

"Well, she's a busy woman." Hutch closed his door and stepping past them all. Aleksi's nose twitched as his scent wafted past. "I'll check with you two early next week. Bob, email me the cloning results, and Aleksi, don't overdo."

"I'll be working on Bob's bear bones." She gave Bob a smile.

"And I'll be in my lab, working on Aleksi's mystery monster."

"Great." Hutch nodded politely to Derrick. "Nice seeing you, Derrick."

"And you, Dr. Hutchinson." Derrick followed them out into the main hall.

Aleksi took a deep breath of aftershave and clean soapy Hutch scent again, and found her eyes following the seat of his jeans as he strode away. She felt an unfamiliar surge of warmth, blinked, and wondered what the hell brought that on. She'd never had such silly musings before, and Hutch was her advisor.

"So, mystery monsters and bear bones." Derrick followed Aleksi and Bob the other direction. "Sounds interesting. Are those the two samples I helped you move?"

"Yeah, but it's mostly grunt work right now. Bob's doing the molecular analyses, and I'm doing the sample prep and morphology."

Bob gave her a strange look. "I'll see you later, Aleksi."

They were going opposite directions at the next turn, so she gave him a smile and a nod. "See you tomorrow for burritos." They waved and went their separate ways. She felt Derrick fall into step beside her and suppressed a shiver of distaste. *Go the fuck away, already...*

"So, this mystery monster. Is that the mislabeled one from the MCZ?"

"Um, yeah. We're still in the dark, pretty much." She gave a shrug, trying to sound boring in hopes that he'd lose interest. She felt bad about putting him onto Oliver's trail. He was new and just trying to get oriented, and she'd sent him to the worst advisor in the department. "Hey, about Dr. Oliver. If she blows you off, I'd say go find someone else. If she's not interested enough to keep an appointment, there's other fish in the sea."

"Oh, yeah. I'm used to the 'too busy' thing. My advisor at Princeton was always *sooo* busy..." He paced her down the stairs and into the MCZ lab wing. "So, Bob said he was working on it with you. So, you two are a team?"

"Collaborating. I'm doing his morphology and he's doing my genetics."

"Genetics?" His face lit up. "You found DNA?"

"Some, but ancient DNA's sometimes like a jigsaw puzzle without all the pieces. I'm hoping we have enough for my dissertation proposal."

"You're still working on a *proposal?*"

She wasn't sure if his tone was sardonic or not, but felt a flare of unaccustomed anger. "It's not as easy as you think."

He followed her down the second flight into the basement. "Oh, I know it's not easy. I'm just surprised. You're second year's almost up. You must be worried."

"Not really. Just busy." She stopped at the door to her lab and turned to face him. "If you're not busy, you're not working hard enough. Which is why I've got to get to work." She smiled politely and opened the door to her lab.

"Oh, right." He put a hand on the wall beside the door. "Hey, I'm having some people over tonight. Nothing big, just drinks and fun, maybe some movies. You want to drop by?"

I'd sooner claw my eyes out, she thought with a cringe. "I'm working late tonight, Derrick."

"Okay, sure. Well, good luck!" His eyes swept the lab as the door swung wide

"Thanks." Aleksi stepped inside, ice water trickling down her spine as she turned her back on him. She wondered at the sensation. Sure, Derrick was kind of creepy, but it wasn't like he was going to attack her. "See you in class."

"Right! Bye."

The door closed, but there was a small safety window near the handle. As she hung up her coat and took her computer bag into the draped corner where her samples awaited, she caught a glimpse of Derrick's face peering in through the glass. More ice water dribbled down her spine, like a centipede with cold feet.

Relax, Aleksi. She reached for protective gear. *He's just new and curious. A spoiled rich kid trying too hard.* She put on a gown, dust mask, and goggles, glancing back toward the door. *It's not like he's a monster.*

Working on the bone bed samples, revealing the once-living remnants from their sheaths of solid rock, time lost its meaning. Aleksi worked methodically, exposing and photographing segment after segment of the jumbled fossils, taking measurements and logging copious notes on her computer. She worked through midday without realizing it, and when a voice from outside the barrier called her name, it was dark outside.

"Aleksi?"

"Yeah?" She straightened from her work and stretched her back, eliciting a sequence of cracks. She could see more than one shape through the translucent plastic barrier. "Who's there?"

"It's Hutch."

Aleksi got up from her stool and moved to the barrier opening. Two men accompanied Hutch; one she recognized as the department chairman, Dr. Vandyke, the other she did not. She removed her safety glasses and mask in a cascade of rock dust.

"I thought I'd find you here working late."

"No rest for the wicked," she said with a smile, nodding to the chairman.

"You know Dr. Vandyke." Hutch gestured to the other man, tall, silver-haired and wearing an expensive suit, though his tie was loose. "And this is Congressman Twain. He's working with me on the pipeline project."

" Dr. Vandyke, nice to see you. Congressman Twain." She snapped off her gloves and shook hands with the two men, smiling through the dust. "Sorry, I'm such a mess, but grinding through rock all day leaves me looking a bit like a dust bunny."

"Not at all!" Vandyke grinned at her, his face flushed. She caught a whiff of whiskey on his breath. "We were just talking with Hutch, and I mentioned the fallout of your switch over to his lab." She opened her mouth to say something, but he held up a hand. "Not to worry! Both Dr. Oliver's and Hutch's records speak for themselves. Frankly, I'm surprised you stuck it out with her as long as you did."

"Well, I probably would have stayed with her, if not for this project." She shrugged. "It's kind of right up my alley."

"Which is why we came to visit you." The congressman's eyes twinkled above that perfect politician smile. "Hutch told us about the bone bed samples and this mystery specimen you've discovered, and I asked if I might be allowed to see them."

"Oh, well, there's really not much to see right now. It's mostly still encased in rock and plaster." She held the drape open and waved an arm at the laden benches. "The one under the drape is the mystery, but I've stopped working on that until we get more information from Bob Tomlin, who's working up some genetic data. We can go in, but you'll have to put on a mask and gloves."

Everyone did, and she gave them a short tour of the work, carefully lifting the drape to show where the plaster had been excavated to expose the ash cast. " Dr. Hutchinson and I took the samples that Bob's working on from here, and here." She indicated the two spots overhanging the edge of the table with a gloved fingertip. "They were kind of hard to get to, so we moved the slab over where it is now to get a better angle. The really curious part was the CT scan." She went to her computer and pulled the image up for them to see.

Vandyke sidled up to peer at the screen. "Hutch told us about that, but he said your preliminary data shows contamination."

"Well, it shows two disparate types of DNA, but we don't know that it's contamination. Bob is thinking that the strange CT is due to two intermingled specimens. We'll see."

"But the CT didn't show a skeletal structure at all?" The congressman peered at the exposed ash cast.

"No. We thought that was due to the heat of the pyroclastic ash, but now that we've found DNA and analyzed some of the ash material, we know it couldn't have been *that* hot." She shrugged again, replacing the drape over the sample. "And these over here, are the bone bed samples."

"You've made good progress." Hutch ran a gloved hand over the newly exposed fossils. "Amazing, actually."

"They're beautiful," the congressman said, and Aleksi looked at him with a new appreciation. Not many people saw the beauty in such things.

"Thanks," she said with a shrug. "I get caught up and can't seem to stop myself. In fact, I missed lunch, *and* dinner, so I better get home and eat, or I'm going to start chewing on these old bones, and I know how Dr. Hutchinson *hates* that."

They all laughed, and Hutch gaped at her.

"Well, we've all just eaten, but it's still early." Congressman Twain gestured toward the exit. "I'd be happy to buy you a late dinner, if you'd join us to continue this fascinating discussion."

"I don't know if we should—"

"Oh, come on, Hutch." Vandyke ushered them outside the barrier and they doffed their gear. Aleksi stripped off her cap and gown as well, taking care not to raise a cloud of dust. "You said she'd made excellent progress. She's probably going to be cooped up in here all weekend chipping away on these things. Let her live a little."

Hutch gave Aleksi a look that she couldn't quite interpret, almost as if he was scared what she might say.

"Well, I'm done with the journal translation, so I wasn't going to work on this anymore tonight anyway."

"Excellent! I know someplace that serves wonderful food, and it's not far." The congressman grinned wide.

"Besides," Aleksi hurried over to the sink to get cleaned up, "if I said no, I'd be breaking one of the four cardinal rules of graduate school."

"And those are?" The congressman arched an eyebrow.

"Never stand when you can sit." She did a quick but thorough job of dusting off with the little hand vacuum as she spoke. "Never sit when you can lie down. Never lie down when you can sleep. And never, *ever*, turn down free food." As they all laughed, she washed her hands and face, then grabbed her coat. "Ready when you are, Congressman."

As she flipped off the lights and they left the lab, Hutch leaned close to whisper. "Who are you, and what have you done with Aleksi?"

"I must be delirious with hunger," she whispered back, enjoying the whiff of his residual aftershave mixed with just a touch of his underlying scent.

Moments after the door closed, it swung silently open again. Derrick Penningly stepped inside, removing the strip of duct tape he'd place over the locking latch of the door. *Simple, no key necessary.* He'd used that trick often; the spring-loaded locking latch was separate from the other regular latches. Taped down, the door would close and appear locked, but the lock wouldn't engage.

Squinted into the darkness, he moved to the dust barrier and slipped inside, breathing in the scents of plaster and decay, of things long dead.

Mystery monster. My ticket to a PhD. If his plan worked, this would be his lab in a very short time indeed. Aleksi would eventually accept one of his invitations to come over, then she'd be his bitch. But he needed to be able to step in, and that meant getting all the information he could. Derrick peered under the sheet into the small gaps where something, probably bone, had been removed. The diffuse light glinted on something within.

Lowering the drape, he turned to the computer that lay under a protective plastic cover on the bench. As he reached out to boot the machine up, a click and voices from outside froze him in his tracks.

Shit! Getting caught burglarizing a lab was a one-way ticket out of Harvard. He needed someplace to hide.

"I told you I was delirious with hunger." Aleksi's voice carried easily through the dust barrier. "I'll just grab it and be right back."

Light flooded the room, and he heard her footsteps crossing the lab. There was only one place he could hide. The harsh fluorescent lights cast deep shadows under the tables, and the drape over the mystery monster almost reached the floor. He ducked down and crawled underneath, holding his breath as he heard the rustle of the dust barrier parting. He watched her shadow as she crossed over to the lab bench.

He tensed, lips curling back from his teeth. *Don't take the fucking computer!*

But she just leaned down and picked up the bag that lay beside the bench and retreated without glancing in his direction.

Yes!

"Got it! Julie would never forgive me if I had to wake her up to get into the apartment." The room darkened and the door clicked closed.

Derrick let out his breath and crawled out from his hiding place, but stood up too quickly. The back of his head cracked the plaster cast, and a cascade of dust fell from the excavated portion of the sample. He drew a sharp breath to stifle a curse, and the shimmering dust filled his sinuses.

It stung like breathing broken glass.

Derrick drew an even deeper dust-laden breath and sneezed into his hands, trying to stifle the sound. His ears popped. He shook his head and listened, his sinuses on fire.

Silence…

That was close.

He emerged from beneath the table dusting the mixture of plaster, ash dust, and some kind of golden glitter from his hair and jacket. Wasting no more time, he went to the computer, and booted it up from sleep mode. There was no password; it was Aleksi's personal laptop, not one of the school's machines.

"Sweet."

He withdrew a flash drive from his pocket and plugged it in. The empty drive came up automatically. He did a search for any files updated in the last week, and saw that most were in two folders, one named "Bears" and another named "Loktev." He transferred the latter to his drive. It was large, and took time. *Patience…* Done, he ejected his drive, put the computer back to sleep, and left the lab as quietly as possible, checking the hall before he slipped out and vanished into the cold Cambridge winter.

17

They arrived at the restaurant in more style than Aleksi had ever been privy to; a limousine complete with bar and privacy screen. They were ushered under an awning with the nondescript moniker of "Abe & Louie's" by a smiling maître d', and relieved of their coats and bags by a hostess at the door. The maître d' escorted them to a comfortable corner booth. Aleksi smoothed her sweater, glad she had worn something reasonably nice instead of a hoodie, and took a seat on the end beside Hutch.

A waiter wearing a white jacket and a solemn smile approached. "Good to see you again Congressman Twain."

"Good to be seen, Danny. Drinks?" The congressman asked, eyebrows arching.

"Best not change horses in the middle of a race," Vandyke said. "Johnny Walker Blue on the rocks."

"Same for me, but make mine neat." The congressman looked at Hutch and Alex. "You were drinking Sam Adams Octoberfest, weren't you, Hutch?"

"Yes."

"And you, Aleksi?" He cocked one silver eyebrow at her.

"A glass of red wine would be perfect." She raised an eyebrow right back. "A Zin, maybe? Something to go with a steak? And a menu?"

"A meat eater! Well, I hope we don't offend the good Dr. Hutchinson."

"No worries." Hutch smiled easily at Aleksi.

"Excellent! Have the steward pick out a nice bottle of old vine Zinfandel for Aleksi here." He turned to her, "And if I can make a recommendation on the steak, the porterhouse is *very* nicely done here."

"Sounds perfect! Thank you."

"My usual for the lady, Danny."

The waiter nodded with a smile and turned away. Aleksi looked to Hutch. "I never asked you why you were a vegetarian."

"The male side of my family is riddled with heart disease and colon cancer. It's not any kind of a moral statement." He gave a little shrug and sipped some water.

"Live fast, die young, and have a good-looking corpse is my motto," the congressman said, though Aleksi would not have called him young or particularly good-looking, though he had the perfect grooming of a wealthy politician. They talked a little until their drinks arrived and Twain raised his glass. "Speaking of youth, may I toast our young lady companion, Aleksi. May your brilliance as a scientist be only out-shown by your beauty."

"Oh, I can't drink to that, Congressman! Brains before beauty for me!" She raised her glass and sipped. Her mouth exploded in a heady swirl of flavors, and she arched her eyebrows. This was *very* good wine.

"Oh? Why?"

"You need to ask a Harvard graduate student *that*, Congressman?" Vandyke laughed with a wry grin. "We don't recruit for looks, and if I remember correctly, Aleksi was Suma Cum Laude at NYU, isn't that right."

"And voted shyest in my class three years in a row." That wasn't really true. She had never gotten enough recognition to be voted anything.

"Oh, surely not!" The congressman knitted his brows at her, suspecting some joke.

"That's why I love paleontology." She stopped, suddenly realizing that she felt totally at ease, sitting here talking to three men, all of them her senior and having quite a bit of power over the future of her academic career. No clenching hands beneath the table, no anxiety, no fear. *What's wrong with me?* She shook off the thought and continued. "Peace and quiet, learning the secrets of things that have been dead for thousands of years; what could be better? And you said so yourself, Congressman, they're beautiful, these things we dig up. There's…something about them. Sometimes, I feel like I can hear them wanting to tell me about themselves." She shrugged and sipped her wine, startled at her own honesty.

"Well, you don't seem shy to me," the congressman said.

"Not to me either." Hutch cast her another quizzical look. "Not nearly as shy as when I first met you, Aleksi."

"I told you; I'm delirious with hunger." She knew that wasn't the case, but it sounded good. Another small sip of wine and she put her glass carefully aside. "And if I drink any more before I eat, you'll find out exactly *how* delirious."

They laughed, and Hutch thankfully changed the subject. Her dinner arrived, and she stared in shock at the inch-thick slab of meat that filled her entire plate.

The congressman chuckled, obviously enjoying his little joke. "You *said* you were hungry, didn't you?"

She picked up her knife and fork and winked at him. "You have no idea, Congressman Twain. Noooo idea."

Hutch was worried when the cab bearing him and Aleksi turned down the street toward her apartment. Congressman Twain had been a wonderful host, and the drinks and conversation had flowed freely. To everyone's astonishment, Aleksi had finished the enormous steak and the last of the bottle of wine in the following hours. Both the congressman and Dr. Vandyke had imbibed a bit too much scotch. Hutch had paced himself and was far from inebriated. Aleksi had been the center of attention, and handled it with humor, confidence, and poise. Throughout the night and during the ride home, Hutch kept looking at her, unsure if he recognized her.

Who are you, and what did you do with Aleksi? It had been a joke, but now, he wondered.

The night had turned cold, the day's rain changing to ice and snow that drifted on the wind like faerie dust. Waiting for the cab, standing in ten-degree wind chill with her coat flapping, Aleksi had called the cold exhilarating. In the back of the cab, she'd fallen silent, sitting there with a quiet smile on her face.

Hutch was seriously concerned.

This was not the Aleksi Rychenkna he'd had to coax into having a coffee with him to discuss a potential research project. *What changed her? Who is she? What happened?*

As the cab's tires crunched to a stop in front of her building, she surprised him yet again. "Are you okay, Hutch?"

"Am *I* okay?" He glanced at her to find her looking him right in the eyes. He blinked and looked away. "I was going to ask *you* that."

"So ask." She got out of the cab before he could open his mouth.

Hutch followed, pulling his coat closed against the icy blast. She stood there on the sidewalk between the snow mounds staring up at the sky, her coat flapping in the wind. "Aleksi, what's gotten into you? You're acting strange."

"I probably drank too much, but I don't feel like it." She turned to face him, coat still open, snowflakes dotting her sweater. "I feel fine. Your turn. What's wrong? You've been looking at me like I grew horns and a tail or something."

"I'm *worried* about you, that's all. You're sick for five days and come out of it…like this. I'm just wondering what happened to you."

"I don't know, but I feel different. Like the world makes *sense* finally." She turned and spread her arms with her hands in her coat pockets, flying into the teeth of the wind. "Maybe the fever knocked my brain into gear or something."

"God! Aren't you freezing?"

"Nope! It feels great. Like I could fly."

"See, that's what I mean. A week ago, you would have never done that, or said that, especially to me." He took her arm and steered her toward the doorway, lowering his voice. "Are you *on* something?"

She tensed at his grip and planted her feet. He looked at her and she was staring down at his hand on her arm, steam rolling from clenched teeth in billowing clouds. Through the sleeve of her coat, a sweater, and the shirt beneath, he could feel her trembling.

"Aleksi! You're *shaking*!"

"What?" Her eyes snapped up to his and the trembling stopped like a switch had been thrown. "Just a shiver, I guess. And no, I'm not *on* anything but a bottle of wine and the first night of my life that I felt like I could actually *talk* to someone." She laughed. "A far cry from that dinner with Persephone, wasn't it?"

"That's just it, Aleksi. What's *happened* to you?"

She shrugged. "No idea, but I'm not complaining." She turned and unlocked the door, then turned back to him, her eyes once again fixed on his. "Why don't you come up and have something warm?"

"*What?*" There was no doubt in his mind what she meant. "What brought *that* on?"

"Something your ex said to me while you and Bob were in the bathroom."

He felt a knot in his gut. *Damn you Persephone.* "Listen Aleksi, she told me about that, and I'm sorry. She can be—"

"She asked if we were fucking."

He swallowed hard. "I know. Listen, she likes to shock people by—"

"When I said that we weren't, she said that was a shame." Aleksi took a step toward him, her coat flapping open again. "She told me that I was desperately in need of a good fuck."

Hutch stared at her in shock. "Aleksi, this is not a conversation we should be having."

"Why not?"

"Because you're acting strangely, we've both had too much to drink, and I'm your *advisor*. It wouldn't be fair to—"

"Fair?" Her teeth flashed white in the streetlight. "It'd be *way* better than *fair*, I think."

"That's what I'm talking about, Aleksi. Think back and ask yourself if you would have said that to me a week ago."

"No, you're right." She shook her head. "I wouldn't have, and I don't know what's gotten into me the last few days, but I don't think it's a bad thing. For the first time in my life, I feel like it's okay to do something for myself, something that might not be the *right* thing to do, but the thing I *want* to do. Come up, and I'll make you a cup of coffee."

"Aleksi." Hutch felt his resolve crumbling, then he stepped back, his teeth clenching and his hands balled into fists in his pockets. "It would be the wrong thing to do. I'm your advisor."

"So come upstairs, have a cup of coffee, and *advise* me." She stepped forward, one hand raising to brush his icy cheek. Her touch felt like fire against his skin. "What do you have to go home to, Hutch? A cold apartment, a cold bed, and a cold floor in the morning."

This isn't Aleksi. I don't know who it is, but this is not her. "Aleksi, I can't. We would *both* regret it, and you *know* it."

"Oh, okay. Have it your way." She whirled away, pausing in the door to look back. "But you know where I live if you change your mind."

"Goodnight, Aleksi." He took another step back, and the loss of the moment, the vanishing opportunity, felt like something had been ripped out of him. One thought gave him solace: *It was the right thing to do.*

"Goodnight." She closed the door and was gone.

Hutch turned away and got into the cab. He told the driver the address of his cold apartment, his cold bed, and his cold floor that would be waiting for him in the morning.

On a whim, Aleksi dashed up the three flights to her apartment, unlocked the door, and slipped quietly inside. She hurried to the window, not even breathing hard from the climb. Looking down, she watched Hutch get into the cab, his breath in the icy air, the tiny snowflakes melting in his hair, the spot on his cheek she'd touched.

Aleksi brought her hand to her lips, inhaling, and licking her finger-tips. *Hutch…the scent/taste* said in her mind. The cab door closed and the car pulled slowly away down the icy street. She watched him until it turned around the corner, fantasizing about what might have happened if he had come up for coffee.

Think back and ask yourself if you would have said that to me a week ago.

No, I wouldn't have. What's happened to me? Aleksi looked at her hand, at the tiny hairs on the back of her fingers. "Who am I?" she whispered, and she realized she didn't really know.

All the memories of being Aleksi, all the feelings of inadequacy, shame, and guilt still lurked deep inside, a cold ball of self-loathing. Two decades of Aleksi stared back at her like a stranger, but the stranger was still her.

Iggy rattled his cage, and she met his reptilian stare in the dark. The tiny scales around his eyes moved as he breathed, his pupils wide, drinking in the sparse light from the street. He looked at her, and she wondered if the same questions might be going through his mind. *Who is this person?*

"I'm me." The answer was so simple, but that wasn't all. "I'm just…" She had no way to finish that, and Iggy didn't answer, except to lick his scaly lips.

Mom equals food. The thought almost made Aleksi laugh.

"Not tonight, buddy. Mom's had too much to drink and needs to sleep. I'll feed you in the morning."

She picked up her things and locked the front door on her way to her bedroom. Boots, sweater, jeans, socks, thermals, bra, and she reached for her flannel pajamas, but stopped. The air felt good against her skin. Goosebumps rose. She could feel them under her fingertips, like braille telling her the same thing Persephone had said.

You, my dear, are in desperate need of a good fuck.

"She was right." Something cold slid down her cheek, and she reached up to touch the tear. "But I'm still Aleksi."

She crawled into bed without the pajamas, the sheets cool against her skin. She lay there thinking about what she'd said to Hutch, wondering if she'd just ruined everything.

Hutch runs from her, his heartbeat loud in her ears as she closes in for the kill. Her long coat flaps like wings in the icy wind. There are snowflakes in his hair, each beautiful crystal distinct. She can smell his scent. A surge of desire mixed with hunger sings in her veins. He looks back at her, terror in his eyes.

"Don't kill me!" he cries as her hands close on his shoulders and she bears him down to the snowy ground. They land as if the snow is a bed of pillows, soft and welcoming.

"What?" She can feel his body against her, and the urge to kill, to feed, vanishes in a heady swirl of desire.

"Don't kill me, Aleksi! Please. I won't hurt you! I promise!"

She breathes in his scent, feels his warmth. "I know you won't hurt me." She revels in the sensation of his skin against hers. His mouth tastes like his scent, and their tongues twine and play with one another. His hands are cool on her skin, guiding her. Gentle. Safe.

"Yes..." He fills her. Sensation spreads through her in a wave...

Aleksi woke in a sweat, heart hammering in her ears, fighting her sheets with the all too vivid dream alive in her mind. For a moment she felt as if she was actually making love to him, as if he still filled her, moving in that delicious undulation that sent waves of pleasure surging through her.

"Holy shit!" She threw off the covers and climbed out of bed. The sheets were damp with sweat, and her underwear was soaked through. "What the...?"

The dream came flooding back, fresh in her mind, and she felt a surge of the same sensation. She'd never felt anything so intense in her life, awake or asleep, and had *certainly* never had a dream so vivid, so tactile, as if she was actually being touched. Her knees were trembling, and sweat rolled down her torso.

"God, please don't let that damn fever be coming back!" Aleksi stumbled to the bathroom and fumbled out the thermometer. She put it under her tongue while she went to the toilet. A shower sounded good, but she knew it would wake Julie. Instead, she toweled off and brushing her sweat-damped hair.

The thermometer beeped, and she looked at it. The display flashed 105.2 in the dark.

"Oh bullshit!" There was no way she was running that high a fever. She tossed the thermometer in the trash and made a mental note to buy a new one.

After downing two big glasses of water, she padded back to her bedroom and donned a clean tee shirt and underwear. The sheets weren't that damp, and she felt cool enough now, so she crawled into bed and tried to get back to sleep. The dream, however, would not leave her mind.

Note to self: don't drink a bottle of wine all by yourself.

She felt herself slipping into a light sleep and the warm sensation of skin against skin returned. Before the dream took her, Aleksi wondered why Hutch would beg her not to kill him as they were making love.

18

Monday afternoon Aleksi finally got a call from Bob about the DNA sequences. The cloning had gone without a hitch, and he'd isolated two different sequences from the first sample.

"I think it's contamination." He sounded tired over the phone. "One of the strands gave me a match to human DNA from a blast scan on Genbank. Whoever dug this thing up must have fouled the sample somehow."

"So, what was the other sequence?" Contamination would be hard to deal with, but not impossible.

"That's the weird part. I don't get any reasonable matches." He sounded frustrated. "I've got five other clones cooking, so I'll have more results by the middle of the week. I don't want to bother Hutch with it until I have more than one data point."

"I agree." She hadn't spoken with Hutch since their ride home in the cab. She knew he'd been right to refuse her proposition, and hoped it hadn't ruined their professional relationship, though she still couldn't make herself stop wondering what would have happened if he'd come up for coffee. "We can take another sample, some of the deep interior residue that would have less of a chance of contamination. But maybe you'll get a match on one of the others."

"That's what I thought. We can also look for more commonly mapped areas. Now that we know we have DNA, we can look for actual genes.

Though if we don't get a match, we might never figure out what this beastie was."

"Don't be so pessimistic! If we don't get a match, maybe we've got some new species, or at least something that hasn't been uploaded into Genbank." She changed tacks. "You sound tired, Bob. Maybe you should knock off early, get some fresh air."

"It's fifteen degrees out, Aleksi. I don't like my air that fresh."

"Go catch a movie or something, then. Take a little brain vacation."

"You wanna go?"

"I'm up to my elbows in these bear samples, but I happen to know that Julie has Monday afternoons off." She had badgered Julie all weekend to let her mention something to Bob.

"Julie, your *roommate*, Julie? I don't know, Aleksi. She's…"

"She's been asking me about you, actually." She grinned into the phone.

"She…*has*?" There was a hopeful if somewhat terrified lilt in his voice.

"Sure! And I also happen to know she's a sucker for chick flicks and popcorn. She's fun, Bob. You should ask her out."

"You promise you're not setting me up to get slammed? She just seems so…I don't know. Out of my league, I guess."

"Oh, Julie dates all kinds of men, and she thought you were nice. That's more of an accolade than she usually gives." She paused to let that sink in. "*Ask* her, Bob. She could use someone nice for a change, and you could use someone fun." *Someone not me.* "It'll be good for both of you."

"Well…and you said she's off Monday afternoons?"

"Yep. She usually works out at home when it's cold like this, then just reads. You want her number?"

"Yeah, I…I do." There was a pause, and she could almost smell his apprehension over the phone. "You're *sure* about this, Aleksi?"

"I'm positive. Call her." She gave him Julie's number.

"All right, I will." There was that hopeful lilt again. It made her smile. "Thanks, Aleksi."

"Don't thank me, Bob, just call her."

When she arrived home for dinner with a pound of roast beef tucked under her arm, she found the apartment empty and a note on the refrigerator door.

Bob called. Movie, and maybe dinner. Thanks! Don't wait up! J.

"Good!" She retrieved a jar of mustard and some greens for Iggy from the refrigerator and brewed a pot of coffee. She spent the evening munching roast beef, playing with Iggy, catching up on her class work and reading.

At eleven thirty, she heard a car stop in front of the building and doors slamming, then a voice she knew. From the window she looked down at Bob's old Nissan idling at the curb, steam pouring out of the exhaust, Julie and Bob stood at on the sidewalk, talking with their hands in their pockets.

"I had a good time," Julie said. "I'd like to do it again sometime."

"So would I." There was an awkward pause, then, "Maybe next Monday?"

"Thursdays are good for me, too. Or we could do a matinee on Saturday; tickets are half price."

"Sounds like fun." Another short pause. "Thanks for coming out with me, Julie. I had fun."

"Kiss her, idiot!" Aleksi whispered, unaware that she shouldn't be able to hear their conversation from three floors up through a double-paned window.

"Well, I better go up before we both freeze. Goodnight, Bob." Julie leaned in, and Bob finally took the hint. They met halfway in a brief but hardly chaste smooch.

"Goodnight, Julie."

"Call me."

"Count on it." Aleksi could hear the smile in Bob's voice.

Aleksi watched Bob get in his car and drive away, and heard the front door of the building close with the clack of the lock. She went back to the couch and continued her reading. The door opened, and Julie slipped through. She peeked into the front room, and Aleksi looked up, trying for a mien of mild surprise.

"Hey. How was it?"

"Nice." Julie doffed her coat and shivered. "He's sweet. Thanks, Aleksi. I needed that."

"My pleasure. Just don't break his heart, okay? He'll blame me."

"No heart breaking, I promise." Julie hung her coat up and drifted off to her room.

Aleksi settled back to read and felt a little tingle of warmth. *Mission accomplished.* The words on the screen blurred, and she blinked. It was nice to see them happy, even if she couldn't seem to manage it for herself.

Wednesday brought more surprises; Derrick Penningly was absent from Aleksi's Comparative Zoology lab, which seemed a reprieve, and Bob called with more news about his cloning results. They weren't good; he'd gotten human DNA from three more of the samples, and the corresponding mystery sequences still didn't match anything in Genbank.

"I think we need to talk to Hutch about this. Maybe rethink things."

"Maybe we could hit happy hour at Grendel's and brainstorm." Her stomach growled like a ravenous beast at the thought of food. She'd been constantly hungry lately.

"Sounds good. I'll ask him and get back to you."

A text message came back in minutes. "Grendel's 5:30, for BS."

She set a timer and got back to work.

Grendel's was packed, as usual, but Aleksi got there early and snagged a corner table. A surly waitress told her she couldn't have a table for four all to herself, but she convinced her that she was expecting two more people and placated her by ordering a platter of chicken wings and an Irish coffee. Hutch and Bob arrived together, and she waved them over.

"Sorry." She gestured to the half-devoured platter. "I had to order something or lose the table."

"No problem!" Bob took a wing and munched as he took his seat. "I owe you one for that recommendation." He smiled and blushed, and she knew he meant Julie.

"Glad I could help." She looked at Hutch, who hadn't even said hello. "So, did Bob tell you what he found?"

"Yes, and it's got to be contamination." He flagged down a waitress, ordered coffee and some kind of vegie burger thing. Bob ordered a beer and another platter of wings. When the waitress left, Hutch continued. "I can't imagine how we could have gotten human DNA from inside the ash cast, unless we contaminated it ourselves."

"Bob mentioned the possibility of two specimens jumbled together in the same cast, which might account for the bizarre CT scan." Aleksi watched Hutch, but he wouldn't look at her. "We know the tooth wasn't human, but what if whatever owned that tooth got caught in the ash fall *with* a human, and we're getting both."

"Which brings up the question of why the sample doesn't have any bones. If the temperature wasn't high enough to cook the DNA, it shouldn't have been high enough to heat-fracture the skeletal structure." Bob nodded to Aleksi. "Aleksi suggested taking another sample, a deeper one, from inside the cast. Something that couldn't have been contaminated by the diggers."

"Why there's no remaining skeletal structure is a mystery I don't know that we can solve. Taking a deeper sample is a good idea, but we'll have to okay it with Quinton first. If he gives the okay, I want you both to do it together. I can't break away, and we need to document that we're not making any mistakes. Video the sample collection. Now that we know we're getting DNA, let's look for something that everything uses, a functional gene, but highly conserved."

"Cytochrome B?" Bob suggested.

"Good idea. Whatever it is, it's got mitochondria. If we can get long enough segments of the DNA surrounding that gene, and still have two different sequences, we know we've got two discrete specimens." Their drinks and food arrived, and Hutch took a bite of his vegie-burger.

"Tomorrow morning?" Aleksi asked Bob. She knew he would want to be free by evening. He had another movie date with Julie. "Assuming Quinton gives the okay."

"Fine with me. I'll meet you in your lab first thing."

"Good."

"Okay, so about this mystery DNA; you didn't get any matches for any of the segments we've cloned?" Hutch seemed to be talking more to Bob than her, even though this was technically her project. She hoped he wasn't going to treat her like a plague carrier because of the other night.

"Nothing near a match we can use for any kind of relatedness. It has more similarities to primate than anything else."

"Primate?" A memory clicked in Aleksi's mind. "You said that canine looked like macaque or baboon."

"Yes, I did." Hutch ate more of his vegie burger and still wouldn't look at her. "If the human DNA is from the sample, not contamination, we might be looking at a human with a domesticated primate. It wouldn't be the first instance of comingled remains being misinterpreted."

"But primate DNA's pretty close to human." Aleksi picked up another chicken wing and stripped the meat off the bone. "Most species are in Genbank. We should have seen a match."

"I don't know." Hutch shook his head and looked at his watch. "Damn. Look, I'm sorry, but I've got to get going." He took another bite of his sandwich and chased it with coffee as he got up. "You two talk this over and shoot me any questions by email. Sorry about the hit and run." He left a twenty on the table and hurried for the door.

"What the hell's up with that?" Bob watched Hutch leave with a furrowed brow. "I've never seen him do that before."

"I don't know." But she did. She'd ruined everything and didn't know how to fix it.

⁓

The sampling went off without a hitch, video recording and all. They excavated down to an area of the cast proximal to the already exposed jaw, and Aleksi brought out a low speed drill and bored a hole in the ash layer. When it punched through, a fine gold-hued dust came out with the bit.

"What do you think that stuff is?" She put the drill aside and picked up a long core sampler.

"No clue. It looks crystalline, like pyrite. It was in the other sample, too, and it seemed to dissolve in EDTA." Bob recorded her putting the long sampler into the hole and withdrawing it, careful not to touch either the edges of the hole or anything else before she tipped the contents—a course dust of grey and gold flecks with a few bits of white and black—into a plastic tube. "That looks exactly the same as the first sample."

"Well, let's hope it is." She labeled the tube, put it in a double sealed baggie and he turned off the recorder. "Okay, molecular man, there's your sample. You need help with the video for the extraction?"

"No, I'll set up a tripod. But thanks." He put the bag in another plain Ziplock and put that in a plastic carry case. "I'll get on this this afternoon and have it in PCR tomorrow."

"Great." She escorted him out of the dust barrier. "Have fun tonight."

"I will, thanks." He doffed his mask, revealing a grin beneath. "Julie's pretty cool. I like her a lot. She knows more about movies than anyone I know."

"Drama student." She smiled at him, relieved to see him at ease with the whole thing. "Just don't break her heart, okay?"

"No worries about that. I still think she's out of my league, but she's fun to hang with."

"Well, have fun, then." She gave him a wave. "And be careful with that sample!"

He gave her a wave and left the lab with another grin.

19

She is chasing him through the snowy Harvard campus. He looks back at her with terror-filled eyes, and she can hear his heart hammering in his chest. She could catch him easily but enjoys the chase. He dodges through the door to the MCZ lab building, and she follows, but finds that she has chased him into her bedroom.

"Please, Aleksi!" His voice trembles with fear. "Don't kill me! I won't hurt you."

She tries to speak but can't. Why would she kill him? But he's already hurt her. She reaches for him, and he flinches, backing away. His legs hit her bed and he falls upon it.

Perfect...

She's on him in a flash, skin on skin. She closes her eyes in bliss. There is a flash of that urge to lash out, to feed. A warm coppery taste floods her mouth. She swallows and has a vision of a thick slab of meat on a plate. She opens her eyes, and Hutch lies beneath her, his chest flayed open, hollow, eyes vacant. Blood drips from her hands, from her chin, and she bends down to feast.

Laughter interrupts her meal and she looks up to see Derrick standing beside the bed, looking at her with that perfect smile. He laughs with those perfect white teeth, and she looks down into Hutch's dead face, realizing what she's done.

· · ·

Aleksi jerked awake, the dream so vivid she could taste the gobbets of warm flesh sliding down her throat—*Hutch's* flesh. Nausea welled up. She flung off the blankets, lurched out of bed, and dashed for the bathroom. She made it to the toilet in time to heave the contents of her stomach into the bowl. The memory rose again, and she heaved dryly, tears streaming from her eyes.

When the nausea finally abated, Aleksi sat there sweating and shaking. After a minute, she flushed the toilet and washed her face in the sink, rinsing her mouth. She dried with a towel and caught her reflection in the mirror. Her face was pale, eyes red and itching like she'd walked through a dust storm. She wondered if she was having some kind of allergic reaction, or maybe food poisoning. That would explain the nausea. Although now, with the dream memory receding, she wasn't nauseous and even felt hungry. She rubbed her eyes again and looked closer at her reflection.

"What the..." She blinked and looked again. Her usually blue-gray irises seemed different, almost hazel in color. She rubbed them again. "Jaundice?" She tried to think of what would cause such a thing. *Hepatitis?* She didn't know much medicine, but thought that affected the whites of the eyes, not the iris.

"This is *not* what I need right now!" She went back to her bedroom and glanced at the clock: four thirty in the morning. She knew it would be useless to try to go back to sleep, so she threw on a robe and went out to get some reading done.

She made coffee and turned on her computer, trying not to make too much noise. She had gone to bed before Julie got home the night before and didn't want to wake her. That thought brought a smile, then a flood of worry for both Julie and Bob. They seemed happy, but what if it went bad? Would they both blame her?

She realized she was pacing the kitchen and clenched her fists. She felt like she was having a panic attack, but not like the ones she was used to. She clenched her hands harder, willing herself to calm. She felt a sharp bite of her nails and looked down at the bleeding cuts in the palms of her hands.

"Holy..." Aleksi hurried to the sink and turned on the water. She rinsed her hands and peered at the four tiny cuts in each palm. She'd never had nails long enough to scratch anything. They got in the way and she tended to bite them short. Now they were longer than she'd ever seen them, with a slight yellowish hue at the cuticle. She grabbed a paper towel and dabbed at the shallow cuts, but the bleeding had already stopped. The pain was gone.

The coffee maker burbled, distracting her. She grabbed her favorite cup, filled it, opened the fridge for milk, and grabbed a few slices of the roast beef she'd bought at the deli the previous day. Wolfing them down and chasing the meat with a sip of coffee, she felt the strange panic attack subside. She looked again at her hands, but the cuts were now just tiny lines. She wondered if she had imagined the blood. The paper towel was still beside the sink, but there was no blood on it, and no sign of blood in the sink.

"What the hell? Now I'm *hallucinating?*"

She sat down with her coffee and tried to read, but the words on the screen couldn't compete with the worry clouding her mind. She needed to do something, to talk to someone, to get some advice or help, but she didn't have anyone. Then, with a tingle of warmth centering in her stomach, she thought that maybe she did.

Malkin gym, where Hutch worked out every morning, opened at six, and Aleksi was at the door at ten past. The place was busy. She had no idea so many people were so health conscious, up before the sun every morning, sweating and straining before the day even started. There were more than two dozen people on treadmills, steppers and cardio bikes, while another dozen lifted free weights or strained at the various machines. Most looked like staff or faculty, with a few students mixed in, and one or two hard bodies. She spotted Hutch, his face flushed as he climbed step after endless step on a stair climber, ear buds tuning out his surroundings.

Unfortunately, a desk, a turnstile, and a heavy-set staff member stood between her and the workout floor. She tried to dial up a smile, but her state of nerves probably made it a grimace.

"Good morning. I need to speak to Dr. Hutchinson. He's right over there on that stepper. I'll just be a second." She pushed on the turnstile but it didn't budge.

The guy behind the desk looked at her tiredly. "I'm sorry, but if you don't have a membership card, I can't let you in. You'll have to wait until he's done working out."

"He's my advisor. I'm a grad student." She fished her student ID from her wallet. "This is important."

"Sorry, but a membership is an extra thing. People pay for it, so I can't just let you in."

"Well, could you just go tap him on the shoulder, then?"

"No, I *can't*. We just opened up, and I'm the only one on the front desk." He stared at her like she was an idiot.

"Okay, how about this: you watch me walk over and tap him on the shoulder and I'll come right back out here and wait for him. How about that?"

"I *told* you; without a membership card, I can't let you in."

"And you can't leave your desk. Yes, I heard you." She looked at him, an unaccustomed surge of anger forming a ball in her stomach. "So, if you can't leave your desk, how do you think you could stop me if I chose to step over this turnstile and go get him myself?"

"I'd call security and have you removed."

"Oh, so there *is* someone else here?"

"No. I'm talking about campus security."

"Oh, but it would take, what, ten minutes for them to get here? I'd be long gone before they even came through the door."

"Look, *honey*, I don't want any trouble."

Honey? Aleksi's nails pressed into her palms like daggers.

"Neither do I. I tell you what, you sit there and forget I ever came in." She vaulted the turnstile and strode onto the workout floor as if he didn't exist, ignoring his shout of protest. Contrary to his claim, he left his desk and caught up with her just as she stepped up to Hutch and caught his attention.

"Aleksi! What are you doing here?" Hutch pulled the ear buds away, staring at her wide-eyed.

"I need to talk to you."

The attendant's thick hand closed around her arm. "You'll have to leave *now*, or I'll call security!"

She grinned at him without humor, the urge to lash out raging through her veins. "Oh, so you *can* leave the front desk after all. Now, please take your hand off my arm."

"You have to leave. *Now*." The man gave a tug, but her feet were planted and she remained where she was. She could feel his flabby fingers pressing on her arm like caterpillars trying to bite into hardwood. She reached up with her other hand and gripped his wrist.

"I will leave as soon as I say what I need to say to Dr. Hutchinson. Now, take your hand off my arm, or I'll take it off...at the *elbow*." She squeezed and saw his eyes widen.

"Hang on a second!" Hutch was off his stepper and between them, his hands on both of them. "Both of you just let go and back off. Doug, she's one of my students, and she wouldn't be here if this wasn't important. Aleksi, I'll be with you in a minute. I've got to shower."

She released Doug's arm, leaving deep fingerprints in his flabby flesh. He would have a bruise. His hand fell away from her arm and he stepped back, staring at her wide-eyed.

"Thanks for your help, *Doug*." She turned to Hutch. "Thanks, Hutch. I'll be at Peet's." She walked away and was out of the building before the guy from the front desk could sit back down. She was shaking, no longer with the urge to rip the man's arm from his socket, but with the realization that she had been ready, willing, and probably able to do just that.

The brisk walk across the quad cleared her head and eased her pounding heart, the icy air seeming to calm her raging emotions. Peet's Coffee wasn't very busy so early, so she had her pick of tables. She ordered a coffee and something to eat, and chose one near the windows. By the time Hutch arrived, there was nothing in front of her but an empty cup and a naked bagel smelling of lox.

"What's wrong, Aleksi?" He took a seat without bothering to get anything for himself. "If this is about the other night, I—"

"This *isn't* about the other night, Hutch. You were right about that; we'd both had too much to drink and it was a bad idea, but you were right about one *other* thing, too." She started to lift her cup, but then realized it was already empty. She took a deep breath. "Something's *wrong* with me. I've changed. I'm having thoughts, and dreams, and I think even waking hallucinations. And that guy back there in the gym, I was ready to *kill* him. I mean *really* kill him, just for grabbing my arm! I don't know what the hell's happening to me, and I'm *scared*, and I don't know who to talk to about it but you."

There. It was all out. He blinked, opened his mouth to speak, then closed it again.

Not good.

"You think I'm crazy, don't you?"

"No, Aleksi, I don't think you're crazy. I think you're hysterical and wired on caffeine." He rubbed his eyes. "What kind of hallucinations are you talking about?"

She told him about her dream, leaving out the fact that it had been him she had murdered and devoured, then cutting her palms with her nails, but finding the wounds already closed when she washed her hands. She showed him her hands, her palms unmarked.

"But now I don't know if I even *was* hallucinating. That guy at the gym, when he grabbed me, I could barely feel his hand, and when I took hold of his arm, I *knew* I could tear it off."

"Now, look, Aleksi. I don't know what's happened, but I don't think you could have—"

She reached across the table and grabbed his forearm, squeezing hard enough to get his undivided attention. "Believe me, Hutch. Something's *wrong*." She released him and spread her hands flat on the table. "Look at my nails. They're discolored, and I swear they're longer than I've ever kept them. And look at my eyes. I think they're changing color. Do you think it's jaundice? Have you ever heard of any strain of hepatitis that can display symptoms like this?"

"Okay, Aleksi. I do see some yellowing of your nails, but your eyes look fine to me." He rubbed his forearm and gave her another one of those looks, as if she were a stranger. "If you think something's wrong, you should probably go to the med center and have some blood work done. Tell them about the fever and your current symptoms, and let docs run you through the mill."

"But, what if…what if I *am* crazy, Hutch?" There was more hysteria in her voice now, not over what she was feeling, but over what would happen if she was right, if she was changed. "Everything I've worked for—"

"Aleksi! Relax!" He stood and held out his hand. "Come on. I'll go with you."

That gesture, that open hand offering help, broke her hysteria like a thin pane of glass. The shards of her worries fell like a shower of ice crystals, like snowflakes melting into little droplets of water, like the ones on the collar of his coat. She took his hand—it was solid and real, and she had no urge to harm him or get away—and let him pull her too her feet.

"Okay. Let's go."

The med center was no busier than Peet's, but the rule of medicine is insurance first, care next. She proffered her student ID and told the desk clerk that she didn't have insurance and didn't have a primary care physician.

"I usually just pay my GYN by the visit, and I don't get sick much. I thought my student status was enough."

"Your student status ensures you urgent care. Is this an emergency?"

"Well, I—"

"It's an emergency," Hutch interrupted. "She had a fever a few days ago, and now is having some secondary symptoms that are worrisome."

"Did you come in when you had the fever?"

"No. I thought it was the flu," she said, picking up on Hutch's ploy, "which wouldn't have been an emergency, would it?"

"No, it wouldn't have been." The clerk produced several forms and handed them over. "Please fill these out and bring them back. I'll have someone see you."

Aleksi took the sheaf of forms and sat down in one of the waiting room's plastic chairs, muttering about the state of medical care in the richest country in the world. The forms were long and ridiculously detailed, as if a physician would use them, not an examination or any actual medical data, to formulate a diagnosis. She finished and returned them to the desk clerk, then went back to the uncomfortable chair and sat down next to Hutch. He looked tired and worried.

"Thanks for doing this, Hutch." She tried to keep her tone level. "I'm sorry, but I didn't know who else to talk to."

"It's all right, Aleksi. At least you realize something's wrong now."

His tone was that of the other night, worried and reluctant. She decided it was probably best to leave that issue alone for now. He had been right about that, too; she never would have propositioned him a week ago. It seemed like that damn fever had changed everything; not just her, but the whole world.

They waited and talked a little about the research. She told him of the progress she'd made on the bone bed samples and taking the second sample with Bob. The conversation fell apart, and they sat there in silence, Aleksi fidgeting with her fingernails, Hutch trying to be surreptitious about glancing at his watch.

"Sorry you ever asked me to be one of your students?" she finally asked, staring at her nails.

"No, Aleksi, I'm not." He reached over and put a hand on hers, stilling her fidgeting fingers. His skin was cool, his touch soft. "We'll get to the bottom of this. I promise. Nothing's going to stop you from getting your proposal in on time."

"But what if—"

"Excuse me, Alex-and-rovna Ry-chen-ka?" The clerk's mutilation of Aleksi's name drew their attention. "Someone will see you. Please go to room four, down that hall."

"Thank you." She stood and turning to Hutch. "And thank you, Hutch. I'm okay now. I just needed someone…you know."

"I know, Aleksi. I know it sounds stupid, but don't worry. You'll get through this."

She smiled and went down the hall to room four and knocked. A voice from inside said, "Come in," so she turned the latch and opened the door. The man seated behind a small desk looked barely old enough to be out of med school. She took a deep breath and went in.

Before the door closed behind her, she heard Hutch whisper, "Excuse me, but make sure the doctor does a toxin and drug screen."

Great, she thought as the door clicked closed.

Hutch left the medical center more worried than ever. He had no idea what kind of psychosis or dementia was affecting Aleksi, but hysterical strength was definitely a part of it. His arm still ached where she'd grasped it. He glanced at his watch and muttered a curse. It was already nine in the morning, and he was supposed to be in his office. Congressman Twain was coming by to talk about the opposition to the pipeline project at nine thirty, and Hutch hadn't even had his first cup of coffee.

He swung by Buckminster's, picked up a large coffee and Danish, and hurried to his office. By the time he got through half of his email, there was a knock on the door.

"Good morning, Hutch."

"Congressman Twain! Good morning!" He stood and shook the man's hand. "Thanks for coming by. Please, have a seat."

"Thank me when you hear what I've got to say." He took a seat and a deep breath. "The opposition from the other side of the aisle has intensified, and I'm not sure it's in our best interest to continue in this format."

"And by, 'in this format,' you mean exactly what?" Hutch lumped one more worry onto what had already become a worry-filled morning.

"I mean our intervention, as it stands, will be defeated. We may be able to do an end around, however, if we piggyback something on another bill. If we put verbiage into something with more support that will block an element of the pipeline, we have a chance." The congressman outlined his proposal, and Hutch saw the wisdom in it. The other bill, an infrastructure initiative that had broad backing on both sides of the aisle, was sure to pass, and the elements that would interfere with the pipeline could be linked to infrastructure with some imaginative verbiage. "On another note, I think I may have found you some funding for that other project. The Russian mystery find? That's got some real front-page potential; nothing like a little international mystery to drum up support."

"Really?" Hutch was flabbergasted. "I knew you found it interesting, but I haven't even submitted a grant yet. We have some money from a private sponsor, but beyond that..."

"Well, this could be good for you, then. This wouldn't be like an NSF grant. More like an investigation into multi-national resources sponsored by our government with matching funds from the Russian National Park Commission. I'd like to talk to you and Aleksi about it if she's available."

"She's not available this morning. She's not feeling well." That was the truth, at least.

"Well, the finagling with the infrastructure bill is going to take some time, and if Aleksi's not available, maybe we can set up a meeting for later."

"Excuse me." The interruption drew their attention, and Hutch blinked at the vaguely familiar face. "Derrick Penningly, Dr. Hutchinson. We met the other day when I was looking for Dr. Oliver. I'm sorry to interrupt, but I just heard you talking about the project Aleksi told me about, and I thought I might save you some time."

"Aleksi told you about her project?" That didn't sound likely.

"Well, sort of." He stepped into the room and held out a hand to the congressman. "Nice to meet you, Congressman Twain. I've been looking for an advisor for next year, and Aleksi said there might be a space opening up with Dr. Hutchinson, and outlined what was happening with the mystery specimen. We thought there might be enough data for two dissertations. I'd be two years behind her, so I thought if I offered my help on the beginning phases, since she's short of time, I would have time to work up a secondary project that rode her coattails, so to speak." The young man smiled disarmingly, and Twain looked at Hutch with a raised eyebrow.

"I spoke to Aleksi this morning, and she didn't mention this."

"Well, she's been a little busy and not feeling well. It must have slipped her mind."

"We'll have to sit down with Aleksi and talk about this, Derrick. I generally pick my own students, and I have a full complement right now." This didn't sound like something Aleksi would do, but then Aleksi wasn't acting like herself.

"Oh, I understand, but I really wouldn't be coming on board until the fall, and Lonnie Westinghouse will be done by then, so you'll be down to four. Until then, I would just be free labor. Just let me tell you my ideas, and you can decide later if you want to take me on, but I *am* familiar with the project."

"I see no reason not to sit down and talk about it, Hutch." Twain looked at his wristwatch.

"All right." Hutch pulled up the research plan on his computer. "I've got a lecture at eleven, but we'll talk and see what you've got, Derrick. If we can pull in the funding that Congressman Twain mentioned, there might be room for two on the project."

"Excellent!" the congressman said with a smile.

"Cool!" Derrick beamed and pulled out a tablet computer. "Well, first of all, you know that Aleksi has come up with nothing that matched the tooth morphology. I've set up an imaging database from the MCZ files that should help us there…"

Aleksi left the medical center frustrated, hungry, and tired of being poked and prodded. The doctor—a third-year resident physician—had been mystified by her symptoms. She was running a very high temperature, near 105 degrees, but was showing no other fever symptoms. They took blood and urine samples, and an embarrassing number of swabs to culture for possible infections. He had no explanation for the discoloration of her nails and sounded like he didn't believe her about the color of her irises, even when she showed him her driver's license and pointed to the entry for eye color. He'd looked in her eyes, nose, mouth, ears, and just shrugged. As to her psychological issues, he simply shrugged again and mentioned stress.

When he suggested admitting her to the hospital, however, she'd balked. She had too much work to do to get stuck in a hospital bed, and she felt fine. Since she was lucid and not a danger to herself or others, they couldn't force her to be admitted. The blood work and cultures would take a couple of days, but he gave her a prescription for a broad-spectrum antibiotic and told her to watch her temperature closely.

She stopped by a deli, picked up a half-pound of sliced ham and ate it on the way to Hutch's office. He wasn't there, but that wasn't unusual, so she went to the lab and got to work. The familiar tasks of chipping away layers of rock to uncover the secrets hidden within quickly soothed her tumultuous thoughts, and she lost track of time.

She recognizes some of them; the pudgy desk clerk at the gym, Derrick Penningly, the young doctor with a needle in his hand, a boy she knew in college who had tried to convince her that she really did *want to have sex with him...they're all around her, trying to grab her, hurt her...She won't let them. She has to fight...*

Flesh parts like a tearing sheet, bones snap like sticks, and faces are torn away, but underneath there are only gnashing teeth and reaching claws. She strikes, claws, fights to get free...

"Aleksi?"

Aleksi snapped awake, unsure of where she was. She wore lab gear; mask, gloves, gown, and her arms and neck ached. She'd been working late, and didn't remember putting her head down on the lab bench. She glanced at the time; it was seven-thirty, but there was sunlight in the lab windows. It was seven-thirty in the *morning.*

"Aleksi? Are you here?" It sounded like Hutch.

"Hutch? Yeah!" She shook her head, banishing the horrible dream from her mind. All the faces, teeth, claws...she shuddered. She doffed her mask and goggles and parted the plastic sheet. Hutch stood at the lab door.

"Aleksi? Are you okay?" He stepped in looking fresh scrubbed, but also worried. "I tried your cell and emailed you, but got no answer."

"I'm fine. I just wanted to get an early start this morning." She didn't want him to know she'd spent the night in the lab; his opinion of her was damaged enough. "With the time I lost at the med center yesterday, I'm feeling a little behind. I didn't even think to check email, and my phone is in my bag. I don't know why I didn't hear it."

"No big deal. I'm on the run, but I've got some good news. I met with Congressman Twain yesterday about the pipeline project, and he mentioned the possibility for some funding for the Russian sample."

"Really?" That was good news. "Did you tell Bob?"

"Just by email. Twain wanted to discuss it and you were out, but then Derrick showed up and mentioned that you'd talked to him about the project."

"Derrick?" She wondered for a moment if she'd heard him right. "Derrick *Penningly?*"

"Yeah. He seems pretty sharp, actually, and knew the project like the back of his hand. He doesn't have quite the skill set that you or Bob do, but he's eager, and had some good ideas. I wanted to say, though, that talking to him about this before coming to me was *not* what I generally like from my students. I'm not saying we shouldn't bring him on board, but come to me first next time, okay?"

"But, I didn't..." Her mind was spinning, still muddled with sleep. What the hell had Derrick told him? A surge of anger infused her.

"Don't worry about it, Aleksi. Like I said, the guy's sharp, and he had Twain eating out of his hand. If we can get the funding, there could be more for a follow-up project, and even a field expedition to look over the recovery site, with matching funds from the Russians. This could really be big, and with Derrick coming on two years after you, there really wouldn't be much of a conflict. He's willing to work as a volunteer during spring and summer semesters, so by fall he'll be ready to jump in with both feet."

"I...um..." She thought furiously; she had mentioned the project to Derrick a week ago, but only in passing. For him to have gotten the kind of details that Hutch was alluding to, he must have talked to someone else, too. Maybe Bob? She had *not* suggested that he come on board as one of Hutch's graduate students, at least not that she remembered. His face swam in her mind, grinning, laughing. Had she? "I think we should all get together to clear up some misunderstandings, Hutch."

"That's fine, but it'll have to be later in the week. I've got legal stuff to do and maybe even a trip down to Washington. This pipeline thing needs work."

"That'll be fine." She needed to talk with Bob and then find Derrick. Her nails pressed against her palms to the point of pain, and she backed off the pressure. "I'll check my phone. Sorry I missed your calls." That, at least, was truer than he would ever know.

"Right." He gave her a smile which suddenly faded. "I almost forgot to ask how things went at the med center."

"Oh, the usual. They took a million samples and gave me a prescription for antibiotics." She shrugged, trying to play it down. "They won't have lab results until Tuesday or so. I feel fine, just...well, you know, different."

"Okay, well, let me know how things come out." He turned to go, then turned back. "And take it easy, Aleksi. Stress can do more damage than a virus."

"Yeah, I know." She wasn't about to tell him about the stress she was feeling right now, and the irrepressible urge to rip Derrick Penningly into tiny bloody chunks of meat.

When Hutch was gone, Aleksi went back and checked her phone. The battery was dead, so she plugged it in and turned it on, then checked her email on her computer. There were two messages from Hutch and one from Bob among the usual student correspondence. Hutch's were straight forward and obviously sent from his phone, asking her to call him.

Bob's was more pointed. It read, "Got email from Hutch about Derrick. We need to talk, ASAP!"

"Shit," she muttered and picked up her phone. He picked up on the first ring.

"Aleksi! What the hell's going on?" He sounded pissed.

"Hi, Bob. Look, something's wrong with this, and I've got to get it straightened out. Can we meet for breakfast? I'm starving and I need coffee."

"Sure. How about Dudley?" His voice was a little calmer, at least.

"I can be there in ten minutes."

"Okay. Okay, I'll see you there."

She packed up her computer, left her phone sitting there to charge and left the lab. The weather had turned relatively warm again, melting the snow to a mire of slush. She didn't even bother buttoning her coat; she needed to cool off and think. By the time she walked into Dudley Café, her head was clearer. The smell of coffee and food helped. She ordered two breakfast sandwiches and a large coffee. By the time she found a seat, Bob was coming in through the door. He didn't even go to the counter but came right over and sat down.

"So, what the hell is going on, Aleksi? I got an email from Hutch yesterday that you invited this Derrick guy in on the project." Bob's voice was loud and angry. "That you did it without going to him first."

"Hang on and listen, Bob." She tried to keep her temper down; she wasn't mad at Bob and understood his mood. "I told Derrick about the project, but not any details, and I *didn't* invite him aboard. Something's up, and I needed to talk to you before I get it figured out. Did Derrick talk to you, at all? Ask you for any information?"

"No, he did *not* talk to me, and he told Hutch he got everything from you. Everything, including *my* sequencing results and the ash analysis, the morphology data that *you* worked up, all of the imaging files, *and* the journal translation." His face was flushed, and she could see the pulse pounding at his neck. "Tell me how the *fuck* he got all that if *you* didn't give it to him, Aleksi? Is that why you set me up with Julie, so you could take this project and pair up with this Derrick guy?"

"What?" She stared at him in shock. "No, that is *not* why I set you up with Julie! I thought you liked her, and I *know* she likes you. That has nothing to do with this! Derrick is a jerk, and he's trying to horn in on *our* project! I'm going to find him and tell him to back off, or I'll get him expelled. I don't know *where* he got all that data, but he didn't get it from *me*!"

Both of their voices were raised now, enough that they were drawing stares.

"Well, I don't *have* a copy of the journal translation, and Hutch and Quinton are the only others who do. If you didn't give it to him, how the hell did he get it?"

"Quinton maybe. He works at the MCZ, you know."

"Then why say he got if from you?"

"I don't *know*, Bob, but I'm going to find out. You've got to trust me on this! I didn't give him anything."

"I'll trust you when you tell this jerk to fuck off, Aleksi!" He stood so quickly that his chair clattered over. "Until then, don't expect any more help from me on *your* project!"

He stormed out of the café amid the stares of several of the other diners.

Aleksi tried to eat and let her temper cool. She didn't know how

Derrick had gotten so much information, but it certainly had not been from her. There was no way she would have forgotten giving him their data. She finished her coffee, tossing the two naked English muffins in the trash on the way out, determined to find out what was going on.

Unfortunately, finding Derrick Penningly was like trying to grab her own shadow. Aleksi had his email address from her class roster, and fired off a terse note, telling him that she needed to speak to him immediately. She got no response. He had no other contact information on file, and his number was unlisted, so she had to wait. She found it hard to concentrate on her work that afternoon and ended up going home early. When she got there, however, Julie met her with a sour look.

"So, what did you say to Bob to get him so upset?"

"There's a guy trying to butt into our project." Aleksi put her bag down, headed for the kitchen and opened the fridge, but nothing looked good. "He told Hutch that I invited him to come on board. He has all kinds of information on the project that he said I gave him, which convinced Hutch that he was telling the truth, so Hutch told Bob." She slammed the refrigerator door and leaned against the counter, her arms folded and her hands clenched. "Bob thinks I'm trying to undercut him, but it's not true. I've got to find this jerk and warn him off."

"Bob's *really* upset." Julie had her arms folded and shoulders hunched in a defensive posture, and her eyes were red.

"What's wrong, Julie? What did he say?"

"He asked me if I knew a guy named Derrick Penningly, and if I was working with you to screw him over."

"He said *that?*"

"Well, not in so many words, but that was the gist of it." Julie sniffed.

"Oh, Julie. I'm sorry." Aleksi went to her, reaching out to offer some support, but Julie backed away. "I'll get this straightened out, I promise."

"Do that." Julie turned and went to her bedroom door and turned back. "I *like* Bob, Aleksi. I like him a lot. If I find out you set us up just to play some game, you'll be looking for a new roommate."

The door closed with a stomach-wrenching finality.

"Great!" Aleksi ground her teeth as she went back to the kitchen. She opened the refrigerator again but there was still nothing that looked good. Her stomach clenched on nothing, and she tried the freezer. She took out a package of hamburger and put it in the microwave to thaw, then went to retrieve her phone from her bag. "Enough of this bullshit." She punched in Hutch's cell number.

"Aleksi? What's up?"

"Sorry to call on a Saturday night, Hutch, but I need to talk to you for a second about Derrick."

"I'm a little busy, Aleksi. If this can wait…" His voice was hushed, and she heard sounds in the background, a woman's voice.

"Look, Bob's really mad, and so am I. I *didn't* ask Derrick to come on board, and I *didn't* give him any of my data or the journal. I don't know how he got them, but it wasn't from me. I don't have his phone number, and he won't answer my emails."

"Why didn't you say that this morning?"

"I didn't know what he had or where he got it, so I spoke to Bob. He said he hadn't talked to Derrick, and accused me of trying to push him out of the project. There are only three copies of the journal translation that I know of; mine, yours, and Dr. Neilson's. *I* didn't give one to Derrick."

"If you're suggesting that he stole it, that's a pretty serious accusation, Aleksi." She heard more noises in the background, other voices. "Look, I can't talk now."

"Just ask Derrick where he got that journal, Hutch. *I* didn't give it to him."

"I will. Goodnight, Aleksi."

"Okay. Thanks. Bye." She hung up, unsure if she'd just done the right thing or not.

The microwave chimed, and she retrieved the hamburger. Without a thought, she ate the barely warm meat right out of the package.

Hutch hung up and turned his phone's ringer off. "Sorry." He put it away and returned to his meal.

"That sounded serious." Persephone speared a butter-drenched scallop from the plate between them and cut it into dainty bites.

"It was." He took a scallop and ate it in four bites. This place was more Persephone's style, but the food was excellent, even though the invitation had come as a shock. "Sometimes I think professors should take courses in psychology just so they can handle graduate students."

"Oh?" She sipped wine and frowned. "Nothing that'll hurt the project, I hope."

"I hope not, but it might be. Aleksi and Bob are having a disagreement over another student. Typical he said, she said situation." He shrugged helplessly. "The kid works for Quinton Neilson at the MCZ, so I can't imagine him stealing anything."

"Stealing? Really?" She put her glass down hard. "Not the specimen."

"Ha! No, the thing weighs about four hundred pounds. Just some data; the imaging and genetics results."

"The same imaging data that you wouldn't loan me?" Persephone pursed her lips and narrowed her eyes; her signature 'I told you so' face.

"Yes, actually, so if they show up on the Internet, you're off the hook." He grinned.

"So good of you to look out for me, Hutch." She speared another scallop. "Which reminds me of why I asked you out: you mentioned funding from Congressman Twain. I'd be careful about him if I were you. I know the man, and he doesn't give *anything* away. If he's going to get money for this project, he'll want something back."

"Like you did?" He endured her glare and sipped his beer. "Sorry, I couldn't resist."

"Well, it might be *exactly* that." She leaned forward. "He's got a reputation with young interns."

"Twain?" Hutch frowned and thought about Aleksi. Every time Twain spoke to him after that night at the restaurant, he'd asked about Aleksi. "I hope not. Aleksi's got enough problems right now."

"You better warn her, Hutch. A girl like Aleksi doesn't have the hutzpah to stand up to someone like Twain." She swirled her wine and sipped.

"I don't know about that." He thought about the night after the restaurant, the morning in the gym, and his sore forearm. "She might surprise you. She certainly has me."

"Oh?" She arched an eyebrow.

"Yes, which brings me back to what you said to her. That didn't turn out well, Persephone. She got the wrong idea."

"No way!" Persephone looked honestly surprised. "She did *not*!"

"As a matter of fact, she was very polite about it, and backed right off." He still felt a pang every time he remembered that night. *It was the right thing to do.* "She wasn't herself, and she apologized later. Like I said, she's got enough problems on her plate." Not the least of which was this situation with Derrick Penningly.

Hutch resolved to get to the bottom of this, and quickly; there was too much at stake. He made a mental note to email Derrick as soon as he got home. He needed to find out who was telling the truth, and who was lying to him. And with Aleksi's recent behavior, he was afraid of what he was going to find out.

2 1

Hutch stepped into his office early Monday morning with just enough time to get this meeting over with and make the flight to Washington. He'd emailed Derrick late Saturday night, asking him to come in, and gotten a reply right away. He hadn't told Derrick why he wanted to talk to him, nor had he told Aleksi about the meeting. He wanted Derrick's side of the story before he went back to Aleksi.

He put his computer in the docking station and turned it on. He'd done his email at home, but there were files here that he needed to back up before he took the laptop on his trip. He logged on just as there was a knock at his open door.

"Dr. Hutchinson. Good morning." Derrick Penningly stood there with a cheerful smile.

"Hello, Derrick. Come in and have a seat. I'll be one second." He started the backup process.

"So, have you had a chance to consider my offer?" Derrick took a seat, smile intact, posture perfect, seemingly oblivious.

"I have, but we've got an issue to clear up first, and I'm short on time, so I'm going to cut right to the chase." He fixed the young man with an even stare. "Where did you get the data files on Aleksi's project, specifically the copy of the translated journal?"

He looked puzzled by the question. "I told you; Aleksi gave them to me. Is there a problem?"

"Yes, there is. She told me that she didn't give you anything, and that she never suggested that you should come on board her project."

"She *what?*" Derrick's jaw dropped, his eyes wide in apparently genuine surprise.

"She said she doesn't know where you got those files, but that *she* didn't give them to you. You say she did. Someone, you or her, is lying to me, and I want to know which one. Now."

"She *did* give them to me! I talked to her the same day I met you, right outside this office. I went to the lab with her, she showed me the samples, then told me to come back later. That afternoon, we talked again, and she put the files on a stick for me. She said I should have a look at them and maybe we could work together. She was a little freaked out that things weren't progressing very fast, and she wanted more help."

Hutch continued to stare at him, looking for signs of a lie. Most people couldn't lie without some betrayal of facial expression or mannerism, but Derrick showed nothing. Less than nothing, in fact. His face remained perfectly neutral. But if Aleksi had given him the data that day, why hadn't she mentioned it that night when they went out with Twain? She'd been very open to discussion that evening, and it would have been the perfect opportunity.

"If you don't believe me, look at the date and time the files were created on my laptop. Here." He dug in his bag and produced a computer. He booted it up and then brought it around for Hutch to see. "See? I created a folder. I even named it Aleksi's research. I went out that night, so I didn't get home until late, but when I did, I loaded these files. See? They all went on at ten fifty-four PM."

"Yes, I see that." Hutch remembered that night all too well, and how strangely Aleksi had been acting. "You didn't come to me for a week after she talked to you. Why wait so long?"

"There was a lot of information to look over, and I wanted to make sure it was right for me." He shrugged disarmingly. "Look, it sounds like she's covering herself for stepping over the line, making me the offer before she spoke with you. She had *also* suggested I might find a spot with Dr. Oliver, but *that* didn't work out so well either."

Hutch frowned at that. It wasn't like Aleksi to do those things, but he hadn't thought she would proposition him, either. "Well, there's no easy way around this. I'll set up a meeting with both of you, but I'm out of town until Thursday night or Friday morning. I'll check my schedule and email both of you." His computer was done backing up, so he shut it down and took it out of the docking station. "I've got to catch a plane to Washington, so you'll have to excuse me, Derrick."

"Oh, sure! No problem." He packed up his computer and backed out of the office. "Don't worry, Dr. Hutchinson. I'll talk to Aleksi and we'll get this misunderstanding straightened out. I just can't believe she told you we didn't discuss this. Is she okay? She seems a little, um...tense."

"She's stressed, and this...misunderstanding is not helping." Hutch closed his door, wondering about Aleksi's condition. She'd as much as admitted that she was having hallucinations, and her personality had definitely changed. She wasn't the same terrified young woman he'd introduced to his other students at Grendel's. But he wasn't about to mention those things to Derrick. "I'll set up a meeting and send you an email."

"Right. Thanks, Dr. Hutchinson."

Hutch nodded and watched the young man walk away, wondering who was lying to him, and how well he really knew Aleksandrovna Rychenkna.

Wednesday was a long time coming for Aleksi. She'd emailed Derrick, copying Hutch, twice a day, but had gotten no response. She thought he would skip the Comparative Zoology lab to avoid her, but when she came in, he was already seated in the back, right next to the girl he'd partnered with the first day. The two were talking, the girl looking shocked, but they fell silent when they saw her. She glared at him, but he just smiled back as if nothing was wrong. She couldn't confront him in a class full of students. She taught the lab with little interest, enduring his smarmy smile throughout and trying not to grind her teeth. When the class was finished, and everyone started leaving, she called him back.

"Derrick, I'd need to speak with you." She had to clean up the lab before she left, but she'd be damned if she let him slip away.

"Oh, I'm sorry, Aleksi. I've got to run off to another appointment." He gave her another smug smile, and the girl he was with stifled a little laugh. "Maybe you could email me."

"No, I need to speak with you *now*!"

"Look, Aleksi." He turned to her with an apologetic shrug. "I'm sorry you're upset, but it's not my fault. I'm not going to play that game. I don't need a grade in this lab." He turned away and left the room.

"You *what?*" The rest of the students were past, but a few glanced back as she followed him out into the hall. "What are you talking about?"

"You *know* what I'm talking about." He raised his hands in an off-putting gesture. "I'm sorry, but I'm not going there with you."

A couple of the students were staring at her as he walked off. She had no idea what he had told them, but with her blood boiling; she wasn't going to let him get away. She dashed back into the lab, grabbed her coat and keys, and locked the door. She'd come back to clean up, but she couldn't lose him. She dashed down the stairs and looked around, but he was already out the door, walking briskly across the small quad toward the street. She hurried after him and caught up just as he reached a shiny blue BMW and opened the door.

"Derrick!" Aleksi grabbed the door before he could close it and wrenched it back. "I don't know what you think you're trying to accomplish with all this, but it's stopping right now."

"What's stopping, Aleksi?" He stood back up out of the car seat, finally meeting her eye to eye. His lips curled back from those perfect white teeth, but it wasn't a smile. "What *exactly* is it that you think I've done wrong?"

A scent flooded her mind. Something about him, something *wrong, dangerous,* set her teeth on edge. She shook her head to clear the dizzying sensation and glared at him. "I don't know how you got those files off my computer, but I've already told both Hutch and Bob that I didn't give them to you. Bob's pissed off and won't do any more work on the project until you back off, so I'm telling you to back off. *Now.*"

"You know you gave me those files, Aleksi. Backing out now won't help you with Hutch." He gave her another toothy, skin-crawling smile. "He can't be happy that you asked me to come on board the project without talking to him first, but denying you did it now is just *pathetic.*"

"Pathetic!" Rage flooded her. She gripped the car door between them, suppressing the urge to take him by the throat. "I'll give you pathetic, you lying piece of shit! If you *ever* come near my research again, or even *hint* that any of it was yours, or tell *anyone* I invited you to work with me, I'll rip out your fucking pancreas and feed it to you!" She reached over and raked her nails across the hood of his car, leaving four parallel scratches.

His eyes widened and his nostrils flared. The sense of danger slammed into her, his eyes, his mouth, lips stretched into a rictus. For a heartbeat she stared into his eyes, poised for him to strike, visions of claws rending flesh surging through her mind. She flexed her hands, felt the tips of her nails against her palms, ready.

"Bitch! That's my car!"

Aleksi banished the urge to lash out and leaned in until their noses were barely an inch apart. "You tell any more lies about me, Derrick, and it'll be your fucking *throat!*"

She whirled away, realizing through the haze of rage that passersby were staring. Not until she got back to the lab and her temper cooled did she notice the flecks of paint and metal under her long, sharp fingernails. She pulled a pair of heavy dissecting scissors from a drawer and carefully cut them short.

2 2

That evening, with Julie sitting on the couch beside her, Aleksi called Bob and laid it all out.

"I see what he's doing now," she explained. "I still don't know how he got the files; he must have hacked my computer, or maybe Quinton's, but he's told Hutch that I gave them to him and asked him to come on board. Then, when I told Hutch I didn't, Derrick's claiming I'm backing out to cover myself for not okaying it with Hutch first."

"So, you saw him today in your comp zoo class?" Bob sounded skeptical but calmer.

"Yes, and I think he's telling lies to the students there, too. They kept looking at me like I'd done something wrong. He's trying to discredit me to make it look like I'm the one who's lying." She paused, but Bob didn't reply. "I'm afraid I kind of lost my temper after class. He just walked away so I chased him down and…um…threatened him."

"You *threatened* him? With what, expulsion?"

"No, though that's probably what I *should* have done. If I can prove he's lying and stole the files, they'll kick him out."

"So, what did you threaten him with?" Bob asked.

"Well, I kind of told him I'd rip out his pancreas, and…um…scratched his car." She cringed at the memory, and saw Julie staring at her in wide-eyed disbelief.

"You keyed his *car?*" Bob laughed over the phone. "Jesus *Christ*, Aleksi, what's gotten into you?"

"I don't know. I just lost my temper. But I definitely did what you asked, Bob. Derrick Penningly has *officially* been told, *by* me, to fuck off." She took a deep breath and let it out. "When Hutch gets back from D.C. we're meeting with him. I'd like you there, too."

"Oh, I'll be there." He sounded nonplussed.

"Good. We'll get this straightened out and get things back to normal. So, you want to come by the lab tomorrow and have a look at your bone bed fossils? I've got six pieces that look good for taking samples for DNA extraction."

"Um…sure. What time?"

"How about noon? I'll bring the burritos."

"Yeah, okay." There was a pause. "Hey, is Julie around? I've kind of got to apologize to her."

Aleksi smiled. "Yeah, she's here. Let me get her." She handed the phone to Julie and left the room, feeling for the first time in days that her life might be getting back to normal.

***

Hutch's phone vibrated in his pocket. He was between meetings, up to his eyeballs in politics, and utterly sick of it. He glanced at the screen and saw "Vandyke."

"What now?" Wondering why he would be getting a call from the chairman, he put his bag down, leaned against a wall and answered. "What's up, Larry?"

"I need to ask *you* that, Hutch. I just got a formal complaint about one of your students."

"What?" He felt a knot in the pit of his stomach. "Who?"

"Aleksi Rychenkna. Seems she keyed a student's car and threatened him."

"She *what?* I don't believe it." He remembered Doug at the gym and thought that it might not be that far-fetched.

"Well, there were witnesses, and this student has some big guns for parents. They're screaming for an expulsion and want to sue the school."

Hutch gritted his teeth. "Let me guess. Derrick Penningly."

"How did you know?"

"Look, Larry, there's more going on here than just a scratch on a car."

He filled Vandyke in on the two sides of the story. "One of the two of them is lying, and right now I don't know who. A week ago, I'd have trusted Aleksi, but she's been sick, and stress has hit her hard. If she's telling the truth, and he stole those files, either from her or Quinton Nielson, that's grounds for expulsion. His big gun parents won't have a leg to stand on."

"You'll have to prove that."

"Look, I'll be back Friday morning, and I'm going to sit down with both of them. We'll look at their computer files and see who's telling the truth."

"Damn it, Hutch. She seemed like a really brilliant young lady. I never would have thought she could threaten someone with violence, even if he *did* try to steal her project. If he did, he's really stupid."

"Maybe he thought his big-gun parents could get him out of it." Hutch had seen that often enough, students who didn't think the rules applied to them because their family had money or power. "I'm in D.C. and I have a meeting in ten minutes, Larry. I'll email both of them tonight that they are officially to calm down, and we'll get this sorted out."

"Do that, Hutch." Vandyke hung up.

Hutch put his phone in his pocket and took a deep breath, trying to focus. "Aleksi, what the *hell* happened to you?"

<hr>

The night had turned cold and blustery when Bob finally left the lab. He was tired but felt good. Things were back on track. He believed Aleksi, and Julie had forgiven his big-mouth accusations. He shook his head thinking about her, wondering how a geeky science nerd had ever gotten together with a girl like her.

"Aleksi," he murmured, answering his own question.

Aleksi had gotten them together, and he'd returned the favor by thinking the worst of her. He even owed her for his dissertation project; if she got a dissertation from the mystery specimen, the already funded bear DNA project was all his, and she had six samples ready for him to take.

"You're an idiot, Bob." He pulled his coat closed against the teeth of the wind as he made his way across the small quad behind Fairchild hall and around the front of the MCZ.

With the weather changing for the worse again, few people were out and about, but Cambridge never really slept. There were always students working or studying somewhere. The MCZ was dark, but Northwest Science was lit up as always. He passed it and keyed into the parking garage side door. The wind slammed the door closed behind him as he started climbing the stairs to the third level. He heard the door slam again just as he reached his floor; someone else was going home after a long day. He glanced down the stairwell out of reflex, but there was nobody there.

With a mental shrug, he pushed open the door to the parking level and started down the row of empty spaces. He was about halfway to his old Nissan when he heard the door slam again behind him. He glanced over his shoulder, but as before, saw no one. A chill shot down his spine that had nothing to do with the cold. Muggings weren't common in Cambridge, but they weren't unheard of, either. There were enough pillars on the level for a stalker to hide behind, but Bob's car was only a couple hundred feet away.

He quickened his steps.

A sound to his left, the scuff of a shoe on concrete maybe, drew his attention, and he thought he saw the flick of a shadow.

"Who's there?" he shouted, not really expecting an answer, but intent on letting whoever it was know that he'd been spotted. He pulled his bag off his shoulder and fumbled his car keys out of a pocket, clenching them in his fist with one key sticking out between his fingers. It wasn't much of a weapon, but it was better than nothing.

Something clicked behind him and to the right, and Bob whirled, but once again, there was nothing there.

"I'm armed!" he lied, hoping it might buy enough hesitation on his stalker's part for him to make it to his car. He broke into a trot. The Nissan was barely fifty feet away. He could make it.

Something went click behind him again, and he glanced back, knowing he wouldn't see anything. The empty garage mocked him. He turned back and ran full out for his car, fumbling the keys. Twenty feet, ten, and he was there. He'd made it. His hand shook as he put the key in the lock and turned it.

He caught a reflection of a shape over his shoulder in the car window, a face, white teeth, eyes glinting in the dim light.

"Little fucker." The voice turned his bowels to water.

Bob whirled his bag around hard, but it was ripped out of his hand. Then he saw the blood, the long, ragged tears in his forearm and the shredded remnants of his hand. Blood pulsed from the tattered stumps of two missing fingers. He opened his mouth to scream, but the next blow struck him across the throat and spun him around.

His own reflection stared back at him from the car window, a flash of surprise before a spray of blood obscured it and his vision dimmed. He slid down the door and lay there, the taste of blood in his mouth and the cold concrete of the parking garage floor pressing against his cheek.

Aleksi snapped awake without knowing what woke her. She blinked, remembering a dream—*faces, blood, claws, and flashing teeth*. They'd become so common that she took them for granted. The clock displayed six ten in the morning; her alarm would go off in twenty minutes. She closed her eyes, trying to banish the dream memory. Then the doorbell chimed, followed by a hard knock on the door, and she realized that must have awoken her.

"Who the hell?" She jumped out of bed, grabbed a robe and went out into the hall. A light flicked on under Julie's door. "Someone's at the door, Julie. I'll get it."

"The door?" Julie's voice sounded sleepy and disoriented.

Aleksi checked that the chain was on before she said, "Who is it?"

"Cambridge Police, Miss. We need to speak to you."

"Police?" Aleksi flipped on the hall light and turned the deadbolt. She put her foot flat on the carpet a couple inches behind the door and opened it slowly. Two men in heavy coats stood in the hall, a shorter one in front and a taller one behind. "Show me a badge."

"I'm Sergeant Jasper, and this is Detective Willis." They both fished in their coat pockets and produced authentic-looking badges, though Aleksi had to admit that she wouldn't have known a false one. "May we come in, Miss?"

"Um...sure." She closed the door, flipped the chain off the catch and opened it again, stepping back. "What's going on?"

"We need to ask you some questions, Miss," the sergeant said as they stepped in.

As Aleksi closed the door, Julie's bedroom door opened. Julie stepped out fastening a robe, her hair a mass of disheveled curls. "What's this about?" She rubbed sleep from her eyes blinking in disbelief.

"And why couldn't it wait until a decent hour?" Aleksi followed up.

"I'm sorry, but it's important." The sergeant looked at them each in turn, then back to Aleksi. "You're Aleksandrovna Rychenkna?"

"Aleksi, yes, and I'll ask again, what's this about?" Aleksi folded her arms and did her best to glare at the two police officers.

"And as I said, Miss Rychenkna, we just have a few questions."

"About what?"

"About where you were last night."

"I was here."

"All night?"

"I got home about seven, worked until about eleven, and went to bed where I slept until about two minutes ago. Now tell me why I need an alibi."

The sergeant ignored her question but turned to Julie. "And you must be Julie Parks." Julie nodded, now fully awake. "Can you confirm that Miss Rychenkna was here all night."

"I went to bed at about ten thirty, and since we don't sleep in the same bedroom, no, I can't."

"And did you phone anyone last night, Miss Rychenkna?"

"I...Yes, I called Bob Tomlin. Why?"

"And what did you talk about?" he asked, once again ignoring her own question.

"We talked about *research*." Aleksi felt herself becoming angry with the cop's manner and bit it back. "We're working together on a project for Dr. Hutchinson, our advisor. Now, that's the last answer you get out of me before you tell me what the *hell* this is about." She clenched her jaw, trying not to grind her teeth.

"Were you here when Miss Rychenkna called Bob Tomlin, Miss Parks?"

"Yes," Julie admitted, a tremor of worry in her voice.

"And can you confirm that they talked about this research project?"

"Yes, I can. I was right there. I talked to him too, after they were done."

"And what did you talk to him about?"

"We're dating. We set up a date for tonight." She glanced at Aleksi, then back to the sergeant. "What's wrong with Bob?"

Jasper looked at Aleksi again, then at Julie, scrutinizing their faces. "I'm sorry to have to tell you this, but Bob Tomlin was murdered last night."

"What?" Aleksi blurted.

"You're lying!" Julie snapped, her voice shaking. She stepped back, and staggered. "What kind of bullshit prank is this? Who the fuck are you, really? I don't believe you're real cops at all!"

"I'm sorry, Miss Parks, but it happened last night at about twelve thirty in the Oxford Parking garage. He was killed right next to his car, and from his cell phone, Miss Rychenkna, you were the last person that Bob Tomlin called."

"I don't believe you!" Julie snapped again, her face pale with panic. "I want to see him!"

"That's not possible, Miss Parks. The body's already been taken to the morgue, and the crime scene is restricted." He turned back to Aleksi. "Did you have any disagreements with Bob Tomlin?"

"Yes, as a matter of fact, but last night's phone call pretty much resolved them."

"And what was the nature of this disagreement."

"Look, I'm willing to answer any questions you have, but I think both Julie and I need to get squared away and maybe have a cup of coffee." She stepped past the two cops and put her arm around Julie's shoulders. "Please. We just woke up."

"We'll only be a few more minutes, Miss Rychenkna. Now, what did you argue about with Bob Tomlin?"

Aleksi ignored the question and guided Julie to the couch. She seemed in shock. "Just sit here for a minute, Julie. I'll get you something." When she turned to the kitchen, the two police officers were standing there, looking grim. She sighed and stepped past them. "We argued about another student, Derrick Penningly, who stole some data from our project and was horning in on the research." She put coffee on and poured a glass of water for Julie. "He told Dr. Hutchinson that I gave him the data and invited him on board, but it was a lie. I told Bob last night that I confronted Derrick and told him to back off."

"And how do you know this Derrick Penningly?" Jasper asked while his partner jotted notes in a tiny pad.

"He's in one of the lab classes I'm teaching, comparative zoology, and he works at the MCZ. I talked to him after class just yesterday." She took the water to Julie and went back to the kitchen, willing the coffee to brew faster.

"And was this conversation with Derrick Penningly heated?"

Aleksi turned and glared at him. "He stole my research and lied about me, Sergeant Jasper. Yes, it was heated. I was angry."

"How angry, Miss Rychenkna?"

"Angry enough to threaten him and key the hood of his car," she admitted, though she was not about to tell him that it was not keys, but her nails that had creased the hood of Derrick's BMW.

"And were you that angry with Bob Tomlin?"

"I wasn't angry with Bob at all. I was just upset that he assumed I was trying to undercut his part in my research project. We were *both* angry with Derrick, and we were all going to meet with Dr. Hutchinson about it tomorrow." She poured two cups of coffee and went back out to the front room. Julie sat there with the full glass of water in her hands, staring into space. She sat down and put the cups on the table. "Julie, drink the water."

Julie took a sip, put the glass down, and picked up her coffee, cradling the cup in her shaking hands. She looked up at the two police men with pleading eyes. "Please. I'd like to see Bob. I've got to see him."

"I'm sorry, but the coroner's performing an autopsy at eight this morning." Jasper produced two business cards from a pocket and handed them each one. "Call me this afternoon, and I'll try to set something up."

Julie glanced at the card and dropped it onto the table, staring into her coffee cup.

"So, are we through?" Aleksi asked, taking a sip of the scalding coffee.

"For now, Miss Rychenkna, but we may have more questions. Please make yourself available to come down to the station for an interview."

"I'll email you my schedule. Just let me know what you need." She tucked the card into her robe pocket, put her cup down and stood. "I'll do whatever I can to help you find whoever killed Bob. He was a close friend." She heard a stifled sob from the couch as she escorted the two policemen to the door.

"Good. Thank you, Miss Rychenkna. Sorry to have woken you up with this."

She opened the door. "I won't lie to you, Sergeant; it's a hell of a way to start the day."

"I know, and I apologize." His tone said that he really wasn't sorry. "Oh, and if I could ask one more question: do you know how we might find Derrick Penningly?"

"No." She wondered why they would ask her with all their resources. "I don't have his phone number, just his email, and I don't have any idea where he lives. You can probably get his information from the registrar's office."

"Right. Good idea. Thank you." He nodded and turned away.

She closed the door and locked it, then leaned her forehead against the wood, her mind spinning. How could Bob be dead, murdered? Sounds of Julie crying intruded upon her thoughts, so she went to her to offer whatever comfort she could. As she sat down, however, she realized that she needed to do one more thing this morning; she had to call Hutch and let him know that one of his students was dead.

So much for the element of surprise," Willis said as they got back into the car. He turned the key, put the heat on full, and reached for his coffee.

"Oh, I think they were surprised enough, at least the Parks woman was. No faking there. The other though..." Jasper reached for his coffee and took a sip; it was cold, but the smell of the fresh-brewed java the girl had made was still in his brain. "Didn't seem like she took it like she ought to. No tears, no denial..."

"Yeah, she did seem more pissed off than distraught." Willis put the car in gear and drove gingerly down the icy street. "The morgue?"

"Breakfast first." Jasper was still trying to puzzle out the Rychenkna woman's response. "The coroner won't start until eight. Banker's hours, you know. And I hate going to an autopsy on an empty stomach."

"Friendly's?"

"Bingo." Visions of fresh coffee, eggs, and home fries blocked out the recent memories of Bob Tomlin's torn throat and mangled hand. "Then maybe the Harvard Registrar's office. I want to talk to this Derrick Penningly."

"Right."

H utch's phone rang precisely at seven in the morning. He was just stepping out of the shower—the hotel had a great mini-gym—so he wrapped the towel around his waist and padded across the floor to the dresser. The caller ID displayed "Aleksi", and he cringed.

"What now?" He'd expected some rebuttal from last night's email, but first thing in the morning? "Good morning, Aleksi. What's up?"

"Sorry, Hutch, but it hasn't been a good morning at all."

"What's wrong?" He could hear the tension in her voice.

"Look, something really horrible has happened, and I don't know how to say it other than to just say it, so here goes." She paused for a breath. "Bob was murdered last night in Oxford Parking garage."

"*What?*" Hutch sat down heavily on the bed, his mind spinning. "How?"

"I don't know. The police came to my apartment this morning at six o'clock and woke me up with the news. I called him last night to straighten out this thing with Derrick, and it was evidently the last call on Bob's cell. They came here and asked a bunch of questions."

"Oh my God." His entire long list of worries had just been trumped. "Murdered? They know it was murder, not some kind of car accident?"

"They told me it was murder but wouldn't give any details. I'm going down to the morgue this afternoon with Julie, my roommate, to see him. They were…um…dating, and she's pretty bad off."

"Yeah, so am I." He tried to think through the spinning in his mind. "Look, Aleksi, I'm back in Boston tomorrow morning. Help the police any way you can, but don't let them screw anything up, okay. They may want to see Bob's lab, and they don't know protocol. They could ruin every sample we took without even trying. Call Dr. Vandyke and let him know; he'll back me up on this. The same goes for your lab. Oh, and call Lonnie and let her know what happened. Tell her to let everyone know."

"Okay." There was another pause. "And what about the meeting with Derrick?"

"I think we better postpone that, Aleksi. The police will want to talk to everyone, and I don't want to cause a confrontation that might be misconstrued." The last thing he needed at this point was a knock down drag out argument in his office. "Everything's on hold until I get back, and I mean *everything*. Understand?"

"I understand." Aleksi sniffed, and Hutch wondered if she'd been crying. "I'm sorry, Hutch."

That, at least, sounded more like the old Aleksi. "Don't be, Aleksi. None of this is your fault."

"Yeah, I know, but…" She sniffed again. "Who would want to kill Bob? I mean, it doesn't make any sense."

"These things never do," he said, trying to sound sure about it. "The police will come up with something. It was probably a mugging gone bad."

"Yeah. Okay. I'd still like to talk with you tomorrow about the project."

"Look, Aleksi, I don't know if we should go into this just yet. Wait for the police to finish their investigation, then we'll pick up the pieces.

"I know it sounds callous, Hutch, but I've got two months to get my proposal in and take my qualifying exams. *Two months.* The graduate coordinator's not going to care about any extenuating circumstances; they'll just tell me I'm out of luck."

"Lawson's not a tyrant, Aleksi. I'm sure he'll let us work something out." He took a deep breath, trying to calm himself. *Bob Tomlin, dead…* "Don't worry about it right now, Aleksi. I'll see you tomorrow, and we can talk."

"Okay. Thanks, Hutch."

"You're welcome. Now, I've got to get dressed and get to work."

"Oh! Okay. Bye then."

"Bye."

He ended the call and fell back on the bed, still trying to wrap his mind around the concept that Bob Tomlin was dead.

The victim died from blood loss due to two severed carotid arteries." The coroner pointed to the four ragged tears that transected Bob Tomlin's neck. The corpse lay on a metal autopsy table, covered to the waist with a thin blue plastic sheet. There was a large Y shaped incision in his torso that had already been closed. The autopsy was finished; Jasper and Willis were getting the condensed version. "The trachea was also damaged extensively, the laryngeal and hyoid cartilages severed. The man's right hand was also severely injured, two digits torn free, the carpals and metacarpals disarticulated."

"Looks like a damn pit bull mauled him." Willis peered down at the mangled hand. "I saw this kid once, a ganger, hopped the wrong fence on a foot pursuit. Damn pit bull took him apart before the patrolmen could even get there. Tore his whole face off."

"This wasn't an animal bite." The coroner stared at Willis as if he didn't appreciate the interruption. "There is no worrying of the tissues, no opposed wounds like teeth coming together would inflict, and we tested for saliva and found none."

"Any guess on the murder weapon, Doc?" Jasper asked.

"My guess is some kind of claw. Maybe a sharpened gardening tool or some type of martial arts weapon."

"You mean like that comic book guy, Wolverine?" Willis tended to irritate people intentionally for the entertainment value. "Should we put an APB out on a guy in yellow spandex?"

"If I remember my Marvel Comics correctly, Detective, Wolverine used blades, so no. Whatever this was, it wasn't sharp. Pointed, yes, but not edged like a knife." He pointed to the origin of the four gashes that had ended Bob Tomlin's life. "See here, and here, the flesh is torn, not cut. This also means that considerable force was required to do this much damage. Whoever your perp is, he's strong."

"He?" Jasper raised an eyebrow. "You saying the murderer couldn't have been a woman?"

"Your suspect's a woman?" The coroner straightened and frowned.

"No suspects yet, Doc, just asking."

"Well, if it was a woman, I wouldn't want to *date* her. She'd have to be a body builder, or maybe a black belt." He shook his head again. "No, I doubt your average woman could do this."

"Maybe she's stronger than she looks?" Willis looked skeptical.

"And maybe we need to talk to Derrick Penningly, and see if he's a martial arts nut with a short temper." Jasper nodded to the coroner. "Thanks, Doc."

"Part of the job." He covered the corpse with the sheet. "Oh, by the way, all internal organs looked normal. I'm running the usual tests, but I don't expect any surprises. On the upside, matching the murder weapon to the wounds should be easy. The spacing of the wounds was slightly irregular and should match the tines of the thing perfectly."

The two detectives left the morgue and headed for their car.

"So," Willis began as he slid in behind the wheel, "do we go to him, or do we call a unit to pick him up and bring him down to the station?"

"We go to him." Jasper rubbed his eyes. He'd been up most of the night at the crime scene.

"You and your element of surprise," Willis grumbled.

"That, and I want to see where this guy lives and if his apartment is full of martial arts junk."

"Ha! We should be so lucky." Willis started the car and pulled out into traffic.

"Don't laugh. It *could* happen." Jasper didn't have much confidence in the claim. They were never that lucky.

W e've come to see Bob Tomlin's body," Aleksi told the receptionist. When the man just looked at her as if he expected more information, she said, "I spoke with Sergeant Jasper. He said we could come down and see him."

"Your names?"

"Aleksi Rychenkna and Julie Parks."

"We usually only let family members in to see the deceased." He said it like it was a law.

"Please call Sergeant Jasper, then." Aleksi produced his card from a pocket. "He woke us up at six o'clock this morning to tell us our friend had been murdered and said we could come down here."

"I'll have to okay this with the coroner." He nodded to the row of industrial-looking plastic chairs. "Please have a seat."

They sat, Julie wrung a handkerchief she'd been crying into all morning, and Aleksi fidgeted. There was nothing to read, not even the 'wash your hands' posters you saw in clinics and emergency rooms. Of course, most people who came here weren't interested in reading. Most of the people who came here weren't interested in anything at all.

Fifteen minutes later a man in scrubs came from down the hall and stopped before them. "I'm Phil Lambert, the coroner's assistant. I can show you Bob Tomlin's body."

"Thank you," Aleksi said, and they both stood.

"This way, please." He didn't smile, but then, Aleksi didn't suppose there was much call for smiling in a job like his.

Lambert escorted them through a pair of stainless-steel doors into the morgue, the air redolent with the scents of antiseptic and old blood. Aleksi wrinkled her nose and swallowed. She hadn't been particularly eager to come down here—she had never seen a dead body before, except for a few open casket funerals as a girl—and didn't relish the thought of seeing Bob's. Julie, however, had been adamant, and Aleksi wouldn't let her go through it alone.

"Just over here." Lambert pointed to a row of gleaming metal doors. He pulled one open, then slid out the drawer from within. The shape on the metal table was covered with a blue plastic sheet. He folded the blanket back carefully, just far enough to expose the face; Bob Tomlin's friendly round features, as peaceful as if he were sleeping.

"Oh, Bobby…" Julie sobbed, reaching forward to touch his pale cheek. The coroner's assistant reached for her hand.

"Please, Miss. I can't allow you to touch the body."

"Leave me alone!" Julie snapped, jerking her hand away.

Her fingers caught the blanket and pulled it down to reveal the four deep gashes that had ripped away much of Bob's throat. The ragged edges of flayed meat looked like something from a horror movie, but too real to be a Hollywood prop. Aleksi's gaze was drawn to those wounds, the gaping flesh, the torn meat, and the tangy sweet scent of blood.

"Oh my God!" Julie staggered back, her hand over her mouth, as pale as Bob's corpse but unable to look away.

"Julie!" Aleksi grasped her to keep her from falling, then glared at the assistant. "Cover him up, please!"

"Sorry, but I warned you." The assistant pulled the blanket back up. "This is why we generally don't allow people to come in here."

"No, please! I'm okay." Julie clutched Aleksi's arm, trembling. "Please! Just his face."

"I'm sorry, Miss, but I can't be responsible for—"

"Please!" Aleksi said, maybe a bit too firmly. She gritted her teeth and forced her temper down, but something had her nerves wound tight. "They were *close*, and his family's from Utah. This might be the last time she gets to see him."

"All right." The attendant pulled the sheet down as carefully as he had before. "But if either of you is not feeling well, let me know immediately."

"Thank you." Aleksi kept a firm hold on Julie as the woman sobbed and stared at Bob's lifeless face.

"Oh, Bobby…" she whispered, trembling like a leaf in the wind.

After a time, Julie nodded and turned away. She muttered her thanks one more time to the attendant and allowed Aleksi to drive her back to the apartment. During the slow drive, however, Aleksi kept recalling the four jagged tears in Bob Tomlin's neck, and how much they resembled her nightmares.

Nice place." Willis stopped the car in front of the high-rent condominium. "The kid must have some cash."

"He's going to Harvard, isn't he?" Jasper got out, gritting his teeth against the slap of icy wind. It was colder now than it had been at six AM. Another Arctic blast. They were entrenched in the typical New England winter schedule; an icy slap in the face every three days. He stamped his feet and stuffed his hands in his pockets.

"Most are on student loans, the way I hear it." Willis joined him on the sidewalk and they strode up to the office entrance. "Those girls' apartment wasn't much, and their furniture looked like garage sale stuff."

"Good point."

They flashed their badges to the bored young woman behind the desk and got directions to Derrick Penningly's unit. Fifth floor facing the river; number five twelve. They didn't know if he'd be home, but had checked his schedule with the registrar, and knew he didn't have classes. Willis pushed the buzzer and they got lucky.

"Yeah?" A clean-cut young man in a Princeton sweatshirt and jeans answered the door, a curious but friendly look on his face. "Can I help you?"

"We hope so, Mister Penningly." Jasper displayed his badge. "I'm Sergeant Jasper from the Cambridge Police Department, and this is

Detective Willis. We'd like to ask you a few questions, if you have the time."

"Uh...sure." He opened the door wide and waved a hand. "Come on in. What's up?"

"Nice place," Willis said as they entered the main living room. It wasn't just a river-front view, but a corner view, with a huge balcony overlooking the river and the city. The furnishings were also top notch, in a kind of macho, black and white motif that screamed money. There was a full kitchen with gleaming appliances, and what looked like two bedrooms. It didn't look very lived in for a bachelor's apartment, however. "Big, too. Just you, or do you have a roommate?"

"Just me, and it's not that big. I use the second bedroom as an office."

"Must have set you back some."

"My father pays the rent, so I really couldn't say." He folded his arms and frowned. "Last time I checked, it wasn't against the law to have money, so if there was something *else* you wanted to talk about."

"We'd just like to ask you a few questions about your relationship with Aleksi Rychenkna and Bob Tomlin." Jasper watched the kid closely; raised eyebrows and a surprised little frown. "You do know them."

"I know Aleksi, but I don't know any Bob Tomlin." He looked suddenly suspicious. "What's this about? What did she tell you?"

"You sure you don't know Bob Tomlin?" Jasper held up a hand at shoulder-height, palm down. "About so tall, brown hair, also one of Dr. Hutchinson's graduate students."

"Oh, wait! Yeah, I did meet him once, I guess, right outside Dr. Hutchinson's office. But I never really talked to him." He was still looking suspicious, but not scared or deceitful. "What did that crazy Russian tell you about me? Did she tell you what she did to my car? Twenty-eight hundred dollars damage, is what! I should have called you on her for that!"

"She did say that you two had a disagreement over some research data, and that she keyed your car. If you want to press charges, all you have to do is file a report. She also said you stole some research data from her, which is a serious crime." *But not as serious as murder*, he thought, still watching the young man's reactions. Most people displayed certain behaviors when they lied, but Derrick Penningly was showing none of them. In fact, he wasn't showing much facial expression at all.

"Is *that* what this is about? She told you I *stole* that data?" He looked suddenly angry, with clenched fists and distended veins in his neck. "She *gave* me that data. I told Dr. Hutchinson that! What I didn't tell him is that after she invited me aboard, she asked me out, and when I told her I didn't think it would be a good idea, she threatened to flunk me out of her lab class."

"The..." Willis made a show of consulting his notes, "comparative zoology class?"

"Yes, that's right. Ask anyone in class; they know what happened." He took a deep breath, suddenly calm again. "At the time, I didn't want to get into a disagreement with her, so I told her I'd think about it. After all, there was still a chance we could work together on the project. Dr. Hutchinson got some real money to back the project, thanks to me, and now she's trying to bump me out of it by telling him I stole the data. Not to mention cover her own ass for asking me aboard without checking with him first."

"Then you got into an argument and she keyed your car," Jasper reiterated, thinking, *Either this guy is a really good liar, or Aleksi Rychenkna left out a few details this morning.*

"Yeah, only it was all her. She chased me down after her class, and I told her I wasn't going to play her stupid game. I mean, I just want to get on board with a good professor and do my work, right? Then she gouged the hood of my car and threatened to rip my throat out."

"She threatened you?" Willis scratched in his pad. "Can you remember her exact words?"

"Not exactly, but it was something like I better back the fuck off, or she'd do the same to my throat." He stopped and looked at them both. "But I don't get it? What's this got to do with Bob Tomlin? Did she accuse him of stealing from her, too?"

"No, Mister Penningly." Jasper decided it was time to drop the bomb. "Bob Tomlin was murdered last night in the Oxford Parking garage."

"*Murdered?*"

Jasper watched him closely, and the astonishment on the kid's face looked genuine. "Yes, Mister Penningly, and coincidently, the injury that killed him sounds *remarkably* similar to what you just described that Aleksi Rychenkna threatened to do to you."

"Holy shit!" Penningly stood there wide-eyed. "I knew she was crazy, but I didn't think she was homicidal!"

"The coroner's report stated that it was unlikely that a woman could inflict the wounds that killed Bob Tomlin."

"Well, she inflicted some pretty serious damage in the hood of my car! Maybe you should check *that* out!"

"Actually, we'd like that very much, Mister Penningly," Jasper said. "Now would be good for us."

"Um…sure." Penningly looked surprised that they took him up on the offer. "Let me grab a coat."

When the kid was out of the room, Jasper exchanged a pointed glance with Willis. His partner just showed him the last page of his note pad. "Threatened to rip his throat out? WTF?"

Jasper nodded; this case was about to bust wide open, and it was only the first day after the murder. With a little physical evidence, they might be able to wrap this up before the weekend.

I can't believe Bob's dead." Lonnie wiped her eyes and stared at the untouched food on the table.

Terry Price, whom Aleksi had only met once, sipped his beer and shook his head while John Alvarez drew circles on the table in the condensation from his glass. Lonnie had suggested they all get together, and Aleksi had agreed that it would be a good idea, but not for the same reasons as Lonnie.

"I took Julie down to the morgue to see him." She sipped her wine just for something to do. The others looked up at her, but their stares didn't intimidate her as they once had. "Julie was dating him and wanted to see him."

"Bob was dating?" John asked, with a sudden hint of his usual sense of humor. "Like, a girl?"

"Yeah. I kind of set them up. She liked him, said he was nice, and she didn't usually get to date nice guys."

"Well, he was that." Lonnie sniffed and raised her glass. "To Bob."

They raised their glasses, and Terry added, "And to the police finding the motherfucker who killed him."

After they clinked glasses and drank, Aleksi took the opportunity to say what she'd come to say. "That's something I wanted to tell you all. I think you should all be careful. I think this might have something to do with our research, and a guy who's trying to steal it."

"Someone's trying to steal the bone bed research?" John furrowed his brow.

"Not that project; the Kamchatka specimen we found. This guy, Derrick Penningly, somehow got my data files, then told Hutch that I'd given them to him. I didn't. He also told Hutch that I asked him to come on board the project, which is *also* a lie." She took a deep breath; they were all staring at her. "He's a post-grad student in my comp zoo lab and works at the MCZ. I think he's been telling lies about me there, too, trying to make me look bad. He wants to come on as one of Hutch's students next year."

"Strange way to go about it, lying and stealing." Terry sounded skeptical.

"But there's no proof." Aleksi met their eyes one by one. "It's his word against mine."

"I don't get it? What's this got to do with Bob?"

Aleksi looked at Lonnie and laid it out. "Bob was upset with me about Derrick. *Really* upset. Yesterday, after class, I cornered Derrick and told him to back off. He called me pathetic, insisting I invited him aboard, then lied to Hutch about it to cover my ass. I lost my temper and threatened him, and…and I scratched his car."

"Jesus *Christ*, Aleksi!" Lonnie gaped at her.

"Yeah, I know. Not like me." She looked down at her wine, then back up at Lonnie. "But that's what I wanted to tell you all. I threatened Derrick with violence, then that very night Bob is killed. I think he might have done it and is trying to frame me for it. With both Bob and me out of the picture, there's nobody to handle either of the projects, and he gets to waltz right in and take over."

"Oh, come *on*, Aleksi." Terry lowered his voice. "You think he *murdered* Bob to secure a research project? That's crazy!"

"I know." Aleksi met Terry's skepticism with a level stare, remembering the danger she'd felt facing Derrick Penningly. "That's why I think he did it."

It's not a perfect match, but it's close." The forensics technician tapped a micrometer on the hood of Derrick Penningly's BMW. "Nice ride, by the way. M-3 limited edition with custom interior. Whoever owns this baby's got some serious disposable income."

"Yeah, his family's loaded." Willis grinned like a wolf. "The kid cried like a baby when we told him we'd have to impound his car."

"So, the spacing between the scratches is different than the wounds that killed Bob Tomlin?" Jasper tried to stay focused. Fatigue was coming down hard now. He'd been going non-stop for eighteen hours, and coffee had lost its effect. "That'll stand up in court?"

"Oh, absolutely!" The tech pointed at the scale color image of Bob Tomlin's torn throat, then at the scratches on the hood of the car. "Spacing's off, but like I said, it's close."

"The woman who did the hood told us she used keys. Could they have—"

"No way," the tech interrupted. "Look here. Run your fingers over those scratches. The metal was actually creased, and some was even removed. No key did that."

The two detectives looked at each other.

"I think we need to have another chat with Aleksi Rychenkna." Willis sounded ready to jump in the car and race down to her apartment again.

"Tomorrow." Jasper shook his head. "I need some sleep and a meal that wasn't deep fried. We'll call her first thing and have her come down for an interview."

"You really enjoy ruining people's mornings, don't you?" Willis turned away from the car.

"It's a hobby of mine." Jasper chuckled and followed.

"One more thing, Sergeant." The technician tapped his micrometer on the damaged hood again, and they both turned back. "There was some *force* behind this to crease the metal like that. If a woman did this..."

"Enough force to do that?" Jasper asked, pointing to the photo of Bob Tomlin's neck.

"Might have to talk to a buddy of mine from MIT to figure that out, but I'd say so."

"Talk to your buddy and get me some hard numbers. I want to know if the same person could have done both of those, and I want to know by tomorrow."

"You got it, Sergeant," the technician said with a grin.

Of course he's grinning, Jasper thought, *I just handed him twelve hours of overtime.* He shook his head and left the garage, thinking only of a cold beer, a hot meal, and a warm bed.

Julie?" Aleksi stepped around the overnight bag next to the door. There were sounds coming from the bathroom, and the door was open, so she peeked in. Julie was rifling through drawers, a handful of items already clutched in one hand. "Hey. What's up with the bag?"

"Oh, hey." Julie gave her a weak smile. She looked terrible. "I'm going home for the weekend. I need to get out of here, or I'll go crazy. And now I can't find my damn barrette!"

"You okay, Julie?"

"No!" Julie slammed a drawer and brushed past her. "No, I'm *not* okay. They guy I was supposed to have a *date* with tonight is lying on a metal slab in the morgue with his throat torn out! I am *so* not okay!" She opened the bag, dumped the items in, and zipped it closed. "I'm going home to try to forget this ever happened."

"I'm sorry, Julie," she said. "If I hadn't set you two up…"

"I know." Julie wiped her nose and sniffed, then picked up her bag. "You know, we never even slept together? So why am I feeling like this? We dated twice and he never even asked me to sleep with him. Tonight was going to be it. I had it all planned."

"Oh, Julie…"

"Yeah, I know. You're sorry." She shouldered her bag and opened the door. "So am I."

The door didn't exactly slam, but Aleksi felt as if she'd just been blamed for everything; Bob's death, Julie's sorrow, the whole thing.

"Maybe it *is* my fault." She went to the kitchen to look for something to eat. In the freezer, the bottle of Stoly sat there next to a package of pork chops. "Perfect."

The meat went into the microwave for thawing, and the vodka went into a glass with a single ice cube.

You killed me, Aleksi?" Bob Tomlin stands beside her bed, a disapproving scowl above the gashes that intersect his throat. "You told him you'd rip his throat out, and this is what happened to me. You did it!"

"I didn't!" She wonders why Bob is in her bedroom. He's dead, in the morgue. "It wasn't me, Bob! I swear!"

"Who then?" He leans forward, the flaps of torn flesh dangling. "Look at your hands!"

She pulls her hands from under the blankets. They are soaked with blood, and her nails are long again, longer than she's ever seen them. There are bits of flesh dangling from them.

"No!" She scrambles back away from him, and falls out of the bed.

Aleksi hit the floor with a thump, startled awake, still half in the dream. Frantic, she fumbled for the light, though the room seemed to glow with the scant light through the drapes. The light flicked on, and there was no blood. Her hands were clean, the dream vivid only in her mind.

She gulped a deep breath and leaned against her bed. The clock read just after three in the morning.

"Goddamn it!" She fought with her twisted pajamas. The fabric tore, and she gaped at her nails; they were indeed long, yellowish in the stark light. She remembered cutting them short only the day before. "What the...?"

Aleksi lurched to her feet, the dream still lurking behind her eyelids. She went to the bathroom and flipped on the light, looking closely at her nails. They were long, all right. She took the clippers in the medicine cabinet and struggled to cut them short, but it was as if the clippers weren't working right. She managed to cut one, then gave up, throwing the useless things back in the cabinet and slamming it closed. In the kitchen, she pulled a pair of heavy shears from the knife block and snipped her nails into the trash, cutting them down to the quick.

Back in the bathroom, she looked closely at her hands. Her nails were definitely yellowed, and she could feel little ridges on them. She rooted through Julie's side of the bathroom and found some not-too-bright nail polish.

25

Not knowing what else to do, Aleksi went to work early on Friday morning. Hutch had said that everything was on hold, but surely that didn't mean she couldn't continue to work on the bone bed samples. Bob's project. Every time she looked at the fossilized bones, she thought of him, of the cold face in the morgue, of the horrible gashes in his neck, of her dream...

You killed me, Aleksi...

She couldn't make herself work on his project, so she did some searches in Genbank with the sequences that Bob had sent her, and started working up a database of relatedness. There was no doubt that one of the sequences was human. They didn't have enough of the genome to get a good fix on who this particular human was, but considering the isotope dating information and the location of the find, it was a safe bet that Asian ancestry was predominant.

The other sequence was a mystery.

She did searches on every one of the sequences they had and got zero matches in Genbank. The closest relatedness she could get was human, and that was only a ninety percent match. Considering a chimpanzee has a ninety eight percent match to human, that wasn't very close. The only thing she could think was that the human had a primate with him, something that didn't have a sequence in Genbank. That was interesting, but hardly dissertation worthy.

She was getting frustrated, and so was almost relieved when her phone rang. She snatched it from her bag, hoping that Hutch was calling to set up a meeting, but the number was not in the phone's memory. *Maybe he's calling from another phone,* she thought, though it was only eight thirty in the morning, and he wasn't due in until nine.

She pushed Talk. "Hello?"

"Good morning, Miss Rychenkna. This is Sergeant Jasper."

"Hello, Sergeant." She refused to say that it was a good morning. What the hell was good about it? Then a thought came to her. "Did you talk to Derrick Penningly?"

"As a matter of fact, we did, and that's part of why I'm calling you. There's quite a discrepancy between what he said, and what you told us."

"That doesn't surprise me at all, Sergeant. Derrick's a liar."

"Yes, well he pretty much said the same about you, Miss Rychenkna. So, what I'd like to do is have you come down to the station for an interview, a formal statement that we can put down for the record, just so we can try to figure out the details of the case, you understand."

Why could cops never speak plainly? "I understand perfectly. You know one of us is lying, and you need to figure out which one, because the one who's lying is a suspect for Bob's murder."

"Well, not exactly, but we do need to hash out some of these details."

"What time would you like me to come in, and where do I go?"

"This morning would be great. The Healy Building, on Sixth Street. How soon can you get here?" He sounded way too eager for Aleksi's liking.

"Well, I don't have a car, and I'd really rather not pay for a cab…"

"I can send a car. Where can we pick you up?"

"Um…how about Oxford Street, in front of the MCZ."

"I'll have a car there in five minutes. Just look for the black and white car with 'Police' on the side in big letters."

Yep, way too eager. "I'll be waiting." She hung up, shut down her computer, stuffed it in her bag, grabbed her coat, and headed out into the chilly morning.

<hr>

Hutch arrived in his office right at nine in the morning in no mood to tackle the deluge of work that had piled up in his absence. Email, he had taken care of while he was in Washington, but there were phone messages, snail mail, and the whole Bob Tomlin situation to deal with. That included priority correspondence with the chairman, the dean, the faculty council, and Bob's parents. The last one was the hardest, by far. He also had a message from the Cambridge Police, asking him to contact a Sergeant Jasper. He called the number and got voice mail, left a message, his cell number, and his lecture schedule.

He was on the phone to Larry Vandyke, trying to figure out more details and formulate a plan for how to handle the fallout from the murder, looking at his watch and deciding if he had time for an early lunch before his lecture, when an email from Persephone popped up.

He opened it and read, listening to Larry rant with the other half of his brain.

"Read about Bob Tomlin in the paper. I'm sorry, Hutch. He was nice, and I made fun of him at dinner. I feel like shit about that now. Call me. I'd like to see you. Life is too short."

Isn't that the damn truth.

He finished his call with Larry, shut down his computer, and left his office.

T*his is delightful*, Aleksi thought as the uniformed officer ushered her into the interview room. The light was harsh and fluorescent, the décor was four featureless pale green walls, four chairs, and one table, all metal.

"Please have a seat, Miss." The officer pointed to one of the chairs on the far side of the table. "Can I get you anything? Coffee, water, a tonic?" She could have cut his Boston accent with a knife.

"Sure. Coffee would be great." She took the seat. It wasn't very comfortable.

"Cream and sugar?"

"Just milk, please. Thanks."

She sat and tapped her foot for five minutes until the officer returned with a small Styrofoam cup.

"Do you know how long Sergeant Jasper's going to be?"

"He got held up with another matter, Miss. He'll be along in a bit."

"Thanks for the coffee." He nodded and left and she took a sip, surprised to discover that it wasn't bad. Unable to simply sit and do nothing, she took her laptop out of her bag and started working on her genetic database. She started an analysis of the two different sequences, looking at sequence differences versus the proteins they would code for. These segments of DNA were junk, and shouldn't code for anything. She didn't know if she'd find anything, but it was something to do. When the door finally opened, she glanced at the time on the computer screen, it was after nine.

"Sorry to keep you waiting, Miss Rychenkna." Jasper came in with a thick folder, his own Styrofoam cup, and an apologetic smile. "We got held up."

"Held up as in delayed, not mugged." Detective Willis grinned as he followed his partner in. "That would have been *wicked* embarrassing."

"No problem." Aleksi shut her computer down, unimpressed with the attempted humor. "I had work I could do."

"Work. You mean your research?" Jasper sat and arranged his folder and coffee. "The research you were working on with Bob Tomlin?"

"Yes. Without Bob on the project, I'm in real trouble."

"How so?"

"Bob was very good at molecular biology and genetics. He was handling the analysis of the samples. Without him, I'll have to do it myself or find someone else to help me. I need to have my doctoral dissertation proposal in and approved by the end of this semester, or I'm out of the program."

"So, whoever killed him might have been trying to ruin your chances to get your proposal in on time?" Willis' eyebrows arched.

"I suppose."

"Academic competition usually isn't a motive for murder, but that could be the case," Jasper said. Aleksi was beginning to think their questions were carefully choreographed. "Any idea who might have a motive to run you out of the program?"

"Yes. Derrick Penningly." She stared at him without blinking, suppressing the surge of adrenalin racing through her veins, the urge to lash out. "Without me or Bob, he would be primed to step into both projects and be Dr. Hutchinson's star student."

"Both projects?" Willis looked almost comically confused. "What other project? I thought you were only sharing one."

She described the projects, the discovery of the mystery sample, the agreement with the MCZ to work it up, and the funding they'd gotten. "So, Dr. Hutchinson agreed that I would use the Kamchatka sample for my dissertation, and Bob would help with the genetics, then he would get the bone bed project, and I would help him with working up the samples and doing the morphology. We both win. We were really excited about it, and we were getting some interesting data. Then Bob was killed."

"So, what happens now?" Jasper asked.

"I don't know. It's not my call."

"Whose call is it?"

"Dr. Hutchinson's."

"What about the funding he just got for this project?"

"It was from a private source."

"Private?" The two men looked at one another. "Do you know this private source?"

"Yes, Dr. Hutchinson's ex-wife, Persephone Terris." She didn't really see how this was pertinent, but it was no secret. "She's a fan of cryptozo-ology, and he thought she might be interested. We all went to dinner with her, Hutch asked her to donate, and she agreed."

"His ex-wife?" The two cops shared another glance. "How much did she donate?"

"Twenty thousand dollars."

"Holy—" Detective Willis blinked and laughed. "Sorry, but twenty grand's a lot."

"Not to her. She's got money." Aleksi shrugged. "Does it really matter?"

"It might. We don't know until we ask." Jasper consulted his file. "And was Derrick Penningly there, at this dinner?"

"No. Why?"

"Because he told us that he was the one who got funding for the project, from a Congressman Twain."

"He *what*?" Aleksi felt a familiar flush of rage and fought it down.

"He said he got the funding for the Kamchatka project in a meeting with Congressman Twain and Dr. Hutchinson. He never mentioned Dr. Hutchinson's ex-wife."

"That was *after* the dinner with Persephone. Her donation was to do the preliminary work. Congressman Twain offered to fund the project. Derrick was there but he didn't *get* the funding. That was when he lied to Dr. Hutchinson and told him that I'd given him the data." Aleksi glared at the two men, who simply stared back. "Next Derrick will be telling you he discovered the sample in the first place."

"He didn't say that, Miss Rychenkna, but he did confirm that you scratched his car and threatened him with violence."

"I told you that."

"Yes, you did, and we had a look at the car." He produced a large color print of a picture of the scratches she'd put in Derricks car. "Look familiar?"

She looked at the picture and cringed. There were four parallel gouges in the paint, and the metal of the hood was creased. "I don't remember doing that much damage. I had my keys in my hand and scratched the hood."

"Do you have those keys?

"Sure." She produced the keys, half a dozen of which were the heavy industrial type issued to fit sturdy lab doors.

"Would you mind if we borrowed them for a few minutes, just so our lab guys can look for paint residue on them?"

"I need them," she said, reluctant to hand them over, not only because she needed them, but because she knew they would find no paint residue on the keys.

"It'll only take a half hour or so. We'll bring them right back."

"Okay." She handed the keys over, and Willis left the room with them.

"Now, about the data that you say Derrick Penningly stole from you. What exactly did that consist of?"

"I don't know, *exactly*, but the data files on the sample, the schematics, the CT scans, and the translated journal; Hutch mentioned those."

"Hutch. You mean Dr. Hutchinson? You call him Hutch?"

"Oh, yeah. That's his official nickname among his students. If you think I'm lying about that, please talk to Dr. Hutchinson."

"We intend to, Miss Rychenkna. Now, are those data files on your computer?" He pointed to her bag. "That computer?"

"Yes, but I'm not going to let you take my computer, Sergeant." Her life was on that computer, and although the data was backed up, she would not hand it over willingly. "Not without a warrant from a judge. Speaking of which, shouldn't you have asked me if I wanted a lawyer?"

"No, Miss Rychenkna; that's only if we arrest you, which we're not going to do." He smiled thinly. "At least not today. But about the computer. If someone hacked it, there may be some trace, some evidence that we can use. Would you mind if I called one of our IT guys in here to have a look at it just to see what he can find? We might be able to confirm if Derrick Penningly *did* steal your data, and that would help you."

"Okay." She pulled the computer out of her bag while Jasper made a call on his cell.

"Johnny? Hi, this is Jasper. You busy? Good. I need your help in interview two. Thanks."

In less than a minute a knock sounded at the door and a young man walked in. He looked barely old enough to be out of high school, let alone college. He was dressed in loose jeans and a tee shirt advertising a heavy metal band named 'Tool'. He had tattoos on his arms, and big disc ear piercings.

"Hey, Johnny. This is Aleksi Rychenkna. She thinks her computer's been hacked, and I'd like you to have a look at it."

"Sure! Hi." He sat down and squinted at her laptop. "Hacked how?"

"I have no idea," she said. "Just don't delete anything, okay?"

"No problem." He hit the on button and arched an eyebrow as it booted up. "No password? This isn't a school computer, then."

"No, it's mine, and I've never used a password."

"You should." His fingers started dancing over the keys and mouse pad so fast that Aleksi couldn't follow. "These files?" he asked, pointing to two folders.

"Well, that's where most of my data is, but..." she looked at him. "How'd you know?"

"We asked Derrick Penningly," Jasper said without apology. "He showed us the files he said you gave him."

"Yep, and he took them at exactly ten twenty-six PM, two weeks ago, Friday." Johnny made a sign with his fingers that she had no idea the meaning of. "That's when his stick drive accessed your computer for the first time, and that was the last time most of these files were accessed."

"So, any idea where you were at that time two weeks ago Friday?"

She thought back. "Yes, I was out with Dr. Hutchinson, Dr. Vandyke, and Congressman Twain."

"And where was your computer while you were out?"

"In my lab." Her eyes widened. "He must have gotten in somehow and took the files. That bastard!"

"Relax, Miss Rychenkna. That just confirms that he stole your data, and frankly it's not my problem. It's a matter for the university, but we'll be happy to help you confirm the truth. Johnny, can you save that and log it as evidence?"

"Sure!" The kid grinned, produced a stick drive from his pocket and popped it into a USB port. His fingers danced again. "Done!" He pulled the jump drive and grinned. "Thanks! Oh, and put a password on your computer. If you had, he wouldn't have been able to do jack."

"Thanks, Johnny," Jasper said in dismissal. The kid left, and, as if it was choreographed, Detective Willis walked in with Aleksi's keys. He handed them over and took a seat.

"So? Did you find your paint residue?"

"Oh, we won't have results from the lab for days." Jasper waved a hand dismissively. "Sorry about not telling you about the computer files, but we had to find out if you were telling us the truth. And it seems you were."

"Why, Sergeant?"

"Because, if you told the truth about that, it's less likely that you're lying about all the rest of it." He gave her a smile that was meant to make her feel like he was on her side. It didn't. "Now, tell me about the relationship between Bob Tomlin and your roommate."

<hr>

She might be telling the truth about Penningly stealing those files, but she lied about the keys." Willis and Jasper watched Aleksi Rychenkna descend the icy steps to the waiting squad car. "No paint, and the forensics guys said no way *those* keys made the scratches in Penningly's car."

"I didn't think so, and it's damn sure they didn't slash open Bob Tomlin's throat, either." Jasper shivered and waved as she got into the car and it rolled away. "Did Johnny get everything?"

"All her emails for the last month," Willis confirmed. "That kid scares me sometimes."

"He scares me *all* the time." He turned and went back inside the building.

"We're in deep shit if anyone finds out he did that without a warrant," Willis said in a stage whisper.

"Aleksi Rychenkna said we could look for evidence on her computer, that's on the recording."

"Did I mention that *you* scare me, too?"

"Good." Jasper gave him a wry smile. "I think we should talk to the good Dr. Hutchinson next."

"Lunch first?" Willis asked. "He has a lecture in a half hour."

"Sure. Your call, but nothing too greasy. My colon's feeling like Hoover Dam."

"Oh, like I *really* needed to know that!"

A leksi?"

She jerked up from her computer. Hutch stood at the door to the lab.

"You okay?" He stepped in and let the door close behind him. He looked like he'd just pulled an all-nighter.

There were two technicians working in the lab, so she couldn't say what she wanted to say, which was something like, "Fuck no, I 'm not okay! Bob is dead, my dissertation is circling the toilet bowl, and now the cops think I'm a murderer!"

Instead, she said, "Not really."

He walked over, hands in his coat pockets, and she could see that he'd just been outside. His lips were pale and he was flushed. "What are you working on?"

"Bob's genetic data. I was looking at the sequences. He told you the others were human, didn't he?"

"Yeah." He took a breath. "Aleksi, we really need to stop on this for now. The police—"

"I found a stop codon." She turned the screen toward him.

"What? Where?" He leaned in to look, and she caught a whiff of that distinctive 'Hutch' scent, soap, aftershave and a subtle undercurrent of *him*.

"In the mystery segment of DNA. One of the disparate regions. The disparity from the nonsense code was complete for about fifty bases, then there's a stop codon. The difference in the code after that point is minimal." She pointed at the two sequences she'd put side by side and the altered portion that coded for the end of an expressed gene; a gene that shouldn't be there.

"What does it code for?" She could hear the insatiable curiosity, a scientist's curiosity, in his voice.

She breathed in, taking his scent in deep, and unconsciously licked her lips. "No idea. The rest of the gene is before the primer portion of the sequence. We could run a reverse primer and get the rest of it easily enough."

He looked at the sequence, then at her. "A retroviral insertion? A protein switch?"

"Could be anything, but we won't know if we don't do the work."

"Look, Aleksi." He straightened from his stoop, his scent fading and her head clearing. "We need to talk."

"We do." She shut her computer down and stuffed it in her bag. "Where do you want to talk?" She reached for her coat.

"Hungry?" he asked without a hint of humor.

"Starving," she admitted, equally sober. "But not for vegetarian."

"Sushi okay? I know a place, but it's across the river."

"Sure."

She followed him out of the lab without another word, through the labyrinth of interconnected buildings, past his office, and to the Oxford Parking structure. They found his car and it hummed to life, taking them out of the building where Bob Tomlin was murdered. They drove across the Charles River and into the city in silence.

"This is off the beaten track," she said as they parked in front of a nondescript storefront displaying only Asian characters on the windows and door. All the glass was painted red, and the characters were in gaudy golden script highlighted in black.

"And not ever likely to make the Fromer's Guide." He opened the door for her. "But it's the best sushi in Boston."

The place was deserted, but it was early, barely four PM, between the lunch and dinner rushes. They were seated by a smiling woman in a beautiful form-fitting white dress that covered her from neck to wrists to toes. It was embroidered with silver thread, twisting scaled shapes intertwining in a confusion of serpentine forms. Hutch asked for a booth, and the red silk tablecloth made a swish sound against their denim pants as they took their seats. The hostess gave them menus and asked if they wanted drinks.

"Water for me," he said.

"Tea please."

When she had gone, he said, "The police called me in for questioning today."

"Me too. They asked about me, didn't they? I think I'm a suspect." She more than thought it. She'd heard Jasper and Willis talking about her as she boarded the police car. They knew she'd lied about the keys making the gouges in Derrick's car.

"Yeah, and Derrick. They asked questions about both of you." He didn't even look at his menu.

"And what did you tell them?" She looked over the sushi menu, circling half a dozen selections of sashimi without rice.

"I told them I'd only known you for a little over a month, but that you were a brilliant young scientist whom I felt privileged to work with." He fixed her with his eyes. "And that's the truth."

"Thanks," she said, not blushing as much as she would have when they first met, but still feeling a rush of heat to her face. "And about Derrick?"

"I told them I'd met him three times, and that he seemed smart, if somewhat aggressive."

"Did they tell you they found proof on my computer that he stole my data?"

His eyes widened. "No. No they didn't. Really?"

"Yep. The night we went out with Congressman Twain, I left my computer in the lab. He got in somehow and downloaded all my research data on the Kamchatka specimen. They found some kind of record on my computer that verified that the files had been downloaded to his jump drive at ten twenty-six that night, and I *know* we were already out of the lab by then."

He looked pensive. "It was close to that time, I think. He must have been waiting until we left and went right in. Goddamn it! The balls!"

The hostess, who seemed to be working as a waitress, too, returned and took their orders, then left, her ivory dress glowing in the low light, the sinuous shapes dancing on her hips. For some reason, Aleksi couldn't keep her eyes off that dress. When the woman was gone, she turned back to their conversation.

"Look, Hutch, I have to ask. Did you tell them, the police, about the other things I told you? The dreams and hallucinations I've been having?"

"They didn't ask about that." He sipped his water and looked at the table.

"And you didn't offer." Her heart pounded with a flicker of hope. Maybe, just maybe, he believed in her. "Thanks."

"Aleksi, do you think that maybe..." He stopped and took a drink of water. "You're *different*, more different than you think you are. You used to be so shy you couldn't meet my eyes, and now I'm the one who has to look away. You've *changed*, and it worries me. When they were questioning me, I remembered what you said about the confrontation with Doug at the gym. That you felt like tearing his arm off, and knew you *could*."

"You're asking if I think I could have killed Bob?" She stared at him, and he looked up from his water. She could see, could *smell* his fear, but there was trust there too. "No, Hutch. Not in a million years. I think Derrick did it to get both me and Bob out of his way."

"But *murder*, Aleksi?" He shook his head. "Seems a little far to go to secure a graduate research project."

"He thinks he can't be touched." She knew she was right, feeling it in her gut. "He's privileged, always had whatever he wanted, and got it with no repercussions. He thinks he can get away with anything."

"Well he's not going to get away with stealing your data, Aleksi, I can guarantee that!" There was steel in his tone now, and he pulled out his phone. "He's out of the program, and the school, as of now."

"What are you doing?"

"I'm emailing Derrick and copying Dr. Vandyke and the faculty council." He stopped and fixed her with a hard stare. "You're *sure* the police found hard evidence that he took your files."

"That's what they said. They looked at his stick drive and found a record on my computer that the files had been transferred to that drive at ten twenty-six two weeks ago Friday. We were at dinner by then, or at least out of the MCZ."

"That's enough for me." He began tapping out an email.

During the process, the waitress brought their food; a wooden plate of fresh fish for her, and a huge platter of vegetable tempura for him. By the time he was finished with the email, she was halfway through her plate.

"There. It's done." He lifted his water glass and she lifted hers. "He's out."

They clinked glasses and she sipped, smiling for the first time in two days. "Thanks, Hutch. For trusting me, I mean. It means a lot to me."

"Don't thank me, Aleksi. Trust is something you *earn*, and you've earned mine." He dug into his meal. "So, this sequence you found. What do you think it means?"

They talked about research through the rest of the meal, and Hutch encouraged her to order another plate of sushi. He tried a piece of Ahi that she thought was particularly good. He made a face, and she laughed. It felt good.

The drive back to Cambridge was quiet until they neared Harvard Square. It was Friday night, and late enough that the icy streets were crowded with pedestrians. Aleksi had been thinking hard all the way back, and finally formed those thoughts into words as they turned onto Oxford Street.

"Hutch, I've got a favor to ask, and I don't know how to ask it."

"About your proposal?" He glanced at her, and she saw the trust there. She felt another flutter of hope in her stomach.

"No. About me." She looked out the car window as he pulled over in front of the MCZ. The building was so familiar; more of a home than anyplace else she'd known. It struck her how odd that was, how odd *she* was. Twenty-two years old, and she'd spent most of her life in schools and museums, studying, learning and researching things that had been dead for millennia. There was so much she hadn't done, so much living she hadn't experienced. She turned back to him and took a deep breath of that clean, spicy, Hutch scent. "Julie went home for the weekend, and the police think I killed Bob. I need an alibi, someone to be with, to confirm my whereabouts. If something else happens..." She bit her lip.

"Aleksi, I don't—"

"I just need someone to watch over me, Hutch. Please." He looked reluctant. "Julie'll be back Sunday evening, so it'd just be for two nights. I'll sleep on your couch, or you can sleep on mine, if you don't mind a noisy iguana shaking his cage in the middle of the night."

"Iguana?" He blinked. "You have an iguana?"

"Iggy." She smiled. "Julie calls him my boyfriend. Would you like to meet him?"

"Sure."

He put the car in gear and they hummed down the icy streets to her apartment.

Aleksi opened the door and ushered him in. At first glance he thought, *Two people live here?* The place was small, with a lived-in look. He remembered his own apartments in Seattle during college and smiled to himself. This was palatial compared to some of them.

"Come on in." She closed the door and showed him around, kitchen, bedrooms, bathroom and finally the living room. "And this is Iggy." To his surprise, she opened the cage next to the couch and the big green iguana hopped into her arms. "Isn't he a cutie?"

"Never considered lizards cute before, but yes." Hutch and the lizard eyed one another.

"He likes to be scratched under the chin." She came closer.

"All right." He did, and Iggy blinked and lashed his tail. "I don't think he likes me."

"He's just jealous. Here, take him. I've got to clean his cage and get him something to eat. If I let him loose, he'll be impossible to catch."

"Um…I've never—"

"It's okay. He won't bite." She handed the lizard over, and he cradled it in his arms, the long claws grasping his coat sleeve for purchase. "See?"

Aleksi made short work of wadding up the dirty newspaper in the bottom of the iguana's cage and disposing of the uneaten food, then laid down new paper and fixed some fruit and veggies in the kitchen. While she worked, Hutch wandered around the living room looking at the books, pictures, and knick-knacks, continuing a careful scratch under the lizard's chin. Iggy seemed content to tolerate this abuse from a stranger, at least for a while.

"Is this your roommate?" He pointed to a picture of a perky blonde with a guy.

"Yeah, that's Julie. Something, isn't she?"

"*She* was dating Bob?"

"Yeah, for all of a week."

"Way to go, Bob," he mumbled, inspecting another picture of her in a bathing suit with several other people on a beach. He tried to picture Bob with her and failed.

"She attracts guys like flies, and most of them have just about as much personality." Aleksi finally relieved him of Iggy. "Bob was the first really nice guy she'd dated in a long time. He was good for her. She's not handling it very well."

He didn't know what to say to that, so he stayed mute.

"So, the couch is here, and I can vouch for its sleepability. I'd let you have Julie's bed, but when there's a man in it she likes to be there, too. She'd never forgive me." She put Iggy back in his cage and brushed her hands on her sweatshirt. "So, will you be my watchdog for a weekend?"

"No offense, Aleksi, but..." Her smile fell, her face transforming from hopeful to downcast in the blink of an eye. He couldn't do it; after what she'd been through, he couldn't turn her down. "I think my place might be a little more comfortable."

Her face lit up like a tree on Christmas eve. "Great! Thanks! Let me just grab a few things."

She ran to her room, then the bathroom, and returned with a handful of clothes and toiletries which she stuffed into her bag. She picked it up and slung it over her shoulder. "Ready!"

"You're bringing your computer?"

"Absolutely! I've got to have *something* to do!" She opened the door and switched off the light. "Besides; the evidence to expel Derrick Penningly is on this computer. It's not leaving my side until he's gone."

They chatted about work on the way to his place, but she fell silent on the ride up the elevator. When he opened his door and ushered her in, that silence broke.

"This is *amazing*." Aleksi stared around the living room in shock, at the lavish furnishings, the view from the dining room window of the Charles River and Boston, and through the living room to the back balcony and Cambridge. "It's *beautiful!*"

"I can't take credit for the décor." He tossed his keys into the bowl on the bookcase beside the door and hung his coat up. "Persephone might be a spoiled brat, but she always had great taste, and was never afraid to spend money on nice things."

"And she *gave* you this?" She drifted around the living room, staring at the leather couches and a low mahogany table, the shelves of books and curios. "That was generous of her."

"Well, I pay the maintenance fee, but yes, it was."

She looked around again, turned to him, and lifted her bag. "Um, where do you want me?"

His brain stumbled on the question for half a second. "Oh! The spare bedroom's been an office for some time, but there's a futon in there. That'll give you more privacy than the couch." He showed her into the room and waved an arm. "The desk is a mess, but the rest is all yours."

"Thanks." She put her bag down and took off her coat.

"Let me grab some sheets and blankets from the linin closet."

When he came back, arms full of bedding, she had doffed her boots and hoodie and was brushing out her hair. She whipped it back into a scrunchie, and kicked her boots toward the closet.

"Here, you go." He dumped the pile in the office chair. They folded the futon down and quickly made the bed. "You want the rest of the tour?"

"Sure!"

He showed her the bathrooms, a small one off the main room, and a huge one that opened both into the living area and the master bedroom. She laughed at the big glassed-in shower, joking that it was big enough for a rugby team. In the kitchen he told her to feel free, opening the fridge and apologizing for the sparse shelves.

"I never really use the dining room." He waved a hand at the elegant dining room table with high backed chairs, and a corner china cabinet. "There's beer in the fridge, or wine in the chiller if you feel like it." He led her back out to the living room. "The TV remote's on the coffee table, and there's Wi-Fi if you want to work online. The password is crazy eco yoga doc five zero five zero, no caps or spaces."

"Fifty-fifty?"

"Just a little self-reminder. Fifty-fifty, work versus life." He shrugged. "All work no play, you know."

"I think my percentages would be closer to ninety-ten." She went to the glass doors and looked out on the dark wintery scene. He could see her reflection in the glass. "Work always seemed safer to me. Less chance of letting anyone getting close enough to hurt me."

"Is that why you set Bob up with Julie?" he asked. "I think he had a thing for you, you know."

"Bob?" She turned around and gave him a little half smile. "Yeah, I… kinda got that. I thought that with us working together it wouldn't be a good idea. They seemed right together. She needed someone nice, and he needed someone beautiful and alive; someone to make him feel good about himself." She looked down. "Someone not me."

"Aleksi, that's not fair."

"Fair?" She barked a laugh, and he heard the pain in it. "Life's not fair, Hutch. You know that." She turned back to the window. "You work and you try to make a life that you can live with, but there's always someone there to kick you in the stomach."

She fell silent and he didn't know what to say. Then he did. "Someone like Derrick Penningly."

"Exactly. There's always someone who will ruin you just because they can." She wiped her eyes and shook her head. "I'm sorry. I'm feeling sorry for myself. Julie hates me, my dissertation's in the toilet, the police think I'm a murderer, and I miss Bob."

"Aleksi, you remember the night you asked me up to your apartment?"

"Yeah." She shook her head and looked down. "Yeah I remember. You were right. We'd both had too much to drink, and it was a bad idea."

"I'm *sorry* that it was a bad idea, Aleksi." She looked back up to meet his eyes in the window. "It would have created a scandal, but don't think that because I said no, that I don't think you're beautiful and alive and brilliant."

She turned around, wiping away tears, her eyes wide. She looked scared. "But...you..."

"Said no." He nodded. "Because it's *still* a bad idea. I'm your advisor. I can't."

"You were right about me, Hutch. I've changed." She stepped up to him, starring up into his eyes, her pupils large, irises flecked with gold that he didn't remember seeing before. "I dream about you every night. I come alive when I catch a whiff of your aftershave. I *know* it's a bad idea for us to get involved, but I can't stop thinking about you."

"Aleksi. Please. We can't. There'll be nine shades of hell to pay."

"I'll pay it. You're worth it." She reached up to brush her fingertips along his neck. "You're the first person in this *world* who has ever made me feel good about being me."

"Aleksi..." He couldn't say it. Not again. *Cold bed, cold apartment, cold floor...* Her touch sent shivers through his entire body.

"Oh my God." Her hand dropped away suddenly, and she stepped back, fear returning to her face. "Your career. I can't let you risk it. Not for me." She turned away again. "I'm sorry. I'm being stupid and selfish."

"Aleksi." He put his hands on her shoulders. "*Wait.* Please."

"Hutch, don't make it harder." She trembled under his hands.

"I want to make it *easier*, Aleksi."

She looked back then, tears streaking her cheeks. "What?"

"You said you'd pay it. So will I." He turned her around and cradled her face in his hands, wiping her tears away with his thumbs. "*You're* worth it."

She stared at him. "But your career..."

"Aleksi, you're here, and you're going to spend the night. Who's going to believe that were *not* involved?" He smiled down into her face, and saw his eyes reflected in hers. "If there's hell to pay, we'll pay it."

She blinked at him. "I can't believe you're saying this to me." She sounded terrified.

"Believe it, Aleksi." He wiped more tears away. "It's real."

She made a sound, half laugh, half sob, all joy. Their first kiss was a little salty, and way more than he had bargained for.

***

F inally!" Willis threw his coat in the general direction of his chair and fluttered an envelope at his partner. "Judges will be judges. Took *hours* to get Haverty to sign the damn search warrants! He wanted to read the whole freakin' case file. I think it was the pics that finally decided him. Danger to the public, and all." He went to the coffee machine and poured himself a cup.

"Well, I don't know if I want to go through this tonight. It's already past six, it's Friday, and it's wicked cold out." Jasper looked at his watch and sighed. He'd hoped to wrap this up by the weekend, but that wasn't going to happen.

"What, you got a date?" Willis bolted half the cup of coffee and sank into his chair.

"It *has* been known to happen." He didn't, other than with a cold beer, his TV, and a frozen dinner, but that wasn't his partner's business. "Just because you're happily married, doesn't mean the rest of us don't have social lives."

"I'm happily married because my husband's a cop and understands cop hours, cop tempers, and cop stupidity." He finished his coffee and put his cup on his desk. "But now that you mention it, neither of these two is a flight risk, and I do owe Charles dinner and a movie."

"Then let's do this in the morning." Jasper pushed himself up from his chair and stretched. "We're more likely to get them both at home anyway. Even Harvard students have social lives, from what I understand."

"Who told you that?" Willis grabbed his coat and grinned.

"That professor guy, Hutchinson. Seems he's pretty strict about keeping his life separate from work."

"Wish I could." Willis laughed. "All I ever get at home is 'this perp,' and 'that perp,' and stories about handcuffs."

"That's what you get for marrying a vice cop."

Willis laughed. "Tomorrow then. Eight okay?"

"Let's start at seven. Element of surprise, you know."

"Okay." Willis grabbed his coat and headed for the door with a wave. "If there's one thing I love, its surprises."

Persephone *was right*, Aleksi thought, as she lay in Hutch's arms, listening to his breathing slow and deepen into sleep. *I did need this, and he* is *very good.*

Thinking back on the last hours, their tumultuous fumbling on the couch, then the floor, discovering things she'd never even dreamt, then a giggling groping shower, and finally a slow, sensitive, rocking experience in his bed that she thought would be the end of her—that if she died that moment, her life would end perfect—she realized that Persephone wasn't right about the second part. Hutch wasn't very good, he was magnificent. Not that she had any great experience with men. She'd had exactly two lovers before tonight, and neither of those had lasted more than two weeks. But Hutch was patient and gentle, strong and thoughtful, and he knew more about pleasuring a woman than any man had a right to.

Lying there, she was happier than she had ever been, but as with all of her happiness, it was tainted. Bob was dead, Julie was torn apart inside, Hutch was risking his career, and Aleksi was happy. It wasn't fair.

Life isn't fair.

Afraid of the dreams sleep would bring, she slipped out of his slack embrace and eased silently out of his bedroom. The sky had cleared, and moonlight streamed down on the crystalline cold scenery. She stood at the window, gazing out at the view in awe. Trees glowed white, covered with icy crystals, each tiny branch distinct. A few cars drove slowly down Memorial Drive, wary of icy streets. She could hear their tires crunching, see the puffs of steamy exhaust and the careful grip of cold hands on steering wheels. An intrepid couple walked along the foot path, arm in arm, their strides synchronous, talking about school, work, children...

I'm so changed, she thought, pressing a hand against the cool glass, feeling the night on the other side. Her hand shimmered with warmth, with life. She felt like she could sense her own blood racing through her veins.

She heard him wake, his first indrawn breath, then a sleepy, "Aleksi?"

"Out here," she said, reluctant to leave the view, the night, the beauty.

"Are you okay?" he asked, and she looked back to see him fumbling with a robe.

"Wonderful." She turned back to look into the crystalline night.

"You look amazing in the moonlight." He sidled up behind her and wrapped her in his robe, his hands cool on her skin. "You're so *warm*."

"Mmmm." She leaned into his embrace, clutching his arms around her, inhaling him. She felt safe. She felt loved. "Thank you, Hutch. For everything."

"My pleasure." He nibbled her neck, sending shivers down her spine.

She felt him stir and reached back under his robe. "Oh, my! Look what *I've* found!" She turned in his arms to fondle him more purposefully, nibbling at his collarbone and neck, feeling the faint stubble beneath her lips, tasting him.

He gave a little moan. "You're going to be the death of me, woman."

The statement, though she knew it was in jest, stopped her cold. Her dreams came crashing in, memories of his flayed flesh, blood on her lips. She pulled back just far enough to look him in the eyes.

"Never." She kissed him hard, pulling him to her and whispering in his ear. "Never say that!"

They made love once more that night. A very slow, tender, and in the end desperate coupling that left them both exhausted. She lay in his arms again, listening to his heartbeat, and let sleep take her. Her last waking thought was, *Please, no dreams tonight*.

But of course, there were.

2 7

She senses him. He is near. She can smell him, hear his heartbeat, feel his pulse in her chest.

> *Prey...*

A memory invades her, flesh against flesh, penetrating warmth, fullness... ecstasy. But she is beyond that. Hunger stirs within her, banishing the memory.

She catches a glimpse of him, pale skin, lithe muscles playing underneath, and her mouth begins to water. Flesh, muscle, sinew, meat...prey.

She spreads her wings and closes in for the kill.

Hutch felt her stir against his back, her warmth like a furnace under the thick duvet. He was too warm, but didn't want to move and wake her up. She was breathing fast, twitching and flexing her hand against his chest, dreaming.

Let her dream, he thought, blinking his eyes open to glimpse the clock. Five ten. He moved slowly, flexing a few muscles one at a time to stretch without waking her. He was pleasantly sore.

Memories of last night sifted through his waking mind, pleasure and guilt all coming back. That he had begun a relationship with a student, breaking one of his own cardinal rules, felt like a knife in his conscience. There would indeed be nine shades of hell to pay, and if Dr. Oliver found out, it would double. But he had needed her, and she him. Bob's death, the loss, the wrenching pain of someone so young, with so much ahead of him, being brutally murdered had left a void in both of them that needed to be filled.

She stirred again, her arms flexing, pulling him close. *Strong...*

More memories of their lovemaking surfaced, and he felt the pulling warmth of desire center in his stomach and move down. God, what a lover she was. Never had he experienced a woman so eager, so willing, so joyous in her body, so centered on giving and receiving, so passionate.

Her hand twitched, fingers flexing against his chest, nails scratching. *Sharp nails!* He griped her wrist, not wanting to wake her, but not willing to get scratched, either. She resisted his grasp, her hand flexing hard against him, her body twisting.

She's having a nightmare, he realized, remembering her stories about bad dreams. He gripped her harder and shook her arm gently. "Aleksi." Her arm flexed hard, nails biting. "Aleksi! Wake up! You're dreaming!"

She pulled harder, nails raking, and her other hand against his back, grasping his shoulder. Pain lanced through him as those nails pressed into his skin.

"Aleksi!" He twisted, keeping his grip on her left wrist and grabbing the other.

She lunged up, flipping a leg over him, grasping him hard between her thighs. One glance at her face told him that something was wrong. Her eyes were vacant, staring at nothing, her face stretched in a rictus of... what? Anger? Rage? Hunger?

Her legs clamped down harder, and she reached for his throat. *She's so strong! Hysterical strength.* Then he saw her nails—no her *claws!* She flexed her fingers and the claws slipped from their sheaths, reaching for him, ready to rip him open.

"Aleksi! No!"

She stared into nothing and strained for his neck, so strong he could not hold her off, but she wasn't very heavy. Hutch brought his knees up, planted his heels and bucked hard, catapulting her forward. Her forehead cracked the headboard, and her arms went slack. Her eyes focused. She shook her head and stared at him in shock, then at her hands, at his grip on her wrists, and panic surged into her face.

Pain lanced through her head, and the nightmare vanished into a reality even more horrible. Hutch lay beneath her, his face contorted in fear, his grip hard on her wrists. There were scratches on his chest, parallel lines of red, not quite bleeding, and her nails...

"Oh my *God*!" Aleksi stared at her hands, at her nails, half an inch beyond the tips of her fingers, ridged and arched. And *sharp*! "No!"

She fumbled back, and he released her. She had to get away from him, had to flee before she hurt him, killed him, tore his flesh into long, bloody strips and feasted on it. She lunged away, but the blankets tangled her legs and she landed hard at the foot of the bed. Still panicked, she scrabbled back, knowing only that she had to put distance between them before she killed him. Her back struck the far wall of the bedroom, and her head cracked against it, stunning her slightly. She blinked, unable to think.

"Aleksi!" His shout pierced her panic. The memories of the bloody nightmare, the horror of waking ready to rip him open with her claws, still blocked her ability to think. Light flooded the room. He was out of the bed, coming to her, but she couldn't let him get close, couldn't touch him, couldn't *ever* touch him again.

"No! Don't!" She put out a hand to fend him off and stared at her fingers. New horror surged through her; her ring and pinky fingers were longer than the others, and at the base of each elongated nail a ring of tiny golden bumps, like fine scales, framed the cuticle. "What the *fuck*?"

"It was a dream, Aleksi." He knelt before her, edging cautiously closer. He held out a hand to brush her trembling leg. "A nightmare."

"Don't touch me!" She pulled away. Tears spilled from her eyes with the horror if it all. "Don't...I don't want to..." She couldn't stop staring at her hands, at the claws, the scales, the scratches on his chest. Memories of the wounds that had ended Bob Tomlin's life flooded her mind, and she choked back a sob. "I can't..." She drew her knees up and clutched her legs to her chest, rocking and sobbing, unable to think.

"Aleksi." His voice was soft, gentle. There was no more fear in his face, only concern. "Hey. It's okay. You didn't hurt me." He reached out again and touched her leg, and she was unable to draw back any further.

"Please..." The tears wouldn't stop, and he wouldn't stop touching her. "Don't...I'm not...safe."

"Aleksi, you're not going to hurt me. You're awake now. This isn't a dream."

Dreams, nightmares, reality…it all blurred in her mind. "How do you know I won't?"

"Because you *won't*." His fingertips gently stroking her clenched forearms. "Remember last night." A suggestion, not a question. "Remember us together. You won't hurt me. Not on purpose."

He smiled at her, gentle, patient, and her heart ached.

"Not on purpose…" The muscles of her forearms eased, and she relaxed from her panicked fetal posture.

"Come on." He stood and offered his hand. "Let me help you."

Aleksi reached out, tentative, careful, and put her hand in his. His grip was firm, cool and solid. She let him pull her to her feet and her knees almost gave way. He grabbed her arms, steadying her, and she clutched him closer, unable to help herself. He drew her into his arms, held her tight and rocked her back and forth.

"Better?"

"I…yes." She did feel better, but all the fear, all the panic lurked under the surface, ready to overwhelm her. She sniffed and pushed him away, steadier now. "But…" She held up a hand between them, turning it to show him the claws, the tiny rows of scales. "What the hell's happening to me, Hutch? I don't…I can't…"

"Shhhh." He took her hand in his. "We'll figure it out, Aleksi. Here." He released her and grabbed his robe from the bedpost. He wrapped her in the soft folds of flannel and gripped her shoulders. "We'll figure something out." He went to the dresser, pulled a pair of pajama bottoms and donned them. "We'll call someone. Get some help."

He lifted the phone from the night table beside the bed and pressed three digits. She heard the tones clearly, one low, then two higher. *911* New panic shot through her.

"What the hell are you *doing*?" Two steps and she snatched the phone from his grasp. She stabbed 'end' hard enough to crack the face.

"Aleksi! What…" His face was slack, a flicker of fear behind his eyes.

"Nine-one-one?" Her ears were still ringing with the surge of panic. She cringed at the cracked face of his phone and put it back on the nightstand. "Sorry about your phone, but *Christ*, Hutch. What the hell do you think the *police* are going to do to me if they see this?" She held up one hand and flexed her claws out.

"Aleksi, I…" His eyes were wide, but then he nodded. "Sorry. I wasn't thinking. You're right. But we've got to do *something*. We've got to get you some help."

"I'm all for help, Hutch, but being locked up in a *cage* isn't my idea of help." She clutched his robe closed and ran a hand through her hair. Several long strands came out in her grasp, and her eyes widened in new panic. "What the *fuck?*"

"Okay. You're right, Aleksi. No police, but we've got to think." He put his hands on her shoulders, gripping her hard. "Something physiological is happening to you. This isn't just nightmares or hallucinations. We've got to get some *medical* help. If it's some kind of infection, some reaction to something, maybe they can arrest it with antivirals or immune suppressants."

"You think this is an *infection?*" A faint memory tickled her mind, drew her eyes to her right palm. *Something…*

"I don't know, Aleksi, but we're both scientists, and this isn't some delusion. It's *real.*" He pulled her face back to his, his palms cool on her cheeks. "I know quite a few doctors in the medical school. If anyone can crack this, they can."

"Doctors." Visions of needles, hospitals, wrist restraints… But she couldn't think of any other option. "I need coffee before I can deal with this."

"Good idea. And maybe something to eat." He took her hand in his and pulled her toward the kitchen.

Y ou look like crap." Jasper lowered his feet from his desk and put his coffee cup down.

"Late night." Willis filled a cup and stirred in an obscene about of cream and sugar. He raised it to Jasper with a weak grin. "Breakfast of champions."

"Dinner and a movie?" Jasper finished his coffee and pulled his Glock from his desk drawer. He checked the piece and secured it in his shoulder holster.

"Yeah. We did an Avengers marathon." Willis brought his coffee to his desk and picked up the search warrants. "I'll never get tired of those movies."

"You just have a thing for men with big muscles."

"Yes, I do." Willis grinned.

Jasper shook his head with a laugh, donned his suit jacket, then his overcoat. "Who do you want to wake up first, Rychenkna or Penningly?"

"Oh, let's do her first. Her place is smaller and won't take as long. If we hurry, maybe we can get them *both* out of bed!" Willis downed his coffee and pulled a travel cup from his desk before heading back to the pot.

"You're evil, you know." Jasper started for the door.

"Well, *yeah!*" Willis filled his cup, snapped on the lid and hurried after him. "I thought you knew that about me. Evil to the bone!"

"Fine, Detective Evil." He pulled the car keys from his pocket and jingled them. "You're driving."

***

utch watched Aleksi push her scrambled eggbeaters around her plate and noticed the tremors in her hands. She wasn't dealing with this very well. He wasn't either, but he had at least been able to eat something.

"My cooking that bad?" He nodded to her plate.

"No, it's fine, I just…" She shrugged. "It tastes funny."

"Fake eggs." He took their plates to the sink. "Sorry I don't have anything else." She had also turned up her nose at granola, yogurt and fruit.

"It's okay."

He turned to see her staring down at her hands. She'd been doing a lot of that. Staring into the mirror was worse; her irises had gone mostly yellow, and the pupils had elongated to vertical ovals. They'd discussed options, but there were few she would agree to, dreading the idea of being stuck in a hospital room or worse while they poked and prodded her. He glanced at the kitchen clock; seven fifteen. He didn't feel good about calling any of his medical friends before eight on a Saturday. He grabbed the coffee pot to freshen her cup.

"I think Jim Bornstein is our best bet." He topped hers off and filled his own. "He's a brilliant physician *and* a scientist, so he'll be able to think outside the clinical box. PhD in Genetics."

"Yeah. Good." She wrapped her hands around her cup. The surface rippled with tiny concentric circles from her tremors. She sighed. "You think he'll be willing to keep it quiet?"

"I don't know. I've known him for years, and he's a solid guy, but he might want you in a hospital for some of the tests."

"What tests?" She looked up at him and her eyes pleaded with his baser emotions.

"I don't know." He put the coffee pot down and covered her hands with his. "He might want to do imaging studies or collect bone marrow."

"Will you ask him to try to keep it quiet?"

"Of course, but I don't think he'll risk his career for me. We're not that close." He gauged her level of calm—not very—and decided to risk a different tack. "I might be able to offer him something as an incentive, though. Or you might."

"Like what?" He could see the suspicion rising up in her.

"This is something I've never heard of, Aleksi." He pulled her hand away from her cup and worked her fingers between his. He could feel the tiny bumps of scales, the ridges on her nails. "It's got to be something like a retroviral infection, or some kind of genetic switch. Bornstein will want to investigate it. If we let him, offer him exclusive rights to publish..."

"I think it's from the Kamchatka specimen." There was more fear in her tone now than since her initial panic. "I think I got infected from it. Remember when I was sick?"

"Holy shit!" The pieces fit together perfectly. He'd read of dormant infections lurking in frozen specimens, but this one hadn't been frozen.

"Yeah, holy shit." She sighed and swallowed some coffee. He heard her stomach growl. "Offer him whatever you think he'll take to keep it quiet. How early can you call him?"

"Maybe eight without causing a stink. He might even be working today. I don't know."

She glanced at the clock. "Good. Look, I hate to ask, Hutch, but I'm starving, and I don't feel much like going out. Could you get me something before you call Bornstein?"

"Sure!" He stood and took another swallow of coffee before heading for the bedroom. "Let me change quick and I'll pop down to the deli. What would you like?"

"Anything red and bloody will do. I'm going to jump in the shower while you're gone."

"Feel free!"

He donned jeans, tee shirt, and running shoes. He heard the water come on before he was ready, so he went through the bathroom on his way to the front door. She was already in the shower, her head under the spray, steam filling the room. He tapped on the glass and she turned to him with a bit of a start.

"Call me if anything comes up, Aleksi." He leaned in.

"Thanks, Hutch." She bit her lip, arms clutched over her breasts as if afraid to touch him.

"Come here." He knew she needed to feel his support, that he wasn't afraid of her.

She leaned in tentatively and kissed him, quick and sweet. He wasn't sure if it was just the shower, or if she was crying again, but there was a smile on her lips.

"We'll get through this, Aleksi. I promise."

"Okay. Thanks."

He smiled and left her. While waiting for the elevator, wondering what to pick up for her at the deli, he realized that she probably hadn't been joking about wanting something red and bloody. He swallowed hard as the elevator doors opened, wondering what he had gotten himself into.

* * *

D on't know why you people can't wait for a decent hour to do these things." The surly landlord mounted the last flight of steps and rifled through his keys. "And I don't know what you want with Aleksi. She's a good tenant and quiet. Not like that roommate of hers, always bringing *men* home."

"We're sorry for the hour, Mister Halifax, but we do have a search warrant, and when she didn't answer the door we became concerned." Jasper traded a covert look with Willis, who just shrugged. *Not a flight risk...right.* Not at home at seven thirty in the morning, and no answer on her phone.

The key clicked in the lock and the landlord swung the door open. "You take anything, I want a receipt."

"Of course, Mister Halifax." He nodded to Willis and the two edged into the apartment, cautious, but without drawing their guns. "Aleksi Rychenkna! This is Sergeant Jasper with the Cambridge Police. We have a search warrant. If you can hear me, please say something."

No answer.

A glance confirmed that the kitchen and living room were empty except for a surly iguana that rattled its cage. They proceeded down the short hall. Both bedroom doors opened easily and neither of the women were home. The rooms were tidy, with no signs of a struggle or any hasty departure.

"Well crap," Willis said. "Bad call on the flight risk thing, I guess. You want Rychenkna's room, or the other?"

"I'll take Rychenkna's." He sighed with frustration. "Don't toss anything too badly. Don't know what we're looking for, but we should know it when we find it."

"Right."

Fifteen minutes yielded absolutely nothing. No murder weapon, no computer, no cell phone. She was gone.

"Not planning to be gone long, either." Jasper met back up with Willis in the hall. "Underwear drawer's full."

"Toothbrushes are missing," Willis said. "They both left on their own. Maybe they're together, gone for the weekend?"

"Well, we can call Parks to find out, but the only other thing we can do is try Penningly's place." He narrowed his eyes at his partner. "Any bets?"

"No way." Willis followed him out of the apartment. "You think they both skipped?"

"Don't know, but something's weird. Sorry to disturb your morning, Mister Halifax." Jasper handed over a card. "If you see either of the young ladies, please give us a call. It's important. This is a murder investigation."

"Murder! Whose murder?" The landlord squinted at the card and pocketed it.

"A young man who was working with Aleksi Rychenkna and dating Julie Parks, so both young ladies may be involved." The door closed with a click, and the landlord locked it. "I'll thank you for your discretion on this. The investigation is ongoing, and the last thing we need is a bunch of rumors flying around."

"The last thing *I* need is a bunch of rumors about murder in my place, Officer Jenkins!" Halifax looked even more surly. "So don't you worry about that!"

"It's Jasper, Sergeant Tony Jasper, and thanks." Jasper led the way down the stairs, thinking that he had enough worries on his mind already, and undoubtedly more to come.

A pound of roast beef, a dozen eggs, bacon and a rotisserie chicken were enough to raise the eyebrows of the checkout clerk at Hutch's favorite deli. The guy knew he was a vegetarian and had never seen him buy meat once in four years.

"Picnic with carnivores," Hutch explained with a sheepish grin, taking back his credit card.

"Have fun." The clerk smiled and shrugged as if it wasn't any of his business, which it wasn't.

Hutch left the shop and started back to his place. He'd only made it half a block when a voice from close behind brought him around with a start.

"Dr. Hutchinson!"

He turned to face Derrick Penningly, and thought, *Oh crap! Here it comes.*

"Hello, Mister Penningly." He squared his shoulders, refusing to be intimidated. "Can I do something for you?" Hutch kept his voice neutral and looked right into his adversary's sunglasses, then recalled that Aleksi thought Derrick was a murderer and swallowed.

"Yes, as a matter of fact, you *can* do something for me." Derrick stopped one step away, gloved hands balled into fists at his sides and shoulders heaving with each breath. "You can tell me what the *hell* you think you're doing with that email you sent. You've got absolutely *no* proof that I did anything wrong. Aleksi's the liar here. *She's* the one who needs to be expelled!"

"I'm not going to discuss this with you, Mister Penningly. If you want to file a grievance, it's well within your rights." He started to turn away, but Derrick grabbed his shoulder and jerked him back around, his grip hard enough to hurt.

"Don't you dare turn your back on me, you pompous fuck! I'm not through *talking* to you!" Derrick's face contorted, lips curling back.

Hutch felt a tickle of fear. *Psychotic, or just angry?* He squared his shoulders and took a deep breath to calm his hammering heart. "There is nothing for us to discuss, Mister Penningly. There *is* evidence that you took data from Aleksi's computer without her permission. That alone is reason enough for expulsion."

"She *gave* me that fucking data, and she got pissed off when I wouldn't sleep with her! I told the cops that!" He thrust a gloved finger under Hutch's nose like a weapon. "They know the truth!"

"Yes, they *do* know the truth." Hutch wondered if Derrick would be stupid enough to attack him in public. He almost hoped he would. With half a dozen witnesses eying them both, it would be enough to get him arrested. "They know you accessed Aleksi's computer when she was out of her lab, with me, the chairman of the department, and Congressman Twain. Your stick drive left a fingerprint on her computer, Derrick. Your story doesn't hold up. Your best bet is to leave the department without a fuss, but if you want to file a grievance, it's your choice."

"Fuck your grievance, *Dr.* Hutchinson!" Derrick seethed, flecks of spittle spraying from between his clenched teeth. "You're protecting that bitch, and I know why! When the chairman finds out you're fucking her, the ball will be back in *my* court!"

Shit! How could he know? But Hutch realized that it didn't matter. Denying it would only bring trouble later, and the truth could pull the fire out from under Derrick's rage.

"There are no set rules governing relationships between faculty and students, Mister Penningly, but there are a number of *laws* concerning the theft of research data, lying about collaboration, and fraud." Again, he kept his tone steady. "Walk away from this before is blows up in your face."

"You stick your laws up your high and mighty ass, Doctor! My father's lawyers will fucking *bury* you!"

Hutch didn't know what to say to that and stood mute.

Derrick Penningly turned on his heel and stalked away, plumes of steam rising from his breath at every step. Hutch turned and started back to his place, thinking that Aleksi might have been right about Derrick all along.

Hello, this is Derrick and I'm sorry I can't take your call. If you're a beautiful young lady, please leave a message and I'll call you *right* back. If you're not, well, no promises."

There was a beep, and Jasper unclenched his jaw enough to say. "This is Sergeant Jasper with the Cambridge Police Department. It's eight in the morning on Saturday the fourteenth. I'm at your apartment with a search warrant. If you don't call me back in five minutes, we will search your apartment without you here. Please call as soon as you get this message."

He hung up. It was exactly the same message he'd left on Aleksi Rychenkna's line. He paced back and forth in front of Penningly's door until Willis arrived with the assistant manager.

"This is Miss Faun." Willis nodded to the severe-looking young woman. "She's agreed, after making a copy of our warrant, to open Mister Penningly's door for us."

"Thank you for your cooperation, Miss Faun," Jasper said. *Not that you had any choice in the matter.*

"My pleasure." She flashed a tight smile as she opened the door and swung it wide.

Derrick Penningly's apartment was much as they remembered it. It reeked of money, but not much in the way of taste. Definitely a rich kid's bachelor pad. Jasper announced them and got no answer. They both put on rubber gloves.

"Do me a favor and check the kitchen," he told Willis. "Looks like the guy likes cutlery. Maybe there's something under the sink."

"Like a gardening tool?" Willis cocked an eyebrow.

"Yeah, like that." There was something about Penningly that he didn't like, but maybe it was prejudice against privileged rich brats. He tried not to let that jade his opinion, but not very hard. "I'll check the bedrooms. Have a look over his DVD collections when you're done in the kitchen. I'm interested to know what he likes for entertainment."

"Right."

They went to work.

Jasper entered Penningly's bedroom to the sound of kitchen drawers being rifled through. His first impression was even worse than the one he'd had from the living room. A larger than life framed picture of a reclining nude woman hung over the headboard of a king-sized black-lacquered bed. The photo was blurred slightly, and there was a red sports car above the nude. The picture screamed "I'm a stud!" loudly enough to send any sensible woman running. Yeah, Penningly was a piece of work, alright.

He searched the bedroom thoroughly without displacing anything, found a pair of padded handcuffs in a drawer beside the bed and a video recorder on a tripod in the closet. *Great*, he thought, glad that he'd taken the bedroom instead of giving it to Willis. He had an even lower opinion of macho rich boys than Jasper, and he didn't want to hear the fallout. He checked the dirty clothes for any signs of blood or rips, just as he had Rychenkna's, and like hers, found nothing. The huge bathroom yielded a copious number of grooming supplies, including a straight razor. He took some hair samples and put them in a small Ziploc. The forensics team hadn't found anything near the murder scene, but this would give them something to compare it to. He gave up and went to the other bedroom.

"Office, huh?" The room did have a desk, but the rest was a blank. The computer on the desk was off, and turning it on only gave him a password screen. If he wanted to know what was on the kid's hard drive, he'd have to get Johnny to hack it. He doubted Penningly would give him the password. He checked the desk drawers, flipped through some magazines, GQ, Sports Illustrated, and a few on Boston. None looked like they'd been read more than once. In the center drawer, he found a rectangular blister pack of pills. There was no label on the back, except for the manufacturer, but he recognized the characteristic + etched onto each white pill. *Rohypnol.* The video camera in the bedroom and the handcuffs, and now this. Derrick Penningly was a piece of work, all right. He put the roofies in a ziplock and pocketed them. If he didn't have a prescription for the drug, this was enough to arrest him. In the waste basket he found a few tissues, one with a speck of blood. It put that in another evidence bag.

"Anything?" he asked as he reentered the living room.

"Other than a *really* tacky choice of DVD's, and a lot of first-person shooter games, no."

"Tacky how?" He joined his partner at the huge entertainment center.

"No slasher movies, or horror. He seems to like guns, fast cars, and bimbos." Willis held up a DVD case that showed all three of those on the jacket. "What did you get?" He nodded at the evidence bags.

"A blister pack of roofies in his desk drawer, a tissue with blood on it from the waste basket, and some hair. He had a video camera set up in his bedroom closet, and padded cuffs in the nightstand. We should download whatever's on that camera and look over his hard drive." He didn't mention the straight razor.

"Well, what now?" Willis put the DVD back where he found it and wiped his gloved hand on his jacket as if he'd touched something slimy.

"Now, I think we need to piss off the Honorable Judge Haverty."

"Arrest warrants?"

"Yep." He nodded to the door and Willis followed him out. "When two non-flight-risk suspects both suddenly go missing and won't answer their cell phones, it's time to bring them in."

"Oh, can I question Penningly?" Willis asked. "I *so* love it when macho boys cry!"

Jasper couldn't help but chuckle. The crack made him feel a little better, but not much; there wasn't much to laugh about in this case.

Derrick felt his phone vibrate in his pocket and pulled it out. He glared at Jasper's name on the display and let it go to voice mail. He wasn't in the mood to talk to cops. His temper was still out of control. *Fucking computer geeks anyway.* One tiny mistake, and he was fucked up the ass.

"Expelled!" He couldn't believe it was real.

All of his plans were being sucked down the drain, just because that arrogant asshole Hutchinson couldn't keep his dick in his pants. The reek of sex on the man had left no doubt.

Derrick's fists clenched. "Fuck them both! I'll fucking kill him *and* that Russian cunt, just like that worthless fuck, Tomlin!" Pain lanced into his palms and he forced his hands open. He'd ruined his gloves.

He had to salvage this, had to get someone on his side, someone powerful. His father, maybe. He'd helped cover up Derrick's previous mistakes, but that wasn't murder. He had to find someone powerful enough to fuck the police, that pretentious shit Hutchinson, and most of all, that bitch, Aleksi.

His tongue flicked out in the icy air to wet his lips. He could still taste the scent of her sex from Hutchinson. The other scent of her came back to him, her delicious rage when she scratched his car. It had hit him like a bolt of lightning, gave him a hard-on.

"Stop thinking with your dick, Derrick!" He stuffed his hands in his pockets and strode for his apartment. He needed to think. He needed help, big name help. Maybe someone to help him plant some evidence that would solidly link Aleksi to Tomlin's murder. He doubted Quinton Neilson would back him up, and Congressman Twain wouldn't want to get involved.

Twain, he thought. That was the kind of power he needed on his side. Could he blackmail Twain into saying that they'd picked up Aleksi after the time he'd downloaded the files? Could he fix this, flip the accusations back at Aleksi, accuse her of fucking Hutchinson for his testimony? But how could he manipulate Twain?

"Ten fucking minutes! That's all I need him to say!" Derrick clenched his fists again, relishing the pain in his palms this time, the piercing, head-clearing rush of it.

He stopped dead in his tracks and looked down at his gloved hands. *Pain? Something...Something not right about that.* He opened one hand and smelled blood, tasted the coppery flavor it in the back of his throat.

"Maybe." Derrick watched his claws retract into the gloved tips of his fingers. "Maybe I *do* have something Twain would be willing to bargain for."

As Hutch merged into the traffic of Memorial Way his phone rang in his pocket. He cursed fluently, pulled it out, and pressed talk. "Hang on, I'm driving." He dropped the phone into the passenger seat.

He wouldn't have answered it if he didn't think it might be Aleksi with something important. Even though he'd only left her a few minutes ago, he was worried about her. When he returned from shopping, she'd been pacing the floor and biting her nails. She claimed it was just too much coffee, but he knew better. At least her nails were short again.

They'd talked while she ate like a starved wolf, putting away half the roast beef and a good portion of the chicken. He'd been surprised she hadn't eaten the bones. He didn't tell her about his confrontation with Derrick, knowing it would only upset her. When eight o'clock rolled around he called Jim Bornstein. Jim had evidently heard the tension in

Hutch's voice and agreed to meet him outside the medical center for coffee at nine. As he left, Aleksi seemed much calmer, agreeing that it would be best if she stayed at his place for a while. She promised to call him if anything came up while he was gone.

That was ten minutes ago.

Hutch found a place to pull off and picked up his phone. "What's up?"

"This is Sergeant Jasper, Dr. Hutchinson. Sorry to call you while you're driving, but we've got a little problem that I think you might be able to help us with."

Adrenalin surged through Hutch's veins the moment he heard Jasper's voice. By the end of the sergeant's claim that he needed help, Hutch was on full alert.

"What can I help you with, Sergeant?"

"We're trying to locate both Aleksi Rychenkna and Derrick Penningly, and wondered if you might know where either of them was."

"Funny you should ask about Derrick." Hutch didn't bother to keep the ire out of his tone. This was the perfect opportunity to draw the cop's attention away from Aleksi. "He accosted me on my way back from the deli this morning, madder than hell."

"Mad at you?"

"Very. To the point that I thought he might take a poke at me."

"Really? Why would Derrick Penningly be angry with you, Doctor?"

"Because I recommended to the dean, the chairman, and the faculty council that he be expelled from Harvard. I've got you to thank for that, Sergeant. If you hadn't found the proof of his stealing that data from Aleksi's computer, he'd still be in the program."

"Well, that explains it." There was a pause, and Hutch imagined him covering the receiver and ordering his minions to hack into the email server to confirm his claim. "So, Miss Rychenkna told you what we found on her computer."

"Yes." He paused just to return the favor. "Should she not have?"

"Oh, no. We didn't tell her to keep it quiet, and it's not our concern really, but I *would* like to know when she told you this."

"Yesterday afternoon." He didn't elaborate.

"You saw her?"

"Yes. I dropped by her lab, we talked, and I bought her a late lunch."

"Do you buy lunch for all your students, Doctor?"

"Occasionally, yes. But with Bob's death, I thought that she might need to talk, and she did."

"When did you last see her?"

Hutch knew this question would come up, and he'd already made his decision how to answer, so there was no hesitation. "Yesterday about six PM. I dropped her off in front of her apartment." Lying to the police wasn't something he took lightly, but all things considered, right now it was low on his list of sins.

"And you don't know where she is right now?"

"If she's not in her apartment or her lab, you might try the library. You have her cell number, don't you?" He knew they did, but couldn't resist the dig.

"Yes, we have her cell number, and she isn't answering."

Good girl, he thought. "Really?"

"*Really*, Doctor." He could hear the veins distending in Jasper's neck. "We also have Derrick Penningly's number, and *he's* not answering either."

"That doesn't surprise me in the slightest. Derrick's turned out to be quite a piece of work."

"On that, at least, we agree, Doctor." Another pause. "If you can spare the time today, I'd like to have you down to the station for a few questions. With both of your students missing, I'm afraid you're our only lead."

"Derrick was *never* my student." Again, Hutch didn't keep the ire from his tone. "And if I'm you're only lead on Bob Tomlin's murder, you've got problems. What time do you want me there?"

"As soon as you can manage would be great."

"I've got a doctor's appointment downtown in thirty minutes. I might be able to make it there by noon, if I'm lucky."

"You've got a doctor that'll see you on Saturday?" There was honest incredulity in the man's voice.

"One of the perks of being a Harvard Professor. We have friends in high places. A medical school and law school right next door." He added the last just to remind Jasper that he wasn't a fool about his legal rights.

"Must be nice."

"It *does* have its advantages. But if I'm late for my appointment, I'll be even later for seeing you, Sergeant, so if you don't mind."

"Oh! Sorry." His tone stated plainly that he wasn't. "Well, if you do see or hear from Mister Penningly or Miss Rychenkna, please tell them to call me. We'll have warrants for their arrests by the time you arrive at the station. If they come in on their own, it'll save trouble."

"Warrants? For *Aleksi's* arrest?"

"Yes, Doctor."

"On what charge?"

"Murder."

"You can't be serious!"

"Its standard procedure to issue warrants when suspects go suddenly missing and won't return calls."

"I understand that, but you can't *seriously* be considering Aleksi as a suspect in Bob Tomlin's murder! She had *no* motive and is in *real* trouble academically as a result of it! Not to mention that she doesn't have a violent bone in her body!" *Except for trying to tear my throat out this morning*, he added to himself.

"Remind me to show you the hood of Derrick Penningly's BMW when you come by today, Doctor. I think you might reevaluate your opinion of Aleksi Rychenkna."

There was something in Jasper's voice that sent a chill up Hutch's spine. "I doubt that, Sergeant, but I'll remind you. I've got to go if I want to make my appointment."

"I'll see you around noon, Doctor."

"See you then." He hung up the phone, dropped it in the seat and pulled out into traffic. Only when he was across the bridge and stuck at a light did he call Aleksi. When there was no answer, he really started to worry. He left an ambiguous message—Whatever he said, the police might hear later—and hung up, then turned his phone to vibrate and put it in his pants pocket.

2 9

Aleksi paced the floor, biting her nails to the quick. She glanced at the clock for the fifth time in the last ten minutes; almost noon. Hutch should be back by now.

She went to the window and watched the people on the street. She could see their breath in the frigid air, hear their voices through the thick glass, count the buttons on the woman's overcoat as she walked her dog down the bike path.

"I wasn't hallucinating." Aleksi remembered her disturbing visual and auditory acuity of days past. "It's me." She raised a hand to the glass and saw that the tiny rows of scales had advanced to her first knuckle. Spreading her fingers, she gaped at the thin line of membrane forming between her last three fingers. "Oh, this just keeps getting better and better!"

Hutch must know something my now, she thought, deciding to give him a call. Being cooped up, even in this beautiful place, was driving her crazy. She went into the guest bedroom and retrieved her phone from her bag, but it was off.

"What the…" Turning it on only earned her a quick bleep of the low battery alarm and a blank screen as it powered back down. "Shit!"

Rooting through her bag, she found the charger and plugged it in. It powered up automatically, and she saw that she had missed four calls; one from her mother, one from Hutch, and two from Sergeant Jasper.

"Shit, shit!" She decided to listen to Hutch's first, hoping for good news. She was disappointed.

"Hi, Aleksi. Hey, I just got a call from the police. Seems they're looking for you. I told them I'd seen you just yesterday for lunch, but they're convinced you've skipped town and want to talk to me. You better give them a call. Bye."

"Perfect!" She had no intension of calling the police, not in her current condition, and he knew that. Was it a warning? She decided to listen to Jasper's message, knowing already what she'd hear. No surprises there, but the warrant for her arrest felt like a nail in her coffin. Her mother's message was mundane. Evidently, she hadn't learned of the murder yet, which was good. Her stomach growled. She was hungry again. She brought her pack and the phone out to the kitchen where she would hear it if Hutch called.

The rest of the chicken vanished as if by magic. She was still hungry, so she munched on slices of roast beef as she paced the living room, wondering if her life would ever be normal again.

T his is ridiculous, Sergeant." Hutch leaned back in the uncomfortable metal chair and rubbed his eyes. "I don't know how many times I can tell you exactly the same story." Eight by ten glossy photos of four deep scratches in the hood of a car glared at him from the surface of the table. He'd feigned enough surprise to fool Jasper, but after this morning, he had no doubt that Aleksi had inflicted the damage with her nails.

"Let's just go through it one more time, please, Doctor." Jasper steepled his fingers in front of his nose. "You dropped by Miss Rychenkna's lab yesterday at about four PM and offered to take her to an early dinner."

"More like a late lunch, but yes, I already told you that." His stomach growled. It was already after three PM, and the questions just kept coming.

"Yes, you did. So, you took her in your car to a swanky Japanese restaurant where you dropped the better part of a hundred bucks on dinner for two."

"I wouldn't call Ichi Ban Sushi swanky, but yes, the bill did come to over fifty dollars, which *is* the better part of one hundred." Hutch bit off the rest of his sarcastic comment, which would have complemented the sergeant's mathematical skills.

"Did you have drinks?" Jasper asked.

"Yes. I think I had two glasses of water. Aleksi had tea, but I didn't count how many cups were in the pot."

Jasper glared at him for a moment. "See, it's *that* kind of crap that is just going to make this interview take even longer, Doctor."

"Oh, is this an *interview*? I was beginning to think that you brought me down here just to be harassed."

"This isn't harassment, Doctor. But keep it up, and you'll get plenty."

"Really? Good. The Harvard Law Review hasn't had much experience in cracking down on police harassment, so this should be good for them."

"The law review? What's that, your own legal team?"

"You could say that. Harvard Law School's top students make it up. They enjoy legal challenges and take every opportunity to practice."

"Students? You're threatening me with a bunch of law students?"

"No, Sergeant. I'm not threatening you at all. That would be foolish of me."

"Yes it *would*, Doctor." Jasper paused and consulted his notebook. "So, why *exactly* did you offer to buy an expensive dinner for Aleksi Rychenkna?"

This was not the first time Jasper had asked that specific question, nor was it the second, third or fourth time. Hutch answered it as he had before and tried not to let his temper get out of control. He had spent enough time in court to not get tangled up by repetitive questioning, so this was nothing but irritating. The questions continued as they had for the past hours, and except for the bit about spending the night with Aleksi and her startling condition this morning, he told the absolute truth. Again, and again.

Did he know Derrick Penningly personally? No, he didn't. Did he know if Aleksi asked Derrick to sleep with him? No, he didn't know whether she had or hadn't, though he hoped she had better taste than that. Did he know Derrick's father was a major contributor to Princeton? Not until you told me two hours ago...

When the clock on the wall showed that it was after four PM, Hutch decided that he'd finally had enough. He stood up from the table and stretched, then, under the startled looks from Jasper and Willis, started for the door.

"Where do you think you're going, Doctor?"

"I'm going home." He paused long enough to give the cop a tired stare. "This is pointless, and I'm tired. This is one of my few days off, and it's been spent here instead of enjoying myself. You can't keep me here without arresting me, and I've done nothing to warrant arrest, so I'm going home. If you think of any *new* questions to ask me, please don't hesitate to call."

"Actually, Doctor, I *can* keep you here if I charge you with obstruction of justice." That stopped Hutch cold, and his glare was no longer tired. "And if you refuse to answer our questions, that's exactly what I'll do."

"Fine." He crossed his arms and leaned against the wall. "Ask a question, Sergeant, but it better be a different question than the ones you've been asking for the past four hours, or I'll be serving you a lawsuit for harassment with your Sunday morning coffee."

"Fair enough." Jasper leaned back in his chair, looking way too comfortable. "Would you mind if we had a look at your apartment?"

Hutch stared at him, taken aback by the question. "Would I *mind*? Without a search warrant, yes, I think I would."

"See, there's the whole obstruction of justice thing again, Doctor." Jasper smiled.

"Go ahead and charge me, then. I'll be home in ten minutes, and your phone will be ringing in fifteen with my lawyers on the other end with that harassment suit." He smiled back. "Are we through playing around, Sergeant?"

"I'll make you a deal, Doctor. You give me one good reason why you don't want me to have a look at your apartment, and I'll let you walk out that door."

"Hmmm. Let me see. Something in the constitution about unlawful search and seizure comes to mind."

"I can have a search warrant in half an hour if you really want to do it that way, Doctor."

One look at the man's face told Hutch that he wasn't bluffing, and he couldn't call Aleksi to warn her with two cops staring at him. In fact, he couldn't' call her at all on his cell phone, because if they did arrest him and took his phone, they would find out about it.

Well, fuck! He could only think of one thing to do.

"Fine. You can have a look at my place, but this is not permission for you to search or seize any of my belongings. I'll meet you there in half an hour. I've got to stop by my office and pick up some things." He might be able to call her from another phone.

"Actually, Doctor, why don't you let me come with you? We haven't had a look at Miss Rychenkna's lab yet, and you can give me a tour."

"All right. I'll meet you in front of the MCZ in fifteen minutes." He might be able to call from one of the phones in the museum before meeting up with Jasper.

"I think I'd rather drive with you. Detective Willis can take our car and meet us there."

"Afraid I'll skip town, too?"

"No, but I've had two suspects go missing in this case. I don't want to lose you, too."

Damn! Jasper was no fool. "Your concern for my welfare is touching."

Aleksi would have gone crazy if not for Hutch's books. She stood by a shelf reading, letting the intriguing ideas of Zen occupy her mind. She had tried to work but couldn't concentrate; her research only reminded her of what she was losing. Her entire career, her life, all she had worked for, was vanishing before her eyes, and there was nothing she could do about it.

She didn't realize it was dark until she looked up at the chime of the elevator. *Hutch! Finally!* She took two steps toward the door before she heard the sound of his voice.

"...still don't know why you want to look at my place, Sergeant."

Sergeant? She stopped cold. *What the hell?* She put the book on the kitchen counter.

"Just curious, Doctor."

Jasper! He brought cops back with him! She was moving before she even thought about what she was doing. Bag, computer, coat, phone, charger.

"With both of our primary murder suspects missing, you must understand that we have to exhaust all the possibilities."

She zipped her bag closed and swept the room with her eyes. Nowhere to hide...nowhere to run. Only one door, and Sergeant Jasper was on the other side. Then her gaze fixed upon the sliding glass door of the living room balcony. She slipped her arms into the straps of her bag and *moved*.

"You think Aleksi and Derrick are hiding in my home? That's just a little ridiculous, isn't it?"

She was at the glass door when his key rattled the lock and through it when it clicked open. Running on adrenalin and instinct, Aleksi vaulted the wrought iron railing as light from the hall scythed through the living room.

She fell.

Light exploded from the balcony overhead as the bracing wind of her decent ruffled her coat and hair. Four floors and a hard parking lot below. She had time to think on the way down, but her thoughts were not panicked, not horror stricken that her bones would be broken and she would lie there bleeding until the police came to drag her corpse away. Instead, she heard Jasper's voice from above…

"Not so ridiculous, Doctor."

…saw she was going to land in an empty parking spot…

"We get lied to all the time."

…and absorbed the impact with her legs. She stepped behind a minivan and stood there, utterly still, her heart beating hard in her ears but not quite drowning out the voices overhead.

"Well I haven't been lying to you, Sergeant." Hutch sounded angry. She heard his keys clatter into the bowl beside the door. "And as you can see, my home is empty."

Their voices were so clear, she wondered if she had closed the balcony door. She had…of course she had…maybe.

"Mind if we look around?" Jasper asked, and she could imagine the thoughtful, raised eyebrow look on his face.

"Oh, I *mind* plenty, but we've already played that game. I'd thank you not to touch anything, though." She heard the refrigerator door open and the 'Tssst' of a bottle being cracked. "I'd offer you a beer, but you're on duty, so I won't bother."

"Nice place." Jasper's voice was closer. He'd moved nearer the windows. Evidently, she had closed the door after all. "A lot nicer than I'd expect from a college professor."

"Not that it's your business, but I got this place in my divorce settlement. My ex-wife has money, and this place was more mine than hers anyway."

"Divorced, huh?" That was another voice, the other cop, Willis. "'Old Path White Clouds'? You read some weird shit, Doc."

"You think *Zen* is weird?" Hutch laughed without humor. She heard the book she'd been reading thump down on the kitchen counter.

"No offense, Doc."

The voices became muffled as they moved into the bedroom, and Aleksi took the opportunity to walk quietly away, her mind a tornado of emotions. Hutch had brought the police back with him, but it didn't sound like he'd done so willingly.

But why not call ahead to warn me? She rounded a corner and started toward her apartment out of reflex. She remembered the message on her phone and realized that he was worried about the police finding out. But he could have called from a different phone before he got home.

Home...

She stopped, realizing that she couldn't go home. If the police were looking for her, they would undoubtedly be looking there. And the lab would be watched, too.

Nowhere to go...

She turned and headed for the nearest subway station, thinking only to put as much distance between her and the police—*and Hutch*—as possible.

W hat do you think?" Willis asked as the elevator doors closed and they started down.

"I think Dr. Hutchinson's a tough nut." Jasper stretched his aching neck and sighed. "He's lying about something, but I don't know what."

"Think he's fucking her?"

"Maybe. There was a lot of hair in his shower drain, but I couldn't very well take a sample with no warrant and him looking over my shoulder. Even if he is, I don't know why he'd protect her from a murder rap. That's some serious shit."

"Wouldn't be the first time a man did something stupid for a *woman*." Willis said it like he thought every heterosexual man on the planet was doomed.

Maybe we are, Jasper thought. As they headed for the car, he went over the hours of the interview in his head. He'd watch the recording again before he went home tonight. Hutchinson hadn't flubbed a single answer, almost as if he had rehearsed them. *Or he's smarter than I give him credit for.*

"What next?" Willis asked as he turned the key and cranked the heater to full blast to defrost the windows.

"We search, watch, and get forensics to go over both Rychenkna's and Penningly's apartments with a microscope." He buckled his seatbelt and tried to order his mind. "Surveillance on Hutchinson, too. Twenty-four seven on the apartments and Rychenkna's lab."

"APB's on the suspects?"

"Yep, and approach with caution. Whoever tore Bob Tomlin's throat open is certainly dangerous."

"Yeah, no shit." Willis put the car in gear and pulled out of the lot. "Anything else?"

"Yes. Email and phone warrants for the suspects, and bank account and credit card activity, too. They're going to need money, and we should be able to track their movements, maybe find them if they're stupid."

"You thinking the two are in this together?"

"Rychenkna and Penningly?" Jasper shook his head, remembering the looks in their eyes, the tones of their voices. "No, they hate each other, all right. I just can't figure where Hutchinson fits in."

"Caught in the middle, maybe." Willis drove gingerly on the icy streets.

"Yeah, maybe. Gotta admit, his precious research has been shot to hell by this whole thing."

"And both students' academic careers, too. If the murder had happened *after* Hutchinson sent that email, we'd have had our motive on Penningly, but to *kill* another student just to make yourself look better? That's just insane."

"Damn straight, it is. And I'm starting to wonder if Derrick Penningly is loony enough to do just that."

Hutch picked up the book and ran his fingers over the cover. "Reading Thich Nhat Hanh, Aleksi?" He put it back down, finished his beer and went to the fridge for something to eat. The chicken, roast beef, bacon and half the eggs were gone. He had missed lunch and knew he should eat, but he didn't feel much like cooking, and certainly didn't want to go out. He grabbed another beer and an apple, and closed the fridge. Tossing the cap in the trash, he saw the empty chicken container.

Evidence, he thought. *Shit!*

Putting beer and apple aside, he did a slow circuit of the condo, looking for traces of Aleksi that the cops may or may not have seen. The spare bedroom was thankfully empty, but she hadn't spent much time there. He did a quick clean up in the bathroom, scouring both sink and shower for her long hair. The drain had quite a lot, actually, and he scooped it into the trash, then bundled up the trash to take out. The bedroom stopped him in his tracks. He had not made the bed, and it was still rumpled.

Should wash the sheets, he thought, and went to the side she'd slept on. He found a few more hairs on her pillow, and, unable to stop himself, lowered his face to inhale the faint remnant of her scent.

His heart skipped a beat.

"God*damn* it, Aleksi…"

He methodically stripped the bed, wading everything into his pillow case, and took it to the washer. When it was running, he gathered up all the trash, including the eggs from the fridge, and took it down to the dumpster. When he got back, his beer was warm. He picked it up anyway, took the book from the kitchen counter to his favorite chair and sat down to read. The white noise of the washing machine, the warm beer, and the simplicity of Zen eased his mind. He didn't think until later that it seemed unfair that he had just removed every trace of Aleksi from his home. He knew he could never expunge her from his memory.

30

Downtown Boston, Saturday night. If *ever* there was a place to be anonymous, Aleksi had found it. Every sports bar in town was packed, with the Celtics and Bruins vying for attention on every flat-screen in the city. She walked through crowds, invisible among so many hooded coats, hats, scarfs and backpacks. She'd been doing this her whole life in Manhattan, ignoring and being ignored, one face among thousands. Before, she'd simply avoided human interaction to shelter herself from her own insecurities; now, she was hiding from the police, running for her life. She didn't know where she was going, where she would sleep, what she would do, but she knew nobody would find her if she just stuck to the crowds.

Her stomach growled at the smells of chicken wings and baby back ribs on the air.

Again already? She wondered if she could find an open table at any of the eateries. They were all standing room only. She found a small grocery doing a brisk business selling beer in small paper bags and walked in. She kept her hoodie up and her face down, knowing there would be security cameras, though she doubted the police would be able to view them all looking for her. In the meat case she picked up a one-pound package of ground beef and took it to the counter. She paid cash. The clerk was so busy he didn't even look at her.

Outside, Aleksi strolled the darker areas, ignoring the fondling

243

couples and exchanges of wrinkled bills for small Ziploc bags. She kept the package of meat under her coat, tore back the cellophane, and ate the raw hamburger in luscious bites, barely chewing. She knew that eating raw meat was not normal behavior, but it tasted *so* good. When it was gone, she ditched the Styrofoam and plastic in a bin and kept walking. She felt better, sated, at least for now. Now, she could think.

"Money."

The police would freeze her account if they hadn't already. She had a credit card, too, but they could block that as well. Could they track her if she took money out of an ATM? Probably, but she had no choice. She found an ATM and took out as much as she could. She stuffed the wad of twenties into her jeans pocket and walked on.

With my luck, I'll get mugged, she thought, watching the crowds for eyes following her.

When she saw an all-night coffee shop slightly less crowded than the sports bars, she walked in without thinking. She bought a large coffee and found an open table in the corner with an outlet nearby. She sat down, plugged in her laptop and phone and logged onto the free Wi-Fi. She wondered briefly if the police could track her down through her email server, but doubted they would have a quick response.

She had a pile of emails, mostly students asking about lab class. She cringed, knowing she would be leaving a lot of people hanging, but unsure what she could do about it. She trashed them one by one, then came across one from Lonnie Westinghouse. She didn't want to get anyone in trouble by sending them a message, but she had to let someone know something. She opened the email and read it.

"Crazy stuff going on. Hutch emailed and said cops were looking for you, and that Penningly accosted him. What a serious dickhead! Are you okay? L."

Aleksi hit reply, and typed, "Not okay. Out for a while. Can't explain. Help Hutch pick up the pieces. The projects are on hold. He needs help. Thanks. A." She read it through once and hit send, wondering if Jasper would be on Lonnie's doorstep in the morning.

Then she saw the last email on the list; it was from Sergeant Jasper. She read it and cringed. She was wanted for the murder of Bob Tomlin. She was to present herself to the Cambridge Police Department as soon as she got this email.

Right, she thought, looking at the tiny golden scales on her fingers. *And monkeys will fly out of my ass!* She hit delete.

She did some surfing, looking for anything she could find about retroviral infections, which got her nowhere, then did some looking into Derrick Penningly's past. Nothing remarkable there; he'd gotten high grades at Princeton. His father was an alumni supporter. Then she found something else; something deep in the old copies of the Princeton student newspaper. There had been allegations of plagiarism involved in one of Derrick's senior research projects, then an assault charge. The allegations and the charge had been dropped for no reason, and Penningly had been exonerated of all wrong-doing. Nothing prior to that except good grades and lots of activities.

But plagiarism and assault were a long way from murder.

Something caught her eye, and she looked up to see two uniformed police officers at the counter. She froze, watching them from the shadow of her hoodie. Neither of them looked too attentive, and they certainly weren't responding to a call. They ordered coffee and Danish, weren't even looking around.

Aleksi unplugged her phone and laptop without taking her eyes off them, just in case she had to run. Thankfully, they didn't sit down to eat, but took their coffee and sweets out the door.

She took a deep breath and let it out slowly. Five minutes later, her heart had slowed, and she could type without her hands shaking. She shut her computer down, packed it up, and left the shop, still unsure of where she would go, who she could trust, and what she would do. With those questions rattling around her mind, she added one more.

"And what the hell are *you* doing, Derrick Penningly?"

When daylight finally lightened his bedroom enough to see, Hutch got out of bed. He had not slept much, and had been plagued by dreams of making love with Aleksi and her changing into some kind of monster. He did a few light stretches, vowing to treat this like any other Sunday until proven otherwise. He needed to clear his mind, to think, to reason this out, figure out what to do.

Winter seemed to have loosened its hold a bit. The temperature was above freezing, and the day promised to be clear and cool. A perfect day to go for a nice long run to clear his head.

As was his usual routine, he made coffee and a breakfast shake, then sat down to do his email. There was nothing from Aleksi, but he couldn't blame her. He did get a reply from Lonnie, however, the content of which caught him off guard.

"Hutch. Msg from A that she is NOT okay. Said you might need some help picking up the pieces. Let's talk. L."

He hit reply and typed, "Monday 0700 her lab. Thanks! H." He hit send, wondering why Aleksi would send an email to Lonnie but not him. Well, at least Lonnie was on his side, and he knew he could depend on his other students to help out with Aleksi's workload, at least through the semester. The research, however, was at a standstill.

"Maybe just pack the whole damn thing up and send it back to the MCZ," he said to himself as he shut down the computer. Then he remembered their conversation about the cause of Aleksi's malady: infection from the Kamchatka specimen. There was no way he could let that out of his hands. He had to get it analyzed properly. Maybe with some work they could figure out some kind of treatment. Maybe, if he could keep this quiet and in the right hands, he could get Aleksi back.

He realized that his thoughts were performing the same spirals that they had been doing all night, so he finished his breakfast, donned running gear and left his apartment.

This is going to be a problem, Aleksi thought as the sun rose above the eastern skyline. Sunday morning, relatively mild temperatures, no real crowds, and anyone who had come out seemed determined to get some exercise. And few wore hoods, parkas or scarfs. She was no longer invisible.

The night had been easy. Daylight was harder. She needed to hide, but where?

Aleksi had never noticed before how many security cameras there were in the subway stations, bus stations, street corners, convenience stores, ATM's, bridges, and even bookstores. Worried about facial recognition programs, she tried sitting for a time, reading a paper on a park bench. Her exhausted mind wandered, and her eyes drifted closed, the snippet of a dream teasing her.

Skin...warm...salty...strong hands on her hips...warmth filling her...Hutch!

She snapped awake, his scent tearing through her mind like a gunshot. Every sense tuned to maximum, she looked around, listened, breathed deep through her nose with her mouth partly open.

There!

She was sitting along the Esplanade, Boston University behind her, the Charles River and MIT filling her view. The bike path was streaming with runners, bikers, and rollerbladers. The false hint of spring had brought them all out, and right there, gliding along like he could run forever, Hutch passed by.

Familiar but recently absent indecision grabbed her. Should she follow him? Chase him down and talk to him? Find out why he brought the police back to his place without warning her? Was he being followed by the police? Was this a trap? There were too many people to tell if anyone was following him, but if there were, she would probably remain unnoticed if she just sat quietly. But watching him, seeing the muscles play in his legs and arms, remembering how they felt under her hands... It was all she could do not to cry out his name.

Don't be stupid! She tore her eyes away and forced herself to relax. *Deep breaths.* His scent faded. She thought for a while; if she stayed put, he might pass back the same way, or he might cross over the Harvard Bridge and run back on Memorial Drive. Should she wait here, or move in hope of seeing him again?

Too risky, she decided. *Got to find a better hiding place.*

She got up and shouldered her pack. Her aching feet found their rhythm easily as she made her way east, across Storrow Drive, and over to Kenmore station. She boarded the first inbound train, intending to go back downtown, maybe find a dark bar or restaurant where she could wile away the day. *Invisible...unseen...alone.*

Hey Lonnie. Thanks for coming."

"Thank me by telling me what the *hell's* going on." Lonnie had her 'no bullshit' face on, and Hutch knew better than to beat around the bush.

"Inside." Hutch pulled his keys from a pocket and opened the door to Aleksi's lab. He flipped on the light and turned to her. "Aleksi's disappeared. The police put a warrant out for her arrest for Bob's murder."

"You are fucking *kidding* me!" Lonnie's eyes widened. "*Aleksi's* wanted? What about that dickhead Penningly?"

"Penningly, too, and he's also vanished. The cops don't know who's telling the truth, so they're trying to bring them both in. Unfortunately, Aleksi can't go to the police." He paused, still unsure exactly how much to tell Lonnie. "Something's happened that I'm not sure I can explain, Lonnie. Remember when Aleksi was out sick for a few days?"

"Yeah." She looked impatient.

"Well, she started acting strangely after that. Strange for Aleksi, that is. Then she came to me and said she was having nightmares and hallucinations, and even some physical symptoms. We went to the med center, but they never found anything but a temperature and an elevated white cell count."

"An infection?"

"That's what we thought." He paused and took a deep breath. "Then there was this whole blow-up with Penningly and Bob was murdered. Anyone who knew Aleksi knew that she could never do anything like that, but with the recent changes, the hallucinations, I was beginning to wonder."

"No way." Lonnie's flat tone booked no argument. "Not Aleksi."

"I agree, but for other reasons than you think." He held up a hand to forestall her argument. "She had nothing to gain and everything to lose by Bob being killed. Derrick Penningly, however, had already stolen research data from her and lied about her asking him to collaborate. If Bob was out of the picture, and Aleksi was framed for his murder, he could step in and fill their shoes."

"You think he killed Bob over a *research* project. That's what Aleksi said, and it's just *crazy*!"

"Crazy for me to think it, or crazy for him to do it?" He cocked an eyebrow. "Because I think that's *exactly* the case. The cops found evidence that he stole the data from Aleksi, so I pulled the pin and sent an email to all the powers that be, recommending expulsion."

"Holy shit!" Lonnie grinned. "Way to kick some ass, Hutch!"

"Well, that was almost exactly what happened when Derrick confronted me Saturday morning. I swear to you, Lonnie, I thought he was going to punch me."

"No offense, but I wish he had. You could have had him arrested on the spot."

"Well, as it turned out, the cops had a warrant for his arrest out later that day when they tried to contact him and he'd vanished. Unfortunately, Aleksi vanished, too, and has the same warrant out on her."

"I don't get it. Why run from the cops?" Lonnie gave him an utterly puzzled look, and he knew he had to tell her the rest of it.

"She's…changed, Lonnie." He kept his voice low, even though they were utterly alone. "And I don't just mean psychologically. I mean *physically*. I actually *saw* the changes. She's contracted some kind of infection, maybe something retroviral. Some kind of gene-switching or something's going on. She didn't want to go to the hospital or to the police for fear that they'd lock her up and never let her out, and I couldn't make her. She agreed to let me have a medical friend of mine have a look, run some tests, but then there was the whole cop thing, and she vanished."

Lonnie looked at him like he'd grown an extra head. She swallowed, opened her mouth to say something, and failed.

"I *know* it's hard to believe, Lonnie, but we think we know where it came from." He nodded to the plastic-draped corner of the lab. "Bob found *human* DNA in the pyroclastic cast sample. We thought it was cont-amination at first, but it was all wrong. There were differences, stop codons where there shouldn't be, fragments that matched perfectly, then others that were vastly different. Like whatever was in that cast was *part*-human, or..."

"Changed." Lonnie's voice trembled.

"Yes. *Changed.*"

"This is like something out of a bad monster movie, Hutch. You're *sure* about this?"

"I'm not sure about anything but the *fact* that Aleksi is showing physi-ological changes that must be taking place at the *genetic* level. I'm not sure it came from that sample, but it's the only thing we could think of."

"So, you didn't ask me here to take over Aleksi's lab classes for the rest of the semester, did you?"

"Well, yes, but I need you to help me secure this sample and put it into storage. We can't let anyone else get infected, and I want it available for a full analysis by my biomedical friends. If it *is* the cause of Aleksi's changes, then we might be able to treat her."

"Um...okay." Lonnie swallowed hard. "I'm in, but how do we keep from getting infected, too? We don't know the vector. It could be airborne, for all we know."

"I don't think so." Hutch led her to the draped corner of the lab. "I've worked up close to it and helped her extract some samples for Bob. Nobody else has gotten ill. Normal precautions should be enough to keep us safe. Besides, the first thing we're going to do is encase it in plastic wrap, then we'll get a lift from Quinton and pack it in Ethafoam."

"Okay."

She reached for the disposable protective gear and began suiting up. Hutch followed suit, and soon they were garbed in everything they needed to keep themselves safe from infection. He nodded to her, pulled back the translucent plastic drapes and stopped dead.

The table that had held the Kamchatka specimen was bare.

"What in the name of..." He looked around the small space, as if a six-foot long slab of plaster could hide somewhere. The bone bed samples were all intact and resting right where they'd been left, but the Kamchatka specimen was gone.

"This is impossible! I saw it here Friday afternoon!"

"Who the hell would steal a plaster cast?" Lonnie's question was probably rhetorical, but Hutch's mind was already whirling ahead.

"Someone who figured out the same thing we did, and didn't want anyone *else* to get their hands on it."

Derrick's plan had worked like magic. Once he showed Congressmen Twain the changes that were occurring to him and told him the source, the government had moved with startling speed. Two panel vans, one carrying the Kamchatka sample, and one carrying him with the four heavy-set goons who had stolen it from Aleksi's lab, crossed the Charles River into the labyrinthine streets of Boston. Derrick flexed his hands inside his gloves and smiled. He felt the claws that tipped his fingers, ran his tongue over the elongating teeth, and blinked with his evolving eyes.

The changes were happening faster now.

He could feel the power in this new thing he was becoming. The cops, Hutchinson, the nose in the air assholes who had expelled him, wouldn't know what hit them. The government was on *his* side now.

The trucks made a half dozen turns, then descended a ramp that led down beneath an old brick building. A security guard checked the first vehicle then tapped in a code that rolled a heavy steel barrier up for them to pass. It boomed closed behind them, and the two vehicles pulled into a parking area populated by half a dozen cars and trucks.

"All right, Mister Penningly. We're here." One of the meatheads opened the door, and they all got out.

Armed guards and white-coated technicians wearing rubber gloves and surgical masks emerged from one of the roll-down doors as the specimen was unloaded. As they started to roll it away, Derrick turned to follow.

"This way, Mister Penningly." The head goon gestured toward another door.

"What? No way. I go with that specimen." He looked around at the guards and felt a sinking sensation. "I should go with them. I've got experience with this thing!"

"Don't worry, Mister Penningly." A lab-coated man stepped forward between the guards, older, balding, with a pinched face and glasses. "I'm Dr. Johansen."

The trolley carrying all the samples vanished behind a stainless-steel door, and Derrick's teeth ground together. "You need my *help* with that thing."

"We've got specialists for this type of situation, and you've provided us with more than enough help. Now, if you'd just follow me, I'll show you to your quarters."

"My *what?*" He didn't move.

"We've put aside a place for you to stay with us here, Mister Penningly. It's quite comfortable, and you must be tired and hungry." Johansen smiled a fake smile.

"I'd rather go back to my own place." He flexed his hands at his sides. They couldn't hold him if he didn't want to stay, though he might make a mess.

"You *must* understand that going home is impossible right now." Dr. Johansen gestured toward the now open door. "The police are still looking for you."

"Twain said you could make that go away." He still didn't move, glaring at the man in white, then the armed guards. They shied away from his gaze. He could smell their fear.

"Oh, we will, we will, but you've got to understand, these things take time." Johansen stepped forward, extending a hand. "Once everything's cleared up, and we find a cure for the infection that's causing these symptoms you're experiencing, you'll be free to go. We can't risk you leaving, you understand. If this is infectious, there could be problems."

"Then you need to find that Rychenkna woman, too."

"We're looking for her, Derrick." Johansen's smile faltered. "We'll deliver on our promises. You've brought us quite a boon. You'll be compensated for your time quite handsomely."

Derrick glanced again at the guards. *Military.* There were too many to kill before they brought those guns to bear on him. He wasn't invulnerable. He nodded to Johansen and started for the door. Guards fell in around him.

"How long am I going to be stuck here?"

"We don't know yet, Mister Penningly." They passed a number of doors, all featureless with keypad locks, as Johansen droned on. "Once the primary analysis is complete, we'll have a better idea. We need to do some research before we can treat your condition." After a few corners, Johansen opened a door and waved an arm to usher him through. "Until we reverse this infection, you'll be our guest."

Prisoner, you mean. He stepped through the door.

"Niiiice place." The rooms were utterly unlike the rest of the facility; soft light, off-white painted walls with shelves of books, magazines and racks of DVDs, with one whole wall a huge entertainment system, and another a window-like screen that displayed a view startlingly similar to the one from his apartment window. The furnishings, too, were similar to his, with a small kitchen area set off to one side.

"There are also a bedroom and a lavish bath." Dr. Johansen waved an arm at the two other doors. "I think you'll find everything comfortable. If you need anything at all, just pick up the phone and press zero."

He went to the kitchen and opened the fridge. It was fully stocked with food and drink, including a bottle of Chardonnay and a variety of beers. He pulled a Sam Adams from the door and cracked it open.

"You pretty much thought of everything." He raised the bottle in toast and drank.

"And if you think of anything we haven't, just call."

"All right." He took another pull of beer and nodded. "I'll sit here like a good boy for now, but I'm not going to be a prisoner." He pointed to the door. "That door's not going to be locked."

"Only from the inside, Mister Penningly." Johansen waved a hand at the door. "You'll have an escort if you want a tour, but that's only to show you the way. And we will want some samples from you for testing."

"Oh, I understand, Dr. Johansen, but *you've* got to understand, too. I'm not your prisoner." He put the bottle down on the counter a little too hard, and the beer foamed up and out the neck. "You can't keep me here against my will."

"You've got nothing to worry about, Mister Penningly. Just relax and enjoy the accommodations."

"I will." Derrick picked the beer back up and took a long pull, surveying his surroundings once more with a scrutinizing eye. "Have your kitchen cook me a steak. Rare. I'm hungry."

Johansen nodded and backed out of the room. "It'll be here in ten minutes." The door clicked closed.

Derrick sipped his beer and looked around the place, perused the books, magazines, and videos. There was quite a selection. *They'll have cameras watching me.* He looked around in disdain at his prison. He would have to put on a good show, until he could find a way to get it out of here. He had to convince them that he could help them, that they needed him for more than *samples*.

Derrick drained his beer and dropped the bottle into the trash. "Home sweet home for now."

<hr>

The cops who had staked out the MCZ in hopes of spotting Aleksi were no help at all until Sergeant Jasper showed up. Tired of listening to them argue with campus police about who had jurisdiction, and who would take the fall for this monumental screw-up, Hutch had finally called Jasper and read him the riot act. Now, at least, there was no arguing, just a lot of ass chewing.

"So, you just thought you'd *watch* four guys in white coveralls take a six-foot long box from the lab we have under surveillance? You didn't even *think* to call the campus police? You didn't *think* it was a little strange that they were working on a Sunday?"

"No sir." The senior of the two plain-clothes officers looked uncomfortable. "We did confront them, but it all seemed to be in order. They had a work order, and it looked legit. They said they worked for the Museum, and that the sample was being transferred to storage."

Hutch had heard that the first time, and immediately called Quinton Neilson; no such orders had been issued. Quinton was even madder than Hutch.

"They had keys to the building and everything!"

"That's impossible," one of the campus police put in. There were cops all over the place now, and quite a crowd of onlookers, not to mention crime scene tape strung all around the area. Forensics teams were taking tire prints, finger prints and foot prints from every conceivable surface. "University keys can't be copied."

Jasper looked at the man as if he was brain damaged. "If you're pulling off a broad-daylight theft, you're not likely to balk at *illegally* copying a set of keys."

The Campus Police officer blushed, but kept his mouth wisely closed.

"I want descriptions of these four men from you two." Jasper pointed at his two officers. "I want times, makes and models of the vehicles, license numbers, and a verbatim account of every word that was said. I also want as good a recollection as you can give me of the work order and any ID's they flashed, as well as the logo on their uniforms, their hair color, clothes, and any distinguishing marks, tattoos, or freaking *dental* work any of them had. You got me?"

"Yes sir."

"And I want to work closely with your department on this, Lieutenant Preece. I'm working a murder investigation; this theft is all yours, but it's probably connected in *some* way. You have security cameras all over campus. We will need to pull them and look for this van. Maybe we got a picture of our thieves."

"You got it, Sergeant." The Campus Police lieutenant, at least, was willing to put the jurisdiction issue aside for now. She ordered her subordinate to have the video footage of every camera on campus pulled for all day Sunday.

Then Jasper turned to Hutch.

"And from you, Dr. Hutchinson, I need to know why the very specimen that was the only contention between my two missing murder suspects and the victim has been stolen."

"*Why* it was stolen is beyond me, Sergeant, but you might ask yourself which of your two suspects has the resources to pull something like this off."

"What do you mean?"

"I mean Aleksi's got no money, no influence, no friends to speak of, and no history of theft. Derrick Penningly's family is rich and influential, and he's already broken into this very lab once when he stole the data from Aleksi's computer."

"Okay, those are good points, but what would he want with that sample?"

"No idea." Hutch shrugged. He couldn't very well tell Jasper his suspicions. Any mention of Aleksi's infection or her changes would only earn him a long stay in a mental institution. "Unless it could incriminate him in some way and he wanted to get rid of it."

"But how could a bunch of old bones incriminate him?" Detective Willis jotted notes continually as they spoke.

"I have no idea." Hutch realized then that he had to say one more thing that might be important. "But we took samples from the specimen. They were being analyzed in Bob Tomlin's lab."

"Any bets that there's been a break-in over there, too?" Willis asked, flipping his notebook closed.

Hutch felt like he'd been kicked in the stomach.

———

These people were pros." Willis examined the blank lab benches, empty drawers, and spotless cabinets.

"No doubt," Jasper agreed. Even the trash had been emptied. He looked at Dr. Hutchinson; the man was pale and shaky. "You okay, Doctor?"

"No." Hutchinson looked at him and swallowed hard. "A priceless archeological specimen has been stolen. Years of work, careers, and one of my student's lives have been lost. I'm *not* okay."

"Were there any other places that samples were taken?" Jasper asked.

"Not physical samples, but there are data files on half a dozen computers and the university server as well." The professor shook his head. "I don't get it. Why take Bob's computer? If they were professionals, like you said, they'd have to know the data was backed up."

"Who else has copies of the data, and where?"

"Well, I do on my laptop, and Aleksi has it all on hers. We sent the preliminary data to Quinton Neilson, the curator of the MCZ, and used a university file-share system for that."

"So, the chances that someone could obliterate *all* of it are pretty slim." Jasper rubbed his jaw and sighed. "Which tells me they didn't *expect* to get rid of it all, but that they wanted everything you had, and Bob Tomlin's computer was the easiest way to get it."

"I think you ought to check your backup files, Doctor," Willis suggested

"Oh, I will."

Dr. Hutchinson was looking a little better, but Jasper couldn't help but think that he had taken the theft of the samples harder than he had taken Bob Tomlin's murder.

"Well, we've got another crime scene, so let's get the forensics team up here and get this taped off." He rubbed his eyes and shook his head. "Hell of a way to start a Monday."

Keys clattered into the bowl and Hutch closed the door. The click of the lock gave him a feeling of security that he knew was false. He leaned back against the door as if trying to close out the world with that thin barrier. He didn't even turn the light on. He didn't want to see anything, hear anything, feel anything.

Everyone from the police to the dean had been hounding him like a pack of wolves all day, and he was mentally and physically exhausted. After the theft yesterday, he'd spent most of the day filling out paperwork and answering questions for the Campus Police, and thought it had been rough. Today had been that to a factor of ten. The hierarchy of the university was all over him, and Quinton Neilson had started the paper storm that was inevitable from the loss of a specimen of inestimable value. The police had contacted him again with more questions. Video surveillance had given them a couple of images of the two vans and the men, but they had all worn baseball caps which obscured their faces. The license numbers of the vans, Jasper had told him, didn't exist. Neither did the shipping company. Everything had been a complete and very professional fabrication.

And without a single scrap of the sample remaining in his possession, and little chance that any of it would ever be recovered, Hutch had no means to have it analyzed, and no hope of finding a cure for Aleksi's condition.

And as a secondary result, his career was in jeopardy. The faculty council was filing an inquiry. He had lost two students—one dead and one fleeing the police—and a priceless artifact in a span of weeks, and they wanted answers.

He opened his eyes, not realizing that they had sagged closed, and went to the kitchen. He put his bag down and opened the fridge. It was after eleven PM, and he hadn't eaten since lunch, but the thought of food nauseated him. He settled for a container of yogurt and a piece of raisin bread. When the refrigerator door closed, he was blinded by the darkness. He fumbled for the switch over the sink and finally found it, then blinked against the flood of harsh light. He fumbled for a spoon and turned to the living room.

Old Path White Clouds stared at him from the kitchen counter.

Goddamn it, Aleksi, he thought, as the flood of memories buried him.

Hutch leaned against the counter and stared at the book while he ate mechanically. When the bread and yogurt were gone, he dropped the cup in the trash and returned to the book. On impulse, he picked it up and flipped through the pages, but there was no trace of her, no smudge of a fingerprint, no ephemeral scent. He had expunged every trace of her from his life.

"God*damn* it!"

Hutch pulled down a tumbler and a bottle of single malt whisky from the cabinet above the fridge. He poured a measure and swirled it in the glass, watching the legs of alcohol stream down the crystal and inhaling the heady aroma of peat and charcoal. He took a sip, picked up the book, and went to his chair. When he turned on the reading light, however, something caught his eye; a square of yellow hovered as if by magic in the center of the glass door to the dining room balcony.

The glass of whisky clacked forgotten to the table. He fumbled with the lock and flung open the door. The winter air hit him like a chill slap in the face, but he had the note from the window in his hand. It was from *her*, from Aleksi. His heart hammered in his chest.

"Coffee, Peet's, 6AM. No cops. A."

"How..." He looked around the balcony for a sign of her, any hint of how she had delivered the note, but there was nothing. No trace. He stared out into the night, the note clasped in his hand against the greedy teeth of the wind. "Where are you, Aleksi?" he asked, wondering if she might be watching from somewhere in the darkness.

He looked down at the note and read it again. He would have to be careful. The police were watching him. If they followed him to Peet's, he would never see her again.

I'm right here." Aleksi watched Hutch from behind a tree in the parking lot.

She also watched the police car parked beneath his balcony, listening to the cops' hushed conversation as steam wafted in interesting patterns from their Styrofoam cups of coffee. They were easy to spot, car engine running to keep them warm, sitting in the dark, watching for her but seeing nothing.

She looked back up to Hutch. He was still standing out on his balcony. "Go inside, Hutch." She glanced back to the cop car, but they were watching the building's entrance, not his balcony. She knew he had not heard her, but he went back in and closed the door. She heard the lock click. Good, he was being careful.

She watched the balcony for a while longer, watched him staring into the night, sipping from a glass of amber liquid. Was he thinking of her? Was he remembering their one night together? She was. She found it difficult, even with all the things occupying her mind, to think of anything else.

After a time, she turned and walked away, invisible in the darkness. She knew where she was going, what she needed, and that there would be more cops waiting for her there. She was getting good at evading police, being invisible, and had learned to stay out of sight in the daylight, to avoid security cameras, to wear a baseball cap and dark glasses when she had to traverse areas where unfriendly eyes or cameras might be looking for her. She had even found a place to sleep, though it wasn't exactly homey.

The Boston subway had become her lifeline, her thread of anonymity and means of travel without being noticed. During the busy morning and evening commute, she was just another face among thousands. A little internet research had given her a hint where she could hide. Disused service doors yielded to her, opening into a labyrinth of old tunnels, a maze of unused caves lined in brick and tile, dark and secure, if not clean.

Her apartment house glowed with heat and light, but on the third floor their window was dark. She spotted the cop car on her way to check the other windows to make sure Julie was asleep. She knew the police had been through her place with a fine-toothed comb, but she could not imagine that they would take all of her stuff, the few things she needed. Another cop car was positioned to watch the fire escape, but there were shadows enough to keep her hidden.

Around the other side of the building, an ancient oak tree rose to dizzying heights, its bare limbs extending far enough toward the eaves for her purposes. She removed her gloves and climbed it with little trouble, trying not to knock too much bark and twigs down. The gap from the tree to the roof was only six feet or so. She landed carefully, knowing the attic apartments were full of sleeping students.

Her bedroom window was in the shadow cast by a streetlight and far from the fire escape. She dug her claws into the gaps of brick and descended. The window had never been locked, with nothing but a thirty-foot drop outside. After slitting the screen, it opened easily. She was through like a whisper and left it open in case she had to leave in a hurry. She didn't think the cops would have an officer in the apartment, didn't think Julie would have put up with it, but she wasn't sure.

She put her empty backpack on her bed and quickly picked a few items she needed from her dresser, underwear, another hoodie, jeans, socks, some tee shirts, her heavy mittens, dark colors. She caught her reflection in the mirror and stopped to stare for a moment before moving on, ignoring the chill up her spine. At her jewelry box—the emerald earrings her father had sent her for Christmas—she dumped the contents into her bag's smallest pocket. She hated to think of selling it, but she would need money when they finally closed out her bank accounts.

The thought of money made her cringe, guilt urging her out of her room into the hall. She heard a rustle from the living room and knew Iggy was awake. She went to the kitchen and picked up the pad and pen beside the fridge. She scrawled, "Pay Rent, Feed Iggy, Find New Roommate," in a bulleted list. She pulled a wad of cash from her pocket, clipped it to the note and left it on the counter for Julie to find. She looked around the kitchen, but there was nothing she needed from here.

She risked venturing out into the living room for a look at Iggy. He sat in his cage—His *clean* cage. *Thanks Julie.* —staring at her. He didn't rattle it to be let out, didn't lash his tail impatiently, didn't seem to recognize her.

Maybe because I'm not me anymore. She blinked hard and turned away. She couldn't take him with her, of course, and couldn't think about what would happen to him. With everything happing to her, concern for a loved pet was one luxury she couldn't afford, which didn't stop her from feeling like shit. There was a lot she couldn't afford to take with her, fragments of a life that wasn't hers anymore.

She walked away and vanished into the night.

———

Persephone girded her nerves and stepped into the Sanctum. Gi-gi was awake, her bed inclined, her ancient eyes flicking over the half-dozen news, information, financial, and entertainment feeds flashing over her flat screens. Speakers mounted near the head of the bed droned out audio tracks to each display, her great-grandmother's amazing mind parsing through the mishmash of sound as easily as her eyes did the video.

Persephone approached and cleared her throat.

An ancient finger twitched on the control and all the screens froze, the audio suddenly silent. "Yes, Persephone?"

"We've had a setback." There had been several, actually, a domino effect of catastrophes seemingly designed to foil her mission.

"Murder..."

Of course Gi-gi knew about Tomlin; the news was all over town. But not the latest developments. "More than that. The specimen has been stolen."

The ancient eyes widened, then narrowed. "Who?"

"I don't know yet."

"Find out." She breathed in sharply, her lips pulled back for a moment. "Why? Something has been discovered. Someone else has learned something that we do not know." She said this like it caused her physical pain. Maybe it did.

"I'll do my best, Gi-gi." Persephone would have to call in some favors for this one. She started to back away.

"And, Persephone..."

"Yes, Gi-gi?"

"Learn what they know and get that specimen. People have killed for it. Be cautious."

"Yes, Gi-gi." Persephone turned and left, the video/audio deluge resuming behind her. *Be cautious...* She knew it wasn't concern for her safety, but concern about discovery that prompted the command. There was no sentiment left in the mind of her great-grandmother.

<hr>

The changes are accelerating." Johansen watched the multiple screens as Derrick Penningly played a videogame. "His reflexes are improving."

"He keeps beating his own high score." The technician pulled up the data and pointed at the numbers, response times, keystrokes per second, and even strategy analysis.

"In only three days. That *is* impressive." He wished the research was progressing as quickly. The samples were an enigma, a confused mish-mash of fragmented proteins, DNA, and RNA that they had only begun to pick apart. The samples taken from Penningly were even worse. The DNA sequences didn't make sense, as if his genome was being rewritten. They had no idea how to stop or reverse the process, even if they wanted to, which Johansen certainly didn't.

"Has he requested anything else?"

"Besides raw meat and alcohol, you mean?"

"Yes, besides that."

"Yes." The technician turned to look at his boss. "He says he's bored. He wants to look at our research."

"Well *that's* not going to happen." Johansen watched Penningly play his video game, clawed hands a blur on the controls. "No, I don't think we can let him out of his cage just yet."

If only he could find Aleksi Rychenkna. Johansen needed to step up the search for her before some fumble-handed cop got his hands on her. There had to be a way to bring her in, something she needed, some vulnerability he could exploit, but so far, he'd only come up with three; her roommate, her faculty advisor, and her parents, none of whom she seemed to be very close to.

No, Miss Rychenkna, we may just have to cut our losses on this one. He turned away from the screen and started back to the lab. *A bird in the hand, after all...*

<hr>

Jasper rubbed his eyes and stared at the white board in the squad room, at all the pictures, diagrams, and notes that made up the case. His eyes found the photographs of the vans, the images of the four men who had stolen the samples. How it connected to the murder of Bob

Tomlin was still a mystery, evidenced by the big red question mark in the middle of the dotted line that connected the thefts to the murder evidence.

"Professional." He frowned and reached for his coffee cup. The coffee was cold and bitter, but so was he, and it kept him alert.

"What did you say?" Willis looked up from the manpower requisition forms he was filling out.

Overtime for surveillance was costing the department a bundle. They had a few ATM transactions from Rychenkna, but they were all over the city. The subway footage was overflowing with images of slim people in coats, hoodies, and hats—*Winter in Boston; what did you expect?*—but none had been confirmed to be either of their fugitives.

"I said, professional." He pointed to the pictures of the van and the men in nondescript uniforms. "Those guys knew every trick. They stink of old school larceny; mob, maybe. Some group that specializes in lifting high-end merchandise."

"But Penningly's family doesn't have connections like that," Willis reminded him. "Plenty of money, but no links to organized crime, and no big expenditures lately that could finance a job like this. The old man's pissed off that his son can't be found, and called every police captain and mayor in the greater Boston area to call them incompetent. They've been estranged for the last two years or so. The kid didn't even go home for Christmas."

"Neither did Rychenkna." Jasper scratched his stubbled jaw. "Who else could arrange this kind of job, and why, other than to protect Derrick Penningly?" He squinted at the photos again. "I mean look at these guys. They look like freaking clones! Perfect posture, cut, walk like guys who know how to move…like goddamn government spooks."

"Oh, speaking of government…" Willis rooted through the pile of paper on his desk and found a sheet. "This came while we were out. Seems the FBI has an interest in the thefts, since the pieces that were stolen were from Russia."

"They're pulling the investigation away from us?" Jasper blinked at him like he'd told him his hair was on fire. "Not the *murder* investigation!"

"No, but they've insisted that we share all our findings with them, including the computer data Hutchinson gave us."

"They're welcome to it, as long as they don't shut us out. We've still got a murder to solve, and at this point, I'll take any help they can give me."

"Hey you two!" They both turned to see Willis' husband Charles coming in. He had a big paper bag in one hand and a drink carrier in the other. "Dinner for three, served with a smile."

Charles struck a pose, smiling like a hundred-watt bulb, and Jasper had to laugh. He was dressed, as always, to the nines; a cream silk jacket, pastel shirt and a tie that probably cost more than Jasper spent on a month's rent. Working vice had its advantages. He often posed as an upscale pimp, and the clothes were part of his job. Charles played it to the hilt.

"Now I know why I married you." Willis rose from his chair to help with the bag and give his husband a kiss of greeting. "You're a godsend."

"And all this time I thought you married me for the sex!" Charles handed over the food and distributed the drinks. "I got those yummy roast beef subs from that place down the square. Dig in!"

"Thanks, Charles." Jasper accepted a wrapped sandwich and a towering cup of Dunkin' Donuts coffee. "You just earned your Christmas Card."

"And it's not even the end of February! Lucky me!" Charles waved a hand at the white board. "Mind if I cover up the gruesome display while we eat. Looking at some poor boy's torn out throat while I'm eating roast beef gives me heartburn."

"Feel free." Jasper bit into his sandwich and chewed in gastronomic bliss. "Wicked sandwich. Thanks, Charles."

"Part of the service." Charles stopped at the white board, not staring at the flayed flesh of Bob Tomlin's throat, but the photos of the shipping crew thieves. "Who are the Fed Four?"

Jasper stopped in mid swallow, nearly choking at the question. He grabbed his coffee and took a pull, swallowing forcefully. "Why call them that?"

"Oh, pu-*lease*! Just look at those *shoes*!" He waved a hand at the photo. "Four pair of identical low-profile combat boots, all the same style, color and make? *Nobody* wears shit like that unless someone makes them, sweetie."

Jasper was out of his chair, the food forgotten. He squinted at the photo, then looked over his shoulder at Willis. "Why didn't we see that before?"

"Because we're not connoisseurs of fine men's footwear." Willis grinned and took another bite of his sandwich. "And my husband's a genius."

"Well, I'll take that as a thank you." Charles reached up and pulled down the screen that covered the board. "Now back to dinner, Sergeant. It's after midnight, and you can't capitalize on my genius until the morning anyway."

"I..." Jasper let Charles pull him away from the obscured board while his mind raced. "Right...midnight...morning."

"You okay, sweetie?" Charles helped Jasper into his chair. "You look a little pale."

"Just thinking." He reached for his sandwich and took another bite, chewing as he let the possibilities sift through his mind. They *might* be government spooks, or maybe some kind of hired mercenaries, but why steal the specimen? And who could swing the kind of weight it would take to organize and execute something like this?

Jasper knew one thing for sure; with the FBI grabbing the jurisdiction of the theft, and evidence pointing to government involvement, he would get absolutely nowhere if he started prying for answers.

"But *murder*..." he mumbled, reaching for his coffee, "...is something else entirely."

3 3

Hutch skipped the gym, drove straight to the Oxford Parking garage—police tail intact—and pulled into an empty faculty spot. The cops, he noticed, parked on the street, no doubt watching the doors. He went to his office, turned on the light, and plugged in his computer.

He left at quarter of six, with the light on and his computer running a virus scan. Fortunately, Hutch could get from his office to the south end of the MCZ building without setting foot outside. From there, he skirted the quad behind the chem labs, crossed Kirkland, and edged along the walk beside Memorial Hall. The dorm quads were silent this early, and he looked back to make sure nobody had followed him. Across Mass. Ave., he passed the transit station and hurried down JFK. He looked back again at Auburn, but there was no sign that he'd picked up a police shadow. It was still dark, but Peet's was lit up and they were just opening the doors. He slipped through, fifth in line, and ordered two coffees and a large apple Danish. When he turned around and scanned the café, he spotted Aleksi's jacket in the corner, the only table blocked from street view. She wore a hoodie and a cap, and he couldn't see her face, but it was her, no doubt.

"Thanks for the note." He sat down with his back to the room. "I bought you a coffee."

Her mittened hands wrapped around the cup. "Thanks."

"Are you okay?" He knew she wasn't but didn't know what else to ask.

"No." She kept her eyes down, but her voice was husky, as if she'd been crying.

"What can I do to help you, Aleksi? The police are watching me, so coming out to meet you probably isn't too safe."

"Why did you bring them to your place?" There was a tremble in her tone, as if she didn't want to hear the answer.

"Sorry about that, but they grilled me for about four hours at the police station, then insisted they see my home. No warrant, but they made it clear that I didn't have much of a choice. I wanted to call ahead, but they wouldn't leave me alone." He tried to peer under the brim of her hat but couldn't see her eyes. "How did you get out of there?"

"Never mind that. Look, Hutch, they've probably got your phone tapped and reading your email, so I don't know how we can communicate. I can't go to the police, and I can't go to a hospital, but I'd like your doctor friend to have a look at my blood or something."

"Something else has happened, Aleksi. The Kamchatka specimen has been stolen. Even the samples in Bob's lab. Someone took everything."

"What?" Her head came up, and he got a glimpse of her eyes. He stifled his surprise—her irises were stark yellow, pupils vertical slits.

"They were taken on Sunday by some fake shipping company. Jasper said it looked professional."

"Why would someone take the samples?"

"I don't know. It doesn't make sense. The only thing I could think was that Derrick arranged it to somehow cover himself, but the samples weren't the incriminating evidence anyway. He's vanished, too, by the way. The cops want you both."

"Well, that's something at least." Her head came up again as someone else came in. "If he took the samples…" Her eyes snapped to his. "Hutch, he knows about the infection, the *source*. He's *got* to be infected, too. It's the only thing that makes sense. *That's* why…"

"But why take them?" He shook his head.

"I don't know, but I think I know how he killed Bob."

"What?" He felt something cold ball up in the pit of his stomach.

She answered him by pulling one of her mittens off. Each of her fingers was now tipped with an inch-long retractable claw, and the golden scales had advanced to cover her whole hand. A fine membrane webbed the space between her last three fingers, and trailed from the smallest up her wrist and under her sleeve. She looked at him then, huge brilliant yellow eyes snapping open and closed under a ridge of brow that glinted with golden scales.

"Oh, Aleksi…" He reached for her hand, but she snatched it away.

"It's progressing faster now, Hutch." She put her glove back on. "I don't know how to explain this, but Derrick…*smelled* strange to me when I scratched his car. Those scratches must have given him an idea how to frame me, so killing Bob would get us both out of the way." She reached out with a gloved hand to clutch his wrist. "Hutch, these changes…they make me feel…they give me violent impulses. If Derrick was *already* aggressive or violent, they might put him over the top."

"You've got to come in, Aleksi. We've *got* to try to help you, treat you, somehow."

She let go of him. "I can't come in. Get a blood kit from one of the bio labs and keep it with you. You can take a sample to Bornstein. If I go to a hospital, they'll never let me out again." She took her coffee and stood. "Thanks for the coffee."

"What else can I do for you, Aleksi?" He reached for her wrist.

"I may need money. My ATM still works, but they'll shut it down soon, and I know they're getting my picture every time I use it."

"Sure. Whatever you need." He squeezed her arm, but she pulled away.

"Thanks, Hutch. Tell Lonnie…something, okay?"

"I will. Be careful."

"I am."

It was all he could do to not watch her as she left the café.

Aleksi sipped her coffee and started toward the Harvard Square transit station. The commute was beginning, and she was one more faceless worker bee in a hive of anonymity. She crossed Auburn and turned up JFK, casting glances into the shop windows as she made the corner. She had no interest in the displays but could see the reflections of what was behind her without turning fully. It was a trick she learned evading the police in the warrens of Boston. It was still early, but there were plenty of people out now, some going the other way, arriving for early classes, others moving along with her, going into the city.

She slowed as she approached the intersection of Brattle Street when something caught her eye. There was a man in a charcoal overcoat, which wasn't unusual, but he wasn't keeping up with the flow, and his gait was strange, arms not swinging much with his stride, as if he was moving with some impediment. His gaze met hers, paused, then swept on. He raised a hand to cup his mouth, and she saw the muscles of his throat moving. He was speaking, but she couldn't hear. She crossed the street and went up the alley that led toward the Garage. At the first plaza she ducked left and sunk down into the shadows behind a dumpster.

She heard his footsteps coming up the alley.

Kill! Strike! Flee! the voice of her instinct screamed, but she fought it down and stayed hidden.

The man in the overcoat emerged from around the corner, his eyes sweeping the little courtyard. He turned a full circle, and she tensed, but his eyes passed over her without pause.

Looking for me.

He hesitated then continued on to look down the narrow alley south into the Garage, and then back over his shoulder, scanning the shadows. She looked into his eyes, analyzing him. Clean shaven, maybe thirty, strong, but moving stiffly, like he was carrying a heavy pack. His gaze swept over her again, and she thanked the darkness, her blanket, her shield. He took the alley, but as he turned, she saw it; a tiny wire curled around behind his right ear to vanish under his stocking cap, like a hearing aid but not.

Cop? She glanced back around the corner. If he had spotted her, which now seemed likely, there would be others.

Aleksi hurried back the way she'd come and surveyed the moving crowd, but saw no other similar overcoats. Another glance confirmed that he was long gone, and she stepped out to continue her way. She headed for the train station, moving with the other people, wondering who the man was, *what* he was, and why she wasn't suddenly surrounded by police. Surely, if he had spotted her, they would have closed in.

But they hadn't.

Aleksi descended the steps into the transit station and swiped her commuter pass through the turnstile, recalling his face, his manner, his gait, forming a search image in her mind. She boarded her train and sat near the exit, eyes low, watching the other commuters via their reflections in the subway car windows. The door hissed closed and she started to breathe easier. Then, as the train pulled into motion, she saw them, two of them now, the man she'd seen and another emerging from the stairs onto the platform. They both moved the same way, hurried but heavy, eyes sweeping the crowd.

A commuter bumped into one of them and she caught a glimpse as his heavy coat whipped open for a moment. The man's pants were bulky, like he was wearing pads under them. A glint of black metal caught her eye, like a pipe, or a stick…or a thick gun barrel.

Darkness enveloped her as the train plunged into the tunnel.

Not cops, but who? Aleksi had much more to worry about now.

The fact is, Quinton, you wouldn't even *know* about the Kamchatka specimen if we hadn't discovered it, so you've really lost nothing." Hutch tried to keep his voice neutral and not squeeze his cracked phone too hard, but he was tired of fending off accusations of incompetence.

"You're right, I've lost nothing, Hutch. *You*, however have lost a priceless artifact. You can't argue your way out of the facts."

"I did *not* lose it. It was *stolen*. It was kept under lock and key. Come on, Quinton, you can't blame us because we were robbed!"

"And what about Aleksi! One of the brightest young students I've ever met, and now she's up on murder charges. You've lost her, too! What the hell is going on?"

"One of my students is *dead*, Quinton!" Hutch's temper flared, his voice trembling. "Don't you *dare* tell me what I've lost!"

"Alright. Okay, that was out of line. I'm sorry, but *damn* it, Hutch, what am I supposed to do? I've got the museum board crawling all over me screaming for blood."

"Tell them to talk to University Police. If you want another ass to chew, try Sergeant Jasper with the Cambridge Police. He's investigating Bob's murder. He's the one who put out a warrant for Aleksi's arrest."

"Why the hell did she run, Hutch? Did she tell you?"

"No. I saw her the day before, and she was worried but nothing more." He felt bad about the lie but didn't know what else to say. "She told me they found evidence that Derrick Penningly stole some data from her computer. Data about the stolen specimen. Don't forget that he worked for *you*, Quinton."

"Not anymore he doesn't."

"Well, right now, I think he's the prime suspect in both the murder and the theft, but nobody knows why he would commit either crime."

"Well, maybe if they find him, they can clear this up." Hutch heard

Quinton sigh on the other end of the line. "Sorry for losing my temper, Hutch, but…well, you know."

"I know, Quinton. Just hang in there. I'll be in touch." He hit end and considered turning the phone off. It seemed he'd done nothing but talk today, and he was tired of it, but there was one more call he had to make. He dialed Congressman Twain and put the phone to his ear.

"Dr. Hutchinson," came the answer. "Been a while."

"Yes, it has. I'm afraid I've got some bad news."

"I heard about that poor Tomlin boy. Terrible, senseless thing."

"That's part of why I called, Congressman," Hutch began, unsure of how to deliver the multiple blow of Bob's death, Aleksi's disappearance, and the loss of the samples. "We've had some additional setbacks as well."

"Really? Nothing serious, I hope?"

"I'm afraid so." He wondered why Twain hadn't asked about Aleksi. Every other time Hutch talked to him, he'd asked how she was progressing. "I'm sorry to say that we had a theft here on Sunday. The entire Kamchatka specimen was stolen from both Aleksi's and Bob's labs. Every trace of it, gone."

"What?"

Still no question about Aleksi. Hutch got a niggling feeling that something wasn't quite right with this conversation. "So, you can see we're a little over our heads. Everyone's upset, and the funding for the project is going to have to be put on hold until we can sort things out and get the specimen back."

"Yes, yes of course. I completely understand."

Still no question about Aleksi. "I'll call you when I know something substantive."

"Any time, Doctor. Anything I can do to help, just let me know."

"I will. Thank you, Congressman."

"No problem at all."

Hutch stared at the phone as the call went dead. Not a single question about Aleksi, when the man couldn't stop talking about her only a week ago. Something wasn't right.

I 'm sorry we haven't made more progress, Mister Penningly, but the DNA of the sample is quite degraded." Johansen stood just inside Derrick's door, hands in the pockets of his lab coat.

Derrick could smell his fear. *Good*, he thought. *He needs to be afraid of me.*

"If we could take another blood sample, and I've scheduled a session to collect bone marrow—"

"No more blood." Derrick raised a clawed hand to scratch at the scales that were forming along his jaw. "And you're *not* jamming a biopsy needle into my pelvis. I'm not giving you anything else until the murder charges are gone and I get my life back."

"But we can't cure you if we can't analyze your condition."

"If you'd let me help analyze those samples, I'd have had an answer for you by now." He went to his refrigerator, jerked open the door, and picked out a flat white package. The paper peeled back from the cool red meat. He tore off a bite and turned back to Johansen, chewing as he spoke. "I *am* a scientist, you know!"

"Actually, I was thinking of directing your specific talents toward another problem, Mister Penningly." Johansen took his hands from his pockets. One held a photo. "You know this woman, Aleksi Rychenkna?"

"Know her? Of *course*, I know her! She's a lying bitch!" He took another bite and chewed. "So, the police haven't caught her yet?"

"They have not, which doesn't surprise me, but neither have my men been able to apprehend her." He returned the picture to his pocket. "We believe that she also has contracted this infection."

"I *know* she has." Derrick took another bite and narrowed his yellow eyes at Johansen. The scent of Aleksi's rage when she scratched his car wafted through his mind. "You need my help with her, don't you?"

"You are as astute as you are perceptive, Mister Penningly. Aleksi Rychenkna seems to have developed a preternatural ability to spot and evade my people. *You*, however, might have better luck."

"Luck has nothing to do with it, Doctor." Derrick stripped away the last of the meat and flicked the denuded bone into the trash. "It's all about skill."

3 4

Aleksi landed on his balcony rail like a dark snowfall and melted into the shadows. There was no note on the window, no sign of him and no light for the two hours since he'd arrived home. She listened, sampled the air, and knew he was inside, in the living room, waiting, alone.

Staying in the shadows cast by the streetlights below, she tested the sliding glass door. It was unlocked. She thought about the men in long coats, about rooftops, high-powered rifles, night scopes, and assassins. Then she thought about Hutch and their brief, wonderful time together.

She would risk it.

In one motion, she eased the door open just wide enough, slipped through, and closed it. She crouched there, a shadow within shadows, listening to her heartbeat, his heartbeat, his breathing, and let the scent of him fill her. He glowed there in his chair, the heat of his body a beacon in her eyes.

"I wondered how you got up to the balcony, but I guess it was easy." He started to stand up.

"Stay down!"

He froze and then sank back down into his chair. "Why?"

"There are...other people, not police, looking for me. They might be watching through the window."

"Aleksi, I don't think—"

273

"I don't know who they are, but they carry guns under their coats, and have ear pieces like spies from the movies."

"Spies?" He paused and cleared his throat. "I may have an idea who they are. You want to talk here, or—"

"Your bathroom. It's the only room without windows. I'll go first, and you follow. Just sand up and walk like you're going there to pee, okay?"

"Okay."

His voice sounded strange, worried, rigid, as if... *He's afraid of me. Good. He'd be a fool not to be.*

She crept across the floor and slipped into the dark bathroom. There was enough light for her, but she imagined he might stumble around, so she hunkered out of his way and listened to him get up and walk toward her. The door closed.

"Can I turn on the light?"

"If you want, but I'll warn you, Hutch, you won't like what you see."

Light flooded the room. She watched him squint and shield his eyes from the glare. Hers adjusted more quickly, though she saw less color than she used to. His formerly royal blue eyes were now gray, his skin dusky instead of that healthy, ruddy hue. He blinked and finally focused on her, crouched in the corner near the sink. She pulled her hoodie back and took off her hat. He opened his mouth to say something, failed, and closed it.

"Don't worry." She stood. "I won't hurt you. I couldn't ever hurt you."

"Oh, Aleksi." He started toward her and a surge of panic shot through her.

She held out one taloned hand and said, "No. Don't, Hutch." He stopped, so much pain in his face, so much sorrow... "You don't want to touch me. It's not safe."

"You said you wouldn't hurt me."

"Yes, but…I don't know. It might…you might get infected."

"I'll be careful, then." He took another step closer, one hand out to brush her scaled cheek. His scent felt like a toxin in her mind, a drug, drawing her in.

She pulled back. "These people following me. You said you might know who they are?"

"Not specifically, but Twain called the other day, and for the first time, he didn't ask how you were doing. Persephone knows him, and said he has a reputation with young interns. I thought back and wondered if he might be planning to come on to you. He asked about you every single time we spoke except the last, even when I gave him the perfect opening."

"Twain..." Could the men in gray coats have been government? *Maybe...*

He looked at her again, closer, and asked, "Does it...hurt?"

"Some." She shrugged and a looked down at her hands, her ring and little finger now far longer than the others, the membrane between them fully formed, trailing all the way up her arm, down her side and leg to her ankle. "Like...growing pains."

"Growing pains?" He gave her a look like he thought she was joking.

"Just a dull ache, in the joints, mostly."

"How do you..." He faltered, shook his head and took a deep breath. "God, Aleksi, how do you survive? How do you stay hidden?"

"It's getting harder," she admitted. "I stay down during the day. At night, nobody pays attention."

"How do you get...food?" He sounded afraid of her pending answer.

"I can buy meat at the small groceries in town without much trouble as long as I can wear my gloves." She indicated the pair of heavy mittens at her belt. "That's going to get harder when the weather warms up. They've all got security cameras, and I'm afraid I'll get spotted. I've done some looking around for meat distributors. They don't have much security."

"But you must sleep somewhere."

"I've found someplace nobody goes to." She didn't elaborate. What he didn't know, he couldn't tell. "I'm doing okay, but I don't know what to do. I've got to find some way to clear this up, Hutch, someone who can help me. Someone I can trust."

"You can trust me, Aleksi." He tried to smile. "And I kinda told Lonnie about some of it, though I don't know if she believes me or not."

"Lonnie? God, Hutch, don't let her get involved in this. I couldn't stand it if her life was ruined, too."

"Don't worry, Lonnie's smart enough to keep her mouth shut. Now." He squared his shoulders as if he was about to give a lecture. "What do you need from me besides money, clothes, food, and a place to sleep?"

She could almost have laughed at his tone, so sure, so matter of fact, as if he wasn't terrified of her.

"I don't think I can risk sleeping here, Hutch, but...um..." She nodded to the shower. "If I could maybe wash up and do some laundry?"

"Of course! Here, let me take your things. I'll run a load while you shower."

"Thanks, Hutch." She handed over her bulging pack and doffed her jacket, hoodie, boots and socks. Then, however, she balked, though he showed no signs of shock at her wiry arms, the thin membrane that trailed up her arm, the claws that extended from her toes. "I'll hand the rest out, if you don't mind."

"Oh. Okay. No problem. Oh, and I have a blood kit. Bornstein agreed to do some tests."

"Okay."

He took the bundle out to the main room and she heard the washer start. She quickly pealed out of her jeans, tee shirt, bra and panties and dumped them outside the door. She turned to the shower, then caught a glimpse of herself in the big mirror and caught her breath, startled by her own reflection.

Monster…

Her hair had receded at the temples and lightened to gold at the roots. The ridge of her brow was even more pronounced, her eyebrows now little more than a line of heavy scales. Her eyes, now bright yellow and slit-pupiled, blinked from enlarged sockets, and her nose had flattened, the nares wider above the thin line of her lips. Her cheekbones were more pronounced, and her chin more pointed, but she could still see her face there, could still see Aleksi behind the monster.

As for the rest, her skin seemed to shimmer in the light, her arms, torso and legs corded with muscle. Her breasts had flattened, and her body hair had completely vanished, replaced by a smattering of golden scales. She looked away, a pit of irrepressible disgust roiling in her stomach. Why had she come here? Why had she risked his life along with hers?

Aleksi turned the shower on and stepped in before it even warmed. Shampoo and soap took away a few layers of filth from living in a subway tunnel. She was lathering her hair a second time when she heard the bathroom door.

Panic shot through her like an electric shock, a cold ball of fear gripping her chest when she realized that Hutch was only wearing a robe.

No! She wiped the soap away and backed into the corner of the shower. "What are you doing?" Terror rimed her voice.

"I need to see you, Aleksi." He didn't reach for the shower door, didn't sound like he was afraid, horrified at her monstrosity. "I need to hold you again. You don't understand how much I miss you, just being with you, touching you." His voice faltered at the last. "If you don't...want me to, I'll leave."

"I..." Aleksi didn't know what she wanted. He said he wanted to hold her, to touch her, but how could he? Could she stand to see the revulsion in his eyes when he really saw her? "I don't know, Hutch. I don't think you want to see me like this."

"Okay, then, how about if I close my eyes."

"What?" She couldn't believe he was saying this. His tone was so flippant, so casual.

"Close my eyes. I'll promise not to look, okay?" Then, in a softer tone, "I just want to hold you again, Aleksi."

"Okay." She didn't know why she said it, why she wanted it, but it was too late to renege. Through the mottled glass she saw his robe drop away, and he reached for the shower door. She huddled back as far back as she could and watched as he eased into the shower and closed the door. His eyes were squeezed tightly closed. "You can open your eyes, Hutch."

He did, and his face changed. She couldn't read what she saw there, but there was certainly shock, surprise...and something else.

"Aleksi...you're...it's..." He paused, his eyes roving over her from head to toe.

Disgusting...monstrous...horrible...hideous! She couldn't bear the thought of him finishing the sentence.

"Beautiful."

"*What?*" She couldn't believe it, couldn't believe him. "Don't *say* that! It's not! It's *horrible*! I'm turning into some kind of a freak!" She clenched her arms around her chest, looking away, blinking back the tears. "Can't you *see*? Can't you see what's *happening* to me?"

Then his arms were around her, holding her, crushing her against his beating heart, and she was crying, sobbing into his shoulder, holding him like she would hold a butterfly, afraid to crush him. Her shoulders heaved and she cried out the unfairness, the horror, the pain, and he held her all the more tightly with every wracking sob.

And it felt good.

The cops were out of their car the moment Derrick and his two keepers stepped out of the big SUV. Derrick kept his hands in the pockets of his heavy coat and squinted through his sunglasses at the two pudgy officers as they approached, flashing badges and asking who they were.

One of his minders pulled a leather billfold from a pocket and flashed it at the cops. "FBI, officer. I'm special agent Prendergast, and this is special agent Watson. We're investigating the theft from the university."

"And we're investigating a murder," one of the cops said.

Derrick kept his face averted. The cop smelled like coffee and fatty deep-fried food.

"Then our jobs overlap very little," his minder said. "You do your job and we'll do ours. Everybody's happy."

"Fine." The cop shrugged like he didn't care, but his tone said he did. "Our guys were already all over that apartment, but if you find anything, we expect full disclosure."

"No problem, officer. Your boss will get our report."

The cops returned to their car, and Derrick followed his escort up the steps and into Aleksi's apartment. They opened the door with a key that fit the lock. He didn't ask how they got it; these guys got whatever they wanted. He would like it even more when they got him what *he* wanted.

"What a shithole." Derrick removed his dark glasses and glancing around the place. It was tiny, cramped, shabby, and smelled like shit.

"Go ahead and have a look around," his head minder said. The guy's name wasn't Prendergast, and the other's wasn't Watson. He didn't know their real names and didn't particularly care to.

Derrick started with Aleksi's bedroom, knowing by scent that it was hers. He looked at her bed, sniffed her pillow. He looked through her dresser and found a tiny empty jewelry box. Her top drawer, where just about everyone on the planet kept their underwear, was mostly empty. He checked the tiny closet, the dirty clothes bin, and found that also nearly empty. The scent from that bin, the mingling of feminine sweat and something else, something not human, something like *him*, set blood racing through his veins. He reached in and pulled out a pair of plain white cotton panties, pressed them to his face and inhaled.

Yes… A flood of scintillating, primal, visceral need burned through his mind.

"She's been here recently." He tucked the underwear in his pocket and left the room.

"How do you figure?" Minder One asked. Minder Two didn't talk much.

"I read the police report and there are discrepancies."

"Like what?"

He raised an eyebrow at the man for questioning him. "Like the six pair of earrings, two rings, and a pendant that used to be in her jewelry box and are now gone. Also, there's not enough in her underwear drawer. She came back, took some clothes, her jewelry, and left."

"So much for police surveillance," the man said with a smirk.

"So much for *your* surveillance," Derrick countered, which earned him a scowl. He just smiled back and stopped at the other bedroom door. He entered and glimpsed a few photos of a perky blonde in the company of several other people. "Where's her roommate?"

"Julie Parks? She's in class. She's a drama student."

"*Perfect.*" Derrick went through her things, memorized her scent, less interesting than Aleksi's, but still… "She might be interesting. Have you questioned her?"

"The police have. She was dating the Tomlin kid."

"*She* was dating Bob Tomlin? No fucking way." He looked again at her picture and licked his lips, remembering the taste of that salty, coppery spray, the gurgle as Tomlin fell to the garage floor clutching at his torn throat. "She must be crushed by the loss and starving for companionship."

"There's nothing to suggest that Rychenkna was particularly close to the Parks woman."

"Still…" Derrick left her room and circuited the kitchen. There was a whiff of Aleksi here. He looked in the fridge, then the trash. Nothing.

The living room was dismal. The couch was threadbare, the TV tiny. They had no DVD player and no stereo. He found the remote and turned on the TV; it came up to the local PBS station. *Typical.* He turned it off and started at the sound of rattling metal from the corner. The scent of shit was stronger here, and he peered around the couch to find a wire cage with a big lizard inside. It stared at him and lashed its tail.

"An iguana?"

"Rychenkna's pet."

"Disgusting." He peered closer at it and wrinkled his nose. "Might as well keep a fucking rat for a pet." He reached for the cage door.

"What are you doing?"

"I'm investigating." Derrick cast the man a glare. "You want to bring someone out in the open, you take something they love away."

"You're going to take her iguana?"

"In a way." He flipped the door open, and before the lizard could escape, he snatched it up, careful not to let his claws pierce its scaly skin.

"Don't do anything we'll have to clean up, Mister Penningly. Those cops got a good look at our faces."

"I was told to find Aleksi Rychenkna." Derrick strolled into the kitchen. "What you've been doing hasn't been working so well."

He stuffed the thrashing lizard in the microwave and slammed the door, then grabbed a post-it note from the fridge and scrawled, "Aleksi, Weld Boat House, midnight." and stuck it to the door.

"You are *not* going to—"

"You want Rychenkna, or not?" He punched in ten minutes and pressed cook. The light came on and the carousel began to turn, but Minder One shoved past and stabbed the cancel key.

"You are *not* going to cook her goddamn lizard!" He grabbed a dish towel and wiped down the keypad.

Derrick stared at the man and grinned. The minder's glare didn't waver. "Fine, Special Agent Gutless. We'll see if it works without sending the filthy little reptile to lizard heaven. I guess it's the message that counts anyway, but a threat doesn't carry the same weight if it's not demonstrated properly. She'll probably write us off as a bunch of pussies."

"You really think she's dumb enough to show up at the boat house?"

"No, but she'll be watching it, and I'll be watching for her. See how that works?"

Minder One waved toward the door. "Now, where to next?"

"I think Dr. Hutchinson's place." Derrick sighed in disappointment and allowed them to escort him out of the apartment. "Fucking tree-hugger's probably got nothing but a bunch of house plants. You gonna get all teary eyed if I nuke his Chia pet?"

Someone was in my apartment, Sergeant, and your goddamn cops let them walk right in!" Julie Parks' call had brought Jasper running like a terrier after a rat, but she had surprised him. She was more angry than upset. "Either you get me some decent protection or you leave me the hell alone!"

"I'll have a talk with my people, Miss Parks." He handed the heavy cage to Willis and smiled at her. "My forensics people will be done in no time."

"And I want someone to get Aleksi's stuff out of here. I'm not sharing an apartment with a murder suspect! I'm going to have to advertise for a new roommate, and I can't do that with her stuff still here."

"We'll contact her parents and see if one of them can come up and pick up her things. Don't worry, Miss Parks. You're safe."

"Bullshit. *Nobody's* safe when someone like Bob Tomlin can get his goddamn *throat* torn out in a goddamn *parking* lot! Just get your people the hell out of here and let me have my life back!"

"We'll be out of here as soon as we can. You have my word." He left the apartment to the forensics team and joined Willis on the stairs.

"So, where are we taking the lizard?"

"The lab first. I don't know if they can lift a print from an iguana, but someone picked him up."

"How do you know it's a him?" Willis lifted the cage higher and squinted. "Not like it's got a package."

"Rychenkna said it was a boy. Didn't you read her statement?"

Willis made a sound of disgust. "Okay, lab first, where to next? This thing's *not* sitting in the squad room."

"Actually, I think I might give Dr. Hutchinson a call about a possible adoption. I'd like to have another look at his place again anyway."

"You'll think he'll take the thing?"

"I don't see why not. They're both vegetarians, and I'd be willing to bet that they're both a lot closer to Aleksi Rychenkna than the good doctor lets on."

<hr>

I appreciate you calling me, Sergeant." Hutch held the elevator door open for the two detectives. He punched his floor and the doors closed. "I don't know what I'm going to do with a two-foot iguana, but I'll be happy to look after Iggy until all this gets cleared up."

"Iggy?" Jasper handed over the cage.

"Yeah, Aleksi told me about him." He peered through the wire. The lizard looked pissed off. Jasper had called him that afternoon, but Hutch couldn't get out of his office until after six. "She said her roommate Julie called him her boyfriend."

The doors opened and Hutch led the way into his apartment. He dropped his keys in the bowl, put the iguana's cage down by the kitchen counter, and waved a hand at the rest of the place. "Feel free to have a look around. I can't believe someone broke into Aleksi's apartment and threatened her."

"Well, they didn't exactly threaten *her*, but the lizard was in real danger," Willis said. "Two minutes from being an iguana pot pie."

"That's just sick." Hutch looked around his place. He doubted that they would find a trace of Aleksi here. He'd done a thorough cleaning after her visit the previous night. "Can I offer you anything?"

"No, thank you. You're being very accommodating, Dr. Hutchinson." Jasper peered around at this and that, checking the refrigerator, the freezer, the microwave, and the oven.

"I know we got off on the wrong foot the other day, but I see how hard you're working on this, and I know Aleksi could *not* have killed Bob Tomlin." He shrugged and pulled a bottle of iced tea from the fridge. "I realized that the more I help you, the sooner this will get cleared up."

"Well, I can't argue with you there, Doctor." Jasper looked around the living room. "If you see anything out of place, please let us know. If they broke into Miss Rychenkna's apartment, they may have broken in here, too."

"Sure." Hutch looked around, not really expecting to find anything out of place. The TV remote wasn't where he remembered putting it, but that was probably nothing. The office was the same as it had always been, and the bathroom was spotless, though his hairbrush was displaced. He knew Aleksi had used it, but he'd been careful about cleaning it thoroughly. He didn't want to give the cops any ideas that she might have been there, so he didn't mention it.

"So, with two of your students gone and that specimen stolen, you must be in a hard spot with the university." Willis looked at him sidelong. "You seem pretty upbeat for a guy on the ropes."

"Attitude determines success." He cocked an eyebrow at the cop. "If you let the negative aspects determine your attitude, your chances of success plummet."

"Sounds like denial to me." Willis turned away to pass through the door into Hutch's bedroom. "So, tell me Doc, did you get a new decorator, or is this part of your positive attitude thing?"

"What?" Hutch stepped into his bedroom and froze, staring at his shredded bed. One pillow and half the bed were torn to pieces. Comforter, sheets and right down to the batting of the mattress were ripped apart, and a yellow post-it note lay on the torn pillow. "Holy *shit*!"

"I'm guessing from your sudden shift in attitude that this is *not* your usual way of making the bed."

"You've got *that* right!" He started forward, then stopped when Jasper's hand closed on his arm.

"Sorry, Doctor, but we've got to get a forensics team in here to look at this before anyone touches a thing."

"Oh. Uh…sure." He could see from where he stood that the sheets and pillow case had been slashed in four parallel strokes, ripped open not unlike Bob Tomlin's throat. But only the half of the bed where Aleksi had lain was destroyed. He lifted the bottle of iced tea to his lips and took a long drink, easing his suddenly dry throat. "You sure I can't get either of you something to drink, because I suddenly feel the need for something stronger than iced tea, and I hate to drink alone."

There must be money in politics. Aleksi peered through the wrought iron gate at Congressman Twain's glittering front door. The place was little less than a mansion, with manicured grounds, gleaming windows, brick drive and more security cameras and motion sensors than the entire Boston subway system. There was a service entrance in the back, but it was flanked by more security cameras. Also, as she strolled around the perimeter, she caught flickers of red at the edge of her vision. If she squinted just right, she could see the ruby beams lacing the yard like a cat's cradle.

She quashed the perverse desire to walk up and knock. There were still some lights on here and there, and one room in particular caught her attention. Northeast corner, ground floor, through the translucent drapes she espied dark paneling and bookshelves. A masculine room. She hoped the Congressman was up late working.

She had left most of her things in her subway cubby but had kept her empty pack. When she reached a shadowed area between two street lights, she melted down into the winter-dead shrubbery and slipped out of her mittens, boots, coat, and socks. For this, she would need a sure grip. She stuffed all but her mittens into her pack and hid it under a shrub, then looked up at the wrought iron fence.

Ten feet, she estimated. *Piece of cake.* Aleksi looked both ways, took three steps and leapt.

She rolled over the top of the iron tines that topped the fence and landed in a crouch, perfectly still, ears straining to hear any sign that she'd tripped some unknown alarm.

Nothing.

From here it was a matter of patience and vigilance. She knew that motion sensors worked on a minimum pixel per second shift. With all the blowing leaves and snow, these had to be calibrated to ignore anything but something large moving fast. The cameras, however, were likely monitored by a person. Her approach might catch someone's attention if they happened to be watching the right camera at the right time. She avoided the melting patches of snow and moved slowly from shadow to shadow. When she finally stood beside the Congressman's house, she felt even more confident of her abilities. At least no sirens blared.

She doubted there was a single window on the ground floor that wasn't wired with an alarm but hoped no such precautions were taken on the small, third-floor attic windows. The house was old, the mortar between the bricks soft and easy purchase for her claws.

Aleksi went up the wall like a spider. At the attic window, she stopped and listened again. Still no alarms. Her claws made short work of the thin frame, and she lifted one pane free. She reached in, felt around the edge for wires, and, finding none, flipped the lock and tried to lift the window.

It wouldn't budge.

"Painted shut." But there was a cure for that, too. She ran a claw around the edge of the casement, digging out ancient paint. When she finished, she tried to lift it again. It slid up, making far more noise than she liked, but she was inside. She stopped and listened, straining for any hint that she'd tripped some kind of alarm.

Nothing.

The room she was in looked disused, an attic remodeled into a kid's bedroom, then mothballed. The bed was stripped, the cupboards and dressers bare, a few boxes and trunks stored along the walls. She moved to the door, opened it, and listened. A faint, rhythmic clicking that she couldn't place, and a distant TV.

Good. The floorboards of the short hallway creaked underfoot as she slipped out. She could smell people and faint food odors. Easing down the stairs, she mentally marked any step that made noise. At the bottom, she took a moment to get her bearings. Two stairs on this floor, one toward the front and one back. She listened again, that tick-tick and the TV, then the distant clink of glass. The Twains were night people. Well, so was she.

She descended the back stairs, feeling each one under her toes before putting her weight down.

Northeast corner, she thought, edging down the hallway. The door to the room she wanted was closed, but the sound of rustling paper and the aroma of expensive whiskey told her that the congressman was inside. She turned the latch slowly and eased the door in an inch, thankful for silent hinges.

This was the moment she was unsure about. Confronting Twain meant letting someone else know about her condition, but from what Hutch had said, Twain knew something. She had to find out what that was and knew only one way. She put on her dark glasses, pulled her hat low, then eased the mittens from her belt and put them on.

Aleksi opened the door just wide enough and slipped through, as silent as a breath of air. She eased the door closed, working the latch to make sure it didn't click.

Twain sat at a broad, leather-covered desk, a tumbler of whiskey in one hand and a thick, loose-bound document before him. He flipped a page, oblivious to her presence. The light was low except for the desk lamp. It was now, or never.

"Working late, Congressman?"

"Wha—"

His reaction was everything she hoped for. The tumbler of whiskey hit the carpet with a thump, and he nearly fell out of his expensive leather swivel chair. By the time he recovered, she stood at his desk, the low lamp illuminating him while her face remained in shadow.

"Who…who the hell—"

"Don't recognize me, Congressman?" He recovered his composure a bit and started to stand up. "Just stay there for now, and please keep your hands on the desk. If you trip an alarm or call for help, I'll be gone before they can get here."

"Al…Aleksi? Holy *Christ*! How did you get in here?"

"Never mind that, Congressman. Besides, I'm here to ask *you* questions, not answer them. Like what do you know about the specimen stolen from my lab, and where the hell is Derrick Penningly?"

"I can have a dozen armed security men here in two minutes." His eyes narrowed in the light, trying to discern her features.

"And I can break a dozen bones in your hands and be out the same window I came in through in twenty seconds." She picked up the inch-thick mahogany and brass pen holder from his desk and snapped it in half. "Go ahead and call for help."

His eyes widened, sweat beading on his lip. "Penningly called me. He said he had something I might be interested in, something he was willing to trade." He swallowed hard, and Aleksi got the impression that he was wishing he hadn't dropped his whiskey. "He told me he'd been infected by some kind of virus that was changing him…then showed me what…what had…his condition. I contacted some people, and they took him in. They confirmed his story and confiscated the specimen."

"*Confiscated?*" Her teeth chirped as she ground them together. "Confiscated is something you do with a court order and the *police*, not with a bogus moving company on a Sunday." She took a breath, suppressed the urge to rip him in half, and continued. "Why take them?"

"To analyze them." His voice was steadier. "They want to isolate the infective agent and see how it works. It's amazing! The changes in Derrick were—"

"Are the same as the ones *I'm* experiencing," she interrupted. "So why frame me for Bob's murder? Just to get me out of the way?"

"Nobody framed you, Aleksi. That was the police. Derrick's been charged, too."

"Well, then they're *half* right, at least, but let me fill you in on something, Congressman: Derrick Penningly killed my friend. He ripped his throat out so he could take his place and steal my research project. If you think that's crazy, then you, too, are only *half* right. These changes…they're not just physical. They give you dreams, nightmares, and violent urges. I've been able to suppress mine, but Derrick's out of control. I don't know where your friends are keeping him, but you better hope it has really strong locks."

"What do you want from me, Aleksi?" He sounded fully back in control now, though she could still smell the fear on him.

"I want the bogus charges dropped, and I want the specimen returned to Dr. Hutchinson. His career's at stake, and your people don't need all of it to do your little science project."

"I can't promise anything, Aleksi. It's out of my hands. But what about you? Part of the deal they gave Derrick was to try to cure his…condition. We could offer you the same."

"I'm not going to be anyone's lab rat. I'm a scientist; I know how that usually ends for the rat. You've got everything you need to do your research." She reached into a pocket and dropped a slip of paper onto his desk. "When Derrick is brought to justice for Bob's murder, and you have a cure for this…thing, you call that number at midnight."

"All right." He picked up the slip of paper. "Anything else?"

"Yes. Tell your friends to call off their goons. I haven't hurt anyone yet, Congressman, but that doesn't mean I won't."

"I'll see what I can do."

"Fine." She turned to go, listening for him to do something stupid like pull a gun from a desk drawer. She almost hoped he would. As it turned out, he surprised her.

"And I'm sorry for what happened to you, Aleksi. Truly."

She looked back and almost believed him, then remembered what politicians did for a living. She left without a word and was out of his house in less time than she'd estimated.

———

This is a waste of time." Minder One scanned the waterfront again with his binoculars.

"Think of it as good practice." Derrick leaned back in the plush back seat of the SUV, watching the late-night foot traffic through the vehicle's tinted windows. Even in the dark, he could see every detail as clear as day. "You're going to have to have someone watching the boathouse every night now, but I think Hutchinson's place is your best bet. She went back to her apartment to pick up some stuff, but she has a thing for the good doctor. I don't know if he's still fucking her. If he is, he's braver or stupider than I thought."

They had been skeptical when he told them the two were doing it. From the police report, Dr. Hutchinson said he last saw Aleksi on Friday, but Derrick knew that was a lie. That was another reason he'd torn up the good doctor's bed; police forensics would be all over it now. Maybe the dipshits could find some trace of her, which would put Hutchinson on the spot. His minders were still dubious, however.

"I'd suggest watching from someplace high up and far enough away that she won't spot you. A rooftop or something." He reached over the back of the seat and opened the cooler, fishing out a soda and a package of cold cuts. He cracked the soda and peeled apart the plastic wrapping on the meat. It wasn't *real* meat, but it was food. "Those stupid cops watching the place can't see into his windows. She can come and go easily without getting spotted. That's where we'll catch her."

His two minders didn't say a thing.

Typical, he thought, downing half the package of cold cuts in one bite. *Dumb-ass grunts.*

Aleksi hunkered in a seat on the subway, head down, feigning sleep, bag of groceries perched on her knee. She watched the people come and go, passing by without recognition. She hadn't seen a cop all night, and now it was late enough that the city was winding down. Time to vanish.

Two more stops then dinner.

She had found a little shop that sold whole smoked hams and bought four. With the accelerating changes, she didn't know how much longer she could keep shopping without drawing attention. A flash of dark color drew her attention to the door as two women wearing Muslim attire came in with a man. The gowns covered them from head to toe, all but their eyes.

Perfect! Why didn't I think of that earlier? She felt for the pre-paid phone in her pocket and decided she'd get another one for Hutch tomorrow night. Maybe he could do some shopping for her. The money he'd given her had surprised her, but no less than his continuing affection, despite her condition. That he wasn't afraid of her, not disgusted by her, was willing to hold her, just hold her close, gave her strength.

The one thing I haven't lost...yet.

Aleksi blinked back tears and focused as the train came to her stop. She scanned the station for men in heavy coats with short haircuts and hearing aids, but saw none. Constant vigilance was becoming a reflex. She rose and passed the Muslim women on the way out, admiring their gowns once again. Garbed like that, she could walk anywhere, and all she'd have to worry about was racial profiling.

She made her way to the service door and slipped through. She'd explored all of the disused tunnels and found four ways in; three were out of view of the ubiquitous security cameras and could be used.

Deep in the disused station, she'd swept an area clear of detritus and vermin. Strangely, the rats didn't bother her; once she moved in, they moved out and hadn't returned, but the cockroaches... She shivered in revulsion. She was careful with her trash and had gotten a Styrofoam cooler to keep food in, which she duct-taped closed and hung in a net of orange construction mesh she'd scavenged. Aleksi sat down on a stack of old bricks and ate, thinking about her conversation with Twain, her time with Hutch, the feeling of his arms around her.

Tomorrow she would get another phone for him and they could talk. She didn't doubt that Twain's friends could track her smart phone, and wondered if they could actually listen in. Maybe a third phone would be best; they were cheap and easy to get, and that way she'd have one to talk to Hutch with, and another that Twain could call. Yes, that would be best.

When she finished her meal, the frequency of the trains told her that it was nearing dawn.

"Sleep, Aleksi." She glared at the bundle of blankets and the sleeping bag she'd picked up at Goodwill. Not that she wasn't tired, and not that her impromptu bed was not comfortable enough. Aleksi had come to loathe her dreams. They were all the same now: violence, blood, tearing flesh… They were so vivid. Upon awakening she remembered images of species long extinct: giant sloths, titanotheres, wooly rhinos, men…

"Why?" Were they dreams, or some kind of genetic memories? What was she becoming, some kind of extinct ice-age predator?

She looked at her hand, so changed now it looked inhuman. *How can this be happening? How could something like this evolve?*

Recollections of the shape in the CT scan of the specimen elicited a shiver of revulsion. She lay down, deep in thought, remembering an old science fiction novel she read, "Protector," by Larry Niven. Was she becoming something like that? Was this a stage of human development triggered by some latent genetic switch hidden in the human genome? No, she had too many violent tendencies, too many dreams of tearing humans to shreds.

Then she realized one detail of her dreams that she hadn't before: *Not humans, only men.* She remembered the urge to fight or flee when Hutch first took her arm, the fleeting urge to lash out. *But why would something evolve to prey only on men?*

36

Y ou said it was important, Congressman." Johansen took a seat in the busy café. He waived to a waiter and ordered coffee and a fruit plate. He hated public meetings like this, especially with politicians, but phones weren't secure. "What is it?"

"Aleksi Rychenkna paid me a visit in my home last night."

That snapped his irritation like a twig. "When?"

"About eleven." His hand trembled as he lifted his coffee. "She went through my security like it was tissue paper. She could have killed my whole family. If you don't do something about this, I will."

The threat was simple; fix it or Twain would go over his head, insist he be replaced. It wasn't an idle threat.

"We've got people on it, Congressman." He accepted his coffee and fruit, lightened the former with milk and sprinkled sugar on the latter. "We've set out some bait that will hopefully flush her out into the open."

"Then what?"

"Rychenkna is a *threat*, Congressman. She's threatened you, and she threatens the security of this project. I'm going to bring her into the project or eliminate her." He sipped his coffee, his hand steady as a rock. "Any way you can help me with that?"

"She told me that Penningly was the one who killed the Tomlin boy, and I believe her. She wants him brought to justice and the charges on her dropped. She also wants the samples returned to Hutchinson."

Johansen laughed without humor. "Did she also want a pardon from the President? A house in the Hamptons? A chartered flight to Switzerland?"

"Don't try to be *funny*, Doctor. She warned me about Penningly. She said the changes bring on violent urges, that he was out of control."

"He is *not* out of control. He is under *precise* control, *my* control, and we're using him to our best advantage." He took a bite of heavily sugared strawberry and chewed. "Now, how can you help me find Aleksi Rychenkna?"

Twain pulled a piece of paper from his pocket and dropped it on the table. "She told me to call her at midnight when I had any news. She wants a cure, Doctor, but she's not going to come in and be your lab rat. She was emphatic about that."

"She won't come in *willingly*, but she *will* come in." He picked up the piece of paper, looked at the number and slipped it into his pocket, smiling without showing his teeth. "You can bank on that."

He's getting home late this evening." Minder One lowered his telescope and squinted at the sky. The light in Hutchinson's apartment had just come on. "Might snow."

"You should watch more closely." Derrick kept his eyes on the distant shape of Hutchinson moving through his apartment. "You might miss something important."

"You really think she'll risk showing up here again after what you did? If she's contacted him, he's told her, and she won't be back." A metal door creaked open onto the roof, and Minder Two approached carrying an insulated pack and a matte black suitcase. "You've sent her to ground, Mister Penningly. She won't risk coming back to anyplace she knows you'll be watching."

"I disagree." He caught a whiff of meat. "She wants to find me as bad as I want to find her. We're the same." His mouth began to water, but he didn't know if it was the aroma of the meat or the thought of finding Aleksi Rychenkna. He rubbed the swatch of cotton in his pocket and brought his fingers to his nose. *Her scent...* She plagued his dreams; his violent *erotic* dreams.

"Dig in, Mister Penningly. It's going to be a long night." Minder Two handed his partner a wrapped sandwich and a cup of coffee, then took his own. He laid out his dinner, then opened the black metal case. The long shape of a rifle nestled in foam padding glinted in the faint light. He lifted it out and attached the stock and barrel to the middle portion that already sported a telescopic sight.

"You're going to shoot her?" Derrick glanced at the distant condominium. "From here?"

"If negotiations fail, yes." The man shouldered the rifle and took a sighting through the scope. Derrick caught a flicker of color from the rifle's frame, a laser range finder, or maybe even a targeting beam. "Not even eight hundred yards." He made some adjustments to the scope.

"You might not want to use that laser too much. I can see the beam. And if I can see it, she can." He reached into the insulated bag, ignoring Minder Two's incredulous look. The meat was wrapped in white paper, cold in his hand. He unwrapped it and ate mechanically, chewing the tender steak a bite at a time, enjoying the flavor but thinking of something else entirely. His eyes never strayed from the distant balcony. When the meat was gone, he crumpled the paper and wiped his mouth on his sleeve.

A car pulling into the condo parking lot caught his eye. "Can I borrow that?" he asked, pointing to the spotting scope.

"Sure. What's up?"

Derrick took the scope without answering and focused it on the car. It had pulled up next to the cop car they'd spotted earlier, and with the scope he could see the occupants. *Jasper and Willis*. He lowered the scope and handed it back. *The fuckers who put the warrant out on me.*

"Nothing. Just the cops checking up on each other. Probably delivering donuts."

The two men chuckled. Their opinion of police was the one thing all three of them shared.

"Look, you don't need me for this, and I've got something I have to do." Derrick turned and started for the door.

"You're not going out on your own, Mister Penningly." It wasn't a question. Minder One's hand drifted to the Taser at his belt. At least he wasn't reaching for a real gun.

"I'm leaving." Derrick glared back at the two meatheads and curled a lip in loathing. "I'll be back in an hour, and you can tell your bosses I was a good boy."

"We can't let you do that." Minder One pulled the Taser, though it wasn't quite aimed at Derrick. Minder Two still had the rifle in his hands, but it was pointed at the roof.

"If you try to stop me, you'll have a whole hell of a lot more to explain to your boss." Derrick narrowed his dragon eyes at the two. "Like how I took that thing away from you and stuck it up your ass."

"If you think you can intimidate—"

Embracing the instincts of the dragon, Derrick lunged.

Minder One raised the Taser and fired. He was quick, and his aim was good, but not good enough. Derrick twisted and watched the two darts fly past. By the time Minder Two raised the rifle, he'd ripped the tendons out of the other man's arm, sending the Taser and three fingers flying. His next blow caught the soldier on the corner of his jaw, just below his ear. His claws struck bone, and the man's entire lower jaw peeled away, blood, meat and shattered bone spraying in an arc as he spun around in a full circle.

Laser light flashed past Derrick's face and he dodged. The report of the sniper rifle hammered his ear despite the silencer. The bullet brushed past him and gouged a hand-sized divot from the concrete. Derrick dodged back and plunged his claws into the Kevlar vest covering Minder One's back. The man was still alive, but wouldn't be for long. The rifle cracked again, and the soon-to-be corpse jerked with the impact. Something grazed Derrick's hip, and he realized that the assassin was shooting *through* his former partner in hopes of putting a bullet in him.

Holding the twitching form of the dying man like a shield, Derrick backed up, crouching as low as he could. Another crack, and something struck him in the chest. The high-powered rifle had punched through the man's body armor, but didn't have much energy left. It felt like a punch, not a gunshot wound.

One more round hit before he reached the edge of the roof, this one spraying blood and bits of the man's spinal column over Derrick's face. The crimson spray tasted like a rare steak. He licked his lips, flung the body forward, and leapt over the edge of the roof before the assassin could fire again. On the way down, he heard the man shouting into his radio.

"Security breech! Security breech! Man down. The asset is on the loose. Repeat, Penningly is on the loose!"

Damn right I am, he thought, flitting from shadow to shadow like a ghost. *And it's time to hunt!*

Ah, the weekend.

Aleksi smiled below her ball cap at the bustling crowds. She was beginning to look forward to Friday night just as much as the teaming throngs of working stiffs. She moved through them, invisible in the mass of humanity, just another faceless street person that everyone avoided. The ratty old coat she'd picked up made the disguise perfect, but she longed for something lighter, something she could move around in more easily during the day, and she was out to do some shopping.

The pre-paid phones were a godsend. Hutch found his in his faculty mailbox in a manila envelope. She called it at noon, and he picked up on the first ring. She had to admit that it was good to hear his voice, but the news that Derrick had ripped up his apartment, specifically the exact spot where she'd lain on his bed, worried her. She feared for Hutch's safety, but there was nothing she could do to protect him.

Other than kill Derrick Penningly. Aleksi stuck to the shadows as she worked her way to the garbage bin.

She'd sent Hutch on a shopping trip. The bin was behind an upscale clothing store where she had seen the outfits she wanted. The image of Hutch going in and purchasing the two long niqab robes amused her, but he'd called her and told her when he was done, and where to find them.

With a quick check up and down the alley, she hopped up to the edge of the bin and looked in. Nobody was likely to care about a street person going through the trash. The bundle lay in the near corner, a big white trash bag with an X on the side. She lifted it out, tore it open and started stuffing the contents into her pack without looking. Something hard was folded into the package, and she paused long enough to unwrap it. It was an IPod wrapped with a tiny red bow and a tag that said, "Happy listening. Love, H".

Love...

She turned it on and flipped through the contents. Audiobooks on Zen, meditation, metaphysics, and yoga. She smiled and stuffed it in her pocket.

Love, H.

Shouldering her pack, she moved on, thinking about the phone in her pocket, about maybe calling him again, thanking him, but it wasn't a good idea. Not yet. Not now. She had one other thing to do tonight, one place to be at exactly midnight. All she had to do was decide where that place would be.

37

I still don't get it," Jasper said as Willis pulled into their parking spot. "Why the notes? He can't expect her to show up. Penningly's got to know cops are watching."

"I figure two possibilities." Willis shut the car off and pulled the keys. "He either doesn't think cops are a problem, or he's trying to flush her out. She might not show, but she might be watching to see if *he* does."

"That's a thought." Jasper didn't like it. They had cops watching the boat house, three apartments and two labs—a real strain on manpower—and had gotten nothing. He opened the door and got out. "Well, I'm for some sleep."

"You kidding. It's Friday night! Why don't you come out with Charles and me?" The driver door slammed and Willis looked over at him with a grin. "No gay bars, I promise!"

Jasper barked a laugh. "Maybe I'd have better luck if I—"

Two luminous yellow points shone in the shadows over Willis' shoulder, like a cat's eyes reflecting the street light, but too high. Man high. They blinked then moved, and he saw a glitter of gold. Hands at the end of long sleeves, fingers tipped in curved talons, raised to strike.

"Look out!"

Willis whirled into a crouch, reaching for his gun, but the shape was faster. The blow spun his partner around, and blood sprayed the driver side window.

"Marty!" The Glock went off three times in Jasper's hand before he even realized he'd pulled it. He clambered over the hood, looking for a target, wondering if he'd hit anything. *God damn, that thing was fast!*

He landed beside Marty and glanced down. Blood pulsed from between fingers pressed to the gaping wound on the side of his neck. His other hand was holding his gun, but it was pointed at the ground, his eyes wide with panic.

"What the...fuck!"

"Don't talk"! Jasper scanned the dark parking lot for something to shoot as he crouched beside his bleeding partner. He pulled a handkerchief from his pocket. "Move your hand for a second."

Willis complied, and blood sprayed Jasper's chest. He held the handkerchief against the huge flap of dangling flesh and pressed it into the wound hard. Willis gasped, and clenched his eyes shut."

"Stay awake, Marty! Eyes open! I need you to watch! Shoot any fucking thing you see. I can't tend you and keep my eyes peeled." That wasn't exactly true, but it opened Marty's eyes.

"Fuck!" Willis swore, blinking against the pain and shock. "Did...you see?"

The bleeding was bad, but he could obviously breathe if he was talking. The blow had caught him just under the ear and tore off a flap of skin and muscle as big as his hand. The blood was bright red and soaked the handkerchief in seconds. He thought about calling it in, but the radio was in the car and their backs were against the driver side door. He didn't feel much like standing up, much less moving Marty, not with some fucking maniac with claws out there. Especially one who could move *that* fast. Besides, gunfire from the police parking lot would summon every cop in the building in seconds.

"Just a glimpse. Hang on, Marty. Help's on the way." Jasper kept his eyes on the shadows, looking for those yellow eyes, ready to put a bullet in one of them. He held the cloth tight against Marty's neck, trying to ignore the warm slickness soaking through it. "Fucking bizarre!"

"Pa...Penningly," Willis hissed, struggling to stay conscious. "Fucking...*claws!*"

"I saw him, Marty. Just be still. Hang on." He heard the commotion of police, shouts, warnings. "Over here! Officer down! Perp with a knife. Ambulance! NOW!"

He knew it hadn't been a knife, but he didn't think anyone would believe him if he told them their murder suspect had just attacked his partner with a hand full of inch-long talons.

———

Aleksi stood staring at the pyramid of Benjamin Franklin's monument in the Old Burial Ground cemetery when her phone rang.

Dr. Johansen stood in a room with a dozen telecommunications technicians and twice as many flat screen monitors displaying the grid of cellular signals that overlaid the Boston metropolitan area. Before they even dialed the number, they knew it was a cell phone, the carrier, and when and where it was purchased. When she picked up, they were already narrowing the search grid.

"Hello?" Aleksi said, walking around to the back side of the monument.

"Miss Rychenkna?"

"Yes. Who is this?" Aleksi stopped in the shadow cast from the street lights. She didn't recognize the voice.

"My name is Dr. Johansen. I work for the United States Government." He watched the screens. They had the tower her phone was connecting through. She was near downtown. He snapped his fingers and held up three fingers to a tech. Team three was scrambled.

"I assume Congressman Twain gave you this number." She peered around the monument, but the Tremont Street was quiet for a Friday night.

"Yes, he did. He told me you paid him a visit." A technician sent a command, and the overlapping cellular network switched to another tower. They started to triangulate.

"I did. Did he tell you that I want my life back?" She could hear the tension in the man's voice, like he was upset or multi-tasking.

"I'm prepared to give it to you, Aleksi. Or as much of it as I can. We're working on a cure." *Someplace west of downtown, near Boston Common.* If she was in the park, it would be open season. Johansen snapped his fingers and called in another team.

"Are you going to cure Derrick Penningly, too?" She let a little of her temper slip into her voice.

"Derrick has been very cooperative, Aleksi. He's given us a lot." The tech switched towers again, and the triangulation kicked in. She was on the east side of the park.

"Did he tell you he killed Bob Tomlin?" She heard a click and looked at the phone's screen. *Two bars?* She'd had a four-bar connection all night. *Trying to find me?*

"He said *you* killed Mister Tomlin, but that is not the issue." They had her. She was on Tremont or Park, near the transit station. "I'm prepared to give you amnesty for any crime you might have committed if you come in."

"Since I haven't committed any crimes, that's a pretty empty offer, Dr. Johansen." His voice was even more stressed now. She scanned the street, listened…nothing.

"What about a cure for your condition? Do you want that?" He signaled for the two teams to converge from the north and the south. If she ran into the park, he had a helicopter standing by.

"Of course, I want a cure. Do you have one?" No way they could have progressed that far so soon.

"Not yet, but we're making progress. It might take some time." The teams were moving into position. "I'd rather have you in a safe location while we work on it."

"You mean a *secure* location, don't you? Someplace you can keep me locked up?"

"Derrick isn't locked up, as I'm sure you know by now."

"No, he's busy rifling through my apartment and threatening to kill my pet. That's not the sign of a stable, cooperative person, is it, Doctor?" She leaned out and listened again. Distant tires squealed, and an engine raced. She moved.

"Derrick has his foibles, but he's been cooperative." The signal was moving, just as the teams were converging. He gave the signal for them to watch for her.

"Derrick is a murderer and a thief, Doctor." Aleksi hopped the wrought iron fence and started toward the transit station. She heard the engines now, racing closer to her. "And you've been keeping me on the line so your men can trap me." A car was coming up Tremont, but slowly.

"What makes you think that, Miss Rychenkna?"

"Because I can *smell* you *lying*, Doctor." Aleksi crossed the street right behind the car. A burst of speed, and she wedged the phone in the gap between the back window and the trunk lid, then dashed into the pillared edifice of Suffolk Law School and listened.

"Change in direction," one of the techs said, pointing at the display. "North on Tremont. Fast!"

"Miss Rychenkna?" he said into the mic. No answer. "She's on the run. Converge and take her. Transmit all data to the teams!" The orders were passed.

Aleksi hunkered in the shadows, watching the car continue up Tremont, and listening to the two powerful engines whine as they raced toward her. A big black Escalade blasted past, and another from the other direction crossed up to block the street in front of the car. Men piled out of both vehicles, weapons drawn, laser light flicking in little red dots on the car.

"Shit." She eased out of the shadows and started down the street.

"Negative contact with target." The team captain's voice cracked over the situation room's speakers. "We found the phone. She put it on a passing car."

Johansen looked at the map. "The transit station! She's going for the transit station! South on Tremont!"

Aleksi heard car doors slam and tires squeal. She glanced back, and the nearer Escalade was burning rubber in reverse. The vehicle suddenly jinked and slid sideways, studded tires throwing sparks from the icy pavement as headlights wheeled around to track her.

She blinked once and ran.

The transit station was half a block, and the Escalade was gaining fast. She was on the wrong side of the street, and there was a fair crowd around the bagel shop on the corner. She dashed across and between the row of newspaper machines and parked bicycles. With all these people around, surely they wouldn't—

A beam of red light lanced over her shoulder and she dodged. Puffs of cement and shattering glass told her that they most certainly *would* shoot her down in a crowd of people. She dodged again and hit the doors of the transit station so hard that the glass shattered and the metal hinges sheared. She was past them before she realized that the doors *pulled* to open. Behind her, the Escalade blasted through the newspaper machines, bicycles, and the melting pile of snow, sending screaming pedestrians scrambling for safety.

Aleksi flew down the stairs, touching every fifth one. She heard the thump of boots behind her, and another red beam winked a jostling pattern as one of her pursuers brought his weapon to bear. She dodged as tile and cement puffed where bullets struck, the gunfire perversely quiet. She reached the bottom and dodged left, right into another ruby beam.

Something hit her shoulder hard, the impact adding to the momentum of her turn to spin her around.

The world wheeled in slow motion. Four men in dark coats, short thick-barreled guns held at their shoulders as they hurried down the stairs. The right side of the ramp and the gates to the Red Line, late night partiers passing through on their way home or downtown. The wall of glaring advertisements for antiperspirant, computers, and cell phones. The turnstile for the Green Line, and more people, some looking up at the commotion.

An image of laser light scything through that crowd, blood and torn meat flying in its wake, flicked into her mind. *Because of me...* They were after her, and people would die because of it, because she was running...

Time to stop running.

She skidded to a stop and looked back, but none of them had come around the corner yet. A flick of movement in the shiny advertisements caught her eye, reflections of dark figures descending the stairs. The leader was three steps up.

Heat surged through her, tingling razor edges along her nerves. *Images, memories, the taste of blood, warm flesh between her teeth...* The dragon came alive within her.

Aleksi dashed toward the point where he would emerge. Two steps. Her feet left the ground. One step, and the muzzle of his weapon came into view. She reached out, the thin metal of the silencer crumpling in her grasp. The muzzle jumped in her hand, and something made a loud crack. She held tight as she flew past him, pulling the weapon with her. The strap over his shoulder came taut, pulling her back, and she cartwheeled. He was heavier than her by a lot, but she used every ounce of her momentum to jerk him off his feet. She swung him in a full arc and released her grip to send him sprawling into another gun-toting assassin.

Laser light flicked out at her and she dodged, launching herself at the startled men. Bullets chewed holes into the woman with the shiny new cell phone, sending plastic, tile, and cement flying, but not a single round touched Aleksi. The lasers told her where the bullets would go, and she spun and whirled to avoid those deadly arcs of light.

Her talons grasped a heavy Kevlar vest. She braced herself against the stairs and flung the man behind her like a ragdoll. He hit the wall fifteen feet away before he touched the floor. The last of the four swung his weapon in a flat arc, lead spewing from the muzzle as brass casings spit from the side of the mechanism. She crouched under the deadly spray and felt the bullets pass her by, then rolled and spun in a low arc, her foot sweeping his legs out from under him.

He fell hard on the stairs, stunned for an instant, and she was on him, one hand crumpling the muzzle of his gun, the other cocked back, ready to rip him open, tear flesh from bone...

No!

Aleksi forced the dragon within her back down where it belonged. The predator had saved her, but she was not a killer. *No...I'm a protector.* The urge to fight the predators, to preserve the lives of the innocent people down the tunnel, had slammed into her like a train. *That* was her purpose.

Aleksi shortened the arc of her blow and buried her claws in his Kevlar vest, lifting him off the stairs, her bared teeth an inch from his nose. A growl unlike anything she had ever heard came from her throat, guttural and feral. She felt such a gut-clenching desire to kill him, to stab her talons into his throat and tear...but she wouldn't. She was *better* than Derrick Penningly.

Aleksi dropped him and grasped his weapon in both hands. Plastic fractured and metal bent before his wide, terrified eyes.

"Tell Derrick that if he hurts a *single* person I care about, if *any* of you do, I'll hunt you down and slaughter you all."

She glanced at the others, but they weren't moving. One might be dead, but she didn't think so; she hoped not. Aleksi dropped the man's mangled gun and dashed toward the Green Line turnstiles, pulling her cap low and hunching her shoulders. Onlookers were staring at her, backing out of her way. One held a cell phone up. Ignoring them, she swiped her travel pass, walked through the turnstile, and boarded her train.

She was halfway home before she realized she was bleeding.

					38

____

The mangled weapon clattered to the table. Johansen looked at it in both disappointment and awe. Military weapons were made to take punishment. This one looked like a Rottweiler's chew toy. The metal frame was bent, and the impact resistant plastic grips were shattered.

"She took my team apart," the tactical officer said. Johansen didn't know his name, but he didn't need to. He also didn't like the tone of the man's voice. There was fear in it.

"I can see that, Captain." He lifted the ruined weapon in his hands and turned it over. "Anyone killed?"

"No. One serious concussion, a broken arm, and a gunshot wound."

"A gunshot wound?"

"Friendly fire. She…threw one of my men at another as he was firing. Two rounds hit his vest, and one lodged in his hip. He'll be fine."

"And the man who was unhurt." He put the weapon down. "I'd like to debrief him."

"Of course."

"He's not to leave this facility until I say so. None of them are."

"They're all covert ops rated, Doctor." The captain said it like that trumped Johansen's order.

"They *better* be, Captain, otherwise they wouldn't have been assigned

304

to this project. *None* of them is to leave the facility until I give the okay. Is that clear?"

"Perfectly clear, Doctor." The man's tone said that he didn't like being ordered around by someone not in the military arm of the department, but Johansen didn't care. He was in charge.

"Good." He glared at the weapon, then back at the captain. "I want options, Captain. Ones that do not include video of your men shooting up a subway station ending up on YouTube. Do you understand?"

"We've got people on that, Doctor. Nothing's going to leak."

"Good." He wished he could say the same about the other incident he had to deal with tonight. The team assigned to Derrick Penningly, or what was left of it, was due to arrive in seconds. One man dead, and Penningly on the loose. How things could possibly get worse, he didn't know.

"Take care of this, Captain, I need options. I'd like to bring Rychenkna in alive, if possible." He looked again at the mangled weapon. "Someone who could do this would be a valuable asset." Johansen needed an asset before this entire project blew up in his face.

In the end, they hadn't needed an ambulance. One look at the bleeding, and six cops had lifted Marty into the back of a police cruiser. With lights and siren, they had arrived at Cambridge Hospital Emergency in less than five minutes. A call ahead had a stretcher waiting at the curb, and a team of scrub-clad doctors and nurses whisked Marty into a treatment room, then straight into surgery. They had controlled the bleeding, but the ER doc had said they needed a vascular surgeon to repair the torn artery.

Jasper and a dozen cops were crowding the waiting room. Someone had brought him a clean shirt and jacket, and he'd cleaned up in the washroom. It had taken him almost a half an hour to get Marty's blood from under his fingernails. Someone else had brought coffee and a stack of Dunkin' Donuts boxes high enough to feed the entire precinct. Jasper didn't feel much like eating, and his hands were still shaking too badly to hold a cup of coffee when his boss walked through the door.

"Christ, Jasper." Commander Fisk looked at him like he was still covered in his partner's blood. "What the hell happened? The duty clerk said Willis had his throat torn out by some kind of animal and you shot up the parking lot."

"Not exactly like that, but close enough." Jasper braced his shoulders and clenched his hands. He knew there would be a formal report, many of them, but this first impression would be the most critical, and he'd been thinking about what he saw, or *thought* he saw, for over an hour. "Derrick Penningly attacked Marty with some kind of claw thing. Fucker was hiding in the shadows. He's completely nuts, sir. He had some kind of mask or makeup on." It could have been makeup…must have been.

"A *mask*? How'd you know it was Penningly if he was wearing a mask?"

"It didn't cover his whole face, just his eyes, some kind of contact lenses. The rest was more like makeup or some kind of paint. I've been looking at his picture a lot, sir. Marty said it was him, too, before he passed out."

"We'll get Willis' statement later." The commander reached for the coffee and filled a cup. "So, did you hit him?"

"I fired three rounds. It was dark, and I was more worried about Marty than hitting anything. I don't know if I got him, but I was firing over the top of the car, so if I did, it would have been in the head. Since he's not lying in the parking lot with a bullet in his brain, I guess I missed."

"Too bad." Fisk sipped his coffee, eyed the donuts, tapped his bulging stomach, and refrained. "Forensics is all over the parking lot, so we'll find out where your rounds went. You're sure only three?"

"Sure, sir." He unholstered his Glock and pulled the clip, then jacked the chambered round into his hand. "Twelve left."

"Fine." Fisk put up a hand at Jaspers offer to hand over the weapon and magazine. "Keep it. They'll want to match it with what they find, so don't clean it or anything."

"Sure." He pocketed the round and the magazine, and holstered the gun.

"Good." Fisk glanced sidelong at Charles, who sat on one of the couches, surrounded by supportive vice cops. "How's Marty?"

"In surgery. They said he's serious but stable. If he doesn't throw a blood clot to his brain, he should be okay."

"Christ, Jasper. How the *hell* did a perp get close enough to lay him open like that?"

"It was dark, sir, and he was fast."

"Good thing he was stupid, too, bringing a knife to a gunfight." He caved and took a powdered jelly donut. "You still want the warrant out on the Rychenkna woman?"

"Not a murder charge, since it's pretty clear who our killer is now, but I'd still like to know why she ran. I say keep the APB and bring her in."

"If we can find her. She's all over the city by her ATM transactions, and her phone is quiet as a grave. She's not stupid."

"She ran, sir. That's stupid. I'll find her." Jasper realized that he still had one lead that might just pay off. Besides himself and Marty Willis, one other person had seen Derrick Penningly recently.

"Do that." Fisk took a huge bite of his donut and chewed, closing his eyes in bliss. After he swallowed, he glared at the donut as if it had committed a crime and dropped the rest in the trash. "Goddamn coffin nails." He wiped the powdered sugar from his face and took a swig of coffee. "I'd like your report in the morning, Jasper, and hand your piece over to forensics for analysis. We'll do the shooting interview then, too."

"Yes, sir."

Fisk glanced again at Charles then looked back to Jasper. "You need to talk to one of the department crisis management shrinks?"

"Not yet, sir." Jasper knew exactly who he needed to talk to.

***

Hutch jerked out of a sound sleep, unsure at first what had woken him. For a moment, he didn't know where he was, then he remembered that he'd sacked out on the couch; his bed was still in shreds. Then the phone rang again, the cheap prepaid phone that Aleksi had given him. He reached for it and swiped the screen, noticing as he did that it was one AM. *Not good.*

"Aleksi? What's wrong?"

"I need some help, Hutch." She sounded shaky. "Someone tried to kill me."

He was off the couch and reaching for his pants before she finished speaking. "Are you okay? What happened?"

"Congressman Twain gave my number to some very determined people. They came after me." She paused, then said, "I've got a bullet in my shoulder, Hutch. I can't get it out by myself."

"*Christ*, Aleksi!" Hutch's mind stumbled; he didn't know what to do. "I'm not a surgeon, but..."

"I was thinking about Dr. Bornstein. Do you think he'd make a house call?"

"I can ask." He thought about his friend and frowned. He'd been skeptical about the blood sample they'd given him, suspecting he was the target of some kind of prank, but then he'd gone silent. Hutch didn't know if Jim believed him or not, but he'd certainly believe if he saw Aleksi with his own eyes.

"Where?"

"I don't think here would be a good idea. The cops are watching me like a pack of wolves." His mind raced. "Can you walk?"

"I'm fine, Hutch. I just need to get patched up."

"Let me call you back in ten minutes. I'll try to set something up."

"Thanks Hutch."

The line clicked dead before he could say what he wanted to say. *Shot? Holy shit! And some kind of government connection...* He pushed those thoughts aside and dialed Lonnie. It rang half a dozen times before it went to voicemail.

"Lonnie, it's Hutch. Call me back on this number. It's an emergency."

He hung up and dialed Jim Bornstein's pager number. He knew he'd answer that if he tagged '911' on the end of his number. Before he could put the phone back in his pocket and find his shirt, his other cell phone rang.

"Damn it, Lonnie, I said to call me on the other—" But when he picked it up, the number and name were not Lonnie's, but Sergeant Jasper's. He thought about answering—He might know something about what happened to Aleksi—but let voicemail take it. He had a shirt and shoes on when his prepaid phone rang. It was Lonnie.

"Lonnie, its Hutch. I need a favor."

"Jeez, Hutch, it's the middle of the night. I *hate* calls in the middle of the night! What's wrong?" She sounded sleepy and pissed.

"Aleksi's been shot, and we can't take her to the hospital. I was thinking the Comparative Zoology lab, but I don't have a key."

"Shot? Holy *shit!*" At least she sounded more awake now. "Now?"

"As soon as you can get there. And pull a tray of autoclaved dissection tools down from the supplies. I don't know where they keep anything."

"Um...yeah. Sure. Give me fifteen minutes. Let's use the third-floor bio lab instead."

"Thanks, Lonnie." His phone beeped with an incoming call. "Gotta go. See you there." He pressed talk to take the incoming call. "Jim? It's Hutch."

"This better not be some kind of joke, Hutch." Bornstein sounded wide awake and angry.

"No joke, Jim. There's an emergency, and you're the only physician I can call."

"What is it?"

"A bullet wound, and I thought you would appreciate the chance to see where that blood sample came from."

There was a long silence.

"Jim?"

"If this is some kind of prank, I'll have your balls on a plate, Hutch."

"No prank. You have my word."

"Where is she?"

"We're going to use the third-floor bio lab on main campus. You remember where it is?"

"I remember. Give me half an hour."

"Thanks, Jim, and please, be discreet."

"Right." He hung up without another word.

Hutch dialed Aleksi's number and wondered if he could get out of the building without being followed by the police.

Clawed fingers probed the wound, picking pieces of fractured bone from the slowly reforming flesh. This predator he was transforming into seemed to heal quickly. That didn't mean it didn't hurt like hell.

Derrick flicked a piece of bone away and held a rag to the wound. "Heal..." He pulled the rag away and fingered the burning track Jasper's shot had left. "Fucking cops."

Derrick licked the blood from his fingers and thrust his hand back in his glove. The cold didn't bother him, but even though he hunkered in the shadows, a passerby might see his claws. He hung back and watched the parade of meat walking past, a hollowness gnawing at his gut. *Hunger...* Dreams, memories of meat and bone shearing between his teeth, made his mouth water. This dragon needed food.

He couldn't go back to Dr. Johansen now, not after killing one of his minders, and his apartment was being watched. With nowhere to go, no shelter, and no food, he stayed in the shadows, face down.

Hungry...

A scraggly figure shambled up to him, a gloved hand extended. "Buck for a coffee brother? Freezin' out here."

The man reeked of alcohol and stale cigarette smoke. Derrick opened his mouth to tell the disgusting bum to get lost, but hunger twisted his gut, and he thought again. He glanced left and right, but foot traffic was sparse, and this spot between a massive pile of filthy snow and a dumpster offered enough privacy.

"Sure, man." He reached into his coat and slipped off his glove.

This close, the man had no defense. Claws pierced flesh. Sticky warmth covered his fingers as he squeezed, crushing fragile cartilage, severing the man's last strangled gasp. Gloved hands batted uselessly at his iron grip, but only briefly. Derrick leaned in close, watching the light of life fade from the man's eyes, relishing it. The dying man's legs folded, twitching spasmodically.

Fresh meat... Derrick dragged the warm corpse behind the dumpster and bent down to feed.

Get that prescription filled and try not to move your arm." Dr. Bornstein donned his coat and took another long look at Aleksi. It had taken the man ten minutes to stop staring at her before he cut the bullet out of her shoulder. "The slug did remarkably little damage. Your scapula should have been shattered but wasn't. Your bones seem to be...well, as changed as the rest of you, like something between cartilage and bone. As for the rest, I'll look into treatments for genetic diseases, but I can't promise anything. I never would have believed the human genome could be altered to this degree. It's a wonder you're alive."

"Thank you, Doctor." Aleksi struggled into her fleece shirt—The wound hurt, and the bandage restricted her movement—and reached for the long, flowing niqab that she'd worn from her hiding place to the Harvard Campus. It covered her completely, and if she kept her eyes down and her hands out of sight, she looked like any one of a thousand Muslim women in the greater Boston area.

"I'll fill the script and get it to you before you leave, Aleksi." Hutch stood and walked with Bornstein to the door. "What do I owe you for the house call?"

"You can't afford me." He looked back one more time at Aleksi and smiled for the first time since Aleksi had met him. "And you've already given me enough. If this ever comes to light, and I can publish... Well, then it is *I* who will owe *you*, young lady. Please try not to get shot again. You risk my Nobel prize with such behavior."

"Yes, Doctor." She didn't feel much like smiling.

He nodded, shook Hutch's hand and left. By the time she had the robe fashioned properly and the hood up, Hutch had the mess of the procedure cleaned up and in a biohazard bag. It would be disposed of in the morning without a second thought by the lab staff.

"Know any all-night pharmacies?" She moved her arm to test the bandage.

"CVS isn't far. Look, Aleksi, there's one more thing I want to talk to you about, but I didn't want to bring it up with Jim here. I got another call right after yours. It was Jasper."

A chill tickled the back of her neck. "What did he want?"

"I'll let you listen to the message." He pulled his phone and played the voicemail for her.

"Dr. Hutchinson, this is Sergeant Jasper. I'm in the Cambridge Hospital surgery waiting room, and will be for another few hours. My partner Marty Willis was attacked by Derrick Penningly a few hours ago. He damn near killed him. I'd like to talk to you about your last meeting with Penningly at your earliest convenience. This is urgent. Oh, and if you get any word from Aleksi Rychenkna, you might want to tell her the murder charges have been dropped, though we still want her for questioning."

Aleksi's mind spun with the news. "Wow." Derrick was out of control.

"Yeah. I thought he might have heard something about the incident at the Park Street station. They're calling that a terrorist situation, by the way. The whole city's looking for you, but not by name. When I heard this…well."

"Yeah." She bit her lip, having given up the nervous habit of biting her nails, since they weren't really nails anymore. "What do you think?"

"I'll have to talk to Jasper, but I don't know how much to tell him. I think Derrick's gone nuts if he's attacked a cop. Why would he *ever* think that would be a good idea?" Hutch shook his head.

"I think he's unstable, Hutch." She'd been thinking about this for a while, remembering his scent, the wrongness of him, the surge of danger. "I think the changes are affecting him differently than me, or his mind, anyway. I don't know why, but there's something *different* about Derrick."

"Different how?" He sat on a lab stool and folded his hands as if she were going to recite scientific findings.

"When I confronted him and scratched his car, when I was close up, he…smelled…dangerous, like I should defend myself." She didn't know how to describe it.

Hutch's eyebrows raised. "When he accosted me outside the deli, he acted like a psychotic. Bared teeth, aggressive, like he wanted to rip me apart."

"I'm sure he did." She knew that feeling. "These dreams I've been having, Hutch, they're *really* violent. Every single one is the same; I'm always hunting, killing…even feeding, but it's always *men*."

"Is that why you attacked me in your sleep?"

"Well, I was dreaming when it happened, but it's more than that. I see things that I've never seen before. Images like memories. Ice-age mammals, vistas, forests…"

"Genetic memories, you think?"

"Yes. I never really bought into that concept, but yes." She took a deep breath and let it out slowly. "If Derrick was always a little psychotic, these memories might put him over the edge."

"They might put *anyone* over the edge."

"I think it's worse than that. If he's having the same impulses I am, but isn't able to suppress them, that would explain his attack on the police and maybe even Bob." She raised a hand and flexed her claws. "This *thing* has evolved to make humans into…something else."

"Evolved?" He sounded dubious.

"It's *specific* to *humans*, Hutch. Think about what Bornstein said. Something in my genome has been…turned on or activated."

"Okay, I'll buy that, and if it can be turned on, it can be turned *off*." He put a hand on her shoulder, her uninjured one. "That's the light at the end of the tunnel, but how does it help us now? I don't think Jasper's going to be able to use that to arrest Derrick."

Aleksi shook her head. "No, if they ever take Derrick, they'll have to kill him. I don't think his government friends are going to be able to control him."

"Maybe we should tell them that."

"Maybe." She sighed and checked the time. It was almost four AM. "If I'm going to pay another visit to Congressman Twain, I'll have to wait until tonight."

"I don't think that's a good idea, Aleksi. He'll have security all over his place. Let me talk to him." He pulled something from his pocket and held it up for her to see. It was the disfigured bullet Bornstein had dug out of her shoulder. "I think I'll show him what he's done."

"You're going to threaten him?" That didn't sound like Hutch's style.

"Oh, no. Not me." He pocketed the bullet and stepped up to her. She had to suppress the urge to step back, to flinch as he reached out to take her hand. He held it between his, warm, alive, kneading her fingers with his. "*You*, my dear, are going to be the threat."

"D r. Dwayne Hutchinson to see Congressman Twain." Hutch had been to the congressman's house once before. It reminded him of Persephone's family estate, which only added to his apprehension.

"Is the congressman expecting you, Doctor?" The voice from the speaker sounded bored.

"No, but tell him that I've got word on that project we were working on together, the one from Kamchatka. It's important." He smiled into the camera and took a deep breath.

"Hang on a moment, please, Doctor."

Hutch leaned back in his car seat and tried to center himself, but the recent conversation with Sergeant Jasper had rattled his calm. Both Jasper and Willis had gotten a close look at Derrick during the attack, and he wanted information. Did Penningly seem deranged? *Yes.* Did he ever threaten him other than the one time? *No.* Did he seem violent? *Very much so.* Did Hutch notice any distinguishing characteristics? *Not really.* What color were his eyes? *He was wearing sun glasses.*

Hutch had recounted the confrontation with Derrick as closely as he could remember, leaving out only the reference to Aleksi. That he couldn't give more details seemed to irritate Jasper. He told Hutch of the attack, the gaping wound in his partner's neck, remarkably similar to the one that killed Bob Tomlin. The conversation played back in his mind.

"Why would he attack a cop, Doctor? He can't be that stupid."

"Not stupid, Sergeant," Hutch had said. "Psychotic."

"You think Penningly's *crazy*, Doctor?"

"I'm not a psychologist, but a pathological fixation on revenge and lashing out violently at a perceived threat seem pretty far down the road to the funny farm."

"You think that's why he killed Bob Tomlin?"

"Revenge against Aleksi, or some kind of male territoriality, maybe."

"Why not kill her instead?"

"When a male lion takes over a pride, he kills the rival male lion and all of his offspring. He doesn't kill the females in the pride."

"Why not?"

"Because millions of years of evolution have conditioned him not to. The females are his only means to expand his genome."

"His genome? You mean he wants to…um…never mind. Penningly told us that Aleksi asked him out, but *he* said no. Are you saying he's got some deranged *romantic* intentions?"

"I'm not suggesting anything. I'm just speculating. Derrick seemed deranged to me. Nothing he's done makes sense if he really wanted me to take him on as a student."

"So what *does* he want?"

"I have no idea."

"Any idea why he hasn't come after *you*, yet, Doctor?"

There was only one answer. "No."

"Do you want protection?"

"Nothing personal, Sergeant, but I don't think it'd do any good."

The wrought iron gate before him swung open, and the voice from the speaker said, "Please drive forward, Dr. Hutchinson. Someone will meet you at the front door."

Hutch drove through, and the gate closed behind him.

Two men met him at the door; security, maybe Secret Service. Congressman Twain was scared. *Good*, Hutch thought as he climbed the granite steps. *He should be.*

"This way, Dr. Hutchinson." One of the two men opened the door and went through. The other waited to follow him.

"Thanks." *Deep breaths…calm…centered.*

They escorted him through the lavishly appointed house to the Congressman's office. It looked more like a library, with dark wood, ceiling-high bookshelves and an impressive desk. Twain stood as Hutch entered. He didn't smile his usual politician smile and didn't extend a hand in greeting. The door closed behind Hutch, but he knew that the two security men were standing on the other side.

"Dr. Hutchinson, please tell me you bring good news."

"I brought you a present, Congressman." He approached the desk and dropped the small piece of mangled lead onto the polished leather surface. "We dug it out of Aleksi's shoulder last night. She's not very happy with being shot."

Twain glared at the bullet, then at Hutch. "Was that a threat, Doctor? Because you will find that I do *not* respond well to that kind of pressure."

"And Aleksi does not respond well to assassination attempts." He refused to be intimidated by the man who had sold Aleksi like a piece of property. "They tried to *kill* her, Congressman. How do you think she's going to respond?"

"That did *not* come from me, Doctor. She told me she wanted a cure for her condition, and I gave her number to the people who are working on one. If she agreed to come in peacefully, they wouldn't have had to resort to violence."

"Violent people always rationalize their actions that way, Congressman. They didn't tell her to stop or try to subdue her, they just started shooting." Hutch could see the pulse beating in Twain's temple. It was fast. "Their attempt and your betrayal of her trust resulted in four injured assassins and one *very* angry young woman. She wanted to come here to talk to you personally, but I talked her out of it."

"She never would have made it through my security, Doctor."

"Did I mention the four assassins she took down like they were paper targets?" Hutch smiled humorlessly. "She *could* have killed them, Congressman, and didn't. By contrast, Derrick Penningly tried to kill the two police detectives who are investigating Bob Tomlin's murder last night. Who would you *really* rather have on your side?"

"I was unaware of that."

"Then maybe you should start asking your friends some questions." Hutch felt the balance of power between them shift. He'd just gained the upper hand. "The police have dropped the murder charges on Aleksi. The two detectives got a good look at Derrick, though they're currently under the impression he's playing dress-up. They still don't know about the changes Derrick and Aleksi are experiencing, but if your friends don't control him, some cop's going to get lucky and put a bullet in his brain."

"I'll relay the message, Doctor."

"Good." Hutch started to turn away then turned back. "One other message you might give your friends, Congressman. If they think they can use this...infection to their advantage, they should rethink their plans."

"Why is that, Doctor?"

"Because they're playing with a fire that is more dangerous than nuclear proliferation, and they don't even know it." He pointed to the mangled bullet on the Congressman's desk. "If one introverted young woman can do *that* to four trained soldiers *after* they put a bullet in her shoulder, what do you think an *army* of infected soldiers could do to the human race?"

"I see what you mean, Doctor," Twain said, but Hutch didn't think he really did.

"Homo sapiens sapiens has spent a million years fighting its way to the top of the food chain, Congressman. Your government friends are very close to putting us on the endangered species list."

"It won't go that far, Doctor. I'll see to that."

"I hope your friends listen." Hutch turned away. At the door, he looked back and added, "For both our sakes."

Persephone stood aside watching the images flick one after another on the wide screen that hung suspended before Gi-gi's bed. With each image, and the continued diatribe of her cousin, Reggie, her heart slipped another inch toward the soles of her shoes.

This is a disaster. She'd stopped listening to Reggie's narrative at the first frame. She knew the story of her failure all too well.

Hacked security camera images of men in overalls and caps removing the specimen she'd been tasked with recovering from the MCZ basement laboratory flicked past. More frames of police crowded around the scene, Hutch among them, looking devastated. Police reports of the assault on one of the officers investigating the Tomlin murder. More images paraded past of men in SWAT gear shooting up a subway station, a figure in a coat and hoodie taking them down. Then finally one she had not seen before blinked on the screen, a woman in a business suit carrying a brief-case. She looked like a lawyer: ghastly hairstyle, no jewelry, minimal makeup, and a sharpness that said, "All business" on her features.

Persephone focused her attention back to what Reggie was saying.

"Inside every disaster lies an opportunity, Great Grandmother."

"What opportunity?" Persephone glanced at Reggie, then Gi-gi's unreadable features. This last image had come as a surprise. She didn't like surprises.

"This is the woman who will take over the government's project concerning the specimen and the two subjects infected by it. Her name is Buckmann. She'll be the new Dr. Johansen." Reggie glanced at Perse-phone, the corner of his mouth twitching. "*She's* our opportunity."

"Excellent." Gi-gi's thin lips stretched wide, lavender eyes turning toward Persephone. "Bring her to me."

"Great Grandmother, if she's to take over as Johansen, she's far up the chain of authority. She's dangerous in the extreme."

"And so will *you* be." Gi-gi's withered hand reached out to touch hers. "Dr. Johansen."

Shit! Persephone swallowed hard. She knew exactly what her ancestor had in mind, and didn't want any part of it, but she had no choice. "Yes, Gi-gi." She examined the woman's picture once again and cringed. *Such dreadful hair...*

4 0

The predator walked among his prey, a wolf in sheep's clothing prowling the ice-shrouded canyons of an urban jungle, yellow eyes flicking from beneath the ball cap he'd taken from the homeless man. *It's like walking down a meat case in a supermarket.* The dragon smiled behind the scarf wrapped around his face.

A woman hurried past the other way huddled in expensive layers of insulation. A whiff of perfume on the chill air, and he turned around to follow her. Her boots crunched on the ice, her coat making a swishing sound against her delicious looking legs. The dragon swallowed and licked his lips. What would she taste like? Would her flesh differ from the homeless man's? Should he exert more caution, or would a dead business woman draw no more attention than a dead vagrant?

Yes...caution. He fell back, girding his hunger, his need. He would feed after dark. It would be safer.

She rounded a corner and passed a stair to a transit station. People milled past. No one looked at him. No one saw the dragon behind the scarf and hat. His lips parted and he drew in a breath, taking in the scent of prey thick on the air. Then *her* scent slammed into his mind, a freight train of sensory overload.

Aleksi!

Derrick scanned the crowd, but she wasn't there. Just her scent... Hunger, yes, but something else overrode that, something deeper, more visceral. Something carnal, even more seductive than her soiled under-wear in his pocket. The scent hammered through his senses into the desires of the dragon. An image flashed into his mind, a dream or memory: *scales against scales, writhing, coupling, biting, clawing for purchase...warmth...release.*

Derrick staggered with the force of the flood, a disturbing mixture of desire and rage. She was like him; they were both dragons. *Aleksi...* There might be something he needed that she could give him...or that he could take from her.

The dragon's tongue flicked out again beneath the scarf to wet his lips, to taste the air for her. Yes, Aleksi was more than just prey.

Persephone stopped the car at the security booth and handed her new identity to the guard. He swiped the card, examined the screen in his booth, then her, and handed the card back. "Do you need an escort, Dr. Johansen?"

"Yes." She didn't say thank you. Persephone would have said thank you, but she wasn't Persephone any longer.

"Someone will meet you."

She nodded and closed the car window. When the door rolled up, she drove in and picked a parking spot. By the time she got out of the car and recovered her briefcase, two armed guards were waiting for her.

"This way, Dr. Johansen."

She followed without a word. *Short steps, straight back, no sway, all business...* She hated this part, the first hours were always the most challenging, delving the woman's memories, mannerisms, foibles, and prejudices to assume this identity. She felt dirty, like she'd just touched something unclean and needed to wash her hands.

The memory of the transformation made her skin crawl, the cocktail of biochemicals and Mary Buckmann's genetic information that had twisted her flesh into the woman's shape, hours writhing in pain as her skin ran like melting wax, then more hours as Gi-gi gave her everything she needed, right down to the name of the boy who Mary Buckmann had dated in high-school, the memory of that horrible night after the prom, the back seat of his car, her torn dress, the slap when she said no, the rape, then the beating from her father when she got home.

Dirty... The memories that weren't hers felt like a violation, and Mary had been through enough of those. *She'll wake up fine. She'll be fine. Just be her, and you'll both be fine.*

The real Mary Buckmann lay in a bed beside Persephone's great grandmother, an IV of mixed medications inducing sleep and forgetfulness. She would get her life back with a gap, but she would get her life back.

Concentrate, Dr. Johansen. If you fuck this up, Persephone won't get anything back.

Persephone's escort paused at the door, and she punched in the security code from Mary's memory. It opened, and they followed her through. The schematic of the facility lay there in her mind. *Business first...always business first.* She strode straight to her office, or her predecessor's office for the next thirty seconds. At that door, she punched in another code and held her left thumb to the small green plate above the keypad. The pad beeped, and the door opened.

"Stay here," she told her escort.

"Yes, Doctor."

She stepped inside and met the eyes of Dr. Johansen. "I'm your replacement."

"Yes." He blinked and stood. She could see the anger, the resentment behind his eyes. "Right on time." He rounded the desk and stopped right in front of her. "Everything's coded over to you. I wish you luck."

Memories...*resentment...men...slap...pain...Business. All business.* "I won't *need* luck."

"Fine." He started for the door. "Be a bitch about it."

"I wasn't called in here to be *nice* to you. I was called in to clean up your *monumental* screw-up." She turned, expressionless, business to the core. "I don't give a *damn* how you feel about me, Doctor."

He flashed her a glare and left the room.

To business. She sat at the desk and keyed in her password, thumbprinted the pad beside the keyboard, and watched the flat screen come to life. She touched the icon for her assistant.

A window opened, displaying a man's round face. "Yes, Dr. Johansen?"

"I need a video conference of my section heads as soon as it can be arranged."

He tapped something off screen. "Five minutes."

"Good." Persephone—*Not Persephone, Dr. Johansen!*—accessed the database and reviewed their progress while she waited. They'd made almost none with regard to the mysterious genome that had infected both

Derrick Penningly and Aleksi Rychenkna. That was good. She didn't want them to. The media hack to expunge the subway video of the shooting with Aleksi had been successful, including the two cell-phone videos and the security camera footage. Also good. An icon blinked on her screen, and she touched it.

"Ready, Doctor," her assistant said.

"Good." She stretched her neck and watched four more windows open on her screen: R&D, IT, Security, and Engineering. They all looked harried, but attentive. "I know you're all busy, so I'll keep this brief. This facility is no longer secure, so we'll be moving the specimens to a holding area."

"This facility is perfectly secure, Dr. Johansen." The head of security clenched his jaw, his Cro-Magnon brow furrowing in displeasure.

"Don't take this personally, Captain. Under normal circumstances, I'd agree with you, but these are *not* normal circumstances. Derrick Penningly is not normal. He knows the location of this facility, and he has repeatedly expressed the desire for access to our specimen. That we cannot allow. I have transportation arriving in four hours. R&D, you will pack everything up in that time for transport."

"Yes, Doctor." The scientist, at least, didn't take exception to her orders. "Will we have another crack at this thing?"

"Once our breech has been sealed, yes. Engineering, every access code into the facility will be changed immediately. Penningly watched while my predecessor punched him in. We can't assume he didn't memorize the codes."

"Yes, Doctor."

"IT, same story. New passwords on your firewalls and separate access for all data files on the specimen. All files will be encrypted."

"Yes, Doctor."

"Security, I want a change in our tactics. Derrick Penningly is no longer an asset, he is a threat. Aleksi Rychenkna is not to be harmed. Our primary objectives are to neutralize Penningly, cover up his mess, and bring Rychenkna in willingly."

"How are we going to manage that, Doctor? She hasn't exactly been cooperative."

"And if I were to put a five point five six millimeter round in *your* shoulder without the slightest provocation, Captain, would *you* be cooperative?"

The man's jaw clenched again, but his mouth remained closed.

"We will bring her in by giving her incentive to cooperate. All of you have your orders. Surveillance is to continue as before."

"And I have a shoot order on Penningly now?"

"You do."

"Very good, Doctor." Security's jaw finally unclenched.

Typical soldier, as long as he had clear orders on who he could shoot, he'd be happy. "Any questions?"

There were none.

"Good." She disconnected and leaned back in her chair. *So far, so good.*

Persephone stood and strode to the credenza where a coffee machine waited patiently. She popped in a K-cup and stabbed the button. While it filled, she caught sight of her reflection in the mirror and cringed.

God above, woman, what possessed you to get that haircut?

41

S o, what's this I hear about you missing work because of some little scratch?" Jasper grinned as he entered the hospital room, one hand bearing a Dunkin' Donuts box, the other a card attached to a flock of shiny balloons. He waved to Charles and deposited the donuts out of the patient's reach. "You cut yourself *shaving* and expect a paid vacation?"

"This was no shaving accident." Willis' voice was a little thick from the meds, but the smile on the half of his face not swathed in bandages was genuine.

"You two are insufferable." Charles stood from his seat beside the bed—he had barely left it for three days—and took the card and balloons. He looked tired and was dressed in an old sweatshirt and jeans; rags for someone with his taste in clothes. He wrapped Jasper in a hug that was clearly not optional. "And such an appropriate gift! Shiny, pretty, and full of hot air!"

"The card's signed by the whole homicide team." Jasper liberated a cruller from the box and took a bite. "Vice wanted to send something, too, but I told them you were in no condition to appreciate a stripper."

"Bullshit." Marty took the card from Charles and fumbled it open.

"I'll be screening all of his presents *personally*, Tony, so you just tell them to send whatever they want." Charles sat back down and took the card from Marty when he was done reading it. He put it with about a dozen others and tied the balloons to one of the flower arrangements that crowded the room.

"The doctors say you're going to be back at work in a couple of weeks. Don't dawdle, huh? We need you back."

"That's bullshit, too, but I appreciate it." Marty pointed to the huge bandage that swathed the left side of his neck and face. "Gonna be scaring children with this face."

"Now who's shoveling the bullshit?" Charles slapped the back of Marty's hand in a scolding gesture. "The doctor said once the swelling's down and there's no danger of clots, a plastic surgeon can touch up the incisions and make him all pretty again. Not that I don't like a man with a few battle scars."

"Any luck finding Penningly?" Willis shifted in bed. He couldn't turn his head, so Jasper moved to the foot of the bed so he wouldn't have to.

"There was another body found last night along the Promenade. A jogger this time. That's three in three nights."

"They sure it was Penningly?"

"Yep. The wounds are similar, and he's…well, the bodies were mutilated." Jasper thought his partner needed to know the truth, if for no other reason than to realize how lucky he'd been. "Some of the organs were missing."

"Oh, my God." Charles turned a little pale and swallowed.

"Too bad you didn't get a decent shot at him." Marty shifted again. "Does the commander want to get my statement today?"

"He might send someone over, but he really doesn't need it. It was Penningly. I saw him." Jasper didn't want to go into what else he saw, or *thought* he saw.

Marty shifted again. "Hon, could you maybe get me a pillow? My leg's gone to sleep again."

Charles looked at Jasper and then back to his husband. "You don't have to fib, hon. If you two want to talk shop, I can go get some coffee." He stood and smiled at them both. "Doctor said no caffeine for Marty, but do you want anything, Tony? There's a Starbucks in the cafeteria."

"Sure. Just a regular coffee with milk. Thanks, Charles."

"For the man who saved my husband's life? You kidding? Anything you want, sweetie." He started for the door.

"Then bring him a tall blonde with big tits," Willis said with another half-grin.

"Anything but that." Charles closed the door behind him.

"So, the doctor says—"

"Cut the bedside manner crap, would you? So, did you tell the commander about Penningly?"

"I told him what I saw." Jasper finished his cruller and talked while he chewed. "I didn't get a very good look."

"You saw his fucking eyes, didn't you?" Willis' voice was hard, almost accusative. "You saw the goddamn *claws* that did this!" He gestured to the thick swath of bandages.

"Yeah, I saw, Marty, but I think it happened too fast to say anything definite. Looked like he had some kind of contact lenses in his eyes, like those ones the goth freaks wear, but yellow. The rest could have been makeup. The claws…must have been some kind of glove or something."

"I know what I saw, Tony. That wasn't a fucking glove on his hand."

"Maybe not, but telling the commander that our murder suspect has *real* claws is more likely to get you a psych evaluation than help solve this thing."

"Damn it, I wish you'd have put a bullet in that fucker!" Jasper could hear the frustration in his partner's voice. "How many shots did you get off? I know I heard two, but…"

"Three, but I didn't hit him. Forensics found the slugs. I managed to hit two cars and a tree." He tapped his partner's foot and grinned. "Don't sweat it, okay? We've got half the cops in the city looking for this freak. The whole Boston PD's hunting him. We'll get him, Marty. Don't worry about it."

"Yeah." Willis closed his eyes and sighed. "I just hope they get him soon. He's not going to stop killing, Tony. He likes what he's doing too much to stop."

"We've got some leads, Marty. We'll get him. I promise you that."

---

*S**leep*, Aleksi thought, staring into the dark, listening to it, feeling it like a living, breathing thing. *Just close your eyes and sleep.* But sleep would not come. It hovered at the edge of her exhaustion like dangling fruit, just out of reach. She knew she needed it but also knew what lurked there waiting for her. *No more dreams...please.* Another train passed; another twelve minutes of her life slipping away.

Mercifully, her phone rang. A glance confirmed that it was the only person on Earth she wanted to talk to.

"Hi." She tried to sound awake, alert, not exhausted.

"Hey there." His voice soothed her frazzled nerves like a cool balm. "Sorry to call during the day. I know you sleep days, but I thought you might like to know what's in the papers."

"I wasn't sleeping. What's up?"

"Another murder."

"Derrick?"

"Yeah, and it's getting weird. The bodies are...were..."

"Eaten?"

"Mutilated, was what the paper said."

"He's hunting, Hutch. He's *feeding* on *people*." Her stomach roiled.

"I also got a call from our favorite congressman."

That got her attention, not that the news of Derrick on a killing spree hadn't. "Let me guess, they want me to come in."

"He said to tell you that things have changed. Dr. Johansen wants to talk to you." His voice brimmed with suspicion. "He gave me a phone number."

"The last time I talked to him on the phone, I got shot. No thanks."

"I thought you might say that." He paused again. "Look, Aleksi, Twain said that the whole project is on hold. Everyone's freaking out with Derrick on a rampage. They need to stop him before some lucky cop puts a bullet in him and they can't explain why what's lying dead on the sidewalk isn't quite human."

"Not human." Those two words felt like a knife in her ribs. "Like me."

"Aleksi. Those were *his* words, not mine. You know I didn't mean it like that." It sounded like he was telling her the truth. She hoped it was the truth.

"So, they want to talk to me about Derrick?"

"That's what Twain said."

"I don't *trust* Twain, Hutch, and I *certainly* don't trust Johansen."

"Neither do I, but I think you ought to consider talking to them. You can take precautions to keep him from finding you. I can help."

"I'd rather not have you with me if all hell breaks loose, Hutch. I can't worry about you if I'm fighting for my life."

"I guess so, but if you need help, let me know. I could even do a phone relay if you want."

"That might work." She rubbed her eyes and sighed. "Let me think about it. I'm kind of tired right now, Hutch, and I can't sleep."

"Did you try the meditation audio I gave you?"

"No." She had listened to some of the Thich Nhat Hanh book, but plugging into the IPod made her nervous. She didn't like blocking out the sounds of her environment. It made her feel vulnerable, blind. "No, I completely forgot about it."

"Try it. It helps me, and it might help with your dreams."

"Really?" She doubted anything would stop her from seeing blood while she slept.

"That's why I gave it to you. I know they're bothering you, Aleksi. There's a lecture on directed dreaming. It might help."

"Thanks, Hutch. I'll give it a try." She'd try anything if it meant sleep.

"Good. I hope it works."

"Okay, well, I better let you go. I'm sure you're busy."

"Never too busy for you, Aleksi. I miss you. Call if you need anything."

"I will." She felt his arms around her and clenched her teeth. *I miss you, too.* "Thanks again."

"Okay. Bye."

She hung up the phone and listened to the echoes of his voice in her mind. The light from the phone died and darkness closed in again. Aleksi rooted around in her pack until she found the IPod and flipped through the menu until she found the meditation audio. She put the ear buds in and closed her eyes, listening to the melodious voice of the narrator. She tried to concentrate, to trust the voice, to relax; anything to control the monster that lived in her dreams.

Darkness settled on the city early in winter. By five it was past twilight, by six, night and time for people to be getting home, for families to congregate around dinner tables, ask what happened at school, snicker at the goofy guy at work, enjoy a glass of wine or a beer. Unwind. Relax.

For Derrick, it was time to hunt.

It was getting hard to evade scrutiny during the day, even with sunglasses, his hands tucked away, and the hat pulled low. The shirt he favored didn't fit very well anymore, and the overcoat was restricting under the arms, but he could hardly take them off. There were police everywhere, and he knew they were looking for him.

"They ought to fucking *thank* me." He turned the corner from Agassiz Road onto Park Drive. The winter-bare trees of Back Bay Fens Park loomed close to the road, the grass crusted with half-melted snow. There were foot trails here, and he knew the worthless dregs of society came here to make their deals: drugs for sex, booze for a spare shirt, food for sharing a squalid shelter of cardboard or a moldy mattress. "I'm doing them a favor. Taking out the trash."

Two figures arm in arm came the other way. They turned onto one of the footpaths. He heard their voices, the low laughter of two women. *Dykes*, he thought. *Probably met in some fag bar and come out here to get high and do each other.* The dragon's tongue licked his lips, tasting the air. They weren't vagabonds, but he was hungry. He turned off the road before the trail and unbuttoned his heavy coat. With two, he would have to be quick.

Sound and scent were enough to keep him on track and out of sight. He shucked the coat and stashed it under some bushes. Closer, edging through the brush, he caught a glimpse of them. The wind gusted and brought him their scent; perfume, the cloying overtone of makeup, cigarette smoke, and something else, something familiar that he couldn't place. Under all of that, the scent of *female*, not the one he wanted, not Aleksi, but definitely female.

Gotta be quick. He increased his pace. *If one screams, I won't have time to enjoy this.* He glanced up and down the trail, but the two were the only ones in sight. There were no other sounds, no other scents nearby. He closed in.

"This is useless," the taller one said, her blonde hair whipping in the wind.

"You think?"

"Total bullshit. Jamison's giving his *girls* the scut work."

What were they talking about? *It doesn't matter. Too close. Too delicious.*

"I don't know. It could—"

A low growl escaped his throat, a feral sound that he knew would draw their attention. It wasn't incaution; it was calculated. He wanted to see their fear, to taste their panic. That instant of terror just before the kill was almost as delicious as the warm gobbets of flesh.

They both turned, and the tall one had time to shout, "Shit!" before his claws tore a raking hole in her neck.

The shorter one opened her mouth to scream, but the spray of blood across her face made her wince, eyes closing reflexively, hand fumbling for something in her pocket. She stumbled back, the hand that had held her friend's arm rising to fend him off. He snatched her wrist, claws piercing, bone cracking. She drew breath to scream, which would ruin his fun, so he grabbed her throat with his free hand. The fragile cartilage of her larynx crumbled and her eyes widened in horror. Derrick grinned and flexed his claws deep into the soft tissue of her neck, relishing the moment.

Sound and impact exploded through him.

A gun! The bitch has a gun!

The smell of oil and metal from the other cops came to him now. He ripped her throat out and flung her aside, glaring down at the bleeding hole in his thigh. She'd fired the gun from the pocket of her coat.

Pain lanced through him, and with it, rage.

The woman who had shot him was still struggling, though the blood flooding from the whole in her neck told him she wouldn't last long. He stomped down on the hand fumbling in her pocket and stabbed his claws into her face, groping deep into her eye sockets. She twitched and thrashed in his grasp, then stilled.

"What kind of a bitch carries a gun in her pocket?" He tore open her coat. The answer to his question hung strapped to her shoulder. A leather harness with an empty holster. He ripped open the inside pocket, and a thin leather case fell out, the silver shield glittering in the dim light. "Fucking cops!"

Derrick stepped back and listened for sirens, for running footsteps, for anything. Tires squealed on the road behind him, and he knew he only had seconds before more cops and guns arrived.

The wound in his leg hurt, but the bullet had not hit bone. Pain was only an annoyance. The bullet had passed through the outside of his thigh, the exit hole twice the diameter of his thumb and bleeding. *That won't do.* He needed a bandage, and he needed to send these cops a warning not to mess with him.

Two birds with one stone, he thought, reaching for the neck of the dead woman's shirt. He tore out a swath from collar to hem and quickly tied it around his leg. That would have to do until he had more time. *Now for the message.*

His claws parted clothing and flesh, and he arranged the two women in a vile parody of love-making. He wanted to do more, but he could hear hurried footsteps now. It was time to leave. He limped a little as he vanished into the foliage. Four cops came running down the path, flash-light beams giving away their position.

"Holy Christ!"

"God, its…"

A flashlight beam swept the darkness, but Derrick stayed low. He heard the sound of one cop retching.

"Call for back-up," another voice snapped. "Cordon off the area. Joey, check to see if either of them is alive."

He circled around and recovered his coat. They might have interrupted his dinner, but they would never forget the message he'd left. They'd think again before they hunted dragons. He dashed through the brush, heading south into the greensward along Fenway. Despite his injury, he knew he could vanish into the maze of university buildings before they could track him down.

He would have to hunt again tomorrow night—he healed faster when fed—but he would change his hunting grounds. Perhaps it would be best if he returned to his home turf. He knew Cambridge better than Boston, and there were specific prey items there that he'd been neglecting. It was time to send another message, one that was sure to bring Aleksi out into the open.

———

The sonofabitch hit again, and this time he picked a couple of cops!" Commander Fisk threw down a stack of eight by ten glossies of a murder scene, and even the hardened faces of the homicide squad blanched. "Two veteran detectives, and he did *that* to them!"

"Holy shit!" one of the team muttered, shifting the photos around. "Fucking sicko!"

"Without a doubt." Fisk glared at Jasper for a moment then let his stare sweep the entire room. "This is now a metro-wide manhunt. Every division of every municipality east of ninety-five from Braintree to Stoneham is looking for this bastard. This started right here in our back yard. I want ideas, options, and stakeouts at everyplace this sonofabitch took a piss for the past year. I want his picture on every goddamn bulletin board and phone pole in Cambridge. Rewards for information, anonymity, get out of jail free cards, whatever it takes!"

"His parents are rich. There'll be a backlash."

"Fuck the backlash. We've got a positive ID of the suspect from two of our own, and unlike our illustrious Sergeant Jasper, one of these fine young ladies managed to hit what she was shooting at last night."

"They shot him?" Jasper was out of his seat. "Did they get a blood trail?"

"Yes. Detective Dempsey shot a hole through the pocket of her coat, and they think it hit him in the leg. Blood in his left footprints. They followed it south into the Longwood area then lost it. Forensics is working it up now to positively ID Penningly." Fisk took a deep breath. "Boston PD said Penningly might not have known the two were cops. They were trolling the parks in plain clothes, trying to flush him out."

"Looks like it worked," one of the junior detectives said.

"Yeah, it worked." Fisk took another deep breath and let it out slow. "Another thing; while the neck and...other wounds are consistent with Penningly's other killings, and the attack on Willis, there was one wound that was different. Dempsey had a compression fracture of her left radius and ulna, near the wrist. There were three puncture wounds where the fracture occurred. They're thinking he broke her arm with whatever weapon he used for the other attacks, but the force applied to break two bones was more than a man could exert. He must have some kind of prosthetic or robotic assist on his hand, which would be consistent with what Jasper told us."

"Some kind of MIT robot nut?" another detective suggested.

"Could be." Fisk tapped the photos with a rigid finger. "I want everyone to look at these, no exceptions. No more dead cops. Let's bring this sick fuck down before he can kill again. Jasper, you're closest to this; I want you to brief anyone who's not up to speed. I want ideas, ladies and gentlemen, and I want them now."

Jasper examined the photos. He'd do as he was told, but he knew where he needed to look for Penningly.

When Hutch's keys hit the bowl beside the door, Iggy rattled his cage hard enough to send it clacking against the kitchen cabinet. The sound brought a smile to his lips, despite the damage to the cabinetry.

"Calm down, you scaly little escapee from the Cretaceous Era! You'll break something!"

"He's just happy to see you."

The voice from the darkest corner of the living room made Hutch's heart skip a beat. The shadows in the corner moved, and he saw her. The hood of her robe was thrown back, revealing her angular features, the hard planes of her face, the prominent jaw, only a hint of Aleksi remaining. She was still changing, still becoming something else. The voice was hers, however.

"Aleksi!" Iggy forgotten, Hutch stashed his computer bag and went to her. She stayed in the shadows, worried, he knew, that unfriendly eyes might see her through the windows. "It's early. Are you okay?"

"I'm fine, Hutch." She returned his embrace, though he could feel her reluctance there, her fear that she might inadvertently hurt him. "I thought about what you said earlier, and I picked up a couple more prepaid phones. If there's a way to do the relay trick, I think I'll—"

The sliding glass door rolling on its track brought them both whirling around toward the balcony. The curtain parted and a grim figure strode into the room.

"Oh, this is just so fucking sweet, I might just *puke*." Derrick Penningly's yellow, dragon eyes glowed in the dim light.

"*Derrick!*" There was more sheer malevolence in Aleksi's voice than Hutch had ever heard. "Tired of killing innocent homeless people yet?" She stepped between them, her arms spread wide, claws extended to their fullest.

I need a weapon, Hutch thought, his mind a whirl of fear, anger, worry, and a sense that he was in very, very deep shit. The closest sharp implement was in the knife block in the kitchen.

"Not even a little bit." Derrick side-stepped across the hardwood floor. Hutch took a moment to look at him, and grimaced. The coat hung open, the shirt streaked with dark stains, a makeshift bandage around one leg, also stained. "They taste like chicken, you know. Isn't it strange that *everyone* tastes like chicken? What do you suppose *you* taste like, Aleksi?"

Aleksi shifted to her right, toward the kitchen, out of the shadows, and Hutch moved with her. He could vault over the counter and the knife block would be in easy reach.

Aleksi sniffed the air. "You *smell* wrong, Derrick. I don't know why, but this thing's made you a monster."

Hutch looked at Derrick in the light and realized that he looked different than Aleksi, not the sleek beauty, smooth scales, clean angular features. His shoulders were hunched, deep-set eyes like holes in a sheetrock wall with someone peering through from behind. Aleksi was right; he was a monster.

"So are you, Aleksi." He edged a step closer, his eyes livid, teeth bared, prominent canines made to tear meat. "We're *both* monsters. You're like me. You *feel* it, don't you?"

"No, Derrick. I'm not like you."

"Come *on*, Aleksi! These meat sacks like Tomlin and your sweet professor aren't what you need! You *need* me! I came here for *you*!"

Hutch edged toward the counter, ready to move.

"You didn't come here for me, Derrick, you came here to die." A sound issued from deep in Aleksi's chest, a growl, a challenge. "And I'm happy to oblige."

The two leapt at each other, claws and teeth flashing. Hutch had seen predators clash before, watched male lions fight for supremacy, big horn sheep and wolves competing for mates, but never had he seen such horrible, flashing violence. Claws swept like scythes, parting the thin material of Aleksi's robe and the thicker cloth of Derrick's coat. Scaly flesh was torn, blood spattering the floor, the walls, the ceiling, all in an instant that left him gaping in horror.

Hutch vaulted the counter, thinking only to put something solid between him and the terrible fray. The thought of a weapon seemed stupid now; a knife against something like *that* was ridiculous. If Derrick killed Aleksi, he would be next, and there was absolutely nothing he could do to affect the outcome. Nevertheless, he pulled the biggest knife from the block.

After the initial clash, the two backed away from each other. Now they circled, both bleeding, clothing in tatters. Derrick's shoulder was torn and Aleksi's robe was ripped open from neck to hip, though Hutch couldn't see how badly she was hurt.

"Come on, Aleksi. You know you want it. We're the only two of our kind. You'll never get another fuck from your pet professor there." Derrick feinted and flung the heavy mahogany coffee table at her. She dodged as if the hundred-pound missile flew in slow motion, flowing out of the way like golden quicksilver. The table smashed into the bookcase, sending volumes and shattered trinkets to the floor with a cascade of splintered wood.

"People aren't pets, Derrick!" Aleksi dashed in, but he dodged, as lightning quick as she.

"No. You're right! They're *prey*!" Derrick lunged, but she pivoted around him, grasping and flinging him into the big flat screen TV. Plastic shattered, clattering to the floor like hail. He crouched among the shards, shaking his head with a feral grin. "They're nothing but an entertaining *food* item."

"Wrong again." She crouched, ready for his next spring.

Watching her, Hutch realized that she was positioning herself not to her best advantage, but to direct Derrick's attention away from him. Also, their strength seemed out of scale with their mass. Wild primates were much stronger than their size suggested; a sixty-pound macaque could break a man's arm. These two were beyond that by orders of magnitude, strong enough to tear a man in half, but weighed only slightly more than a hundred pounds. He found the fight both horrible and mesmerizing.

"This…thing was made to *protect* humans, not to prey on them. It's the only thing that makes sense."

"Then why the dreams, Aleksi?" He circled again, his back now to the kitchen. "You have them, too. I *know* you do. You *feed* on humans in your dreams. We're the same."

"Not all humans, Derrick, only *men*, and they're not dreams." Her claim stopped him. "They're genetic memories of what we were before."

"Want to hear *my* theory?"

"Not really."

"We're the next stage in human evolution. I'm going to father a new *race* with you. A *better* race! But first, I have to eliminate the competition." He whirled toward Hutch, yellow eyes wide, claws ready to tear.

Hutch barely had time to raise the knife before Derrick leapt, but Aleksi was already on him. The impact of her attack saved Hutch's life. Claws that would have torn his head from his shoulders missed the end of his nose by an inch. They crashed onto the sink counter, the thick marble cracking, cabinetry splintering under the onslaught.

Hutch crouched down beside Iggy's cage, knowing he should move, get out of the way of the terrible mayhem, but transfixed by the horrible beauty of the conflict. They were both so fast that he could barely see them move, so powerful that every blow they deflected or absorbed would have killed him. Aleksi grasped Derrick's thick coat and twisted, pivoting his mass around hers and propelling him over Hutch, over the counter to crash into the dining table. Before Hutch could stand to look, Aleksi dove after him. Another crash, and Hutch rose to peer over the barrier.

Amidst the wreckage of the splintered table, Aleksi sat astride Derrick, his wrists pinned to the floor in her taloned grasp. She couldn't strike, but she had him immobilized for the moment.

"Oh, so you like it on top." Derrick bucked hard, arching his back and pushing with his legs.

Aleksi flew forward but twisted and maintained her grip on her opponent's wrists, claws deep in his flesh. She landed with her feet under her and jerked hard, flinging him against the wall. The sheetrock buckled, but the steel studs beneath only bent. Now Aleksi stood between her foe and the kitchen.

Derrick's grin faded. Blood flowed freely from gashes in his arms and shoulder. Aleksi was scratched, but not as deeply. Her robes hung in tatters, but her claws were extended, ready. He glared at her and glanced at the open glass door.

"There's no place you can run, Derrick." Aleksi's voice dripped venom. "You came here for *me*. Finish what you started."

"I *always* finish what I start!" Derrick flexed his hands. He tried to grin, but it was now more of a grimace. He had misjudged her and realized his mistake. "I *will* finish with you! Just not today."

Derrick dashed for the open door, but Aleksi was right on his heels. One sweeping claw caught his flapping coat and spun him around. They missed the open door and crashed through the heavy plate glass, Aleksi's claws reaching for his throat as they plunged over the balcony rail.

The beast within her had finally been set free. All the rage and frustration melded with the instincts of the dragon. Finally, she could kill something that deserved killing.

Falling in a glittering spray of shattered glass, Aleksi had an amazing span of time to think. They tumbled as they fell, sky and earth flashing past in a sickening vertigo. Claws reached for her, and she couldn't fend them off. He raked her shoulder but couldn't get a grip. Neither of them could alter their trajectory, but both struggled to land on top. Winter dead trees, parking lot crowded with cars, two astonished faces looking up through a windshield, and the glaring street lights all whirled past. Derrick flung one arm wide, his tattered jacket and the membrane from his elongated fingers to his ankle biting into the wind to tumble them over.

The hood of the unmarked police car was slightly softer than asphalt.

Sheet metal buckled under the impact, the windshield shattering beneath Aleksi's head. The blow would have killed a human, but only left Aleksi dazed. Derrick lay on top of her, pressing onto her chest. Exclamations from the two police officers in the car and the hiss of air escaping the airbags pierced her momentary confusion.

"Say you want me, and I won't kill you."

A surge of revulsion at Derrick's voice in her ear sent adrenalin lancing through her like lightning. She shoved him up, but he had a grip on her shoulders. His hips ground into hers, but she couldn't get a leg up to pitch him off. He grinned down at her, pulling against her thrusting arms, kicking to force her legs apart. She couldn't *believe* he was actually trying to rape her on the crumpled hood of a police car.

A pencil-thin beam of light swept between their faces, bobbled for a moment then flicked into Derrick's disheveled hair. Horror crossed his face. Even as he released his hold on her, she reached for him. All she had to do was hold him still for half a second, and someone else would finish this for her. Her claws grasped the fabric of his coat, but he tore away.

The shockwave of a bullet passing through the space where his head had been buffeted them both. Derrick tumbled away. She lunged after him, claws digging furrows in the hood of the police car. The laser wobbled and swung toward Derrick.

"Stop! Police!"

"Shit!" She ducked and dashed for the shadows.

A muzzle flash caught Derrick like a strobe. Snow spat up beside her as she leapt behind a car. With something solid between her and the guns, she had a few seconds to think. One of the cops shouted something ridiculous, while the other yelled into his radio, calling for help. Derrick was nowhere in sight. Tires squealed, and she hazarded a glance to see how many police cars were closing in.

Three black Escalades raced down the street toward the parking lot.

"Shit-shit-*shit!*" She had to move, but where?

Then she saw a heavy storm grating only twenty feet away. She was moving before she could talk herself out of it.

Bullets spalled against pavement and metal, but her claws were in the grating before anything hit her. She wrenched the heavy cover up as another salvo roared. The steel grating rang with the impact of a bullet, but she was already dropping through the hole. The grating clanged into place above her as her feet splashed into icy water.

The darkness here was thicker, but she knew it was her friend. She tried to remember which way it was to the river and dashed into the gloom, claws scrabbling for purchase on the tunnel walls.

By the time Jasper arrived, the place was crawling with feds. Three big SUV's had disgorged SWAT armed mystery men like giant kiddy cars spewing clowns in a circus. Despite his own flashing blue lights and badge, a stone-faced man held up a hand at the parking lot entrance, the ID in his other hand unfamiliar. It wasn't an FBI badge.

He got out of his car. "Who the hell are you guys?" There were half a dozen more squad cars hot on his heels, blue lights strobing through the night.

"Federal agents, sir." Well, at least they were polite. "We've cordoned off the area. We'll let you have the scene as soon as we've seen to a few things."

"I'm Sergeant Jasper, Cambridge Homicide, and those are my men." He pointed to the two officers who were surrounded by a ring of feds. "I need to speak with them." He started forward, but the fed put his hand up again.

"I'm sorry, sir, but nobody enters the scene until we've seen to a few things."

"What *things*?" Tires squealed behind him and uniformed police got out. He glared at the man before him, then gaped as he saw that his two detectives were being guided toward one of the waiting SUV's. "Those are *my* men!"

"Your men will be returned to you when they've been debriefed, Sergeant." Jasper turned to see a woman in a dark suit approaching with two more fed clones in tow. "This scene is ours for now."

"And who the hell are you? That wasn't an FBI badge he flashed, and I have jurisdiction in this city!"

The woman stopped three feet in front of him and held up her ID close enough for him to see. The picture wasn't very flattering, but the broad blue letters "D.H.S." sure were.

"My name is Dr. Johansen, and the whole of the United States is my jurisdiction. This has become a matter of national security. Your men will be debriefed and returned to you, this scene will be sterilized, and we will thank you for your cooperation." She put the ID away. "That's how this is going to happen, Sergeant Jasper."

"You are not taking—" Motion at the doors to the condo building caught his attention, and he turned to see Dr. Hutchinson being escorted by two more dark suits toward yet another SUV. "You can't just kidnap people like this!"

"It's not kidnapping, its detention, and we certainly *can* detain anyone we wish, Sergeant."

Jasper heard in her voice that her list of potential detainees included police detectives. He gritted his teeth, forcing down his temper.

"I want some kind of contact information before you leave here, Doctor." He nodded to the dozen cops who had fanned out behind him. "Or *nobody's* leaving."

"Of course." She handed over a white business card.

A glance showed him only an embossed seal of the Department of Homeland Security, her name, followed by PhD, and a phone number.

"This is hardly proper identification, Doctor. I need some kind of—" His phone rang, but before he could even answer, Johansen told him who was calling.

"That's the chief of the Cambridge Police Department, Sergeant. He's going to tell you to give us your full and complete cooperation."

He gave her a withering glance and answered his phone. Damned if she wasn't right, even about the full and complete part. He could only say, "Yes, sir," and hang up. He ordered his people to set up a perimeter and watched the show. As they dismantled the damaged police car, he made the connection.

National security...professionals wearing combat boots...missing specimen... But he couldn't figure out why the Department of Homeland Security would want a bunch of old fossils.

43

In the back of an Escalade, with grim-faced federal agents seated to either side and tinted windows obscuring his view, Hutch knew only vaguely where they were when they finally turned into a parking structure.

The vehicle stopped at a security check, then proceeded through a roll-up steel door. They parked, and the man to his left opened his door and the one to his right nudged him to slide out. There wasn't much else he could do. Another Escalade pulled up, and six more people got out. The men all seemed cut from the same bolt of cloth, short hair, cut, but the woman among them stood out. She was shorter, severely tailored, and didn't look at him as they all moved toward another door.

Then his phone rang.

They all stopped as if controlled by the same puppeteer. The woman turned, her eyes fixing on him before the second ring.

She touched the lapel of her coat and said, "Cellular call incoming. Parking garage, level B-two. Isolate and triangulate." She stepped up to him. "Answer your phone, Dr. Hutchinson."

He pulled the prepaid phone from his pocket and pressed the green icon. "Hello."

"Are you okay, Hutch?"

Her voice...she's alive!

"I'm fine. How are you?"

The woman stared at him, not giving any direction or instruction.

"Alive. Derrick got away."

"Aleksi, some people came. They got there before the police."

"I saw them. They're the ones who tried to kill me."

"I'm with them now."

Silence… Then she said, "They're tracing this call, Hutch."

"Yes, we are," the woman said, as if she'd heard Aleksi's voice on the other end. Maybe she had.

"They're listening, too, Aleksi."

"Great. I better—"

"Give me the phone, Dr. Hutchinson." The woman held out a hand.

"A woman with them wants to talk to you, Aleksi. I've got to hand over the phone."

"Just do whatever they say, Hutch. This has nothing to do with you."

"Okay." He handed over the phone.

"Miss Rychenkna, this is Dr. Johansen." After a short pause, she added, "No that's not my real name, and neither was it my predecessor's. He's been replaced. I'm sorry for what happened earlier."

Hutch heard Aleksi's raised voice over the phone and could not help but smile. She had certainly expanded her vocabulary.

"That was before Derrick Penningly escaped our control. He's gone completely rogue, Miss Rychenkna. I'd like to talk to you about how we might work together to resolve this issue."

Another stream of expletives.

"I'm not asking you to come in. We can talk by phone or meet in person. You choose the time and place, and I'll be there."

Aleksi said something too quiet for Hutch to hear, but the woman's raised eyebrows were enough to tell him that it wasn't expected. She looked at her watch.

"Can you give us a half hour?" She pulled the phone away from her ear and covered the receiver. She started to mouth something to one of her associates, but Aleksi interrupted her.

"No. Now or never. And bring Hutch." He heard that clearly and smiled.

"That's impossible, Miss Rychenkna. Dr. Hutchinson is in our custody."

"He shows or I don't! And no goddamn snipers, or I'll disappear and you can deal with Derrick Penningly on your own."

Dr. Johansen paused, seeming to consider. "Very well, Miss Rychenkna. We'll be there as soon as we can."

"Fine."

Johansen looked at the phone, and Hutch knew Aleksi had hung up. She touched her collar and said, "Position?"

Hutch heard no answer, and a glance confirmed that she and her cadre all wore earpieces.

"Okay, assemble a team." She gestured to the SUV. "Dr. Hutchinson, it seems we're going for a ride."

"Were to?" He couldn't very well say no.

"The Prudential Tower."

What the hell? Hutch thought as they stuffed him into the back seat of the Escalade. *What in the world are you thinking, Aleksi?*

I just hate this 'Word From On High' bullshit, sir. They walked away with two of our people and the primary witness!" Jasper was still livid; by the time the feds had let them onto the scene, there had been nothing left to investigate. "They even took our fucking *car*!"

"I don't like it any more than you do, Jasper, but my hands are tied. When my boss says shut up and follow orders, I do just that. You'd be wise to follow suit." Fisk hadn't moved from behind his desk since Jasper arrived. It was almost midnight, and the forensics team was still crawling all over Hutchinson's apartment and the condo parking lot, not that there was anything to find. The feds had been thorough.

"I'll follow orders, sir, but I'm worried about our people." He was worried about more than that, but it was the only lever that might move Fisk's ass out of his chair.

"And don't suggest for a second that I am *not*, Sergeant." Fisk's glare would have scared a rookie detective into submission, but Jasper was no rookie.

"I'm not suggesting anything, sir, but you should have seen how they took over the scene. That Johansen told me the chief was calling me before I even answered my goddamn phone!"

"Well, if it'll make you feel any better, the Boston PD got the same call. We're off the case until further notice. National security."

"They must have loved that, with two of their cops dead." Jasper tried to imagine the rug being pulled out from under a cop-killer investigation.

"Well, there was not much they could do, but yeah, everyone's fuming over this. There's also a gag order to the press and all evidence is being confiscated."

"Nice." Jasper rubbed his eyes, wondering what the hell he could do to bypass the bullshit. The answer was, not much. "What about that blood work on Penningly? Did they at least get a match?"

"No, and you're not going to like that either. They fucked up the sample somehow. Not only was the blood not Penningly's, it wasn't even human. They think maybe a dog or rat contaminated it."

"You're kidding me?" Jasper thought back to the scene at the condo parking lot. *Not human...* The hood of the unmarked police car had been crumpled and cut up like something out of Junk Yard Wars.

"I don't kid about shit like that, Jasper." Fisk took a deep breath and let it out slow, a sure sign that his temper was coming down. "For now, we just move on. Anything you find out about this case should come directly to me and I'll pass it up the line."

"Fine." Jasper's mind clicked to the only other lead they had. He didn't want a replay of what had happened at Hutchinson's apartment. "I think we should warn the guys watching Julie Parks."

"Think he'll go after her?"

"He might, and the feds aren't going to do jack-shit to protect her." He started for the door, then turned back. "I'll tell you one more thing, Commander; after seeing the hood of that car and the inside of Hutchinson's apartment, I'm going to want something with a little more knock-down than my Glock the next time I see Derrick Penningly."

The indignant assurances of the Prudential Building security guards that *nobody* could have gotten onto the Skywalk floor after hours seemed only to amuse Dr. Johansen. Nothing amused her entourage of four dark coats. Hutch found the entire situation maddening. He practiced his breathing during the long elevator ride up the tower, trying to calm his nerves. Aleksi had to know that she was cornering herself by arranging a meeting at the top of a fifty-story building.

Trust is something you earn, he remembered telling her, *and you've earned mine.*

He had no choice but to trust her now, though after the fight with Derrick, he didn't see how she could be in any condition to defend herself. He didn't know if their IDs were legitimate, but that his escorts were with the government, he had no doubt. Nobody else could intimidate the police and spirit away witnesses and evidence like that.

The elevator chimed and the doors opened. Two of the dark coats moved out of the elevator and took station to either side of the doors.

Johansen gripped his arm with one slim hand. "Shall we, Doctor?"

He felt like jerking out of her grasp but settled for giving her a scathing smile. With two more goons behind him, there wasn't much else he could do. They walked into the open viewing area that surrounded the restaurant, the floor to ceiling glass displaying an expansive vista of Boston. The two men behind them looked left and right, but there was no sign of Aleksi.

A ruse? he wondered, unable to guess Aleksi's motive for such a ploy other than to distract them from her real whereabouts.

Johansen spoke into her lapel. "Team one. Once around. No guns."

The two stationed by the elevator began a slow circuit of the viewing floor and restaurant, their hands in plain sight, though Hutch had no doubt that they could produce weapons readily enough. They completed their circuit and shook their heads.

"Well, it would seem that Miss Rychenkna has sent us on a wild goose chase."

"Or you need people with better eyes."

The voice spun everyone around, hands reaching into coats, but still there was no one there.

Hutch smiled. "I'm here, Aleksi."

"I know." Her voice sent a thrill up his spine.

Johansen nodded to her men, and they started to fan out.

"Keep them right where they are, Doctor." Aleksi sounded very different when she spoke to Johansen, harsh and suspicious. "If I see one gun, you'll be the first person to die."

"Nobody's going to die here, Miss Rychenkna." Johansen nodded to her men again. They took station on either side of her, hands empty. "Do we talk face to face, or do you stay hidden?"

Shadows moved where the ceiling met a support column, and Aleksi dropped to the floor. She landed without a sound and then rose from her crouch to step into the open. She still wore her tattered niqab, the hood back. She kept her hands folded in front of her, clutching the torn and bloodstained cloth closed. Her eyes scanned the group, lingered on Hutch's for a moment, then shifted to Johansen.

"Thank you for bringing Dr. Hutchinson."

"Thank you for agreeing to meet."

"I'm sorry about your home, Hutch." Her eyes never left Johansen.

"It's just an apartment, Aleksi. Just things. It's not important." He smiled at her, wanted to go to her, take her in his arms and hold her, but knew he couldn't. "I was thinking about remodeling anyway."

"I'm just glad you weren't hurt."

"I'm fine."

Her eyes flicked to his for a moment, then back to Johansen. "I'm here to listen to you, Dr. Johansen, but you may as well know now that I'll never come in to be your guinea pig."

"I'm not asking you to."

"And I want you to release Dr. Hutchinson. He's not a part of this and he's lost enough already."

"Right now, we're keeping him, but our only interest is to find out how much he knows about…your condition."

"Less than you do, if you had Derrick in your lab. How did that work? Did you offer him amnesty for murdering Bob Tomlin if he came in and told you where to find the samples that infected us?"

Hutch felt Johansen's grip tense on his arm. The scathing suspicion in Aleksi's tone made her nervous.

"Something like that, but I wasn't the one who made that deal, Miss Rychenkna. It was a bad call, and we're trying to rectify that mistake."

"And how's that working for you?"

"Admittedly, not very well. Derrick's out of control. That's why I took over this project from my predecessor and why I wanted to speak with you." She let go of Hutch's arm and held out her hands imploringly. "You seem to be very much *in* control, and quite capable of confronting Penningly. I'd like to know why you think you're less mentally impaired by the changes you're going through, and I need to know how to find and neutralize Penningly."

"Let me ask you something first. You did blood work on Derrick. What did you find?"

"The results were inconclusive. The DNA in the samples was…unstable."

"No, it wasn't. It was changing, being rewritten by the infection. Gene switching, recombination, recoding. It seemed unstable because the changes aren't complete yet."

"What will he…and you be when the changes *are* complete?" There was less incredulity there than Hutch would have suspected.

"I don't know, but I won't be the same as Derrick Penningly. We're… different. This…" She raised one clawed hand and extended the two webbed fingers fully, now a foot longer than her other digits. "…evolved to protect humans, but in *him* it didn't. It may work differently in men than women. Whatever he is, the changes, his violent impulses, are out of control."

"Interesting." Dr. Johansen licked her lips and cocked her head in a mannerism that sparked a twinge of familiarity in Hutch. "So, how do we get him?"

Where have I seen that before? He looked closely at the woman again, but her face sparked no memories.

"Watch more closely than you have been, but you already know that." Aleksi took a couple of steps closer, into the brighter light. Her angular features glowered at them, the prominent brow and hard cheekbones framing her bright yellow eyes like a glittering golden sculpture. "As to how to neutralize him, I don't know if I want to tell you. Anything that will help you kill Derrick will help you kill me, which you've already tried to do twice."

"The first time was not under my direction, as I said, Miss Rychenkna, and the second time we weren't aiming at you, only Penningly." Now it was Johansen's turn to use a hard tone. "That *won't* happen again. You're much too valuable to us alive."

"How so?"

"This meeting proves it." She flicked a hand, a graceful gesture that sparked another twinge of familiarity. "You're willing to speak with us. You're an asset, Miss Rychenkna. We don't waste assets."

"I know what you're thinking, and you're wrong, Doctor."

"What *am* I thinking, Aleksi?"

"You want to create some kind of…weapon out of this." She gestured to her own face with one clawed hand, and Hutch noticed Johansen flinch. "You're playing with a fire you can't control. It's more dangerous than anything the human race has ever discovered. It'll destroy civilization if you let it loose."

"We have no intention of letting it loose, Miss Rychenkna." Johansen sounded like a parent telling a child that there was no Santa Claus. "We only want to understand it, to discover how it evolved, and why it vanished. I would like *your* opinion, as a paleontologist, why there is no fossil record of it."

"I'm still formulating theories about that, but you've had more time with the specimen than I did. The interior of the sample was crumbled to dust, but not from heat fracturing. There was nothing left, but it was still infectious."

"How could this evolve, Aleksi?"

"I don't know." Aleksi lifted her webbed fingers again. "I have dreams… genetic memories that aren't consistent with what I'm…experiencing. I'm not sure what I'm going to be."

"Any theories on that?"

"Some. Unless your laboratory comes up with a cure, and, no offense, I don't think that's very likely, I'll find out eventually."

"Not likely, perhaps, but it *is* possible." Johansen took a short step forward. "*Work* with us, and I promise you, we'll try."

"You'll forgive me if I don't trust you, Dr. Johansen." She smiled, and her pronounced canines glinted in the light like knives. "Your people shot me, remember?"

"I'll concede that we've not earned your trust." She stepped back and nodded toward Hutch. "I'll agree to free Dr. Hutchinson on the condition that he agrees not to speak to anyone or publish anything about you or this project, and I'll see that your name is cleared. We can manufacture any story you wish to satisfy the press and your family."

"And what do you want in return?"

"Help us neutralize Penningly."

"You mean kill him for you."

"That, or lure him into a position where we can capture him."

"If you think you can capture—" Aleksi's head cocked, and her eyes snapped into hard slits. "I should have *known* better than to trust you!"

"Wait, Aleksi!" Johansen shouted, but Aleksi was already moving. "They're just for surveillance! We're not—"

But her assurances were cut off by the crash of shattering glass and the whir of helicopter rotors.

Tempered glass exploded around Aleksi in a glittering cascade, ten thousand diamonds falling with her as she ripped free the last tatters of her shredded robe. As the fabric fluttered away, she saw that the helicopter she'd heard was still some distance off, but too close for comfort. In the open side door a black-clad man held a rifle.

Aleksi flung her arms wide, extending the two elongated fingers that she usually kept folded down along her forearm. The membrane that had formed between those fingers and all the way to her ankles, snapped taut like a sail in a hurricane. She couldn't actually fly yet, but she was betting her life that she could glide enough to evade her enemies.

She banked to the northeast, but immediately knew that her glide angle was too steep. Instinct told her that if she tried to flatten her trajectory, she would stall. She needed someplace to land or…

Without thinking, she banked back to the right, aiming for the rounded glass monstrosity of another building. She pulled up hard, aiming for one of the terraced rooftops. Wings billowed, clawed toes scraping the lowest terrace an instant before she barreled right into one of the glass walls. Thinking of all the bugs she'd seen hit windshields, she folded her wings and balled her fists.

The glass shattered, and she slammed through office furniture as she tucked and rolled. She came to her feet and burst through a door into a maze of cubicles. She kept moving, dashing the length of a long, open isle and glancing to her left for an opening. A balcony there drew her attention and she turned, increasing her speed again. Movement through the windows caught her eye before she plunged through the glass and launched herself into the air.

The helicopter had followed her decent, but the pilot had not predicted her change in direction. It banked around the building, its rotors a deadly disc of flashing blades. She caught a glimpse of the pilot's astonished face, mouth agape, as she plunged past, missing the rotors by mere feet with her wings fully extended. The prop wash buffeted her, but she was already banking away, swooping around another building, this one mostly gray concrete. She spied her goal and pulled up, killing her speed in a stall as she approached the roof of the Boston Public Library.

The ceramic tiles of the pitched roof shattered under her feet, but she managed to keep her balance, scrambling to the north end of the building. She launched herself into the air once more, but this was just a short jump in comparison to her previous dizzying plummets. She cleared a bus as it passed on Boylston Street, and arrested her flight by grasping one of the ornate light poles in front of the Old North Church. Her claws screeched against the steel pole as she swung around it once and dropped to the sidewalk. A passing couple turned to stare, eyes wide, mouths hanging open. She could only guess what they were thinking as she folded her wings and dashed into the Copley St. subway station.

At this point, she wasn't concerned if she was caught on someone's cell phone camera or one of the security monitors. Let Johansen worry about that. She had clothes stashed in the tunnel, and seven minutes until the next train passed. Aleksi would be just another faceless figure in the crowd when she caught the train at Arlington station.

4 4

Persephone sat back in Dr. Johansen's chair and watched the video again from the beginning. She had a DHS analysis team going over it frame by frame, harvesting every bit of technical information they could, but still, she watched it again. She couldn't get enough of it, her mind awhirl.

Dragons…

She'd read the transcript of Hutch's conversation with Congressman Twain. Would a race of dragons put humans on the bottom of the food chain, even exterminate mankind? Gi-gi had been right about one thing; such a thing was not to be trusted in the hands of the US Government.

Her computer chimed, an icon flashing on the screen. Mary Buckmann's memory told her it belonged to the Director. He was probably watching the same video. She touched the icon.

"Yes, sir."

"This project has become too high profile, Doctor. Control it or end it."

"Containment is our primary goal, sir."

"There's been another murder."

"Where?"

"You'll get the details. We have a clean-up team on it already."

"Very well."

There was a pause, then, "Are you sure it's Penningly doing this, not Rychenkna?"

"Positive, sir."

"Then get him."

"We will." The call ended. She tapped another icon on her screen and said, "Bring Dr. Hutchinson to interview room one."

"Yes, Doctor."

Persephone pushed herself to her feet, wobbling with fatigue. She hadn't gotten much sleep since she assumed Buckmann's identity, but there would be time for sleep when it was done. She fished a small bottle of pills from her jacket pocket and shook one into her palm. It went down with the last swallow of her coffee. By the time she arrived in the interview room, she'd be as sharp as a razor.

***

D r. Hutchinson, I hope you slept well." Johansen entered the room bearing two big cups of coffee. "Strong and dark with milk no sugar, right?" She sat down and pushed one cup across the table to him.

"Yes." He didn't reach for the coffee, though the smell set his mouth watering. "And, as a matter of fact, I didn't sleep well at all. When are you going to release me?"

"Just as soon as we reach an agreement, Doctor." She sipped her coffee and leaned back in her chair, looking as fresh as if she had just spent a day at a spa. "I'm prepared to do everything Aleksi asked for in return for her help, but I need yours as well."

"To keep your secret?" Hutch didn't like secrets and he didn't like lies. This woman was full of both. Any agreement from her was worthless. They would do whatever they wanted to further their own ends, regardless of what they promised him.

"That and work as our liaison with Aleksi Rychenkna."

"And if I don't agree?"

"Then your life goes down the toilet, Aleksi becomes a target instead of an asset, and we find Derrick Penningly on our own, probably after he's killed a dozen or so more people." She withdrew a folder from her bag and placed it before him. "Those are his victims so far. Two of them were cops." She flipped open the folder, and the eight by ten glossy photo of an eviscerated woman glared up at him. "Tell me you don't want to help us stop this."

Hutch stared at the photo, his stomach clenching on his unappetizing breakfast. He tore his eyes away and picked up the coffee. He managed to swallow a sip and breathe. "You know that Derrick wants to do that to me, too."

"The thought had crossed my mind." That stony mien, humorless, lifeless, stared him down.

Bait...they want to use me as bait. "Not that I expect you to tell me the truth, but do you plan to kill him before, or after he's taken the bait?"

"Before, Doctor, but we can't watch you twenty-four seven." Johansen reached into her bag again and slid his two cell phones across the table. "You *do* have someone else out there watching over you."

"I don't want Aleksi anywhere near Derrick Penningly." He swallowed and closed his eyes. The image waiting for him there resembled the woman in the photo, but with Aleksi's face.

"She's proven that she can take him, Hutch. Let her do what she was *made* to do."

"What do you mean, *made* to do?"

"If she's right, this...affliction evolved to *protect* mankind." She sipped her coffee and eyed him evenly.

"From what?" Hutch didn't trust her, but the scientist in him was curious.

"From ourselves, maybe." She licked her lips and cocked her head at him, that same familiar gesture. Where had he seen that? "Mankind evolved in a dangerous world. We weren't on the top of the food chain then and needed protection. Now we are. I want to keep us there."

It made sense. Hutch tried to imagine an evolutionary pathway that would yield something like Aleksi and failed. He looked at the two phones. "You've got those bugged."

"You wouldn't believe me if I told you we didn't."

"True."

"So, take them, and help us stop Penningly."

"And agree to keep your secrets."

"Yes."

He took another sip of coffee. It was good, strong with just the right amount of milk. *How the hell do they know so much about me? How much more do they know?* He knew that their threat to ruin his life wasn't idle. They could manufacture evidence and have him arrested as a terrorist just to ensure his silence. But there was that glossy picture staring at him, screaming at him, pleading with him to end this slaughter of innocents.

"All right." He put the coffee down and picked up the two phones. "I agree to keep this as quiet as I can, not publish any findings or go to the authorities. Frankly, they wouldn't believe me anyway, and my career would be ruined."

"I'm glad you see it our way, Doctor." She smiled and closed the folder.

"Just keep one thing in mind, Dr. Johansen."

"What's that?"

He longed to wipe that smirk of superiority from her face. "Whatever I agree to, Aleksi makes her own decisions. I can't guarantee anything from her, and she'll *never* trust you, not after what you did to her."

"I'm not asking for your guarantee, Doctor, just your cooperation." She stood and picked up her coffee. The door opened, and the two guards who had escorted him in stood there waiting. "She'll agree because it's the only thing she can do."

"What do you mean?" Hutch stood and picked up his coffee.

"She's alone. She needs someone, and you're the only someone she's got."

Hutch wondered if they would ever let Aleksi go, if they would offer her a cure for her condition, assuming they ever found one. He also wondered what Johansen wasn't telling him.

Some questions you'll never get an answer to, Hutch. He followed his escort out of the room. He was halfway home before he had one final revelation: *She called me Hutch. Why would a woman I've never met before call me Hutch?*

Gobbets of bloody flesh splashed into the icy Charles River, the least appetizing bits of Derrick's most recent kill. He crouched in the shadowed framework of the Boston University railroad bridge, his taloned feet gripping the rusty steel girders.

This is more like it. He ate at a leisurely pace, watching the waterfront along MIT and the southern shore. Figures jogged or strolled along the pedestrian paths. A lone biker rode past, braving the cold and darkness. *So many...like lambs in a slaughterhouse, waiting for me to get hungry.* He tore another bit of the fatty flesh from bone and chewed thoughtfully.

He scratched at the thick scab on his shoulder. His other injuries ached, but the dragon healed quickly. His thigh felt stiff and hot, but with food and rest he would be fine. And there was plenty of food.

He tore off another hunk of meat and dropped the denuded limb into the water. The arm sank. Yes, this was much better, a leisurely meal with a water-front view and an easy means to dispose of the offal. No traces for the cops or Johansen's goons to hunt him down with.

"Hunting…" he mumbled around a bit of gristle. He looked to the northwest but couldn't see Hutchinson's condo from here. There were other bridges near there. They weren't as concealing as this one, but he could hide there and watch, at least until morning. He knew a number of good hiding places for daytime but couldn't watch from any of them. No, his hunting would have to be at night. Nobody missed homeless people, and with the river to dispose of the bones, nobody would discover his activity.

Derrick had only one problem left.

Aleksi… He didn't understand her attachment to Hutchinson. Sure, she had fucked him, but that didn't mean anything. They were too different now. Was she keeping him like a favored pet?

"You're talking about the woman who kept a lizard." He swallowed and picked out another choice bite. It didn't matter why Aleksi felt the need to protect Hutchinson, so long as she did. It would make her that much easier to find. Then he would make her understand, show her that he was the only one for her. His teeth sheared through the fatty muscle easily. He would feed and heal, then find her.

And there was plenty of food.

<hr>

Hutch opened his door and cringed. His home was a wreck. Then he heard a cage being rattled against the kitchen counter and his concerns shifted one hundred eighty degrees.

"Oh, Iggy! Damn! You poor thing." He dropped his keys in the bowl and hurried to the kitchen. Thankfully, the refrigerator was one appliance that had been spared the mayhem. He recovered a wide range of fruits and vegetables for the ravenous iguana. In short order, he had the cage door open, Iggy in a firm grasp, and was feeding him halved cherry tomatoes and bits of romaine lettuce.

"I suppose this is male bonding." He offered up a slice of cucumber. Iggy ignored it, so Hutch popped it into his mouth. "Two vegetarian guys hanging out, huh?" He offered a wedge of slightly rotten strawberry and was redeemed.

He put Iggy on the floor next to the bowl of diced food, and quickly cleaned the cage. Then, he turned to the fridge for his own dinner. Yogurt sprinkled with granola, a few of the lesser spoiled strawberries, some cucumber slices and bleu cheese dressing to dip them in. Add a cold beer and he had dinner for one. He sat at the kitchen counter and surveyed the damage while he ate. The thick marble counter near the sink was cracked, and the cabinetry was knocked askew. The dining and living rooms were utterly trashed, splintered wood, broken plastic, and glass everywhere. The condo manager had at least taped plastic over the shattered glass door to keep out the elements. Tomorrow he would have to contact his insurance company. He doubted he was covered for a battle between dragons, but a tale of home invasion and vandalism wouldn't be too far from the truth.

With dinner finished, and Iggy stuffed and torpid enough to return easily to his cage, he put the dishes in the sink. It was bent and would have to be replaced. He went to his phone, checked messages, and then plugged in his computer to do some damage control. Eighty-four emails and six phone calls later, he checked his watch—ten thirty—and decided for a shower and maybe something to take his mind off his troubles. Bed and a book sounded way too good to refuse.

After a shower, he felt better, and he opted for a whiskey in addition to the book. He went to the bedroom, put the book and glass on the nightstand and shrugged out of his robe.

"Reading Zen again?"

Her voice went through him like an electric shock. He turned to the shadows beyond the open closet door and saw two faintly reflective golden orbs. They blinked then rose. Aleksi stood from her crouch and came into the soft light. She was garbed once again as a street person, but had traded the coat for a loose-fitting poncho that looked like a blanket with a hole cut for her head.

"Actually, it's a brain vacation book." He pulled his robe back on and nodded to the book on the night table. "You'd call it make believe. Something to take my mind off...things."

"Off me, you mean."

"No, Aleksi. Not you." He rounded the bed, but she backed away. "Are you okay? When you fell, I—"

"I'm fine, Hutch. This...thing heals quickly, as long as I have food. It's you who's in danger. I'm surprised they let you go."

"I agreed to stay quiet and to talk to you about Derrick."

"That's why I'm here, Hutch. We need to talk about this." She shifted, her movements slow, deliberate. Was she injured and hiding it? "Derrick showed up here because *I* was here. He's looking for *me*, not you. That's why he didn't kill you earlier. He's probably watching your place every night. Just being here, I'm putting you in danger."

"That's not true, Aleksi." He didn't like where this was going or the pain in her voice. "You saved my life last night. If you hadn't been here, he would have killed me."

"If I hadn't been here, he would never have shown up! He's after *me*. He won't rest until he…finds me."

"Kills you, you mean."

"I don't think so, Hutch. The way he was fighting, the things he said…" She hugged herself, her long claws gripping her arms so tightly that they pierced the fabric of her poncho. "I think it's mating behavior. We're the only two…like this in the world, Hutch. Think about it."

"I don't want to think about it." He took a step closer. "Listen, Aleksi, Johansen wants to use me as bait. She wants to take Derrick out when he comes for me."

"She's wrong. He won't come for you, Hutch. He's after *me*! He came here because he knew I care for you." Her gaze fell to the floor. "I need to leave."

"But if you leave, there's nothing to keep Derrick from *killing* me."

"If I leave, he won't have a *reason* to kill you." She looked up, then away, her golden eyes closing tight. A tear slipped down the angle of her scaly cheek and fell from her chin. "Please don't make this any harder, Hutch."

"I'm trying to make it *easier*, Aleksi." She looked at him, and he saw the memory of the last time he'd said that to her flash across her face. He reached out for her, but she backed away.

"Hutch…don't."

"Don't leave me. Don't let him win. If the feds want to use me as bait to draw Derrick into the open, then *use* me! If you think he's after you, then the only way you can expose him for them is to be with me! You said so yourself!"

"Or I could hunt him down myself." She sniffed and wiped away her tears. "He's feeding on *people*, Hutch. All I've got to do is think like him, watch for him, and I'll find him. He won't kill me. Not if he thinks I'm…interested."

"You *can't* be serious, Aleksi." The cold ball of dread that had been sitting in Hutch's stomach exploded into a full-fledged panic, his heart suddenly racing. "You can't let him—"

"I have no intention of letting him do anything, but letting him think I *might* will get him close enough for me to kill him." Her voice was cold now, a predator he didn't know.

"Do you think you can, Aleksi?" He wasn't talking about her physical ability to overpower Derrick; he was talking about her taking a life. "You're no killer."

"Killing Derrick won't be murder, Hutch. It'll be an execution for what he's done." It wasn't really an answer, but it was enough. He had to trust her.

"Promise me you'll come back to me when this is over." He took another step closer to her.

"I…can't, Hutch." She hugged herself tighter, her shoulders shaking. "They'll never let me be, and if I'm near you, they'll use that."

"I don't care."

"I do."

They stared at one another for a very long while, eyes of gold and blue fixed upon one another, communicating more than could ever be said.

"I've got to go, Hutch." She started to move past him, but he raised his hand to forestall her.

"You can't!"

"Please, Hutch, I—"

"No, I mean not until morning. You said yourself that Derrick will be watching my place. He could be watching now." He put his hands on her arms, his fingers interlacing with hers. "You can stay until morning, can't you?"

"I…I shouldn't."

"Bullshit."

She smiled, some of the pain ebbing from her eyes. "Yep, pretty much."

"Then stay." He pulled her into an embrace, feeling the tremors in her wiry frame, wanting only to ease them somehow. "Stay with me, Aleksi."

"I'll stay," she whispered in his ear, and it felt like the weight of the world lifted from his shoulders. Her arms enfolded him, the sinewy wing membranes wrapping him like a blanket. Her embrace was gentle, her breath warm on his neck. "Until morning."

45

"Hey, Dr. H!"

"Hi guys." Hutch dropped his keys in the bowl and waved to the two contractors putting the last touches of plaster on the new sheetrock. His condo looked more like a construction project than a war zone now. "You're working late."

"Just finishing up. Out of your way in ten minutes."

"No worries. I'm going for a run, so just lock the door when you leave."

"Sure, Doc!"

He stashed his work things in the office, then went to his bedroom and changed into sweats. It was cool out, but there had been a break in winter's grip and people were out in droves enjoying it. The days were getting longer; there was a sliver of twilight at five PM. There had not been a murder reported since he'd last seen Aleksi four days ago; no sign of her or Penningly, and not a word from the mysterious Dr. Johansen. He was feeling strange with the silence, wondering if it had all been taken care of by the government, Derrick dead, Aleksi either dead or captured. His life seemed to be returning to normal; nothing to worry about but work and himself.

He picked up his IPod, plugged in, and waved to the workers on the way out. Some quick stretches in the entryway, and he was out the door. He looked for the ugly green Ford that had been stationed outside his place for what seemed like forever, but even the police surveillance had vanished. That, he wouldn't miss.

An easy warm-up jog took him to the nearest crosswalk, and he stretched some more while waiting for the light. Once on the Memorial walkway, he let the music and rhythm of his feet take his unease away. His mind drifted through the details of work, Lonnie's upcoming dissertation, his search for a new student to take on the bone bed project. He would have to hire a technician for some of it; there had been too big a hole left behind with the loss of both Bob and Aleksi.

Loss. Hutch thought about the concepts of loss, death, and aloneness, about Aleksi stretched out on an autopsy table, her beautiful golden skin flayed open for analysis.

He picked up his pace, passed the boat houses and kept going under the Elliot Bridge. Past the American Legion hall, the trail went to gravel and the number of people thinned. Winter-dead trees crowded in, limbs rattling in the wind. The cold, ice-strewn waters of the Charles seemed to swallow up the heat of the day, and his breath came in clouds of fog. When the trail met back up with the street, he decided to cross again. He wasn't in the mood for a wide paved trail, the backstreets of Cambridge would give him something to look at, something to feel.

He found himself staring at Cambridge Cemetery beyond the empty parking lot through the spindly shrubs. The expanse of simple and elaborate headstones stretched on for what seemed like forever. *So many bones,* he thought, remembering Aleksi's love of them.

On impulse, he crossed the tangle of dead vegetation and began running along the twisting paths and circuitous roads, winding his way through the graves. Aleksi was still officially only missing. Her parents had called the university, but there was nothing to tell. He wondered if they would eventually erect a headstone for her. Maybe he should, just for closure. It would give him someplace to think of her, someplace to talk to her. If he had that, maybe she wouldn't invade his every waking moment and plague his dreams.

With a start, Hutch realized that it was too dark to read the smaller inscriptions on the headstones. He turned for home and found one of the main roads leading toward the parking lot.

"Running alone at night through a *cemetery*, Doctor?" A figure stepped out from behind a tall monument. "That can't be healthy."

"Derrick." The sight of him, the angular features, filthy coat draped over hunched shoulders, bare feet sporting longer claws than he remembered Aleksi ever having, brought more than a surge of fear; it brought a flicker of hope. *If Derrick is still alive, maybe...* "You've been quiet lately."

"Have I?"

"The police haven't found any more of your handy work."

"The police couldn't find their asses with both hands." He glanced around and took a few steps into the shadow of another tall headstone. "Where's Aleksi?"

"I don't know." Running would be worse than useless. "She said she was leaving, that she didn't want to put me in danger. She knew you were looking for her."

"I don't believe you." Derrick's yellow eyes flicked around the shadows. "She wouldn't leave you unprotected. She knows I'd come for you."

"She thought you were only watching me to find her. She left to find you." He didn't know how much truth to tell, but anything to keep Derrick talking, to keep those claws from his throat, seemed like a good idea. "She said she needed to find you, that she understood you."

"Bullshit!" Lips curled back from teeth like knives. He moved closer, but still in shadow. "*Nobody* understands me, least of all *her*!"

"Why least, Derrick?" Hutch started backing up slowly. "She's more like you than anyone else in the world."

"That's the first true thing that's come out of your mouth." He stepped closer, his clawed hands emerging from the drape of his coat. "Maybe this will bring her out."

"Killing me won't solve your problems, Derrick."

"Who said I was trying to solve anything?" He advanced, and Hutch backed up, fighting the urge to run.

"They're working on a cure, Derrick. Johansen said they would try to—"

"Who said I *wanted* one?" He moved closer, stalking like a cat playing with a mouse.

"You don't need to do this, Derrick!"

"Oh, I do." He strode forward, and Hutch stumbled back, thinking only to put something, anything between him and those claws. "I *really* do."

Light swept across them, tires squealing. Derrick whirled, squinting into the glare of the high-beam headlights. The car engine screamed, the vehicle barreling up the narrow drive, straight at them. Hutch dove out of the way, more out of reflex than any conscious thought, and when he looked back, Derrick was gone. The car squalled to a stop only feet away, the passenger door flying open to reveal a wide-eyed Sergeant Jasper.

"Get in!"

There was no argument. Hutch scrambled into the car, and before he could even slam the door, they were burning rubber in reverse.

"Tell me that was Derrick Penningly!" Jasper flung an arm over the seat, eyes fixed out the back window as the engine whined to a dangerous pitch.

Hutch opened his mouth to answer, but something struck the top of the car. He barely had time to glance up before three long claws cut parallel furrows in the roof, the fabric of the headliner ripping in a wide swath.

"Shit! Hang on!"

Hutch was already hanging on, but his grip failed when Jasper flung the wheel over and the car slewed around. Tires howled in protest as Jasper slammed into forward and hammered the gas pedal to the floor. That the reckless maneuver had not shaken off their assailant became evident when claws pierced the roof again. Tearing sheet metal screeched. Hutch crouched low, eyes glued to the car's roof being pealed back like wrapping paper on Christmas morning.

Jasper swore and fired his pistol into the roof.

The muzzle blast hammered Hutch's ears in the confined space. How many rounds Jasper fired, he was unsure. While his ears were still ringing, the cop slammed on the brakes. Hutch took the impact of the dashboard on his forearm and caught a glimpse of something tumbling over the hood.

Hutch blinked, and the shape before the car coalesced into Penningly, the ragged coat gone, clawed hands spread wide, yellow eyes glowing. The thin membranes between his arms and torso were riddled with holes, and one bullet had left a crease along his chest. His lips parted in a feral grin, and even as Jasper flung his door open and leveled his gun to fire, Derrick leapt.

Something dark flashed past, too fast to follow, and Derrick Penningly was gone. Movement and sound through the ringing in his ears drew his attention to the right, and there, tumbling among the grave markers, two dragons fought in a tangle of wings, claws, and flashing teeth.

"Aleksi!"

Aleksi hated the thought of having to thank that asshole, Jasper, for saving Hutch's life, but she had to admit, if not for him, she wouldn't have arrived in time. That was the problem with watching from hiding; she had to stay far enough away to keep hidden, but when the shit hit the fan, she was too far away to reach him quickly.

Thanks to Jasper, however, she finally had him.

Her lunge sent them both flying into a row of low headstones. A three-inch-thick slab of pitted granite arrested their trajectory and very nearly broke several of her ribs. Claws raked her shoulder as she rolled into a crouch, ready to spring if he dodged or fled. He stood his ground, eyes wide, his grin a mouthful of razors.

"I *knew* you'd come." His tone dripped vengeance, satisfaction, and bloodlust. "You can't resist me, Aleksi. We're the *same*."

"We're *not!*"

He lunged, but she swept his raking claws aside, scoring a shallow scratch on his forearm. She darted in low, but he flipped up and over her head effortlessly. She heard shouting from Hutch and Jasper but dared not look away.

"You're weak and slow, Aleksi." He circled, feinting and dodging. "What have you been eating, rats and stray dogs?" He lunged again, and she met the attack, her claws interlaced with his. Pain lanced through the backs of her hands. For an instant, they stood face to face. "You're starving yourself for no reason. The city's full of meat for the taking!"

"I don't eat people, Derrick!" She twisted, claws ripping free as she sent him sprawling into a headstone. The stone snapped under the impact. "And I'm fast enough to kill you."

"You *sure* you want to kill me?" He flipped to his feet, quick as a striking snake, and came at her, apparently unfazed. "You'll be all alone, if you do."

"I *like* being alone," she lied, ducking under a slash of his claws that seemed almost playful.

She barreled into him, intending to pin him to the ground, but he tucked and they rolled smack into another headstone. She grasped his wrists to keep his claws from her throat and arched, but his legs tangled with hers to keep her from bucking him off. He leered down at her, saliva dripping down onto her face, teeth an inch from her nose, but she pushed him back up.

Green laser light flickered between them.

They both saw it, and Derrick flung himself back. A headstone splintered into a spray of shrapnel as a bullet passed between their faces. He lurched up trying to escape, but their tangled legs tripped him. He sprawled flat and rolled.

A huge plume of earth flew up from another rifle shot. Whoever was firing was hampered by distance, the time between the squeeze of the trigger and the bullet reaching its target was probably a full second; a lot of time for a dragon. Aleksi would have to hold him still long enough to let the sniper do his work or kill him herself.

Derrick dashed for the cover of a large monument, but the sniper knew how to lead his target. Polished granite spalled across his shoulder and back, gouging scaled golden flesh into lacerated meat. She dove into the wedge of darkness behind a stone, unsure if the sniper might have orders to kill them both. So far, he had only targeted Derrick; Johansen might not have lied after all.

Aleksi heard more yelling; Jasper and Hutch arguing, but she couldn't divert her attention from Derrick for an instant. If she looked away, she might lose him in the chaotic shadows of the cemetery. He crouched behind a monument, biding his time for a few seconds. A few seconds was all she needed.

While his attention was on the sniper's pending shot, she examined his posture, and knew which way he would run. Alexi circled, scrabbling low behind a row of stones, claws finding easy purchase in the loam. She heard the impact of a bullet meeting granite and lunged from hiding.

Right into Derrick's path.

They met like two express trains on the same track, but she was ready for the clash and he was not. Despite his greater weight, her momentum bore him over backward. Her claws lanced deeply into his upper arms, piercing bone. They landed in a tangle of leathery wings and scaly flesh, but the moment they stopped rolling, her advantage of surprise was lost.

He kicked hard and flipped her off, trying to twist free of her grasp, but her claws were set deep, and though lighter, she was by no means weak. She rolled, fighting to keep him still, hold him steady just long enough. A shot shattered a century-old headstone a foot from Derrick's head, sending him into a frenzy.

"Let go, you crazy bitch!" He tore one arm free, a huge flap of muscle spraying her with blood. "They're trying to kill us!"

She flung her legs up and clamped them around his hips, lancing her free claws into his chest. "Not us! Only *you*!"

He surged up on powerful legs, but she refused to let go and they tumbled behind a huge marble monument. Laser light flicked through the night but couldn't reach them.

"Now!" He leered at her, ignoring her talons in his ribs, blood flecking his lips. "Now, you're mine!"

He drew her close. Eyes of topaz bore into hers, jaws gaping. She tried to thrust him to arms-length, refusing to let go, her legs like a vice around him. He pressed down hard, pulling her into his teeth, bucking between her legs in a sick parody of copulation. She flexed her claws, ribs splintering in her grasp, but still he pulled her closer.

Derrick Penningly's head exploded in a shower of flesh and bone, the impact ripping him out of her grasp. Her right ear rang with the deafening gunshot. Derrick's corpse twitched convulsively, a death rattle. She flung him away and rolled to her feet.

The crack-crack of a shotgun action brought her eyes up into those of Sergeant Jasper. He had the weapon aimed right at her chest, the smoking muzzle her death sentence.

"NO!" Hutch crashed into him, one hand grasping the gun's barrel.

The blast tore through the darkness, but missed by a wide margin.

"Goddamnit, let go!" Jasper smacked the stock of the shotgun into Hutch's chest and wrenched the weapon free. "I wasn't going to shoot her, for Christ sake!"

"What?" Hutch clutched his bruised ribs and stepped between them again. "But you…"

"She saved our lives." Jasper jacked another round into the shotgun but didn't point it at her. "I wasn't going to shoot her, but…she's…" He blinked at her. "You *are* Aleksi Rychenkna, right?"

"I was." She heard distant sirens, and closer the rev of engines.

"Well, then I'm sorry." Jasper stood up straighter and let the weapon dangle from his hand. "And thank you."

Tires squealed on pavement, four black SUVs roaring up the road toward them.

"Thank me by telling them you never saw me." She turned to Hutch. "Goodbye, Hutch."

Aleksi Rychenkna turned and vanished into the night, ignoring the protests of the only man she had ever truly loved.

<hr>

A leksi! Wait!" Hutchinson took a step and stumbled.

Jasper grabbed his arm and watched her go. He hadn't been sure she wasn't going to rip his throat out after he shot Penningly and wasn't about to take the chance. He looked at the onrushing fleet of SUV's and knew they'd take Penningly away, rob him of his victory. There were too many questions that would never be answered. Tires squalled to a stop and federal agents piled out, weapons drawn.

"Good to see you alive, Dr. Hutchinson." Dr. Johansen approached flanked by a dozen more men and women in dark coats and rubber gloves.

"Good to be alive, but your man across the river was a little slow."

"I'll let him know." Her attention turned to Jasper, and her eyes flicked down to the gun in his hand. "We're taking Derrick Penningly, Sergeant."

"Can't stop you," he admitted, "but it leaves me holding nothing."

"No, you can't stop us, but don't worry, your boss will receive an explanation that will cover everything." She nodded to the men who were already slipping Penningly's remains into a black plastic bag. Others were cleaning up every trace of evidence. A team was even attacking his car, removing a large section of the roof with a pair of noisy electric shears. "Until you receive orders from your commander, you're not to speak to anyone about this incident. Is that understood?"

"I don't take orders from you." Half a dozen pairs of eyes suddenly flicked his way. "But if I want to keep my job, I'm pretty much forced play along."

"That is exactly correct, Sergeant." She glanced over her shoulder at the approaching squad cars. "I trust you can provide a ride home for Dr. Hutchinson."

"No problem."

"Goodbye, Dr. Hutchinson. I hope we never meet again. Don't do anything that will make our reacquaintance inevitable."

"I won't if you don't, Dr. Johansen." Jasper admired the steely eyed stare Hutchinson leveled at the woman; the man had nerve. "Leave Aleksi alone."

She smiled, but there was no mirth there.

As the fleet of police cruisers pulled up, blue lights flickering through the night like winter lightning, Johansen turned away and boarded one of the SUV's. The cops started to block their exit, but Jasper called them off.

There was no point in a confrontation now; it would only come back to bite him later. He'd have enough trouble explaining this whole thing.

"I'd love for you to tell me about this someday, Dr. Hutchinson."

"You really don't want to know, Sergeant Jasper." Hutchinson took a deep breath, closed his eyes for a moment and let it out slowly. He opened his eyes and looked around the shadows. Jasper knew who he was looking for, but he could see that the man held no real hope of seeing her again.

"You're wrong, Doctor." He clapped the man on the back and gestured toward a waiting squad car. "I really, *really* would." He met Hutchinson's incredulous stare with a laugh. "Unofficially, of course."

Persephone watched the flames consume the remains of Derrick Penningly.

Reggie closed the door of the incinerator and put a hand on her shoulder. "Glad that's over?"

"Eager to get my own face back." The fatigue was coming down hard now, the stimulants wearing off. "Can you drive, Reg? I'm a wreck."

"No problem, cuz." He grinned and helped her into the big SUV they'd used to transport the remains from the federal storage facility.

The vehicle still rode low with the weight of the specimen and all the samples. Mary Buckmann would have a lot of questions thrown at her, and absolutely no memory of the last ten days to answer them. The Director would be furious. Persephone regretted using the woman, but there had been no other option.

They drove out of the industrial area south of town and got on the expressway. She leaned back in the seat and let her eyes close, the flash of passing street lights behind her lids alternating with the image of the despair on Hutch's face as he stared into the darkness of the cemetery. She knew him, knew that look. She'd seen it once before when he asked her for a divorce.

Oh, Hutch, you have the absolute worst luck with women...

She must have drifted off to sleep, for when she opened her eyes, they were pulling up in front of the house. Reggie must have called ahead; half a dozen family members stood ready to help them with the cumbersome specimen. One more task before she could sleep.

It took them the better part of an hour to muscle the thing down into the Sanctum. Gi-gi lay there watching as they wheeled the trolley up beside her bed, the plaster cast still wrapped in plastic.

Her wizened hand reached out to touch it, and his thin lips twitched. "Thank you, Persephone. Thank you all. We can begin work in a few days, but I imagine my great granddaughter wants some rest."

"Yes, please," Persephone said as the others turned to go. *Sleep...It's over...I can sleep.* Persephone rounded the bed to lay down on the other gurney, rolling up her sleeve.

"Just relax, cuz." Reggie pulled an IV pole over and swabbed her forearm for the needle. "You'll be yourself in no time."

"Persephone?"

She turned to look at her great grandmother. "Yes?" *Please, just let me sleep...* A needle pierced her arm.

"I have a proposal I would like you to consider." Gi-gi's wizened hand patted the plaster-encased specimen of the dragon, and she felt a cold chill trickle down the back of her neck.

"I don't think..." Cool fluid rushed into her arm, and darkness enclosed her mind.

Quite a story." Sergeant Jasper leaned back in his chair and sipped his beer, looking around at the first honest to God spring day they'd seen yet this year.

"Yes, it is." Hutch sipped his own beer. "And not likely to ever make the evening news." He'd told Jasper everything, even about his one single night with Aleksi. It still haunted him.

"No, I don't suppose it will, but it's nice to know the truth." Jasper stared up at the startlingly blue sky, unreal after months of winter gray.

A team of industrious gardeners was planting seedlings in the long boxes that edged the Daedalus' rooftop. The splashes of green looked out of place, alien to Hutch's winter-attuned eyes. Spring was supposed to mean life, renewal, growth. He felt none of that.

"People like Johansen, or whatever her name is, manufacture truth."

"Yeah." Jasper sipped his beer again and sighed. "And that really just stinks like a ton of shit, doesn't it?"

"Yes, it does."

"Do you think they'll ever do anything with that…whatever?"

"With Penningly as an example, they'll be careful, but eventually…yes, I think they probably will try to use it for something." That scared him more than anything. "Which also stinks like a ton of shit."

"Yes, it does." Jasper's eyes slid over to look at Hutch sidelong. "What about Aleksi?"

"Vanished completely." Hutch tried to sound casual, though he doubted he fooled the cop. "I just hope she's someplace safe."

"Going to be hard to hide her...condition when summer comes." He gestured to a few of the other patrons, dressed in light jackets and dresses. "No overcoats or hats."

"I suppose." Hutch had been thinking about that, too, wondering how she would survive. Unfortunately, he hadn't been lying; he'd not seen her in the three weeks since Derrick was killed. He needed to change the subject. "How's your partner?"

"Good, but it'll be a while until he's recovered from the surgery. Penningly really did a job on him. Plastic surgeon had a field day."

"Good that he's okay." Hutch was glad someone would recover from this.

"So, you're life's pretty much back to normal, huh?" Jasper waved to a passing waitress.

"Yep. Boring old professor with a boring old career and way too much work on his hands." He tipped his beer and drained the last of it. "Speaking of which, I better get back."

"Let me buy you another, Doc. It's a beautiful spring day, and the view is lovely." He smiled at the pretty waitress as she reached across the table for Hutch's empty glass.

"Thanks, but no." Hutch reached for his wallet. "I really do need to do some work this afternoon. I've got two new students to interview."

"On a Saturday?" Jasper beat him to the draw and dropped a twenty on the waitress's tray. "I've got this. Keep it."

"Thanks!" She smiled at him and walked off.

"Yep. Both will be entering the graduate program in the fall, so they'll be coming on board in a few months." He stood and stretched. "Got a lot of work to catch up on."

"Yeah, I guess we all do." Jasper stood and held out a hand. "Call if you ever need someone to shoot the shit with, Doc."

"I will, Tony, and thanks again." He shook Jasper's hand. "Sorry it had to turn out this way."

"I'm not." He sounded genuine. "Case closed, bad guy dead, no loose ends. Who could ask for more?"

Loose ends...

Hutch could think of one thing more he could ask for but wasn't about to bring it up. He settled for a smile and a nod and followed Jasper down the stairs and out of the restaurant. They parted with another handshake and a wave, and Hutch walked casually through campus to his office. The weather was hardly balmy, but it was clear and warm enough to prompt a deluge of students to spread blankets and lawn chairs out on the quads.

Spring, he thought. *Life, growth...* His thoughts spiraled as they had been doing a lot lately. The next thing he knew he was reliving the best night of his life, the night he could never truly relive, the love he would never experience again.

He navigated to his office in a haze, but the familiar surroundings and more work than he could possibly finish soon diverted his thoughts. He'd been working way too much lately, but it was the only thing he had to stave off depression. The two interviews went well; the students were eager, smart, enthusiastic, and grateful for having a project to jump right into.

But they were *not* Aleksi Rychenkna.

At five PM he packed up his computer, grabbed his jacket and left his office. *Are you alive, Aleksi?* he wondered as he shouldered his bag and headed for the parking structure. The place was virtually empty, and once again, his thoughts drifted. This was where Bob died, where Penningly murdered him. He barely noticed when he reached his car, staring at it like he didn't recognize it as his.

He didn't even have his keys out.

"You're going senile, Hutch." He fumbled through his pack.

"No, you're not."

Hutch froze. He looked around, but there was no one, just shadows. But that voice... Had he imagined it? It had been different, but *hers*. He was sure of it.

"Aleksi?"

No answer. Not a sign of her. *Had* he imagined it? Maybe. A memory of her dropping from the shadows like a wraith revisited him, and he realized that if she didn't want to be seen, he wouldn't see her. But if she had spoken...

"Or I really *am* going crazy."

Hutch found his keys and opened the car door. He had his bag on the passenger seat and was putting the key in the ignition when he saw a folded yellow post-it note tucked under his windshield wiper. He was out of the car and had it in his hand in a heartbeat. He peeled it apart and peered at the note.

"Fifty-fifty or ninety-ten?" he read aloud.

He glanced around again but there was still no sign of her. The note was from Aleksi, without a doubt, but why be so cryptic? He looked at the note again and thought about it. Was she watching him? Worried about him? Lately, he had been closer to her professed percentages of ninety-ten.

Hiding behind work. He knew he was, but also knew *why* he was hiding.

Aleksi was hiding, too, from the eyes of those who thought of her as an asset, *their* asset. They were undoubtedly watching him as well. Was that why she had stayed away?

"We can't hide forever." He slipped the note in his pocket. "And my door is always open."

Without another look around, he got in his car and drove home. He had too much to think about during the drive, too much to feed the depression that he knew was getting worse. He dumped his keys in the bowl and went to the kitchen to let Iggy out of his cage for their evening ritual. The iguana patrolled the kitchen floor while Hutch chopped fruit and vegetables for their evening snack, but when he looked down, the ungrateful lizard was nowhere to be seen.

"Iggy?" He put the bowl down and rattled the cage, which usually brought the lizard running.

Nothing.

"Iggy, where the hell..."

He looked in all the iguana's favorite places, under the couch, by the big potted bamboo in the corner, in the laundry nook, but he was nowhere to be found.

"Fine. Come out when you're hungry, then." He picked a few pieces of grape from the bowl and popped them in his mouth, opened the fridge and grabbed a beer, then took his computer bag to the office. He plugged the laptop in and left his beer beside it while he went to change into his weekend clothes. He hung his jacket in the big walk-in closet without bothering to turn on the light and kicked off his shoes. A little scratch from the back of the closet caught his ear, and he realized where Iggy must have gone.

"You shouldn't hide back here, Iggy. I'm likely to step on you."

"He's not hiding."

Hutch's heart skipped a beat. He peered into the shadows, reaching for the light switch.

"Please, Hutch. No lights." Something rustled and he caught a glint of the diffuse light from the shaded window reflecting from her golden eyes. "Iggy might not be hiding, but I am."

He squinted, his eyes adjusting slowly to the gloom, and saw her hunkered down in the corner. Aleksi held the Iguana in her arms, scratching under his chin with her claws.

"He misses you." His voice came out scratchy. He cleared his throat. "*I miss you.*"

"You shouldn't." She stood, taller than he remembered, but didn't move from the darkest corner of the closet. "I'm not me anymore, Hutch."

"Bullshit."

She ignored his comment. "And they're still looking for me." Her voice sounded strange, a little slurred, huskier. "I shouldn't have come here. They probably still have your place bugged." She started for the door.

"I don't care." He stepped into her way. "They won't hurt you, and they can't touch me."

"Why not?"

He didn't know which statement she was questioning, so he answered both. "Johansen said that you were an asset, remember? They don't waste assets. They can't touch me because I've made sure that doing so would be more trouble for them than it would be worth." He smiled at that; he might not like Persephone very much, but he had no doubt that if he suddenly disappeared, the files he had given her would end up on the front page of every newspaper in New England.

"You're not safe, Hutch. Neither of us is safe."

"*Life* isn't safe, Aleksi. Now put Iggy down, because I'm going to give you a hug and I don't think he'll like it."

"Hutch, I..." She took a step back toward her dark corner. "You shouldn't."

He reached for the light switch and flipped it on. They both blinked, and he saw that the changes had continued. Her face was even more angular, the ridge over her eyes more pronounced, but he could still see her there beneath the mask. There were tears on her golden-scaled cheeks, and fear in her eyes. He reached out a hand and brushed the dark garment she wore like a voluminous poncho.

"Please, Hutch. Don't..."

"Why not?"

"Because it's..."

"Not safe?"

"Yes."

"I don't want to be safe, Aleksi. I want to be your *friend*." He gripped her shoulders and looked into her large, yellow eyes. "Now put down the lizard and give me a hug. I've got a two-pound porterhouse in the freezer with your name on it, and a bottle of old vine Zinfandel in the chiller that we are going to share."

"That sounds good."

"Which part, the hug, the steak, or the wine?"

"The *friend* part." She stepped back and put Iggy down. "I could use one."

"You've got one, Aleksi." Their embrace was awkward, her membranous wings got in the way, but they got it sorted out in the end. She took a deep breath and let it out slowly, warming his neck. Their hearts beat against one another, inches apart, slowing to a steady, warm cadence.

It wasn't safe.

Nothing was safe.

But it felt good.

ACKNOWLEDGMENTS

Many thanks to my wife, Anne, for her intimate knowledge of the Boston Area, for dragging me on foot throughout Boston's back bay, Cambridge, and the Harvard campus, as well as her expertise in genetics.

FALSTAFF BOOKS

Want to know what's new & coming soon from
Falstaff Books?

Join our Newsletter List
& Get this Free Ebook Sampler
with work from:
John G. Hartness
A.G. Carpenter
Bobby Nash
Emily Lavin Leverett
Jaym Gates
Darin Kennedy
Natania Barron
Edmund R. Schubert
& More!

http://www.subscribepage.com/q0j0p3

ABOUT THE AUTHOR

Born and raised in Oregon, Chris met his wife and soulmate, Anne, while attending graduate school in Texas. Since then they have been gaming together since 1985, sailing together since 1988, married since 1989, and writing together off and on throughout their relationship. Most astonishingly, they have not killed each other during the creation or editing of any of their stories…although it was close a few times. Since 2009, the couple has been sailing and writing full-time aboard their beloved sailboat, *Mr Mac*. They return to the US every summer for conventions, always happy to sign copies of their books and talk with fans. Visit Jaxbooks.com for more.

ALSO BY CHRIS A. JACKSON

From Jaxbooks

A Soul for Tsing

Deathmask

Blood Sea Tales

The Pirate's Scourge

The Pirate's Truth (coming 2019)

The Pirate's Curse (coming 2020)

Weapon of Flesh Series

The Cornerstones Trilogy
(with Anne L. McMillen-Jackson)

The Cheese Runners Trilogy
(novellas – also on Audible)

From Dragon Moon Press

The Scimitar Seas Novels

From Paizo Publishing

(also available as audiobooks)

Pirate's Honor

Pirate's Promise

Pirate's Prophecy

From Privateer Press

Blood & Iron (ebook novella)

Watery Graves

From Fantasy Flight Games

The Deep Gate (Lovecraftian horror novella)

www.ingramcontent.com/pod-product-compliance
Lightning Source LLC
Chambersburg PA
CBHW051559100726

47898CB00001B/155